THE WORLD'S GREATEST MYSTERIES . . .

- WHY ARE THERE PYRAMIDS IN EGYPT, THE YUCATAN, AND CENTRAL AMERICA?

- WHY ARE THERE SIMILAR LANGUAGES CARVED INTO THEIR STONES?

- DID ATLANTIS REALLY EXIST?

- WHAT IS THE STRANGE FORMATION IN THE SEA OFF THE BIMINI ISLANDS?

- WHO PUT THE STATUES ON EASTER ISLAND?

- DO UFOS REALLY EXIST?

. . . ALL HAVE THE SAME ANSWER.
IT'S ELEGANT.
IT'S SIMPLE.
IT'S ABSOLUTELY TERRIFYING.

AREA 51

AREA 51

ROBERT DOHERTY

A DELL BOOK

Published by
Dell Publishing
a division of
Random House, Inc.

ISBN: 0-440-22073-4

Printed in the United States of America

Published simultaneously in Canada

March 1997

20 19 18 17 16 15 14 13

OPM

To Craig Cavanaugh,
who helped with the idea
and was the first one
to read the manuscript

AREA 51

Prologue

It came alive into darkness, wondering what had caused it to wake and aware at the same time that it was much weaker than ever before. The first priority was time. How long had it been asleep? The weakness gave the answer. Dividing half-lives of its power source, it calculated that almost fifty revolutions of this planet around the system star had passed since last it had been conscious.

The data from sensors was examined and found to be indeterminate. Whatever signal had tripped the alarms and kicked in the emergency power had to have been strong and vital but was now gone. Its sleep level had been so deep that all the recorded data showed was that there had been a signal. The nature of the signal, the source of the signal, both had been lost.

The Makers had not anticipated such a long time before resupply of the power source. It knew there was not much time left to its already very long life before the power supply slipped below the absolute minimum to keep it functioning even in hibernation.

A decision needed to be made. Should it divert power to sensors in case the signal were repeated, or should it go back to deep sleep, conserving power for time? But if the signal had been vital, and the sensor log said it was indeed so, then there might not be much time left.

The decision was made as quickly as the question had

been posed. Power was allocated. The sensors were given more power to stay at a higher alert status in order to catch a repeat of the signal. A time limit of one planetary orbit about the system star was put on the sensors, at which time they would automatically awaken it and the decision could be reconsidered.

It went back to a lighter sleep, knowing that the decision to divert power to sensors for an orbit would cost it almost ten orbits of sleep when the power got lower, but it accepted that. That was its job.

NASHVILLE, TENNESSEE
T—147 HOURS

The grocery bag Kelly Reynolds was holding ripped open as she unlocked her mailbox and a twelve-pack of Diet Coke burst open on impact with the ground, sending cans everywhere. It had been that kind of day, she reflected as she gathered in the errant cans. She'd spent it interviewing local bar owners on Second Avenue for an article she was writing, and two of her five appointments had failed to show.

She stuffed the mail into the remnants of the bag and made her way to her apartment, dropping the entire mess on the table in her tiny kitchen. She filled a mug with water and pushed it into the microwave, setting the timer, then leaned back against the counter, giving herself the two minutes before the beeper sounded to relax. She studied her reflection in the kitchen window, which looked out onto a back alley in Nashville's West End. Kelly was short, just over five feet, but big boned. She carried her weight well thanks to her morning routine of sit-ups and push-ups, but the combination of bulk and lack of height made her look like a compressed version of a person who should be four inches taller. Her hair was thick and brown, streaked with gray for the last ten years. Kelly had made the effort to keep the original color for a year or so, then had given up, accepting what time had dealt her after forty-two years on the planet.

The microwave dinged and she removed the mug and placed a tea bag into it, allowing the water to soak through. While she was waiting for that, she pulled out the mail, interested most in the thick brown envelope that she'd noticed as the cans had fallen. The return address made her smile: Phoenix, Arizona. It had to be from Johnny Simmons, an old friend from her graduate days at Vanderbilt. Actually, more than an old friend, Kelly reminded herself as her mind focused on those years a decade and a half ago.

Johnny had caught her on the rebound after her first husband had dumped her. She'd anchored her psyche in his emotional harbor for several months. When she'd finally felt like something of a whole human being again, she'd discovered that while she truly cared for Johnny, she didn't have that special spark for him that she felt was necessary for an intimate relationship. Johnny had been very nice about it and they'd backed off, not speaking to each other for a while, then slowly reentered each other's lives, testing the waters of friendship.

Kelly felt they had cemented that friendship after three years when Johnny had returned from a photojournalist assignment into El Salvador, where he had been documenting right-wing death squads. He'd holed up in her apartment for two months, decompressing from that ordeal. One or the other would call every month or so and they would catch up on their lives and know there was someone out there who cared. Last she'd heard, he was also working freelance, doing articles for whichever magazine was willing to cough up some money.

She slit the envelope open and was surprised to see an

audiocassette fall out along with several pages. She picked up the cover letter and read.

Hey Kelly,   3 Nov 96

I was trying to think of who to send a copy of this tape to, and you were the first name that popped into my head—especially after what happened to you eight years ago with that joker from Nellis Air Force Base in Nevada.

I got a package in the mail last week that included a letter and an audiotape—no return address and post-marked Las Vegas. I think I know who sent it, though. He wouldn't be hard to find. I want you to listen to it. So go find a Walkman or go over to your stereo now. Don't pass go, don't collect two hundred dollars, and take this letter with you. I mean NOW! I knew you were still standing there. Put the tape in, but don't start it yet.

Kelly smiled as she walked over to her stereo system precariously perched on a bookcase made up of cinder blocks and planks of wood. Johnny knew her and he had a good sense of humor, but even the humor couldn't erase the instant bad feeling the Nellis Air Force Base reference had evoked. That Air Force intelligence officer had destroyed her career in filmmaking.

Pushing away the negative thoughts, Kelly put the tape in, then continued reading.

Okay. I'll give you the same information that was in the letter I received with the tape. In fact, I'll give you a copy of the letter that came with it. Next page, if you please.

Kelly turned the page to find a Xerox copy of a typewritten letter.

Mister Simmons,

In this package you will find a tape recording I made on the evening of 23 October of this year. I was scanning the UHF wavelength. I often listen in to the pilots out of Nellis Air Force Base conducting operations. It was while doing just that, that I picked up the exchange you will listen to.

As near as I can tell, it is between the pilot of an F-15 (Victor Two Three), the control tower at Nellis, which uses the call sign Dreamland, and the flight commander of the F-15 pilot (Victor Six).

The pilot was taking part in the Red Flag, force on force, exercises at Nellis. These exercises are where the Air Force trains its fighter pilots in simulated combat. They have a whole squadron of Soviet-style aircraft at the Groom Lake complex on the Nellis Reservation to use in this training.

I'll let you draw your own conclusions from the tape.

You want to talk to me, come to Vegas. Go to the "mailbox." You don't know what that is, ask around and you'll find it. I'll come to you.
The Captain

Kelly turned the page. She smiled as she read.

Listen to the tape now.

Using her remote, she turned the stereo on and pushed play. The voices were surprisingly clear, which made Kelly wonder at the machinery used to make the tape. This wasn't someone holding a tape recorder up to a radio speaker. There was a clear hiss of static at the end of each transmission and three distinct voices, as the letter had indicated.

"Victor Two Three, this is Dreamland Control. You are violating restricted airspace. You will immediately turn on a heading of one-eight-zero.

"Victor Two Three, this is Dreamland Control. Repeat, you are violating restricted airspace. Turn immediately on a heading of one-eight-zero. Over."

A new voice cut in, this one with the muted roar of jet engines in the background.

"Victor Two Three, this is Victor Six. Comply immediately with Dreamland Control. Over."

"Six, this is Two Three. I'll be out of here in a flash. Over."

"Negative, Two Three. This is Dreamland Control. You will comply with our instructions ASAP. Over."

The commander came back on.

"They got you, Slick. Comply. You know we can't mess with restricted airspace. Over."

"This is Two Three, I will— What the fuck! I've got— Christ, I don't know what the hell it is. A bogey at three o'clock and climbing. I've never—"

The quiet, implacable voice of Dreamland Control cut in.

"Two Three, you will immediately cease transmitting, turn on a heading of one-eight-zero and descend for a landing at Groom Lake. That is a direct order. Over."

The pilot of the F-15 was growing more agitated.

"This thing has no wings! And, man, it's moving. It's closing on me. We got a live one! I'm—"

There was a hiss of static.

"—was close!" Static. "On top of—" Static. "—my God! It's turning—" Static. "Jesus! It's—" The voice was suddenly cut off.

"Two Three! This is Six. What's your status, Slick? Over."

Silence.

"Break, Dreamland Control, this is Victor Six. Do you have Two Three on scope? Over."

"Victor Six, this is Dreamland Control. You will return to Nellis Airfield immediately. The exercise is canceled. All aircraft are ordered grounded immediately. You will remain in your plane until cleared by security personnel. Over."

"I want to know the status of Two Three. Over."

"We've lost Two Three from our scope. We are initiating search and rescue. Comply with orders. There are to be no more transmissions. Out."

The tape ended. Kelly sat still for a few seconds, considering what she had heard. She knew the name Dreamland well. She picked up Simmons's letter.

Yeah, I know exactly what you're thinking, Kelly. It could be a hoax or a setup like they did on you. But I talked to a friend of mine over at the local Air Force base. He said that some of that sky out there near Nellis is the most restricted airspace in the country, even more so than that over the White House in D.C. He also said that pilots in the Red Flag exercises sometimes try to skate the edges of their aerial playing field on the regular Nellis Range and gain a tactical advantage by cutting across the restricted airspace. If that pilot did wander over the Groom Lake/Area 51 complex or try to cut a corner, he might have seen something he wasn't supposed to. Obviously he ran into *something*.

You know me. I'm heading out there to take a look. There's enough interest in all of this that even if I get nothing about the pilot, I ought to at least be able to write a couple of articles about the Groom Lake complex. Maybe *Technical* or some other science-type magazine will buy.

So I'll be out there on the night of the ninth. Now, I plan on being back home the tenth. I don't want to hang around there any longer than I have to. I'll give you a call, regardless, on the tenth by nine in the morning. At the absolute least if I can't quite make it home by then I'll change the message on my answering machine by remote before 9:00 A.M. on the tenth.

I know all this sounds melodramatic, but when I went down to El Salvador—a place no one remembers nowadays—it stood me in good stead to have someone waiting on a call. Held the assholes off from beating me too bad or keeping me forever when I got caught in places I wasn't supposed to be. So if you don't hear from me by 9:00 A.M. on the tenth, it means I got caught. Then I trust you to figure out what to do. You owe me, bud!

Wish me luck. By the way, if by chance—da-da-de-dum—drumroll, please, I get scarfed up by the authorities, you have a copy of the tape and the letter, and also I've enclosed a key to my apartment.

Thanks.

All of my love, all of my kisses!

Johnny

Kelly didn't need to check the calendar. The ninth was this evening. She gathered the tape out of her stereo and took it, along with the letters, to her desk. Then she used the key around her neck to open the file drawer. She withdrew a file labeled "Nellis" and laid it on the desktop.

Flipping it open, she saw that the first document inside was a typed letter on official Air Force stationery. The signature block at the bottom indicated it was from the Public Affairs Officer at the base: Major Prague.

"Asshole," Kelly muttered as she remembered the man. She place Johnny Simmons's letter and the tape inside, then replaced the folder in the drawer and locked it. The surface of the desk was clear, except for a silver-framed black-and-white photo of a young man dressed in khaki. He wore a black beret, and a Sten gun was slung over his shoulder.

She was thoughtful as she kicked back in her chair and considered the photo. "Sounds like Johnny has nibbled at the hook, Dad." She tapped a pencil against her lip, then sighed. "Damn you, Johnny. You're always causing trouble, but this time I think you may have gone too far."

NELLIS AIR FORCE BASE RANGE,
VICINITY GROOM LAKE
T—144 HOURS

"Wait here," Franklin ordered as he braked the battered Bronco II to a halt. There was no flash of brake lights. He had pulled the fuse for them prior to turning onto this dirt road. Johnny Simmons leaned forward in the passenger seat and squinted into the darkness. He had to assume that Franklin was so familiar with the road that he was able to drive it without headlights. Although the road did stand out as a lighter straight line on the otherwise dark ground, the trip through the dark was unnerving.

Simmons rubbed his forehead. They were up several thousand feet in altitude and he felt a bit of a headache from the thinner air. He was a tall, thin man, his pale skin liberally sprinkled with freckles. Simmons appeared to be much younger than his thirty-eight years and his disheveled mane of bright red hair only added to the youthful image.

Franklin walked to one side of the road and disappeared into the darker countryside for a few minutes, then his shadow crossed the road and was gone for a few more minutes. When he returned, he was holding four short green plastic rods in his hands.

"Antennas for the sensors," he explained. "I found the sensors last month. I wondered why the camo dudes were always onto me so quick. They'd show up within twenty minutes of me hitting this road. Then they'd call in the sheriff and it was just a plain hassle."

"How'd you find the detectors?" Simmons asked, covertly making sure the voice-activated microcassette recorder in his jacket pocket was turned on.

"I used a receiver that scanned the band lengths. I drove around and stopped when I picked up something transmitting," Franklin said. "Right at 495.45 megahertz."

"Why four antennas?" Simmons asked. "Wouldn't two do?"

Franklin shook his head. "They're deployed in pairs on either side of the road. That way they can tell which way you're going by the order they're tripped in." Franklin talked quickly, eager to impress Simmons with his knowledge.

The simple logic quieted Simmons for a few moments. For the first time he wondered if he was biting off more than he could chew here. Since Area 51 wasn't listed on any topographic maps, and all roads leading onto the Nellis Reservation were posted with no trespassing signs with ominous threats printed in red, Simmons had sought help. He'd met Franklin in Rachel, a small town on Route 375 that ran along the northeast side of the Nellis Reservation. Franklin was the person he'd been pointed to by "experts" in the UFO field as the man to see about getting a look at Area 51, the place the Air Force pilot had been overflying when he'd been accosted by Dreamland Control and whatever unknown object the pilot had seen.

Simmons hadn't been too surprised to find Franklin a young bearded man who looked more like he ought to be doing poetry reading at a college than leading people to look at a classified government facility. Franklin worked out of a small, dilapidated house where he self-published a monthly newsletter for UFO enthusiasts. He'd been thrilled when he'd seen Simmons's credentials and publishing history. At last someone with a little bit of credibility and pull, had been the way Franklin had put it, and he'd promised to put Simmons as close to Area 51, the code name for the Groom Lake complex, as he possibly could.

Simmons wondered if Franklin might not be the "Captain" who had sent him the tape and letter, but he didn't think so. There didn't seem to be any need for the subterfuge, and Franklin had seemed genuinely surprised to see him. They'd passed the "mailbox" farther back on the dirt road about twenty minutes ago and there had been two cars and a van parked there. UFO watchers had waved at the Bronco as they drove by. The mailbox, which was an actual small battered metal mailbox on the side of the road, was the last safe place to observe the sky over the Groom Lake/Area 51 complex. To Johnny it was obvious that the watchers there weren't surprised to see Franklin's truck drive by.

Franklin threw the truck in gear and rolled forward about a hundred feet. "The sensors pick up ground vibes from passing vehicles, but they don't trip on people walking or animals. Then they transmit that information back to whoever is in charge of security for this place. Without the antennas they can't transmit. We're out of range now. Back in a second." He stepped out and was gone for several more minutes as he screwed the antennas back into the sensors.

They went another two miles down the road, then Franklin pulled off into the lee of a large ridge that rose up to the west like a solid, sloping black wall: White Sides Mountain. Simmons stepped out, following Franklin's lead.

"It's going to get colder," Franklin said in a low voice as he pulled a small backpack out of the rear of his truck.

Simmons was glad he had packed the extra sweater. He pulled it over his head, then put his jacket back on over it. It had been reasonably warm in Rachel, but with the departure of the sun, the temperature had plummeted.

They both turned as they heard a low roar coming in from the eastern horizon. The sound grew louder, then Franklin pointed. "There. See the running lights?" He snorted. "Some of the people who camp out at the mailbox mistake aircraft running lights for UFOs. When a plane's in its final flight path the lights seem to just hover, especially since it comes in almost straight over the mailbox."

"Is that the 737 you told me about?" Simmons asked.

Franklin giggled nervously. "No, that's not her." The airplane banked over their heads and disappeared over White Sides Mountain, descending for a landing on the other side. A second one, just like the first, came by less than thirty seconds later. "Those are Air Force transports. Medium-sized ones, probably C-130 Hercules. You can hear the turboprop engines. Must be bringing in something. They haul in pretty much all their equipment and supplies to Area 51 by plane."

They heard the abrupt increase in the whine of engines and the sound lasted for a few minutes, then silence reigned again.

He held out his hand. "Camera."

Simmons hesitated. The Minolta with long-range lens hanging around his neck was as much a part of his clothing as the sweater.

"We agreed," Franklin said. "A whole lot less hassle all around if the sheriff shows. You saw the negatives and prints back at the office that I've already taken of the complex. They were taken in daylight, too, with a better camera than you have. Much better than you could get at night even with special film and long exposure."

Simmons removed the camera, the loss of the weight around his neck an irritant. He also didn't like the idea of having to pay Franklin for photos he could take himself. Plus what if they spotted something happening? He had noted Franklin stuffing a camera into his backpack when they were leaving earlier in the day. Simmons understood Franklin's scam: he wanted exclusive footage if anything happened and he wanted to make extra money selling his own photos. Simmons handed his camera to the younger man, who locked it in the back of the truck. Franklin grinned, his teeth reflecting the bright moon hanging overhead. "Ready?"

"Ready," Simmons acknowledged.

"Let's do it." Franklin took a few deep breaths, then headed for a cut in the steep mountainside and began striding up. Simmons followed, his boots making a surprisingly loud clatter in the darkness as he scrambled up the loose rock.

"Think we were spotted?" Simmons asked.

Franklin shrugged, the gesture lost in the dark. "Well, we know the sensors didn't pick us up. If there was a camo dude out there in the dark and he saw my truck going down the road, then the sheriff will be here in about a half hour. We'll see the lights from above. The camo dudes, who are the outer perimeter security people for the complex, will drive by on this side of the ridge, maybe even come up prior to showtime if they saw we had cameras, another good reason not to bring them. The fact we haven't seen anyone yet means there's a good chance we weren't spotted. If we weren't spotted, then we can spend the whole night up top without getting hassled."

"Doesn't the Air Force get pissed at you for messing with their equipment?" Simmons asked as Franklin led the way.

"Don't know." Franklin giggled again, the sound irritating Simmons. "I imagine they would if they knew it was me. But they don't, so screw 'em. We're still on public land and will be the whole way," Franklin explained, slowing a bit when he recognized his paying guest's more modest pace. "But if the sheriff comes here, he'll confiscate the film anyway, so it's easier to simply not haul the weight up. Plus, we got us sort of a gentleman's agreement. This is the only spot left in the public domain that you can see the runway from since the Air Force purchased most of the northeast section last year. Most people stay back at the mailbox because they don't want to get hassled, but we aren't doing anything illegal by climbing this mountain.

"But soon it won't be legal to come here," Franklin continued. "The Air Force is trying to get this land too. Once they get it you won't be able to see into the lake bed from anywhere in the public domain. And you sure as hell can't overfly this place.

"Earlier this year they seized a bunch of the land over that way"—Franklin pointed to the north—"from the Bureau of Land Management, which had control of it. I used to watch from there occasionally."

Franklin gave Simmons a hand as they made it over the lip of the cut onto the side of the ridge proper. "They wanted it all, but the law says that over a certain acreage, there have to be hearings, so the Air Force seized up to their limit the last couple of years and they'll probably do it again this year, until they get all they want, piece by piece."

Simmons would have liked to ask a few more questions but he was too winded to do anything but grunt.

"We have another eight hundred feet of altitude to make," Franklin said.

THE CUBE, AREA 51
T—143 HOURS, 37 MINUTES

The underground room measured eighty by a hundred feet and could only be reached from the massive hangars cut into the side of Groom Mountain above via a large freight elevator. It was called the Cube by those who worked in it—the only ones who actually knew of its existence other than the members of Majic-12, the oversight committee for the whole project at Dreamland. *Cube* was easier on the tongue than the room's formal designation, Command and Control Central, or even the official shortened form: C^3, or C cubed.

"We've got two hot ones in sector alpha four," one of

the men watching a bank of computer screens announced.
There were three rows of consoles with computers lining
the floor of the room, facing forward. On the front wall a
twenty-foot-wide by ten-high screen dominated the room.
It was capable of displaying virtually any information that
was desired, from maps of the world to satellite imagery.

The Cube operations chief, Major Quinn, looked over
his man's shoulder. Quinn was of medium height and build.
He had thinning blond hair and wore large tortoiseshell
glasses to accommodate the split lenses for both distance
and close up. He ran his tongue nervously over his lips,
then glanced at the back of the room at a figure sitting at
the main control console.

Quinn was perturbed to have intruders nosing around
tonight. There was too much planned, and most importantly, General Gullick, the project commander, was here,
and the general made everyone nervous. The general's seat
was on a raised dais that could oversee all that went on
below. Directly behind it a door led to a corridor, off of
which branched a conference room, Gullick's office and
sleeping quarters, rest rooms, and a small galley. The
freight elevator opened on the right side of the main gallery. There was the quiet hum of machinery in the room
along with the slight hiss of filtered air being pushed into
the room by large fans in the hangar above.

"What happened to the sensors?" Quinn asked as he
checked his own laptop computer terminal. "I've got a
blank on the road."

"I don't know about the road," the operator reported.
"But there they are," he added, pointing at his screen.
"They might have walked in, skirting the sensors."

The glowing outlines of two men could clearly be seen.
The thermal scope mounted on top of a mountain six miles
to the east of White Sides Mountain was feeding a perfect
image to this room, two hundred feet underneath Groom

Mountain, twelve miles to the west of where the two men were. Thermal was extremely efficient in this terrain at spotting people at night. The sudden drop from daylight temperature made the heat difference between living creatures and the surrounding terrain a large one.

Quinn took a deep breath. This was not good. It meant the men were past the outer security, known to locals as the "camo dudes," but known in here as Air Force security police, with low-level clearances, who could turn them away or could bring in the sheriff to run them off. Since the Air Force security police didn't know what was really going on at Area 51, their use was restricted to the outer perimeter. Quinn did not want to alert the inner security personnel yet because that would require informing the general of the penetration. Also, he was getting more and more concerned about some of the methods the inner security people used.

Quinn decided to handle it as quietly as he could. "Get in the security police."

"The intruders are inside the outer perimeter," the operator protested.

"I know that," Quinn said in a low voice. "But let's try to keep this low key. We can pull a couple of the security police in as long as the intruders stay on that side of the mountain."

The operator turned and spoke into his mike, giving orders.

Quinn straightened as General Gullick turned from the massive screen. It was currently displaying the world's surface in the form of an electronic Mercator conformal map.

"Status?" the general snapped, his voice a deep bass that reminded Quinn of James Earl Jones. Gullick walked down the metal steps from his area toward Quinn. The general was over six and a half feet tall and still carried himself as erect as he had when he was a cadet at the Air

Force Academy thirty years ago. His broad shoulders filled out his blue uniform and his stomach was as flat as when he had played linebacker for the Academy team. The only obvious differences the years had made were the lines in his black face and the totally smooth-shaven skull—a final assault on the hair that had started to turn gray a decade ago.

It was as if he could sniff trouble, Quinn thought. "We have two intruders, sir," he reported, pointing at the screen. Then he added the bad news. "They're already in sector alpha four."

The general didn't ask about the road sensors. That explanation would have to come later and wouldn't change the present situation in the slightest. The general had earned a reputation as a hard-nosed squadron leader in the Vietnam war, flying F-6 Phantoms in close support of ground troops. Quinn had heard rumors about Gullick, the usual scuttlebutt that went around in even the most secret military unit, that the general, as a young captain, had been known for dropping his ordnance "danger close"—inside the safety distances to friendly ground units—in his zeal to kill the enemy. If some friendlies got injured in the process, Gullick figured they would have been hurt in the ground fight anyway.

"Alert Landscape," Gullick snapped.

"I've got the air police moving in—" Quinn began.

"Negative," Gullick said. "There's too much going on tonight. I want those people gone before Nightscape launches." Gullick turned away and walked over to another officer.

Quinn reluctantly gave the orders for Landscape to move. He glanced up at the main screen. Just above it a small digital display read T–143 HOURS, 34 MINUTES. Quinn bit the inside of his lower lip. He didn't understand why they were launching a Nightscape mission this evening with the

mothership test flight only a little under six nights away. It
was just one of several things that had been occurring over
the past year that didn't make sense to Quinn. But the
general brooked no discussion and had gotten even mood-
ier than usual as the countdown got closer.

Quinn had worked in the Cube for four years now. He
was the senior ranking man not on the panel—Majic-12—
that ran the Cube and all its assorted activities. As such he
was the link between all the military and contract personnel and Majic-12. When Majic staff was gone, as they often
were, it was Quinn who was responsible for the day-to-day
operation of the Cube and the entire Area 51 complex.
Those below Quinn knew only what they needed in order
to do their specific jobs. Those on Majic-12 knew everything. Quinn was somewhere in the middle. He was privy
to much information, but he was also aware there was
quite a bit that he wasn't given access to. But even he had
been able to tell that things were changing now. The rush
on the mothership, the Nightscape missions, and various
other events were all out of the norm that had been established his first three years assigned here. The Cube and all
it controlled was abnormal enough; Quinn didn't appreciate Gullick and Majic-12 adding to the stress.

General Gullick crooked a finger and Quinn hastened
over to stand with him behind another operator whose
screen showed a live satellite downlink, also with thermal
imaging. "Anything at the mission support site?" Gullick
asked.

"MSS is clear, sir."

Gullick glanced over at a third officer whose screens
showed multiple video feeds of large hangars with rock
walls—the view of what was right above them. "Bouncer
Three's status?"

"Ready, sir."

"The C-130's in?" Gullick asked, this time focusing on Quinn.

"Landed thirty minutes ago, sir," Quinn replied.

"The Osprey?"

"Ready to go."

"Start the recall."

Quinn hastened to do as he was ordered.

2

"Sprechen Sie Deutsch?"

Mike Turcotte turned with a blank expression to the man who had spoken. "Excuse me?"

The other man chuckled. "I heard you came here from those high-speed counterterrorist boys in Germany, but I like that response. Don't know nothing, didn't come from nowhere. That's good. You'll fit in well here."

The man's name was Prague, at least that was how he had introduced himself to Turcotte earlier in the evening when they'd met at McCarren Airport. Upon meeting him Turcotte had immediately sized up the other man physically. Prague was a tall, lean man, with black eyes and a smooth, expressionless face. His build contrasted with Turcotte's, which was average height, just shy of five feet ten inches. Turcotte's physique was not one of bulging muscles but rather the solid, thick muscular physique some people are born with, not that he hadn't maintained it over the years with a constant physical regime. His skin was dark, natural for his half-Canuck, half-Indian background. He'd grown up in the forests of northern Maine, where the major industries were lumber and hard drinking. His shot out of town had been a football scholarship to the University of Maine at Orono. That dream had been crunched during a game his sophomore year by a pair of defensive backs from the University of New Hampshire. His knee had been reconstructed, then his scholarship terminated.

Faced with the prospect of going back to the logging camps, Turcotte had enlisted the aid of the lieutenant colonel in charge of the small army ROTC program at the university. They'd found a friendly doctor to fudge on the physical and the army had picked up where the football team had fallen off.

Turcotte had graduated with a degree in forestry and received a commission in the army. His first assignment had been with the infantry in the Tenth Mountain Division. The pace at Fort Drum had proved too slow and first chance he had, Turcotte had volunteered for Special Forces training. The warrant officer giving him his Special Forces physical had looked at the scars on his knee and signed off on the paperwork with a wink, figuring anyone crazy enough to try Special Forces wasn't going to let a little thing like a reconstructed knee stop him.

But it almost had. During the intense selection and assessment training the knee had stayed swollen, causing Turcotte intense pain. He'd walked on it nonetheless, finishing the long overland movements with heavy rucksack as quickly as he could, as his classmates fell by the wayside. After starting with two hundred and forty men, at the end of training there were slightly over a hundred left and Turcotte was one of them.

Turcotte had loved the Special Forces and served in various assignments up until his last one, which had not turned out well in his view. Now he had been handpicked to be assigned to this unit, of which he knew nothing except it was highly classified and went by the designation of Delta Operations, which made Turcotte wonder if the name had been deliberately chosen to be confused with Delta Force, the elite counterterrorist force at Fort Bragg with whom he had worked occasionally when stationed with Detachment A in Berlin—a classified Special Forces unit responsible for terrorism control in Europe.

There wasn't even any scuttlebutt about Delta Operations, which was rather amazing among the close-knit Special Operations community. It meant one of two things: Either no one was ever reassigned out of Delta Operations and therefore no stories could be told, or those reassigned out of it kept their mouths completely sealed, which was more likely. Turcotte knew civilians found it difficult to credit, but most military men he had worked with believed in the oaths of secrecy they swore.

But the thing that concerned Turcotte was that there were two levels to this assignment. As far as Prague and Delta Operations knew he was just another new man with a security clearance and a background in Special Operations. But Turcotte had been been verbally ordered by the DET-A commander to stop in Washington on his way from Europe to Nevada. He'd been met at the airport by a pair of Secret Service agents and escorted to a private room in the terminal. With the agents standing guard outside the door he'd been briefed by a woman who'd identified herself as the presidential science adviser to something called Majic-12, Dr. Lisa Duncan. She'd told him that his real job was to infiltrate Delta Operations, which provided security for Majic-12, and observe what was going on. He was given a phone number to call and relay what he saw.

To all of Turcotte's questions Duncan had been evasive. She couldn't tell him what he was supposed to be looking for. Since she was on the Majic-12 council, that made him suspicious. She had not even told him why he was being selected. Turcotte wondered if it had anything to do with what had just happened in Germany. Beyond that wondering, the naturally suspicious part of his mind, which years of work in Special Operations had cultivated, wondered if Lisa Duncan was who she said she was, regardless of her fancy ID card. This might be some sort of test of his loyalty set up by Delta Operations itself.

Duncan had told him he was not to inform anyone of his meeting with her, but that had immediately put him in a bind the minute he had met Prague at the Las Vegas airport. Withholding that information meant he was already in subtle conflict with his new organization, not a good way to start an assignment. What was real and what wasn't, Turcotte didn't know. He'd decided on the plane from Washington to Las Vegas to do what Duncan had said, keep his eyes and ears open, his mouth shut, and ride whatever roller coaster he had been put onto until he could make up his own mind.

Turcotte had expected to be driven straight out to Nellis Air Force Base from the airfield. That was the destination listed on his orders. To his surprise they had taken a cab downtown and checked into a hotel. Actually they hadn't checked in, they'd walked right past the desk and taken an elevator directly up to the room, which had a numerical keypad instead of a traditional lock. Prague punched in the code.

Prague had shrugged at Turcotte's concern about reporting in to Nellis, as they entered the lavishly furnished suite.

"Don't sweat it. We'll get you in tomorrow. And you're not going to Nellis. You'll find out, meat."

"What's with this room?" Turcotte asked, noting the *meat* comment. It was a term used for new replacements to combat units that had suffered high casualties. Certainly not the situation he was in now, at least he hoped not. There was only one other way to decipher the phrase, as a slam. Turcotte didn't know why Prague would do that except to test his tolerance levels, which was an accepted practice in elite units. Except it usually involved professional tests of physical or mental capabilities, not insults. Of course, Turcotte knew there might be another reason for Prague's attitude: maybe he knew about the meeting in Washington and it had been a test. Or, that Duncan was for real and Prague knew Turcotte was a plant. All this thinking about plots within plots gave Turcotte a headache.

Prague threw himself down on the sofa. "We have all these rooms on a permanent basis for R and R when we come into town. We get taken care of real well, as long as we don't screw up. And no drinking. Even on R and R. We always have to be ready."

"For what?" Turcotte asked, dropping his large kit bag and walking over to the window to look out at the neon display of Las Vegas.

"For whatever, meat," Prague returned easily. "We fly out of McCarren on Janet tomorrow morning."

"Janet?" Turcotte asked.

"A 737. Goes out every morning to the Area with the contract workers and us."

"What exactly is my job and—" Turcotte paused as a loud chirping filled the air and Prague pulled a beeper off his belt. He turned off the noise and checked the small LED screen.

"Looks like you're about to find out," Prague said, standing. "Grab your gear. We're going back to the airport now. Recall."

NELLIS AIR FORCE BASE RESERVATION
T−143 HOURS

"I wonder what their electric bill is?" Simmons muttered, staring out across the dry lake bed at the brilliantly lit complex nestled up against the base of the Groom Mountain Range. He put his binoculars to his eyes and took in the hangars, towers, and antennas all laid out alongside the extremely long runway.

"Looks like you might have come on a good night," Franklin commented, sitting down with his back against a boulder. They'd arrived at the top of White Sides Mountain ten minutes earlier and settled in on the edge of the mountaintop, overlooking the lake bed.

"Might just be for the C-130's," Simmons commented.

The transport planes were parked near a particularly large hangar and there was some activity going on around them. He focused the glasses. "They're not unloading," he said. "They're loading something onto the planes. Looks like a couple of helicopters."

"Helicopters?" Franklin repeated. "Let me see." He took the binoculars and looked for a few minutes. "I've seen one of those type of choppers before. Painted all black. The big one is a UH-60 Blackhawk. The two little ones I don't know. They fly UH-60's around here for security. I had one buzz my truck one day down on the mailbox road."

"Where do you think they're taking them?" Simmons asked, taking the binoculars back.

"I don't know."

"Something's going on," Simmons said.

McCARREN FIELD, LAS VEGAS
T—142 HOURS, 45 MINUTES

The 737 had no markings on it other than a broad red band painted down the outside. It was parked behind a Cyclone fence with green stripping run through the chain links to discourage observers. Turcotte carried his kit bag right on board after Prague joked that they could carry any damn thing they wanted onto this flight—there was no baggage check.

Instead of a stewardess a hard-faced man in a three-piece suit was waiting inside the plane door, checking off personnel as they came in. "Who's this?" he demanded, looking at Turcotte.

"Fresh meat," Prague replied. "I picked him up this evening."

"Let me see your ID," the man demanded.

Turcotte pulled out his military ID card and the man scanned the picture. "Wait here." He stepped back into what had been the forward galley and flipped open a small portable phone. He spoke into it for a minute, then flipped it shut. He came out. "Your orders check out. You're cleared."

Although his face showed no change of expression, Turcotte slowly relaxed his right hand and rubbed the fingers lightly over the scar tissue that was knotted over the palm of that hand.

The man held up a small device. "Blow."

Turcotte glanced at Prague, who took the device and blew into it. The man checked the readout, quickly switched out the tube, and handed it to Turcotte, who did the same. After looking at the readout the man gestured with the phone toward the back of the plane.

Prague slapped Turcotte on the back and led him down the aisle. Turcotte glanced at the other men gathered on board. They all had the same look: hard, professional, and competent. It was the demeanor that all the men Turcotte had served with over the years in Special Operations had.

As Prague settled down next to him and the door to the plane shut, Turcotte decided to try to find out what was going on, especially since it now seemed they were on alert. "Where are we headed?" he asked.

"Area 51," Prague replied. "It's an Air Force facility.

Well, actually it's on Air Force land, but it's run by an organization called the National Reconnaissance Organization or NRO, which is responsible for all overhead imagery."

Turcotte knew that the NRO was an extensive operation, overseeing all satellite and spy-plane operations with a budget in the billions. He'd been on several missions where he'd received support from the NRO.

"What exactly do we do?" Turcotte asked, pressing his hands against the seat back in front of him and pushing, relieving the tension in his shoulders.

"Security," Prague answered. "Air Force handles the outer perimeter but we do the inside stuff, since we all have the clearances. Actually," he amended, "Delta Ops consists of two units. One is called Landscape and the other Nightscape. Landscape is responsible for on-the-ground security of the facilities at Area 51 and for keeping tabs on the people there. Nightscape, which you are now part of . . ." Prague paused. "Well, you'll find out soon enough, meat."

Turcotte had been in enough covert units to know when to stop asking questions, so he shut up and listened to the engines rumble as they made their way north toward his new assignment.

WHITE SIDES MOUNTAIN
T—142 HOURS, 26 MINUTES

Simmons reached into his backpack and pulled out a plastic case and unsnapped it.

"What's that?" Franklin asked.

"They're night vision goggles," Simmons replied.

"Really?" Franklin said. "I've seen pictures of them. The camo dudes here use them. They drive around wearing

them, with all their lights out. They can scare the shit out
of you when they roll up on you in the dark like that when
you think you're all alone on the road."

Simmons turned the on-switch and the inside of the lens
glowed bright green. He began scanning, keeping the goggles away from the bright lights of the facility itself, which
would overload the computer enhancer built into them. He
checked out the long landing strip. It was over fifteen thousand feet long and reputed to be the longest in the world,
yet its very existence was denied by the government. Then
he looked over the rest of the lake bed, trying to see if
there was anything else of interest.

A small spark flickered in the eyepiece and Simmons
twisted his head, trying to catch what had caused it. He
looked down and to the right and was rewarded by another
brief spark. A pair of four-wheel all-terrain vehicles were
making their way along a switchback about four miles
away. The spark was the reflection of moonlight off the
darkened headlights. Each of the drivers had goggles
strapped over the front of his helmet.

Simmons tapped Franklin and handed him the goggles.
"There. You see those two guys on the ATVs?"

Franklin looked and nodded. "Yeah, I see 'em."

"Are they the 'camo dudes' you were telling me about?"

"I've never seen them on ATVs before," Franklin said,
"but, yeah, those are camo dudes. And, actually, I've never
seen them on the inside of the mountain before. They always came up on us on the other side." He handed the
goggles back. "They can't get up here on those things anyway. The closest they can get is maybe a mile away."

"Have you ever pulled the road sensors before?" Simmons asked suddenly.

Franklin didn't answer and Simmons took one more look
at the two ATVs coming toward them, then turned off the

goggles. "You've never played with the sensors before, right?"

Franklin reluctantly nodded. "Usually we get stopped down below by the outer security guys. The sheriff comes, confiscates our film. Then most of the time he lets us climb up."

"Most of the time?" Simmons asked.

"Yeah. Sometimes, maybe three or four times, he told us to go home."

"I thought you said this was public land," Simmons said.

"It is."

"So why did you leave those times?"

Franklin looked very uncomfortable. "The sheriff told us he couldn't be responsible for our safety if we continued on. It was like a code between him and me, man. I knew that was when I was supposed to go back to the mailbox and watch."

"And what happened those nights?" Simmons asked.

Franklin didn't answer.

"Those are the nights you spotted strange lights doing unexplainable maneuvers in the air on the other side of the mountaintop. This mountaintop," Simmons said with a bit of heat in his voice.

"Yeah."

"So this is the first time you've ever been up here and they didn't know you were up here. This might be a night you were supposed to go back to the mailbox."

"Yeah."

That explained why Franklin was carrying the only camera, Simmons realized. Franklin was using him as a cover in case they were caught, probably hoping that Simmons's status would help him with the authorities. Simmons took a deep breath as he considered the possibilities. It was dangerous, but there was a chance here for a big story. "I guess we'll just have to see what happens, then."

They both turned their heads as they again heard the whine of jet engines in the distance.

"That's Janet," Franklin said as the 737 descended overhead to a landing on the airstrip. He sounded concerned. "It's early. It usually doesn't come until five forty-five in the morning."

Simmons looked through the goggles. The two ATVs had turned around and were now heading away. He thought that even more strange than the 737 coming early.

GROOM LAKE AIRSTRIP, AREA 51
T—142 HOURS, 13 MINUTES

The 737 came to a halt a quarter mile away from the two C-130's. Turcotte followed Prague off and into a small building next to a hangar. Up against the base of a large mountain there was a cluster of buildings, several hangars, and what appeared to be a couple of barracks buildings, along with a control tower for the runway.

"Stow your kit bag there, meat," Prague ordered.

The other men were opening wall lockers and pulling out black jumpsuits and putting them on. Prague led Turcotte over to a supply room and began tossing him pieces of equipment, a similar jumpsuit leading the way, followed by a combat vest, black balaclava, black aviator gloves, and a set of AN-PVS-9 night vision goggles—the hottest technology in the field.

Prague unlocked a large bin and pulled out a sophisticated-looking weapon. Turcotte nodded in appreciation. The NRO was supplying these guys with top-of-the-line gear. Turcotte took the weapon and checked it out. The gun was a 9mm Calico, with telescoping butt stock, built-in silencer, hundred-round cylindrical magazine, and mounted laser sight.

"It's zeroed in on the laser out to one hundred meters, flat trajectory," Prague informed him. "Out from there you raise about an inch per fifty meters." Prague looked at him. "I assume you have your own personal sidearm?"

Turcotte nodded. "Browning High Power."

"You can carry that, but only use it as a last resort. We like to stay silenced." Prague also handed him a headset with boom mike. "Voice activated, it's preset to my command frequency. Always have it on and powered," he ordered. "If I can't talk to you, you'd better be fucking dead, because you don't want to see or hear me again."

Turcotte nodded and slipped it over his head, sliding the main battery pack on a cord around his neck.

Prague slapped him on the shoulder, much harder than necessary. "Get changed and let's roll."

Turcotte zipped up the coveralls and tugged on the combat vest, filling the empty pockets with extra magazines for the Calico. He also appropriated a few flash-bang grenades, two high-explosive minigrenades, two CS grenades, and placed them in pockets. He took his Browning out of his kit bag and slid it into the thigh holster rigged below the vest. For good measure he added a few more items from his kit bag: a leather sheath holding three perfectly balanced and highly honed throwing knives handmade for him by a knifesmith back in Maine went inside the jumpsuit, strapped over his right shoulder; a coiled steel wire garotte fitted inside one of the suit's pockets; and a slim, double-edged commando knife with sheath slid down the outside of the top of his right boot.

Feeling fully dressed for whatever might occur, Turcotte joined the other men by the doors to the hangar. There were twenty-two men and Prague was apparently in charge. He spotted Turcotte.

"You stay with me tonight, meat. Do what I tell you to do. Don't do nothing you aren't told to. You're going to see some strange things. Don't worry about anything. We got it all under control."

If we have it all under control, Turcotte wondered, *why do we need the guns?* But he kept his mouth shut and looked out at what the other men were watching. A UH-60 Blackhawk helicopter, blades folded, had already been placed inside the first C-130. Two AH-6 attack helicopters—"little birds," as the pilots referred to them—were also being loaded onto the second one. The AH-6 was a small, four-man helicopter with a minigun mounted on the right skid. The only unit that Turcotte knew of that flew the AH-6 was Task Force 160, the army's classified helicopter unit.

"Alpha team, move out!" Prague ordered.

Four men with parachutes casually slung over their shoulders walked onto the tarmac toward a waiting V-22 Osprey that had been sitting in the dark, unnoticed until now in the lee of the large hangar. Another surprise. Turcotte had heard that the government contract for the Osprey had been canceled, but this one looked very operational as each of its massive propellers began turning. They were on the end of the wings, which were rotated *up*—a position that allowed the plane to take off like a helicopter, then fly like a plane as the wings rotated forward. The Osprey was moving even before the back ramp finished closing, lifting into the sky.

Turcotte felt a surge of adrenaline. The smell of JP-4 fuel, the exhaust from the aircraft engines, the sounds, the weaponry, all touched his senses and brought back memories—some good, most bad, but all exciting.

"Let's go!" Prague ordered, and Turcotte followed the other men on board the lead C-130. The interior could easily fit four cars end to end. Along each side of the plane facing inward was a row of red canvas jump seats. The skin of the aircraft wasn't insulated and the roar of the four turboprop engines reverbrated through the interior with a teeth-rattling drone. Several chest-height, small round portholes were the only windows to the outside world. Turcotte noted several other pallets of gear strapped down along the center of the cargo bay. There were other groups of men already on board, some dressed in gray jumpsuits, others in traditional army green.

"The ones in gray are the eggheads!" Prague yelled in his ear. "We baby-sit them while they do their stuff. The green ones are the pilots for the choppers."

The ramp of the C-130 slowly lifted and closed and the interior lights glowed red, allowing the people inside to maintain their natural night vision. Turcotte glanced out one of the small portholes at the airfield. He noted that the V-22 was out of sight. He wondered where the four men were jumping. Out of the corner of his eye something large and round was moving about thirty feet above the flight strip, between them and the mountain. Turcotte blinked. "What the—"

"Keep your attention inboard," Prague ordered, grabbing his shoulder. "Your gear good to go?"

Turcotte looked at his leader, then closed his eyes. The image of what he had just seen was still clear in his memory, but his mind was already beginning to question itself. "Yes, sir."

"All right. Like I said, just stick with me for this first one. And don't let nothing you see surprise you."

The plane shuddered as it began to slowly move. Turcotte took the Calico submachine gun and placed it in his lap. He swiftly fieldstripped it down to its component parts, balancing them on his thighs. He lifted up the firing pin and checked to make sure the tip wasn't filed down. He put the gun back together, carefully checking each part to make sure it was functional. When he was done, he slid the bolt back and put a round in the chamber, making sure the select lever was on safe.

"What do you think is going on?" Simmons asked nervously, wishing he had his camera. The first C-130 was moving ponderously toward the end of the runway. The other smaller plane had taken off like a helicopter and disappeared to the north.

"Holy shit!" Franklin exclaimed. "Do you see that!"

Simmons twisted and froze at the sight that greeted him. Franklin was up and running, stumbling over the rocks, heading back the way they had come. Simmons reached for the small Instamatic camera he had secreted inside his shirt when the night sky was brilliantly lit for a few seconds and then Simmons saw and felt no more.

Turcotte held on to the web seating along the inside skin of the aircraft as the nose lifted, and then they were airborne. He caught a glimpse of a bright light somewhere out in the mountains through the far portal. He glanced over at Prague, and the man was staring at him, his eyes black and flat.

Turcotte calmly met the gaze. He knew the type. Prague was a hard man among men who prided themselves on being tough. Turcotte imagined Prague's stare intimidated less-experienced men, but Turcotte knew something that Prague knew: he knew the power of death. He knew the feeling of having that power in the crook of the finger, exercising it with a three-pound pull, and how easy it was. It didn't matter how tough you pretended to be at that point.

Turcotte closed his eyes and tried to relax. It didn't take a genius to figure out that he wasn't going to get anything up front here. Wherever they were going, he'd find out when they got there. And whatever he was supposed to do when they got there, he'd find out when they told him. It was a hell of a way to run an operation. Either Prague was incompetent or he was deliberately keeping Turcotte in the dark. Turcotte knew it wasn't the former.

Vicinity Nebraska/South Dakota Border
T—141 Hours, 15 Minutes

The V-22 Osprey circled the south shore of Lewis and Clark Lake at ten thousand feet. In the rear the team leader listened on the headset of the satellite radio as he was fed the latest from the Cube.

"Phoenix Advance, this is Nightscape Six. Thermals read clear of humans in MSS. Proceed. Out."

The team leader took off the headset and turned to the three members of his team. "Let's go." He gave a thumbs-up to the crew chief.

The back ramp slowly opened to the chill night sky. When it was completely open, the crew chief gestured. The team leader walked to the edge and stepped off, followed closely by the other men. He got stable, arms and legs akimbo, then quickly pulled his ripcord. The square chute blossomed above his head and he checked his canopy to make sure it was functioning properly. Then he slid the night vision goggles down over his crash helmet and switched them on.

Glancing above, beyond his chute, he could see the other three members of his team hanging up above him, in perfect formation. Satisfied, the team leader looked down and oriented himself. The target area was easy to see. There was a long section of shoreline with no lights. As he descended, he checked the terrain through the glow of the goggles and started picking up more details. The abandoned ski lift was the most prominent feature he was looking for, and once he spotted it, he pulled on his toggles, aiming for the high terminus of the lift. There was a small open field there, where years ago beginning skiers had stumbled off as the chairs deposited them.

Pulling in on both toggles less than twenty feet above the ground, the team leader slowed his descent to the point that when his boots touched down it was no more of a jar than if he had stepped off a curb. The chute crumpled behind him as he unfastened his submachine gun. The other men landed, all within twenty feet. They secured their chutes, then took position underneath the top pylon of the ski lift, on the highest bit of ground within ten miles. From there they could oversee the jumbled two miles of terrain lying between them and the lake.

The area was called Devil's Nest and it was rumored that Jesse James had used it as a hideout over a century ago. The rolling plain of Nebraska abruptly dropped off into sharp hills and ridgelines, starting right where the men were and running up to the edge of the man-made lake— the result of the damming of the Missouri River ten miles downstream. A developer had tried to turn it into a resort area a decade ago—hence the ski lift—but the idea had failed miserably. The men weren't interested in the rusting machinery, though. Their concern lay in the center of the area, running along the top of a ridgeline pointed directly at the lake.

The team leader took the handset his commo man offered him. "Nightscape Six Two, this is Phoenix Advance. Landing strip is clear. Area is clear. Over."

"This is Six Two. Roger. Phoenix main due in five mikes. Out."

In the air Turcotte watched Prague speak into the satellite radio, the words lost in the loud roar of the engines. He could feel the change in air pressure as the C-130 descended. A glance out the window showed water, then shoreline. The wheels of the 130 touched earth and the plane began rolling. It stopped in an amazingly short distance for such a large aircraft and the back ramp opened, as the plane turned around, facing back down the runway.

"Let's go!" Prague yelled. "Off-load everything."

Turcotte lent a hand as they rolled the helicopter off and into the shelter of the nearby trees. He was impressed with the ability of the pilots. The runway was little more than a flat expanse of rough grass between dangerously close lines of trees on either side.

As soon as they had the helicopter and equipment out, the plane was heading back down the strip, the ramp not even fully closed as the plane lifted off into the night sky. Less than a minute later the second plane was landing and the process was repeated. In a few minutes they had all three helicopters and personnel on the ground.

As the sound of the second plane faded into the distance, Prague was all business. "I want camo nets up and everything under cover, ASAP. Let's move, people!"

3

CAIRO, EGYPT
T−137 HOURS

"I don't know what's wrong with this thing," the graduate student said, twisting knobs and adjusting controls on the machinery in front of him. The sound of his shrill voice echoed off the stone walls and slowly died out, leaving stillness in the air.

"Why are you so sure there's something wrong with the machine?" Professor Nabinger asked in a quieter voice.

"What else could be causing these negative readings?" The student let go of the controls of the magnetic resonance imager that they had carried down here, with great effort, into the bowels of the Great Pyramid.

The effort had taken two forms: in the past twenty-four hours the actual physical effort of carrying the machine through the narrow tunnels of the Great Pyramid of Giza down to the bottom chamber and, for a year prior, complex diplomatic effort to be granted permission to bring the modern equipment into the greatest of Egypt's ancient monuments and turn it on.

Nabinger knew enough about the politics of archaeology to appreciate the opportunity he was being given to use this equipment here. Of the original seven wonders of the ancient world the three pyramids on the West Bank of the

Nile were the only one still standing, and even in ancient times they were considered the greatest of the seven. The Colossus at Rhodes—which most archaeologists doubted had even existed as reported—the hanging gardens of Babylon, the Tower of Babel, the Tower of Pharos at Alexandria, and other reported marvels of early engineering had all disappeared over the centuries. All but the pyramids, built between 2685 and 2180 B.C. They were weathered by the sand long before the Roman Empire even rose, were still there when it fell, centuries later, and were standing strong as the second millennium after Christ's birth approached.

Their original face of hand-smoothed limestone had long ago been plundered—except for the very top of the middle pyramid—but their bulk was so great that they had escaped most of the ravages of the wars that had swirled around them. From the Hyksos invasions from the north in the sixteenth century B.C. to Napoleon, to the British Eighth Army in World War II, the pyramids had survived them all.

There were over eighty pyramids still standing in Egypt, and Nabinger had seen most of them and explored their mysteries, but he was always drawn back to the famous trio at Giza. As one came up on them and viewed the three, the middle pyramid of Khafre appeared to be the largest, but only because it was built on higher ground. The Pharaoh Khufu, more popularly known as Cheops, was responsible for the building of the greatest pyramid, farthest to the northeast. Over four hundred feet tall and covering eighty acres, it was by far the largest stone building in the world. The smallest of the three was that of Menkaure, measuring over two hundred feet in altitude. The sides of all three were aligned with the four cardinal directions and they went from northeast to southwest, from largest to smallest. The Great Sphinx lay at the foot of the middle pyramid—

far enough to the east to also be out in front of the Great
Pyramid, off the Sphinx's left shoulder.

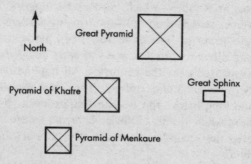

The pyramids drew tourists and archeologists and scientists and evoked awe among all. For the tourist the size and
age were enough. For the scientist the exact engineering
defied the technology of the time in which they were built.
For the archaeologist not only was the architecture amazing, but there was the unsettling question of the *purpose* of
the buildings. That was the question Nabinger had struggled with for years, not content with the answers offered up
by his colleagues.

They were commonly assumed to have been tombs for
the pharaohs. But the problem with that theory was that
the sarcophagus discovered inside of each of the pyramids
had been found empty. For years that had been blamed on
the plundering of grave robbers, until sarcophagi with the
lids still on and the seals on those lids still intact were
found, and they were empty also.

The next best theory, and one that logically followed the
previous one, was that perhaps the pyramids were cenotaphs, funeral memorials, and the bodies had secretly been
buried elsewhere to prevent the graves from being plundered.

A more recent theory took a totally different approach.

There were those who postulated that, to the Egyptians, the finished pyramid was not so important as the process of building; that the purpose of their construction was a desire by ancient pharaohs to employ and draw together their people during the annual three months the Nile flooded and agricultural work came to a standstill. Idle hands led to idle minds that could possibly think thoughts the pharaohs would not have approved of. So, this theory went, the pharaohs placed ten-ton blocks of stones in those idle hands.

Another theory favored by the more optimistic traditionalists was that the final resting place of the pharaohs in the pyramids had not been discovered yet. It was perhaps hidden deep in the bedrock underneath the massive stone structures.

There were many theories, but none had yet been proven. It was a search to discover and prove the purpose of the pyramids that drew Peter Nabinger to them every year for six months. The leading Egyptian expert at the Brooklyn Museum, he had been coming here for twelve years.

Nabinger's area of expertise was hieroglyphics: a form of writing using figures or objects to represent words or sounds. His philosophy was that the best way to understand the past was to read what people of the time had to say about their own existence, rather than what someone digging up ruins thousands of years later had to say.

One thing Nabinger found most fascinating about the pyramids was that if they had not been there now, in the present, for everyone to see, it was doubtful anyone would believe they had ever existed, because of the almost total lack of reference to them in ancient Egyptian writings. It was almost as if Egyptian historians of years gone past had assumed everyone would know about the pyramids and therefore there was no need to talk about them. Or, Nabinger sometimes suspected, maybe even the people of the time of the pyramids' building weren't quite clued in themselves as to the reason they were being built. Or maybe, Nabinger also wondered, maybe it had been forbidden to write about them?

This year he was trying something different, in addition to his main project of recording all the writing and drawings on the interior walls of the Great Pyramid. He was using the magnetic resonance imager, the MRI, to probe deep underneath the structures where the eye could not go and physical excavation was prohibited. The waves emitted by the imager could safely invade the depths and tell him if there were more buried wonders. At least that was the theory. The practice, as his graduate assistant Mike Welcher was pointing out to him, was not living up to the anticipation.

"It's like"—Welcher paused and scratched his head—"it's like we're being blocked by some other emission source. It's not particularly powerful, but it is there."

"For example?" Nabinger asked, leaning back against the cool stone walls of the chamber. Despite all the time he'd spent inside the pyramid over the years, there was still a feeling of oppression in here, as if one could sense the immense weight of stone pressing down overhead.

Nabinger was a tall, heavyset man, sporting a thick black beard and wire-rimmed glasses. He wore faded khaki, the uniform of the desert explorer. At thirty-six he was considered young in the field of archaeology and he had no major finds to stake his reputation upon. Part of his problem, he would readily acknowledge to his friends back in Brooklyn, was that he had no pet theory that he desired to pursue. He only had his pet method, searching for new writings and trying to decipher the volumes of hieroglyphics that still remained untranslated. He was willing to accept whatever they yielded, but so far his efforts had not turned up much.

Schliemann might have been convinced that Troy actually existed and thus spent his life searching for it, but Nabinger had no such convictions. Nabinger's work on the pyramids was one of detailing what was there and searching for its explanation, an area that was perhaps one of the most heavily studied in the field of archaeology. He had hopes that perhaps he might find something with the MRI, something that others had missed, but he didn't have a clue as to what. Hopefully, it might be a new chamber with not only whatever was in it, but also new, unseen writings.

Welcher was looking at the readouts. "If I didn't know better, I'd say we're getting interference from some sort of residual radiation."

Nabinger had been afraid of this. "Radiation?" He glanced across the chamber at the group of Egyptian laborers who had helped haul the MRI down here. The head man, Kaji, was watching them carefully, his wrinkled face not betraying a thought. The last thing Nabinger needed was the laborers walking out on them because of the threat of radiation.

"Yeah," Welcher said. "To prepare for this I worked with the MRI in the hospital and we saw readings like this once in a while. They came up when the reading was affected by X-rays. In fact, the technician told me they finally had to write up a schedule for the machines so they wouldn't be on at the same time, even though they were on different floors of the hospital and both heavily shielded."

It was information not widely known, but Nabinger had read reports from earlier expeditions that had used cosmic ray bombardment to search for hidden chambers and passages in the Great Pyramid and their reports had been similar: there was some sort of residual radiation inside the pyramid that blocked such attempts. The information had not been widely disseminated because there was no explanation for it, and scientists didn't write journal articles about things they couldn't explain. Nabinger often wondered how many unexplained phenomena went unreported because those who discovered them didn't want to risk ridicule since there was no rational explanation for their findings.

Nabinger had hoped to have better luck with the MRI because it worked on a different band-width from the cosmic-ray emitters. The exact nature of the radiation had never been detailed, so he had not been able to determine if the MRI would be blocked also.

"Have you tried the entire spectrum on the machine?" he asked. They'd been down here for four hours already, Nabinger allowing Welcher to handle the machine, which was his specialty. Nabinger had spent the time painstakingly photographing the walls of the chamber, the bottom of the three in the Great Pyramid. Although extensively documented, some of the hieroglyphics on the wall had never been deciphered.

The notebook in his lap was covered with his scribblings, and he had been centered totally on his work, excited by the possibility that there might be some linguistic connection between some of the panels of hieroglyphics here and newly found panels in Mexico. Nabinger did not concern himself with *how* such a connection could be, he just wanted to decipher what he had. And so far, a very strange message was being revealed to him, word by laborious word. The importance of the MRI was diminishing with every minute he studied the writings.

A year ago Nabinger had made some startling discoveries that he had kept to himself. It had always been accepted that there were certain panels or tablets of markings at Egyptian sites that were not classical hieroglyphics but appeared to be some earlier picture language called "high runes." While such sites were few—too few to provide a database sufficient to allow a scientific attempt at translation—enough had been found to cause some interest. What Nabinger had stumbled across were pictures of similar high runes from a site in South America. After a year of very hard work over the few samples available—combining them with those from Egypt—he believed he had manage to decode a couple of dozen words and symbols. He needed more samples, though, in order to feel comfortable that the little he had achieved was valid. For all he knew, his translation could be totally false and he had been working with gibberish.

Kaji snapped some commands in Arabic and the laborers rose to their feet and disappeared back up the corridor. Nabinger cursed and put his notebook down. "Listen here, Kaji, I've paid—"

"It is all right, Professor," Kaji said, holding up a hand roughened by a lifetime of manual labor. He spoke almost perfect English with a slight British accent—a surprise to Nabinger, who was often exasperated by the Egyptian tactic of retreating behind a pretended ignorance of English to avoid work. "I have given them a break outside. They will be back in an hour." He looked at the MRI machine and smiled, a gold tooth gleaming in the front of his mouth. "We are not having much luck, yes?"

"No, we're not," Nabinger said, used to the strange syntax.

"Professor Hammond did not have much luck with his machines, either, in 1976," Kaji noted.

"You were with Hammond?" Nabinger asked. He had read Hammond's report in the archives of the Royal Museum in London. It had not been published due to the failure to discover anything. Of course, Nabinger had noted at the time, Hammond *had* discovered something. He had discovered that there was residual radiation inside the pyramids that shouldn't be there.

"I have been here many times," Kaji said. "In all the

pyramids. Also many times in the Valley of the Kings. I spent years in the desert to the south before the waters from the dam covered it. I have led many parties of laborers and watched many strange things at sites."

"Did Hammond have any guesses why his machine didn't work?" Nabinger asked.

"Alas, no." Kaji sighed dramatically and ran his hand lightly over the control panel of the MRI, getting Welcher's attention. "Such a machine is expensive, is it not?"

"Yes, it—" Welcher halted as Nabinger shook his head, now partially seeing where this was leading.

Kaji smiled. "Ah, Hammond, he had no readings. His man on the machine, he, too, said radiation. Hammond did not believe it. But the machine, it would not lie, would it?" He looked at Welcher. "Your machine, it would not lie, would it?"

Welcher remained quiet.

"If the machine does not lie," Nabinger said, "then something must be causing the readings."

"Or something was *once* here that still causes the readings," Kaji said. He turned and headed back toward the other side of the chamber, where a large stone sarcophagus rested.

"The sarcophagus was intact but empty when they broke the seals," Nabinger said sharply, referring to the first expedition into this chamber in 1951. There had been great excitement over the discovery of the chamber and particularly of the sarcophagus found inside with its lid still intact and sealed. The mystery of the pyramids was about to be solved, it was thought at the time. One could imagine the dismay when the seals were broken and the lid was opened, and there was nothing in the stone box.

The interior of the Great Pyramid contained three chambers. One entered the pyramid either through the designed polar entrance on the north side, or one blasted just below that by a caliph in later centuries. Both linked up with a tunnel that descended through the masonry and into the rock beneath the pyramid. That tunnel ended in an intersection hewn out of the rock where two tunnels branched off. One headed up to the middle chamber and the Grand Gallery, which led to the upper chamber. The other, more recently discovered tunnel headed down into the bedrock to the lower chamber. It was the lower chamber that Nabinger and his crew were presently working in.

THE GREAT PYRAMID

The Upper Chamber or "King's" Chamber

The Grand Gallery

The Middle or "Queen's" Chamber

The Lower Chamber

"I was here in 1951," Kaji said. "Yes, the sarcophagus was empty then."

"Then?" Nabinger repeated. He'd worked with Kaji before at other sites and the man had always been honest. When he'd first hired the old man years ago, Nabinger had checked with several others in the field and Kaji had come highly recommended.

"Hammond, he thought me an old fool, and I was young then," Kaji said. "I am older now. I tried to talk to him, but he did not wish to talk." Kaji rubbed the fingers of one hand lightly in the palm of the other.

Nabinger knew what that meant. Kaji wanted to be paid for his information, as Nabinger had suspected, but that was only natural. The professor thought furiously. He had rented the portable MRI. The contract was billed by day of use, and he had enough funds from the museum for eight days of use. If he air-shipped it back tomorrow, he would save five days of billing. That was a substantial amount of money, at least from an Egyptian standpoint. The only problem was explaining his receipts and billing forms to the accountant back at the university. But there was no sense in continuing to use a machine in a place where it yielded no information. He also considered the runes he was deciphering in this chamber. Those alone would make the expedition worthwhile. The MRI had been a long shot anyway.

Nabinger looked at Welcher. "Take a break."

Welcher left the chamber, leaving the two men alone.

"Ten thousand pounds," Nabinger said.

Kaji's face was expressionless.

"Twelve thousand and that is all I have." Nabinger knew that was over a year's salary to the average Egyptian.

Kaji held out his hand. Nabinger reached into his pocket and pulled out a wad of bills, the week's wages for the laborers. He would have to go to the bank and draw on the expedition account to pay them now.

Kaji sat down cross-legged on the floor, the money disappearing into his long robe. "I was here in 1951 with Martin's expedition when they opened this chamber, but it was not the first time I was in this chamber."

"Impossible!" Nabinger said sharply. "Professor Martin broke through three walls to get into here in 1951. Walls that were intact and dated. The seals on the sarcophagus were the originals with four dynasties marked—"

"You can speak impossible all you like," Kaji continued in the same quiet voice, "but I tell you I was in here before 1951. You have paid for my story. You may listen or you may argue, it matters not to me."

"I'll listen," Nabinger said, beginning to think he had

just wasted quite a bit of the museum's money and wondering if he could make it up by skimping elsewhere on the expedition fund. His mind automatically began figuring the exchange rate on the pound to dollar.

Kaji seemed satisfied. "It was nine years before Martin's expedition, during the Second World War. In 1942 the British ruled here in Cairo, but many were not happy with that. The Egyptian nationalists were willing to trade one set of rulers for another, hoping that somehow the Germans would be better than the British and grant us our freedom. In reality we did not have much say in the process. Rommel and the Afrika Korps were out to the west in the desert and many expected him to be here in the city before the end of the year.

"It all began in January of 1942 when Rommel began his offensive. By June, Tobruk had fallen and the British were in retreat. They were burning papers in the Eighth Army headquarters here in Cairo in preparation to run. They were all afraid. And Rommel kept coming. The British army fell back on El Alamein.

"I was working in Cairo," Kaji said, waving his hand above his head. "Even in the middle of war there were those who wished to view the ancient sights. The pyramids have seen many wars. There were many people for whom the war was a fine opportunity to travel and make money. I gave tours above. And sometimes, if the person paid enough so I could bribe the Egyptian guards, I took them inside. Many wanted to see the Grand Gallery," he said, referring to the massive passageway hundreds of feet above their heads that had twenty-eight-foot ceilings and led up to the center of the pyramid and the uppermost chamber.

Kaji spread his hands. "I cared not who ruled Cairo. The pyramids have seen many rulers and they will see many in the future. And the pyramids and the other sites, they are my life.

"The Germans were only a hundred and fifty miles away and it looked as if they could not be stopped. In early July, General Auchinleck was relieved and Churchill sent a general named Montgomery to relieve him. No one thought much of it here. It was assumed the British would fall back to Palestine, where they would block the canal with sunken ships, and the Germans would get Cairo.

"That was when I was approached by a party wanting to go inside this pyramid. They spoke strangely, but they paid well, which was all that counted. I bribed the guards and we entered, using the caliph's entranceway late at night, which was also strange.

"We moved through the descending corridor until we linked up with the original ascending tunnel leading to the Grand Gallery. But they did not want to go up, nor did they want to go to what we now call the middle chamber, but was then called the lower chamber. They had paper with them with drawings on it." Kaji pointed at the walls. "I did not get to look at it for very long, but the writing was very much like that on these walls. The symbols that cannot be read." His eyes turned to the notepad in Nabinger's lap. "Perhaps you are starting to understand those symbols?"

"Who were these men?" Nabinger asked, flipping the notepad shut.

"They were Germans," Kaji replied.

"Germans? How could they have gotten into Cairo? The British still held the city."

"Ah, that was the easy part," Kaji replied. "Throughout the war Cairo was one of the major centers for espionage, and all sorts of people came and went freely."

Kaji's voice became excited as he remembered. "Cairo was the place to be in World War II. All the whores worked for one side or the other or many times both. Every bar had its spies, most also working for both sides. There were British spying on Germans who were spying on Americans

who were spying on Italians and around and around." Kaji
chuckled.

"There were fortunes made on the black market. It was
no trouble for the Germans to send these men into Cairo.
Especially that July when everyone was more concerned
about preparing to flee or how to ingratiate themselves
with the invaders than about strange groups of men moving
in the dark."

"Where did the Germans get their drawings from?"
Nabinger asked.

"I do not know. They used me to get inside only. From
there they took charge."

Nabinger asked the question closest to his heart. "Did
they know how to read what they had?"

"I do not know," Kaji repeated, "but they had someone
with them who could understand it in some manner, that
was for certain. There were twelve of them. We went to the
dip, where the tunnel turns and heads up toward the
Grand Gallery, and halted. They searched and then began
digging. I became frightened and upset then. I would be
blamed, because the guards knew me and knew that I was
leading this party in. They were destroying my livelihood
with their picks and shovels.

"The German in charge"—Kaji paused and his eyes lost
their focus—"he was an evil man. I could see it all about
him and especially in his eyes. When I complained he
looked at me, and I knew I was dead if I opened my mouth
again. So I stayed silent.

"They worked quickly, digging. They knew exactly what
they were doing because inside of an hour they broke
through. Another passageway! Even through my fear I was
excited. Nothing like this had happened in my lifetime or
many lifetimes before me. This passageway led downward,
toward the ground beneath the pyramid. No one had ever
thought of that before. No one had ever considered if there

was a passage into the ground. They had always searched
for ways to go up.

"They went into it and I followed. I did not understand
what they were saying but it was easy to see they were
excited also. We came down the tunnel"—Kaji pointed behind him—"as you and I did earlier today. There were
three blockages set up in the passageway. I could see the
original writings on the walls and knew we were entering
parts that had not been seen by a living man in over four
thousand years. They tore through the blocking walls as
quickly as possible, leaving the rubble behind.

"The tunnel ended in stone, but the Germans didn't let
that stop them as they had not let the three other walls
stop them. They used their picks and broke through. And
then we were in here. And the sarcophagus was there just
like you see it in the pictures of Martin's expedition, with
the lid on and the seals intact. In the air I could feel the
presence of—"

Kaji paused and Nabinger blinked. The old man's voice
had drawn him in, the effect magnified by being in the very
room he was talking about.

Kaji looked at the center of the floor where the sarcophagus had once been. "The Germans were not archaeologists. That was certain. The way they broke through the
walls showed that. And the fact that they broke the seals
and lifted the lid. In 1951 Martin took six months before
his men opened the lid, carefully detailing every step of the
operation. The Germans were into it in less than five minutes after entering. They were interested in nothing but the
sarcophagus. Not the writings on the walls here, not the
seals. Nothing but the stone box."

"Was it empty?" Nabinger asked.

"No."

Nabinger waited, then could wait no longer. "Did they
find the pharaoh's body?"

"No." Kaji sighed and all the energy seemed to drain out of his body. "I don't know what it was that they found. There was a box inside the stone. A box of black metal. Metal such as I had never seen before nor have seen since." He gestured with his hands, indicating a rectangle about four feet high by two in breadth and width. "It was this size."

Nabinger shook his head. "This is all a story, Kaji. I think you have taken my money for a story that is a lie."

Kaji's voice was calm. "It is not a lie."

"I've seen the pictures Martin took. All the walls were intact. The seals on the sarcophagus were intact and the original ones. How do you explain that if these Germans did what you said? How did the walls get put back up? The seals put back on? Magic? The pharaoh's ghost?" Nabinger was disgusted.

"I am not sure," Kaji admitted. "I do know, though, that the Americans and the British sealed off the Great Pyramid for eight months in 1945, while the war was ending. No one could go in. Maybe they put everything back. It would have been difficult but possible. When I went down with Martin all the walls were back up as you say. It made me wonder, but I knew I had seen them broken through earlier."

"Why didn't you tell Martin?" Nabinger asked.

"I was just a laborer then. And he would not have believed me, as you do not believe me now."

"Why are you telling me?"

Kaji pointed at Nabinger's notebook. "Because you are interested in the special writings that no one can read. The Germans had those writings. That is how they found the chamber."

"This makes no sense," Nabinger exclaimed. "If the Germans came in here and ransacked the chamber, then why would the Americans and British cover it up?"

Kaji remained silent.

"Ah!" Nabinger threw his hands up in disgust. "There were no Germans in here in the first place. How many times have you sold this story, Kaji? How many others have you stolen from? I tell you, I will not allow you to get away with it."

"I have not lied. I was here." He reached inside his robe and pulled out a dagger.

Nabinger started, thinking for a second he had pushed the old man too far, but Kaji held it by the blade, offering the handle. Nabinger carefully took it.

"I stole that off one of the Germans. They all wore them."

Nabinger felt a chill as he looked at the handle. A miniature, very realistic ivory skull was at the end, and swastikas were carved into the bone handle along with the lightning bolts that indicated the infamous SS. He wondered what animal the bone had come from, then decided that was information he was better without. The gleaming steel was intricately detailed. Nabinger squinted—there was something written there. There was a word on the one side:

THULE

and on the other side a name:

Von Seeckt

Nabinger had heard of Thule. A place of legend, written about by Ptolemy and other ancient geographers as the northernmost inhabitable land, north of Britain. He had no idea what that had to do with the Nazis or the pyramids.

"Who was Von Seeckt?" Nabinger asked.

"He was the strange one in the group," Kaji said. "Ten of the twelve were killers. I could tell by their eyes. Two were different. One was the man who read the symbols and pointed the way. Two of the killers guarded him always. As if he was not there of his own free will.

"The second man: Von Seeckt—which is why I stole only from him—he was different also. He was not one of the killers but he wanted to be there. He was very excited when they found the black box. That was when I was able to take the knife. They gave him the box and he put it in a backpack. He carried it with him when they left. It looked heavy, but he was a strong man."

"That is all they wanted?" Nabinger asked. "Just that black box?"

"Yes. As soon as they had it we went back out. They had a truck waiting and drove away to the north. I ran and hid. I knew the guards would look for me when they found the broken walls and the empty chamber. But they never came for me. I never heard a word, which was strange also."

Nabinger held on to the dagger. "How do I know you didn't get this on the black market? It does not prove your story."

Kaji shrugged. "I know it is true. I do not care if you believe it is true. I am at peace with Allah. I have told the truth." He pointed at the MRI. "I was reminded to tell you this story because when the Germans opened the sarcophagus and pulled out the box, the man I stole the dagger from had one of those"—Kaji paused as he searched for the word—"a small machine that made noise when he pointed it at the big black box. It chattered like a locust."

"A Geiger counter?" Nabinger asked.

"Yes. That is what I have heard it called."

"The black box was radioactive?" Nabinger said, more to himself than Kaji. Nabinger looked at the Egyptian, who returned his gaze levelly. Although there was no logical reason to believe the old man, for some reason Nabinger did. What had been sealed in the sarcophagus? What had the ancient Egyptians possessed that was radioactive? There was no doubting that the MRI was picking up some form of residual radiation.

Nabinger sorted the story out in his mind. There was only one clue to pursue: the name on the dagger. Von Seeckt. Who was—or probably more appropriately—who had he been?

"What are you doing?" Kaji asked, as Nabinger tucked the dagger into his waistband.

"I am keeping this," Nabinger said. "I paid for your story and this is the only proof."

"I did not agree to that," Kaji said.

"Do you wish me to tell your men of your deal? Of the money I just gave you?" Nabinger asked. "They would want their share."

Kaji eyes narrowed. Then he stood and shrugged. "You may keep it. It is an evil thing. I should have gotten rid of it long ago."

4

"This is Johnny. I'm out of town for a bit. Back on the tenth. Talk to you then. Leave a message at the beep. Bye."

Kelly slowly put the receiver down, not bothering to leave a message. It was after nine in the morning on the tenth. "Oh, Johnny, you've done it now," she whispered to herself.

There was no doubt in her mind that Johnny Simmons was in trouble. He had a strange sense of humor, but he wouldn't have sent her that tape and letter as a joke. She knew he was dead serious when he went on an assignment. After the little he had related to her about what had happened in El Salvador, she could well understand his seriousness. He had listed nine in the morning three times in his letter. He would not have forgotten or blown it off. At the absolute minimum he would have changed his message by remote as he had said he would.

She turned on her computer and accessed her on-line service. To find out where Johnny was, she would have to follow him, and information was the way to start.

There were two avenues of investigation to pursue, and she knew they were the same two areas that Johnny would have looked into before he went on assignment. The first would be to get background information about Area 51 and Nellis Air Force Base. The second would be to get more specific and look into the UFO phenomenon as it related to Area 51.

Kelly had more than a glancing background in the field of UFOs, which was why, in addition to their friendship, Johnny had sent her the package in the first place. Her trouble eight years ago with the Air Force at Nellis Air Force Base had had to do with that subject and had for all practical purposes destroyed a promising career in the documentary filmmaking field. What had appeared at the time to Kelly as an excellent opportunity had turned into a disaster.

Kelly took the package Johnny had sent her and went through it one more time, this go-around making notes of key words on a legal pad. When she was done, she looked at what she had:

Las Vegas Postmark
The Captain
23 Oct. transmissions, Nellis AFB
   Red Flag
   F-15
"Mailbox"
Dreamland
Groom Lake

Kelly accessed her on-line data base and set up a Boolean keyword search. She started with the date in question, combining it with *Nellis Air Force Base,* and drew a blank. Then she switched to both the twenty-third and twenty-fourth of October and accessed any news about F-15's. This time she got a hit. She drew up the article, from the *Tucson Citizen,* dated the twenty-fourth of October:

F-15 Crashes, Pilot Killed

Officials at Davis-Montham Air Force Base confirmed last night that an F-15 fighter jet from the 355th Tactical Training Wing crashed during training yesterday on the Luke Air Force Base reservation.

The pilot, whose identity is being withheld pending notification of next of kin, was killed in the crash.

The aircraft went down in rough terrain and recovery operations are under way.

(No further information was available at press time.)

Kelly checked, but there was nothing on the crash in the following day's paper, which was unusual. Kelly flipped open her atlas. Luke Air Force Base was in Arizona, hundreds of miles from the Nellis Air Force Base Range. She hit the delete key. This had nothing to do with what she was looking for.

Then she paused. Or did it? How often did F-15's crash? Not exactly every day of the year. Was it just coincidence? Kelly did not believe much in coincidence. She felt her gut tighten further. What had Johnny stumbled upon? If this F-15 was the F-15 on the tape, the Air Force had gone through a lot of trouble to point the finger in a different direction from Nellis and Area 51. And not only was the plane reported as having crashed, the pilot was dead. He had been very much alive on that tape.

Next, Kelly tried *mailbox* in conjunction with UFOs. This produced three hits, all of which identified the mailbox as an actual mailbox along a dirt road outside of the Groom Lake complex where UFO enthusiasts gathered to watch for strange craft over the mountains. Obviously the man who had sent Johnny the tape—the Captain—was one of those people. At least she now knew where she could find that link in the puzzle if she needed it.

Trying *Dreamland* and *Groom Lake* brought her a wealth of stories about the site there. They were both cross-referenced to *Area 51*, which was another one of the many names for a place whose purpose was unknown and whose existence was officially denied.

There were many theories, and Kelly was familiar with most of them. There were some who claimed the government had contact with aliens at the site, and they were trading for information and technology. The more radical theorists stated that, on their side of the barter, the humans were allowing the aliens to conduct mutilations on cattle and other livestock and also—from the truly radical fringe—to abduct humans for various nefarious experiments. There were some who even claimed that the aliens were interbreeding with the humans. Kelly shook her head. These were the sorts of stories that made headlines on the tabloid rags at the checkout counter, not something that legitimate journalists pursued.

Another theory was that Area 51 was the place where the government was testing its own supersecret aircraft and that the F-117 Stealth fighter had been test-flown out there. The latest "secret" plane that was supposedly being tested was called Aurora and guesstimates had the plane—no one quite knew what it looked like—flying anywhere from Mach 4 to Mach 20 and being capable of going high enough to place satellites into orbit.

The official government line was that the Groom Lake/Area 51 complex didn't exist, which was a most interesting position considering the fact that the Air Force had been gobbling the terrain around the area for the past five years as quickly as it could.

Obviously, *something* was going on at Area 51, Kelly decided from all the information in front of her. And she knew that Johnny must have done the same search, in fact, a much more in-depth one. And after completing that search he had felt it was worth going out there and taking the chance that the tape he had been sent was a fake or, given that Johnny knew about her own Nellis experience, a setup.

Shifting through several of the articles, two names kept popping up: Mike Franklin, a self-styled Area 51 expert living in the town of Rachel, just outside the Nellis Air Force Base range complex; and Steve Jarvis, a scientist who claimed to have worked in the Groom Lake/Area 51 complex and actually seen alien craft that the government was test-flying. Johnny would have seen the same names.

Kelly picked up the phone and got Franklin's number from information. She dialed and waited as it cycled through five rings. Just as she was about to hang up, somebody came on the line. The voice on the other end was a woman's and she sounded upset. "Yes?"

"I'd like to speak to Mike Franklin. This is Kelly Reynolds."

"Mike's not here," the woman said.

"Do you know when he'll be back?"

"He's not here," the woman repeated.

"I'm doing an article on UFOs for a major magazine," Kelly said, used to occasionally getting the cold shoulder, "and I'd like to talk to—"

"I said he's *not here!*" the woman snapped. Just as quickly the voice on the other end started sobbing. "Mike's dead. He was killed in a car wreck last night."

Kelly's hand tightened on the phone. "Where did the wreck occur?"

"On Route 375, about fifteen miles outside of town."

"Was he alone?"

"What?"

"Was he alone in the car?"

"Yes. The state police say he must have run off the road, maybe trying to avoid hitting a deer. They acted like he must have been drunk. But Mike never drank that much. He didn't like it. And someone went through all his stuff here at the house. When I got here this morning I could tell, even though they tried to put it all back in place. I'm scared they're going to come back here."

"Who are they?" Kelly asked.

The woman gave a high-pitched laugh. "Them. You know."

"No, I don't," Kelly said. "Who are you talking about?"

"Forget it," the woman said. "Mike shouldn't have been doing whatever he was doing. I told him."

"What's your name?" Kelly asked.

"I'm not talking to no one. I'm getting out of here. I don't know what Mike was doing and I don't want to know no more." The phone went dead and Kelly slowly lowered the receiver.

"Oh, Johnny, Johnny," she said softly. "You hit the nail on the head, I think, but it looks like the nail was harder than you thought."

Kelly stood and looked at the dry-erase board where she kept all her appointments and job assignments for the next several weeks. There was nothing that couldn't be put off for a while with a few phone calls.

After making her work calls she dialed a travel agency and booked a flight out of Nashville into Las Vegas, departing at noon. Then she called information and got the number for a Steve Jarvis in Las Vegas. A male voice answered. "Hello?"

"Is this Steve Jarvis?"

"Who's calling?"

"This is Kelly Reynolds. I'm a freelance writer doing an article for—"

Jarvis cut in. "My fee for a print interview is five hundred dollars. That gets you one hour."

"Mr. Jarvis, I'm just trying to find—"

"Five hundred dollars, one hour. Cash or a money order. No checks. No free questions."

Kelly paused and gathered in her emotions. "Can I see you this evening?"

"The elephant bar at the Zanzibar. Be there at seven on the dot."

"How will I recognize you?" Kelly asked.

"I'll recognize you," Jarvis replied. "Wear red. Something sexy. Order a slow, comfortable screw from the bartender."

Kelly clenched her teeth. "Listen, I'm a professional and I'm coming out to Las Vegas to do a legitimate job. I don't need—"

"Obviously," Jarvis cut in again, "you don't need to interview me, then. It was nice talking to you, Miss Reynolds."

Kelly waited. He didn't hang up; she didn't either. Electronic Mexican standoff.

Finally Jarvis spoke. "Do you have the money? Five hundred? Cash?"

"Yes."

"All right. Just ask the bartender for me. He'll point you in the right direction. I'll be there at seven."

As Kelly hung up the phone, a flicker of doubt crossed her mind. Was she overreacting to the situation?

She reached down and pulled the Nellis file out of her desk and stared at it for a few minutes while she thought. Once before she'd been down this path. But this time was different. She wasn't just after a story. There was Johnny, out there somewhere, hopefully still alive.

But that didn't mean she had to walk in blind. She looked up the article on Jarvis again and checked some-

thing. Then she picked up the phone and made another
call.

CAIRO, EGYPT
T—134 HOURS, 40 MINUTES

Peter Nabinger was also trying to answer questions, but he
didn't understand the information that was appearing on
the computer screen in front of him. He was in the research section of the University of Cairo, using their database to check on Kaji's story. He was glad he had access to
such a sophisticated system as the university's computer,
because much of what he was looking for had been reported only in academic and scientific journals or out-of-
print books, and the computer held hundreds of thousands
of such abstracts. The system also had the advantage of
holding practically every bit of information about Egypt
and Cairo that had ever been recorded.

There was no record of Germans in the Great Pyramid
during World War II; not that he had expected to find any.
But, sorting through bits and pieces of local newspaper
articles from 1945, it *did* appear that access to the Great
Pyramid had been restricted for several months during that
year and that some strange Allied military activity had centered around the building, as Kaji had said.

Cross-referencing the word *Thule* with the Nazis brought
a surprising result. Nabinger had been familiar with the
word *Thule* in the traditional sense from ancient mythology: a northern, inhabited region. The Nazis, however, had
perverted that concept—and many other myths and legends—for their own purposes and they had used the science of archaeology to try to support their claims.

Even nonarchaeologists knew about the Rosetta stone,
found in 1799 when Napoleon's army had invaded Egypt.

In many ways the stone had been the key that opened up study of ancient Egypt, because when Champollion finally broke the code to the traditional Egyptian hieroglyphics and deciphered it, a wealth of information was unleashed.

Despite his having studied the history of archaeology in college and graduate school, the information Nabinger was now reading was new to him. What Nabinger had never been told was that in 1842 the King of Prussia had led an expedition to Egypt that had done further work on deciphering ancient Egyptian texts and markings. A German Egyptologist named Richard Lepsius had accompanied the king and remained there for three years, producing drawings and measurements of all three pyramids.

Over the years that followed, the Germans had invested quite a bit of time and energy in the study of the pyramids, hieroglyphics, and high runes. Obviously—if Kaji's story was true—that effort had borne some fruit.

In the decade just prior to World War I various German groups had used myths and archaeology to weave a strange and convoluted web of doctrine to support their racial and anti-Semitic philosophies. The swastika, a symbol that had been used by several ancient peoples, was resurrected. List, an early influence on Hitler, used his own false deciphering of high runes to justify his beliefs.

Nabinger stopped scrolling the computer for a second and stroked his beard. Although the deciphering of the Rossetta stone had greatly increased understanding of hieroglyphics, it had been of no help in the deciphering of the high runes. Nabinger's own feeling was that the high runes were older than hieroglyphics.

Nabinger remembered Kaji's comments about the Germans using some sort of map with markings on it to find their way. What had the Germans uncovered? Had they discovered a way to decipher high rune text that still remained unknown to the rest of the world? Were they using

some ancient document or perhaps something drawn by
Lepsius in the nineteenth century? Or had they simply
used a map, copied from someplace, and still been unable
to read the high runes?

Nabinger *had* heard about the German fascination with
the myth of the Holy Grail and the search for the lance
supposedly used on Jesus after his crucifixion, but his in-
structors in school had laughed away the Nazis as amateurs
in the scientific field of archaeology, more interested in
propaganda than science. But perhaps, Nabinger wondered, there had been other searches with better results?
Nabinger thought of his own hypothesis connecting the
high runes in South and Central America with those in the
pyramid. He knew he would be laughed at also if he tried
to publish his results.

Nabinger read on. At the end of World War I many of
the occult groups that had been born in Germany prior to
the war grew in strength, feeding off the deep and bitter
dissatisfaction of the people with the defeat and peace im-
posed on their country. The name Thule was appropriated
as a cover for these groups.

Nabinger straightened. In 1933 a book had been published in Germany called *Bevor Hitler Kam (Before Hitler
Came)*. It was apparently about the connection between
Hitler's National Socialist movement and the Thule movement. The interesting thing was that after publication, the
author disappeared under mysterious circumstances and all
copies of the book that could be found in Germany were
collected and destroyed by the Nazis. The author of the
book was named Baron Rudolf von Sebottendorff.

Checking, Nabinger was surprised to see that the computer had an abstract on the book. Sebottendorff had
taken the ancient myth of Atlantis and the myth of Thule
and reinvented them with his own sick motivations.

According to Sebottendorff, Thule was reported to have

once been the center of a great civilization, but was subse-
quently destroyed by a great flood. This concept was based
on an earlier theory postulated by the Theosophical Society. Nabinger said a brief prayer for the computer that
gave him the ability to cross-reference so quickly as he
requested information on this latest piece of information.

The Theosophical Society was founded in 1875 in New
York City by a woman named Madame Helena Blavatsky.
Her theory had the inhabitants of Atlantis—or Thule, as
the Nazis had named it—representing the Fourth Race,
the only true line of man, which of course, the Nazis found
very convenient to use in their Aryan-race theory. According to the abstract the inhabitants of Thule looked very
much like the figures carved into stone on Easter Island.
Nabinger ran a hand through his beard. How the hell had
she made that connection?

Nabinger started to feel like he was getting off base, but
he read further. The fall of the true line of man—the
Atlanteans or Thulians—had come about because they had
mated with lesser beings. Voilà, the master race needed
purity, which also worked quite well into the master-race
theory of the Nazis.

So the Nazis had been interested in Atlantis? What did
that have to do with Egypt? He sat back in the chair and
closed his eyes. Unsettling thoughts floated through his
brain as he reviewed what he knew and what he had just
learned. Why had the Nazis destroyed the book and what
had happened to Sebottendorff? There didn't appear to be
any direct connection here with Kaji's story other than the
word *Thule* inscribed on the dagger, but Nabinger was used
to having to dig intellectually as well as in the dirt. Perhaps
there was more here than was readily apparent.

Nabinger opened his eyes and went back to the abstract
on the book. Apparently the book had been destroyed and
information about it suppressed because Hitler wanted

people to think all his ideas had begun with him and were
not borrowed from other sources.

Nabinger decided to press on for a bit along the present
avenue of research. A search on Atlantis brought a large
number of references—over three thousand. Obviously the
Germans had not been alone in their interest. Nabinger
searched the titles until he found one that seemed to give
an overview of the history of the fabled continent.

Atlantis was often regarded as a myth mentioned in original source only by Plato. Most historians thought Plato
had made the tale of Atlantis up to stress a point and that
it was only a literary tool. For those who did think it represented an actual place, the fingers pointed to various locations. Some believe it to be the island of Thera in the
Mediterranean, which was destroyed by a volcanic erup-
tion. The crater of the volcano Santorini had been investigated by leading oceanographers, searching for clues.
Others placed it in the middle of the Atlantic Ocean. The
Azores were mentioned—the Lake of the Seven Cities on
the island of São Miguel was a body of water in a volcanic
crater. The main city of Atlantis was supposed to lie beneath that lake, or so the supporters of that site claimed.

Nabinger scanned down, skipping most of the middle of
the article, looking to see what the latest theories were.
Recent discoveries of large stones closely fitted together
off the islands of Bimini in the Bahamas had caused quite a
bit of excitement several years previously and the enigma
of their creation and location had never really been adequately explained. That struck a bell with Nabinger. A
speaker at an archeological conference he had attended
the previous year had been from Bimini and had spoken of
the site. And, if he remembered rightly, there were high
runes there, too, that couldn't be deciphered.

Nabinger put his briefcase on the table next to the computer and dug through. He had a binder in there with in-

formation that he always carried with him when he went overseas to work. In the back were several pages of document protectors, each sized to hold twelve business cards. He found the card of Helen Slater, the woman from Bimini who had spoken at the conference. He removed it and put it in his breast pocket.

Nabinger hit the F-3 key to print out the article and moved on to another article. This one described a nineteenth century American congressman, Ignatius Donnelly, who had published a book called *Atlantis: The Antediluvian World,* which had been a best-seller in its own time. Donnelly's hypothesis was based on similarities between pre-Columbian civilizations in America and Egypt. Nabinger felt like he was reading the beginning of his own unpublished paper on the high runes. Both cultures had had pyramids, embalming, a 365-day calendar, and a mythology about an ancient flood. Donnelly's theories had been torn apart by scientists of his own day, which didn't surprise Nabinger. The same connection had been made by people in this century and received the same chilly reception, which was the major reason Nabinger's paper was still unpublished.

Done with that article, he decided to get back to what had led him here: the cross-reference with the Nazis and Atlantis. The Nazis had launched expeditions during World War II to the cold wastelands on both ends of the earth, in search of both Atlantis/Thule and relics such as the Holy Grail. And also to Central America, where there were pyramids, not quite as large or of the exact same design as those in Egypt, but with high runes also.

Nabinger stroked his beard. What had the Nazis found that had led them back to the Great Pyramid and to a chamber that had been undisturbed for over four thousand years? Had they broken the code on the runes and found out important information? Was there something written in these other locations about the pyramids? If Kaji's story was true, at the very least they had found information that had told them of the lower chamber.

Nabinger cleared the screen and went back to the word search. He slowly typed in the name Kaji had given him:

Von Seeckt.

One hit. Nabinger accessed the article. It was a fifty-year anniversary article about the atomic bomb being dropped on Hiroshima. It detailed the development of the atomic bomb during World War II. Nabinger scanned down. Von Seeckt's name was listed as one of the physicists who had worked on development and testing of the bomb.

But Von Seeckt had been with *Germans,* according to Kaji. How had he ended up in America in the middle of the war? And why had the Germans brought a nuclear physicist into the Great Pyramid? And, most importantly, what had Von Seeckt discovered and carried out of the lower chamber in 1942?

Nabinger's fingers halted over the keyboard as something he had written earlier in the day came back to him. He reached into his backpack and pulled out his sketchpad. He'd been working on the panels in the lower chamber that stood at the head of where the sarcophagus had once been. The partially deciphered rune text was there in pencil:

POWER SUN
FORBIDDEN
HOME PLACE (???) CHARIOT (???) NEVER
AGAIN
(???) DEATH TO ALL LIVING THINGS

Curses against interlopers in the monuments of ancient Egypt were not unknown. Did this curse relate to what Von Seeckt had taken out of the pyramid? And why had the Allies hidden all record of the invasion of the pyramid and the discovery of the lower chamber? It had to be something much more important than some simple archeological find.

There was a way to find out. The end of the article stated that Von Seeckt was still alive and living in Las Vegas. Nabinger turned off the computer and stood. Budget be damned, there was a mystery here, and he was the only one who was on its trail. He left the university library and walked into the nearest travel agency to book a return flight to the States that evening, with one stop en route to see Slater in Bimini.

Once he knew when he would be arriving, he rang through the long-distance operator to information in Nevada. There was a Werner Von Seeckt listed and Nabinger copied down the number. After he'd dialed it, he found himself talking to voice mail. As the beep sounded, Nabinger quickly composed his message:

"Professor Von Seeckt, my name is Peter Nabinger. I work with the Egyptology Department at the Brooklyn Museum. I would like to talk to you about the Great Pyramid, which I believe we have a mutual interest in. I just deciphered some of the writing in the lower chamber, which I believe you visited once upon a time and it says: *Power, sun. Forbidden. Home place, chariot, never again. Death to all living things.* Perhaps you could help shed some light on my translation. Leave me a message how I can get hold of you at my voice-mail box," and Nabinger left his number.

5

"About a year, give or take six months, without treatment. With treatment you can add perhaps another half a year."

The old man didn't blink at Dr. Cruise's pronouncement. He nodded and rose to his feet, a black cane with a wide silver handle grasped in his withered left hand. "Thank you, Doctor."

"We can start the treatments tomorrow morning, Professor Von Seeckt," Dr. Cruise hastily added, as if to cushion his earlier words.

"That is fine."

"Would you like something—" Cruise paused as the old man held up his hand.

"I will be fine. This is not a surprise. I was informed this would most likely be the case when I was hospitalized earlier this year. I just wanted to confirm it, and I also believe I was owed the respect of your telling me yourself. My security will take me home."

"I'll see you at the meeting later this morning," Cruise said, stiffening at the implied rebuke in Von Seeckt's words.

"Good day, Doctor." With that Werner Von Seeckt made his way out into the hallway of the hospital and was immediately flanked by two men wearing black wind-breakers and khaki slacks, their eyes hidden behind wrap-around sunglasses.

They hustled him into a waiting car and headed to the airstrip at Nellis Air Force Base, where a small black helicopter waited to whisk him back to the northwest. As the helicopter lifted off, Von Seeckt leaned back in the thinly padded seat and contemplated the terrain flitting by underneath. The American desert had been his home for over fifty years now, but his heart still longed for the tree-covered slopes of the Bavarian Alps, where he had grown up. He had always hoped he would see his homeland before he died, but now, today, he knew he wouldn't. They would never let him go, even after so many years had passed.

He unfolded the piece of paper on which he had written the message he had taken off his answering service while waiting in Cruise's office. *Power, sun. Forbidden. Home place, chariot, never again. Death to all living things.* He remembered the Great Pyramid.

Von Seeckt leaned back in the seat. It was all coming around again, like a large circle. His life was back where it had been over fifty years ago. The question he had to ask himself was whether he had learned anything and whether he was willing to act differently this time.

THE DEVIL'S NEST, NEBRASKA
T—132 HOURS

Underneath the camouflage netting that Turcotte had helped rig during darkness, the mechanics made the three helicopters ready for flight, folding the rotors out and locking them in place. The pilots walked around, making their preflight checks.

On the perimeter of the primitive airstrip Turcotte was lying on his stomach in the middle of a four-hour guard shift, looking down the one asphalt road that led up to the airstrip. The road was in bad shape. Plants and weeds had sprouted up through cracks, and it seemed obvious this place had been abandoned for quite a while. That didn't mean, of course, that someone in a four-wheel-drive vehicle couldn't come wandering up and stumble over their mission support site. Thus Turcotte's orders to apprehend anyone coming up the road.

The question that still had not been answered—albeit Turcotte had not asked it out loud—was what mission this site was set up to support. Prague had given orders through the night, but they had been immediate ones, directed to the security of this location, not shedding any light on what they would be doing once the sun went down this evening.

THE CUBE, AREA 51
T—130 HOURS, 30 MINUTES

The conference room was to the left of the control center as one got off the elevator. It was soundproofed and swept daily for bugs. The Cube had never had a security compromise and General Gullick was going to insure that the record remained intact.

A large, rectangular mahogany table filled the middle of the room with twelve deep leather chairs lining the edges. Gullick sat at the head of the table and waited silently as the other chairs were filled. He watched as Von Seeckt limped in and took the chair at the other end of the table. Gullick had already been briefed by Dr. Cruise on the confirmation of Von Seeckt's terminal condition. To Gullick it was good news. The old man had long ago outlived his usefulness.

Gullick shifted his attention to the youngest person in the room, who was sitting to his immediate right. She was a small, dark-haired woman with a thin face, dressed severely in a sharply cut gray suit. This was Dr. Lisa Duncan's first meeting, and while inbriefing her on the project was one of the two priorities on the meeting schedule, it was not the primary one in Gullick's mind. In fact, he resented having to take time out at such a critical juncture in the project to get a new person up to speed.

There was also the fact that Dr. Duncan was the first woman ever allowed in this room. But, since Duncan was filling the chair reserved for the presidential adviser, it paid at least to give the appearance of respect. The fingers of Gullick's left hand lightly traced over his smooth skull, caressing the skin as if soothing the brain underneath. There was so much to do and so little time! Why had the previous adviser been reassigned? Duncan's predecessor had been an old physics professor who had been so enraptured by what they were doing upstairs in the hangar that he had been no trouble.

A week ago Kennedy, the CIA representative, had been the first to notify Gullick of Duncan's assignment and this visit. Gullick had ordered the CIA man to look into Duncan's background. She was a threat; Gullick was convinced of that. The timing of her sudden assignment and this first visit couldn't be coincidental.

"Good afternoon, gentlemen—and lady," Gullick added with a nod across the table. "Welcome to this meeting of Majic-12." Built into the arm rest of his chair was a series of buttons and Gullick hit one of them, lighting up the wall behind him with a large-scale computer image. The same image was displayed on the horizontal console set into the tabletop just in front of Gullick for his eyes only:

INBRIEF PRESIDENTIAL ADVISER

CURRENT STATUS OF BOUNCERS

CURRENT STATUS OF THE MOTHERSHIP

PROJECTED TEST OF THE MOTHERSHIP

"This is today's schedule." Gullick looked around the table. "First, since we have a new member, introductions are in order. I will begin from my left and go around the table clockwise.

"Mr. Kennedy, deputy director of operations, the Central Intelligence Agency. Our liaison to the intelligence community." Kennedy was the youngest man in the room. He wore an expensive three-piece suit. If they weren't a quarter mile underground he'd probably have been wearing sunglasses, Gullick thought. He didn't like Kennedy because of his age and his aggressive attitude, but he most certainly needed him. Kennedy had thick blond hair and a dark tan that looked out of place with the other men at the conference table.

"Major General Brown, deputy chief of staff, Air Force. The Air Force has overall administration and logistics responsibility for the project and for external security.

"Major General Mosley, deputy chief of staff, Army. The Army supplies personnel for security support.

"Rear Admiral Coakley, assistant director, Naval intelligence. The Navy is responsible for counterintelligence.

"Dr. Von Seeckt, chief scientific counsel, Majic-12. Dr. Von Seeckt is the only man in this room who has been with the project from the beginning.

"Dr. Duncan, our latest member, presidential adviser to Majic-12 on science and technology.

"Mr. Davis, special projects coordinator, National

Reconaissance Organization. The NRO is the agency through which our funding is directed.

"Dr. Ferrel, professor of physics, New York Institute of Technology. Our chief scientific counsel and in charge of our reverse engineeering work.

"Dr. Slayden, project psychologist, Majic-12.

"Dr. Underhill, aeronautics, Jet Propulsion Laboratory. Our expert at flight.

"Dr. Cruise, MD."

Gullick wasted no further time on the people. "I would like to welcome Dr. Duncan to our group for the first time." He looked down the table at her. "I know you have been given the classified inbriefing papers on the history of the Majic-12 project, so I won't bore you with that information, but I would like to run through some of the highlights of our operation as it currently stands.

"First, everything and anything to do with the project is classified Top Secret, Q Clearance, Level 5. That is the highest classification level possible. Majic-12, which is the official designation for the people around this table, has been in existence for fifty-four years. Not once in all those years have we had a security breach.

"Our primary mission is twofold. First is to master flying the bouncer disks and reverse-engineer their propulsion system." He flicked a button and an image of nine silvery disks appeared, lined up in a massive hangar. It was hard to tell details from the photo, but five of the disks appeared to be identical to one another, while the other four all differed slightly.

"We have been flying bouncers for thirty-three years and keep double flight crews current on their operation. But we have not had as much success discerning their method of propulsion." He glanced down the table and arched an eyebrow.

"I'm current on that research," Duncan said.

Gullick nodded. "We are continuing flights of the bouncers to keep the flight crews current and also to continue tests on the propulsion system and their flight characteristics. We have several prototypes of the bouncer engine, but have not yet succeeded in engineering one that functions adequately," he said, understating the massive problems they had encountered over the years and eager to get past the failures of the past and on to the future.

"Our second purpose—the mothership—is a different story altogether." An elongated black cigar shape appeared on the screen, again nestled inside a hangar with rock walls. It was impossible to tell the scale of the ship from the photo, but even in the two-dimensional projection it gave the impression of being massive.

"For all these years the mothership has defied our best scientific minds, but we finally believe we have gained enough knowledge of the control system to activate the propulsion system. That is currently our number-one priority in the project. It will—"

"It will be a disaster if we activate the mothership," Von Seeckt cut in, looking at Duncan. "We have no clue how it operates. Oh, these fools will tell you we understand the control system, but that has nothing to do with the mechanics and the physics of the engine itself. It is like inviting a man into the cockpit of an advanced nuclear bomber and believing that the man can operate the bomber because he can drive his car and the yoke of the bomber is very much like the steering wheel of the car. It is madness."

Gullick's left eyebrow twitched but his voice was calm. "Thank you, Dr. Von Seeckt, but we have been over all that ground already. We will never understand the mothership if we do not attempt to investigate it. That is the method we have used on the bouncers and—"

"And we still don't understand the bouncers' propulsion systems!" Von Seeckt threw in.

"But we're flying the bouncers and using them," Doctor Ferrell, the physicist, said. "And we are getting closer every day to figuring them out."

"It is dangerous to play with tools we don't understand!" Von Seeckt cried out.

"Is this test dangerous?" Duncan asked, calm in contrast to Von Seeckt's wavering and excited voice.

Gullick looked across the table at her. Just before this meeting he had studied the classified file Kennedy had amassed on her. He knew more about her than she probably remembered about herself. Thirty-seven, twice divorced, a son in private high school back in Washington, a doctorate in medical biology from Stanford, a successful career in business, and now, due to her friendship with the First Lady, a political appointee to perhaps the most sensitive post in the administration. Of course, Gullick knew, the President didn't fully comprehend the importance of Majic-12. And that was one of the Catch-22's of the secrecy surrounding the project. Because they couldn't really tell anyone what was going on, they were often neglected in the big scheme. But there were ways around that and the members of Majic-12 had long ago perfected those ways.

"Ma'am," Gullick said, reverting to the military form of addressing a woman, "everything is dangerous, but test-flying is probably the most dangerous occupation in the world. I flew experimental aircraft early in my career. Over the course of a year at Edwards Air Force Base, eight of the twelve men in my squadron were killed working out the bugs in a new airframe. And here we are dealing with alien technology. We didn't design these craft. But we do have an advantage," Gullick added. "We are dealing with technology that works. The largest danger I faced as a test pilot was *getting* the technology up to speed so it would work.

Here we know these craft fly. It is a matter of figuring out *how* they fly."

Gullick turned his chair slightly and pointed at the mothership sitting in its cradle of steel beams. "We are currently slightly over one hundred and thirty hours from the first test flight. But before we attempt that, we simply are going to start it up and see what happens. That is the reason this meeting is scheduled for today: so you can see for yourself in a few hours that there is no danger. To use Dr. Von Seeckt's analogy—but in the proper perspective— we are simply going to put our man in the pilot's seat and have him turn the engines on and then off. The craft won't go anywhere. And our man is not a child. We have the best minds in the country assembled here working on this project."

Von Seeckt snorted. "We had the best minds back in eighty-nine when—"

"That's enough, Doctor," Gullick snapped. "The decision has been made. This is an information briefing, not a decision briefing. At thirteen hundred hours local time today the mothership's engines will be turned on for ten seconds and then immediately turned off. The decision has been made," he repeated. "Now, shall we move on with the briefing?" It was not a question designed to be answered with anything but assent.

For the next thirty minutes the meeting went as scheduled with no further interruptions. Gullick formally brought it to a close. "Dr. Duncan, if you would like, you might want to take a tour of the hangar and our other facilities and be present when we conduct the test on the mothership."

"I would like that very much," she replied, "but first I'd like a moment alone with you."

"If you would excuse us, gentlemen," Gullick said. "Designated personnel, please wait outside," he added.

"There's quite a bit that I don't understand," Lisa Duncan said as soon as the room was clear.

"There's quite a bit *we* don't understand," General Gullick amended. "The technology we are working with here *is* overwhelming at times."

"I'm not talking about the technology," Duncan said. "I'm talking about the administration of this program."

"Is there a problem?" Gullick asked, his voice chilling the room.

Duncan was blunt. "Why the secrecy? Why are we hiding all this?"

Gullick relaxed slightly. "Numerous reasons."

"Please enumerate them," Duncan said.

Gullick lit a cigar, ignoring the NO SMOKING signs that adorned the walls of the Cube conference room. Government bureaucracy found itself into even the most secret of locations. "This program began during World War II, and that was the reason it was initially classified. Then there was the Cold War and the requirement to keep this technology—what we did understand of it—out of the hands of the Russians. One study by our staff even found a high possibility that if the Russians ever discovered that we had this technology it would upset the balance of power and they might launch a preemptive nuclear strike. I would say that's a damn good reason to keep this secret."

Duncan pulled a cigarette out of her purse. She pointed at the ashtray for Gullick's cigar. "Do you mind?" She didn't wait for an answer as she lit up. "The Cold War has been over for over half a decade, General. Keep counting the reasons."

A muscle twitched on the right side of Gullick's jaw. "The Cold War may be over, but there are still nuclear missiles pointed at this country by foreign countries. We are dealing with technology here that might totally change the course of civilization. That is sufficient—"

"Could it be," Duncan cut in, "that all this is classified simply because it's always been classified?"

"I understand what you're saying." Gullick attempted a disarming smile that didn't work. He ran a finger over the file folder that held Kennedy's report on Duncan and restrained an impulse to throw it at her. "It would be easy to see the secrecy surrounding Majic-12 as simply a leftover from the Cold War, but there are deeper implications here."

"Such as?" Duncan didn't wait for an answer. "Could part of those deeper implications be that this project had been founded illegally? That the importation of people such as Von Seeckt to work in it—in direct violation of law and a presidential order in force at the time—and other activities since then would open up personnel involved in this program to criminal prosecution?"

The glowing red numbers set into the desktop next to the computer screen read T–130H/16M. That was all that concerned Gullick. He'd talked to a few of the others about how to handle Duncan and now it was time to start with what they had come up with.

"Whatever happened fifty years ago is not our concern," he said. "We are worried about the impact publicizing this program will have on the general population.

"Dr. Slayden, the program psychologist," Gullick said, "is on our staff for this very reason. As a matter of fact, we will have a briefing from Dr. Slayden at eight A.M. on the twelfth. He'll be able to explain things better then, but suffice it to say that the social and economic implications of revealing what we have here at Area 51 to the public are staggering. So staggering that every president since World War II has agreed that the utmost secrecy should surround this project."

"Well, this president," Duncan said, "may think differently. The times are changing. An immense amount of money has been poured into this project and the return has been minimal."

"If we fly the mothership," Gullick said, "it will all be worth it."

Duncan stubbed out her cigarette and stood. "I hope so. Good day, sir." She turned on her high heels and walked out the door.

As soon as she was gone, the Majic-12 men in uniform and the representatives from the CIA and NRO came back in. All attempt at being cordial slipped from Gullick's demeanor. "Duncan's fishing. She knows there something more going on."

"We need to have Slayden give her the data on the implications of revealing the project," Kennedy said.

"I told her about Slayden's briefing and she's got his written report already," Gullick said. "No, she's looking for something more."

"Do you think she has something on Dulce?" Kennedy asked.

"No. If there was any suspicion about that, we'd know about it. We're wired into every intelligence apparatus this country has. It has to be something else."

"Operation Paperclip?" Kennedy asked.

Gullick nodded. "She made a point of mentioning that Von Seeckt and others were recruited illegally. She knows too much. If they pull on that thread too hard, this whole thing might unravel."

Kennedy pointed at the folder. "We can go hard with her if we need to."

"She's the President's representative," General Brown warned.

"We just need time," Gullick said. "I think Slayden's psychobabble will keep her occupied. If not"—Gullick shrugged—"then we go hard." He looked down at the computer screen and changed the subject. "What's the status of Nightscape 96-7?" Gullick asked the director of Naval intelligence.

"Everything looks good," Admiral Coakley answered. "The MSS is secure and all elements are in place."

"What about the infiltration by that reporter and the other person last night?" Gullick asked.

"We've cleaned it all up and there's an added benefit to that situation," Coakley said. "That other fellow's name was Franklin. A UFO freak. He's been a pain in the ass for a long time working out of his house in Rachel. We no longer have to worry about him. He's dead and we have an adequate cover story in place."

"How did they get inside the outer perimeter?" Gullick demanded, not appeased at all.

"Franklin unscrewed the antennas from the sensors on either side of the road," Coakley replied. "We got that off a cassette recorder we found on the reporter."

"I want that system replaced. It's outdated. Go with laser sensors on all the roads."

"Yes, sir."

"And the reporter?"

"He's been transferred to Dulce. He was a freelancer. We're working on a back story for his disappearance."

"It won't happen again," Gullick said, his tone of voice indicating it was not a question.

"Yes, sir."

"What about Von Seeckt?" Kennedy asked. "If he makes any more trouble, Duncan might start asking more questions."

Gullick rubbed the side of his temple. "He's become a liability. We'll just have to move up his medical timetable. We'll take care of the good doctor and insure he won't cause any more problems. He outlived his usefulness to this program a long time ago. I'll talk to Dr. Cruise."

THE DEVIL'S NEST, NEBRASKA
T—130 HOURS

"What's that?" Turcotte asked.

The man in the gray flight suit looked up. "Laser firing system," he said shortly, snapping shut the metal case on the sophisticated machinery that had drawn Turcotte's attention.

Turcotte had never seen a laser that was packed suitcase size, but the technician did not seem amenable to discussing the technology. Another question to add to all the others.

"Get some sleep. You'll need the rest," Prague said, appearing suddenly at his shoulder. "We'll be ready to move after dark and you won't get any sleep for a while." Prague smiled. *"Sleep good, meat,"* he added in German.

Turcotte stared at him for a second, then walked over to where the other off-shift security men were dozing in the shade offered by several trees. He grabbed a Gore-Tex bivy sack and slid into it, zipping it up around his chin. He thought about everything he had seen so far for about five minutes, wondering what Prague had been told about him. He finally decided he didn't have a clue what was going on or what Prague knew, and switched his brain off.

As he fell asleep, his mind shifted to other scenes. Prague's final words in German echoed through his brain and Turcotte fell into an uneasy slumber with the echo of gunfire and German voices screaming in fear and pain.

THE HANGAR, AREA 51
T—129 HOURS, 40 MINUTES

Lisa Duncan had read the figures and studied the classified photos, but they had not prepared her for the sheer size of this operation. Flying into Area 51 on board one of their black helicopters, she had been impressed with the long runway and the aboveground base facilities, but that impression had been dwarfed by what was hidden out of sight.

Taking the elevator up from the Cube, she and her scientific escorts entered a large room carved out of the rock of Groom Mountain. This was the hangar, over three quarters of a mile long and a quarter mile wide. Three of the walls, the floor, and roof—one hundred feet above their heads—were rock. The last side was a series of camouflaged sliding doors that opened up onto the north end of the runway.

The true size of the hangar could only be seen on the rare occasions, like now, when all the dividers between the various bays were unfolded and a person could look straight through from one end to the other. Duncan wondered if they had done that to impress her. If they had, it was working.

She was still bothered by her confrontation with General Gullick. She'd been briefed for the job by the President's national security adviser, but even he had seemed uncertain about what was going on with Majic-12. It actually wasn't that surprising to Duncan. In her work with medical companies she'd often had to deal with government bureaucracy and found it to be a formidable maze of self-propagating, self-serving structures to negotiate. As Gullick had made very clear: Majic-12 had been around for fifty-four years. The unspoken parallel was that the President whom Duncan was working for had been around for only three. She knew that meant that the members of Majic-12 implicitly believed they had a greater legitimacy than the elected officials who were supposed to oversee the project.

The CIA, NSA, the Pentagon—all were bureaucracies that had weathered numerous administrations and changes

in the political winds. Majic-12 was another one, albeit
much more secretive. The issue, though, was why were
Gullick and the others in such a rush to fly the mothership?
That issue and other disturbing rumors about Majic-12 operations that had sifted their way back to Washington was
the reason Duncan was here. She already had some dirt on
the program, as she'd indicated to Gullick; but that was
past dirt, as he'd indicated in return. Most of the men involved in Paperclip were long dead. She had to find out
what was presently happening. To do that she had to pay
attention, so when her guide spoke up, she put away her
worries.

"This is the hangar we built in 1951," Professor Underhill, the aeronautics expert, explained. "We've added to
it over the years." He pointed at the nine silvery craft
parked in their cradles. "You have all the information on
how and where we found the bouncers. Currently, six are
operational."

"What about the other three?" she asked.

"Those are the ones we're working on. Taking apart the
engines to see if we can reverse-engineer them. Trying to
understand the control and flight system along with other
technology."

She nodded and followed as they walked along the back
of the hangar. There were workers on each of the craft,
doing things whose purpose was unclear. She had indeed
studied the history of these craft, which seemed simply to
have been abandoned in various places some time in the
past. From the conditions of the locations they were found
in, the best guess had been about ten thousand years ago.
The craft themselves seemed not to have aged at all.

There had been very few answers about the origin or
purpose or original owners of the craft in the briefing papers. Something that didn't seem to concern the people out
here very much. That bothered Duncan, because she liked

thinking in analogies and she wondered how she would feel if she had left her car parked somewhere and came back later to find that it had been appropriated and someone was taking the engine apart. Even though the bouncers had been abandoned long ago, centuries might be just a day or two in the relative time scale of the original owners.

"Why does everyone out here call them 'bouncers'?" she asked. "In the briefing papers they were called 'magnetic-drive atmospheric craft' or 'MDAC' or simply 'disks.' "

Underhill laughed. "We use the 'MDAC' for scientific people who need a fancy title. We all call them 'disks' or 'bouncers.' The reason for the latter, well, wait till you see one in flight. They can change directions on a dime. Most people who watch them think we call them 'bouncers' because they do seem to suddenly bounce off an invisible wall when they change direction—that's how quick they can do it. But if you talk to the original test pilots who flew them, they called them 'bouncers' because of the way they got thrown around on the inside during those abrupt maneuvers. It took us quite a while to come up with the technology and flight parameters so that the pilots wouldn't be injured when they had the aircraft at speed."

Underhill pointed at a metal door along the back wall. "This way, please."

The door slid open as they approached, and inside was an eight-passenger train on an electric monorail. Duncan stepped into the car along with Underhill, Von Seeckt, Slayden, Ferrel, and Cruise. The car immediately started up and they were whisked into a brightly lit tunnel.

Underhill continued to play tour guide. "It's a little over four miles to Hangar Two, where we found the mothership. In fact, that's the reason this base is here. Most people think we picked this site because of the isolation, but that was simply an added benefit.

"This part of Nevada was originally being looked over to

be the site of the first atomic tests early in World War II, when the surveyors found that the readings on some of their instruments were being affected by a large metallic object. They pinpointed the location, dug, and found what we now call the mothership in Hangar Two. Whoever left the ship here had the technology to blast out a place big enough to leave it and then cover it over."

Duncan let out an involuntary gasp as the train exited the tunnel and entered a large cavern, a mile and a half long. The ceiling was over a half mile above her head and made of perfectly smooth stone. It was dotted with bright stadium lights. What caught her attention, though, was the cylindrical black object that took up most of the space. The mothership was just over a mile long and a quarter mile in beam at the center. What made the scale so strange was that the skin of the ship was totally smooth, made up of a black, shiny metal that had defied analysis for decades.

"It took us forty-five years before we were able to break down the composition of the skin," Ferrel, the physicist said, as they exited the tram. "We still can't replicate it, but we finally knew enough about it to at least be able to cut through it."

Duncan could now see scaffolding near the front—if it was the front and not the rear—of the mothership. The ship itself rested on a complex platform of struts made of the same black material as the skin. The rock sides of the cavern were also smooth, and the floor totally flat.

They walked alongside the struts, dwarfed by the sheer mass of the ship above them. Underhill pointed at the center as they passed it. "We call it the mothership not just because of its size, but also because there's space in the center hold to contain all the bouncers and about a dozen more. There are cradles in there that are the exact dimensions to hold every bouncer. We believe this is the way the bouncers got here to Earth, as they are not capable of leaving the atmosphere on their own power."

"But we still can't even open the external cargo bay doors." Von Seeckt spoke for the first time. "And you want to start the engine," he added accusingly, glaring at Underhill.

"Now, Werner, we've been through all that before," Underhill said.

"It took us forty-five years to simply get in," Von Seeckt said. "I was here for all forty-five of those years. Now in the space of a few months, you want to try and fly this!"

"What are you so worried about?" Duncan asked. She'd read the file on Von Seeckt and personally, given the man's background, she did not much care for him. His constant complaining did little to ameliorate that impression.

"If I knew what I was worried about, I'd be even more worried," Von Seeckt answered. "We don't understand at all how this ship works." He stopped to catch his breath and the other members of the party paused also, over three quarters of the way to the nose.

Von Seeckt continued. "I believe part of the propulsion system of this craft works using gravity. In this case it would be the gravity of our planet. Who knows what it would do if it got turned on? Do you want to be responsible for affecting our gravity?"

"That's my area of expertise," Ferrel said, "and I can assure you there are no problems."

"I feel so much better," Von Seeckt snapped back.

A voice on a sound system echoed through the cavern: "TEN MINUTES UNTIL INITIATION. ALL PERSONNEL ARE TO BE INSIDE PROTECTION. TEN MINUTES."

"Gentlemen, enough," Underhill ordered. They were at the base of the scaffolding. "We can see the inside later, but for now, let's go over here." He led the way toward a small doorway in a concrete wall. A metal hatch closed behind them and they were inside a blast bunker. "We have two men on board in the control room. They are simply going to turn on the engine, leave it on for ten seconds, and turn it off. They are not going to engage the drive. It's sort of like starting a car engine but leaving the transmission in neutral."

"We hope," Von Seeckt muttered.

"FIVE MINUTES."

"You are witnessing history," Underhill said to Duncan.

"We have every possible monitoring device set up here," Ferrel added. "This should give us what we need to understand the engine."

Duncan glanced over at Von Seeckt, who was sitting in one of the folding chairs along the back wall of the bunker. He seemed uninterested in what was going on.

"ONE MINUTE."

The countdown now started by the second, reminding Duncan of the space shots she had watched as a youngster.

"TEN.

"NINE.

"EIGHT.

"SEVEN.

"SIX.

"FIVE.

"FOUR.

"THREE.

"TWO.

"ONE.

"INITIATION."

Duncan felt a wave of nausea sweep through her. She staggered, then leaned over, feeling the contents of her breakfast in Las Vegas come up. She fell to her knees and vomited on the concrete floor. Then, just as quickly, it was over.

"ALL CLEAR. ALL CLEAR. PERSONNEL MAY LEAVE PROTECTION."

Duncan stood, feeling the taste of acid in the back of her mouth. The men all looked pale and shaken also, but none of them had thrown up.

"What happened?" Duncan asked.

"Nothing happened," Ferrel replied.

"Goddammit," Duncan snapped. "I *felt* it. Something happened."

"The engine was turned on and then off," Ferrel said. "As far as what the effect we felt was, we'll have to analyze our data." He pointed at a television screen. "You can see from the replay that nothing happened." And indeed, on the screen, the mothership sat completely still as the digital readout in the lower right hand corner went through the countdown.

Duncan wiped a hand across her mouth and looked back at Von Seeckt, who was still in his seat. She felt embarrassed to have thrown up, but Ferrel's response to her brief illness seemed a bit nonchalant. For the first time she wondered if the old man might not be as crazy as he sounded.

In the conference room Gullick and the inner circle of Majic-12 had watched the test on video, although there had been nothing to really see. The mothership had simply sat there, but the data links indicated that the power had indeed been turned on and the ship seemed to function properly.

Gullick smiled, momentarily erasing all the stress lines on his face and scalp. "Gentlemen, the countdown continues as planned."

The data was being read before it was fully cognizant. The signal came from the northeast. The power reading was not accurate enough to give distance to the disturbance. A quick time check showed that it had not been long since the last time it had been awakened.

This time, though, it knew what had caused the disturbance. The data from the sensors matched information in its memory. The nature of the signal was clear and it knew the source.

Action had to be taken. Valuable energy would have to be expended. As quickly as the decision had been made, execution was begun. The order was given. The next time this occurred, it would be ready and have forces in place.

"Steve Jarvis?"

The bartender grimaced and pointed toward a booth at the rear. As Kelly walked toward it, she studied the man sitting there. She hated to admit it, but he didn't look like the flake she had expected. Jarvis had straight black hair and wore wire-rim glasses. He was well dressed in a sport coat and tie. Not at all what she had expected from both the subject matter and the discussion on the phone. He was eyeing her as she approached and she could see his disappointment. He must have had hopes for someone taller and with more curves, she assumed.

He stood. "You have the money?"

So much for second impressions, Kelly thought. She pulled out an envelope and handed it to him. Johnny *really* owed her now, she thought. Jarvis looked in the envelope, thumbed through the bills, and then sat back down, signaling for the waitress. "Would you like a drink?"

"My tab or yours?" Kelly responded.

Jarvis laughed. "Yours, of course."

"I'll have a Coke," she told the waitress while Jarvis ordered his "usual."

"What do you want to know?" Jarvis asked as he finished off the drink he had in front of him in one gulp.

"Area 51," Kelly said.

Jarvis laughed again. "And? There's a whole lot going on out there. Anything in specific?"

"Why don't you just start and I'll get specific as you go along," Kelly replied.

Jarvis nodded. "Okay. The usual, then. First, of course, you want to know how I know anything about Area 51, right?" He didn't wait for an answer. "I worked there from May 1991 to March 1992. I was a contract employee hired by the NRO, the National Reconnaissance Office. I worked on propulsion systems, trying to reverse-engineer . . ." He paused. "Well, let me back up slightly. You know what they have out at Groom Lake, right?"

"Why don't you tell me?"

"Nine alien spacecraft," Jarvis said. "They're in a hangar cut into the side of the mountain. The government can fly some of them, but they don't know how the engines work. Thus they can't replicate them. That's why I was called in."

"Where'd the government get these craft?" Kelly asked.

Jarvis shrugged. "Got me. I don't know. Some say we traded for them, kind of like an interstellar used-car lot, but I don't believe that. Maybe we just found them. Maybe they crashed, but the ones I saw seemed intact and showed no sign of having crashed."

"Why'd they bring you in?"

"To figure out the engines. I did my dissertation at MIT on the possibility of magnetic propulsion. We already use magnets on things such as high-speed trains, and the military has been working on a magnetic gun for a long time. But all those systems generate a magnetic field of their own, which requires a lot of energy. My theory was that since the planet already has a magnetic field, if there was some way we could manipulate and control that field with an engine we would have an unlimited source of energy for an atmospheric craft."

"So the government just hired you out of the blue and took you to a top-secret installation?"

"No, they didn't hire me out of the blue. I had worked for the government before down at White Sands. A joint contract with JPL working on the possibility of using a long, sloping magnetic track on a mountainside to launch satellites into orbit."

"Not many mountainsides at White Sands," Kelly said.

Jarvis smiled, but it didn't quite reach his eyes. "Are you trying to test my credibility?"

"I paid you five hundred dollars," Kelly said. "I get to ask the questions."

"Okay, you're right," Jarvis agreed. "There aren't any mountainsides at White Sands. We were simply working on the theory on a small scale. Best we ever got up to was a one-to-thirty model. You can do that using a sand dune."

"So they brought you up to Area 51," Kelly prompted, making a notation in a small notebook.

"Yeah. It was weird. I reported to McCarren Field here in Vegas and they put us on this 737 and flew us out there. I had a Q clearance already from my previous work, so that was okay. But, boy, they had the tightest security I've ever seen. You couldn't fart without someone looking over your shoulder. Those security people were scary, walking around in these black windbreakers, wearing shades and carrying submachine guns."

"Did you stay out there at Area 51?"

"No. They shuttled us back and forth every day on the 737. The only people who live out there are the military people, as far as I could tell. All the scientific people and the worker bees—they were on that plane."

"That plane flies every day?"

"Every workday. It's an unmarked 737 with a red stripe down the side."

"Get back to Area 51," Kelly said, flipping a page. "What was it like?"

"Like I said, tight security. Everything out of sight. The saucers were inside a big hangar. They had three of them partially disassembled. Those are the ones I got to work on.

"They were about thirty feet in diameter. Silver metal for skin. Flat bottom. About ten feet in from the edges on top the saucer becomes hemispherical to a flat semicircle top, about five to eight feet around."

Jarvis finished his drink and ordered another before continuing. "The bitch of working on the engines was that there really weren't any. That really threw the military guys for a loop. You know how a jet fighter is designed: basically a large engine with a small place for the pilot to sit. Well, the disks were mostly empty on the inside. There were these sort of man-sized depressions in the center. I guess where the crew sat.

"Anyway. Getting back to the engines that weren't. I told you my theory: magnetic propulsion working off a field of energy that is already there. Most conventional engines take up a lot of space because they have to produce energy. The disk engines simply had to redirect energy. There were coils around the edge of the disk, built into the edge and the floor." Jarvis smiled. "That also explains why they are saucer or disk shaped. The coils are circular and need to be in order to be able to redirect the energy in any direction."

Kelly found herself falling under Jarvis's spell. His words made sense, which was her second surprise of the day. She had to remind herself what she had learned on her last phone call earlier today before heading to the airport.

"The setup of the coils was relatively simple. The problem was that we couldn't replicate; hell, we couldn't even describe the metal that made up the coils. It actually wasn't a metal. It was more of a . . ." Jarvis paused. "Suffice it to say it was different and the best minds we had there couldn't figure it out."

"Why did they terminate your contract?" Kelly asked.

"Like I just said, we couldn't figure it out so there was no need to keep us around. I assume they brought other people in."

"What do you know about a man named Mike Franklin?"

"The nut who lives up in Rachel?"

"He's dead," Kelly said, watching Jarvis carefully.

"Took them long enough" was his only reply as he took another drink.

"Took who long enough?" Kelly asked.

"The government." Jarvis leaned forward. "From what I heard Franklin was a jerk. He led people up there on White Sides Mountain to look down at the Groom Lake complex. They would catch him and tell him not to come back but he kept coming back. What did he expect?"

"You don't seem very interested in how he died," Kelly said. "You just seem to assume it was the government that killed him."

"Maybe he had a heart attack." Jarvis shrugged. "I don't really give a shit."

"Aren't *you* worried about the government coming after you? You seem to be more of a threat than Franklin was."

"That's why I'm talking to you," Jarvis replied. "That's why I went on that talk show last year. That's why I keep myself in the public eye."

"I thought it was the five hundred dollars," Kelly replied dryly.

"Yeah, the money helps. But I really do it to keep the spooks off my ass. The government won't kill me because it would raise too many questions and actually make my story more valid. But they *have* blackballed me. I can't get a research job anywhere, so I make my living as best I can."

"I thought it might simply be because you never graduated from MIT," Kelly said.

Jarvis carefully put his drink down. "Our hour is almost up."

Kelly looked at her watch. "Not even close. You did work at White Sands, but the records show it was on the basic construction of a new research facility, not in the facility itself. In fact, there is no record of you receiving a degree any higher than a BS from the State University of New York at Albany in 1978."

"If you have any more questions you'd better ask them before your time is up," Jarvis said.

"Did you talk to a man named Johnny Simmons?"

"I don't recognize the name."

Kelly described Johnny, but Jarvis maintained ignorance. She decided to go back on the attack.

"I checked with Lori Turner, who interviewed you last year for cable TV. She says most of your background doesn't check out. That makes me doubt your story. That means either you're a liar or a plant to feed false information. In either case it tells me your story about Area 51 is bullshit."

Jarvis stood. "Time's up. Been a pleasure." He turned and walked out of the bar.

"Great," Kelly muttered to herself. She needed a way into Area 51 and Jarvis obviously was not the way. She'd just pissed away five hundred dollars and gotten nowhere. Her hope had been that Johnny had contacted Jarvis.

She looked down at the notes she had made during the interview. What would her dad do in this situation? He'd always said the best way to overcome an obstacle was to approach it in a manner that was least expected. He'd also said that in the case of getting into a place that was guarded, approach it not at the weakest place, but at the strongest because that was the least-expected avenue.

What was the strongest thing about Area 51, from what Jarvis and the research said? "Security," Kelly muttered to herself, still looking at her notes. They had to have people employed to do their security. Driving out to the Groom Lake area would certainly bring her into contact with the security people, but Johnny had done that and he was gone.

She circled 737 on her pad. That was it. Tomorrow morning she would go out to the airfield and see if anyone got off the plane. If they did, she'd follow them and see what she could turn up. And if tomorrow morning didn't work, then there was always tomorrow evening.

8

"We're green," Prague announced to the men gathered around him in the dark. "Our eye in the sky says the objective is clear. I want all three birds airborne in two mikes. Move out." Prague headed toward one of the small AH-6 helicopters and gestured at Turcotte. "You're with me, meat. Backseat."

Turcotte grimaced. The *meat* comment was getting real old, but now was not the time to face it down. He followed Prague and joined him in the helicopter. Prague took the seat up front next to the pilot, while Turcotte had the entire backseat to himself. The doors were off and the cold night air swirled inside, making Turcotte regret he had not put on long underwear. He wished he had been better briefed on what was going to happen. He zipped his black Gore-Tex jacket up tight over his coveralls and took the headset that was hanging on the roof and placed it on, over the small plug already in his ear for the FM radio on the team frequency.

Because he was on the same bird as Prague—the mission commander—Turcotte was immediately plugged into the mission's secure satellite communications traffic as they winged their way to the southwest over the fields of Nebraska.

"Nightscape Six, this is Cube Six. Status. Over." The voice on the other end sounded familiar to Turcotte, but he couldn't quite place who Cube Six was.

Prague replied from the front seat. "This is Nightscape Six. En route to Oscar Romeo Papa. Will hold there. Over."

Turcotte followed the military terminology easily—ORP stood for "objective rally point," the last place friendly forces held before hitting an objective. Except in this case, Turcotte still didn't have a clue what the objective was, nor was he impressed with how friendly the forces around him were, if Prague was to serve as the example.

The other, deep voice continued. "Roger, this is Cube Six. Break. Bouncer Three, status? Over."

A new voice came on the air. "This is Bouncer Three. Airborne and en route. Over."

"Roger. Wait for my command. Cube Six out."

The pilot of the AH-6 swept even lower over the cornfields, the UH-60 Blackhawk following just to the rear and above. The other AH-6 flew trail. The corn gave way briefly to pasture with cattle breaking in all directions as the helicopters came over, then the terrain turned back to corn. Turcotte had never seen this many fields, even in Germany. It seemed like all of Nebraska was one big checkerboard of cultivation and ranching. Through his night vision goggles he could see an occasional patch of trees off in the distance, sometimes with lights peeking through the trees, indicating that was where the farmers and ranchers lived. *What are we going after out here?* Turcotte wondered.

The pilot pulled back on the cyclic and reduced throttle. Turcotte could see Prague checking their location on a ground positioning receiver (GPR). Prague gave a hold signal to the pilot.

"Cube Six, this is Nightscape Six. At Oscar Papa Romeo. Request final clearance. Over."

"This is Cube Six. Eye in the sky still shows you are clear for a twelve-kilometer radius. No traffic within eighteen klicks. Proceed. I say again, proceed. Out."

"Roger. Out." Prague pointed out the windshield and they were swooping across the dark sky again. "Phase one initiated. Start the watch."

THE CUBE, AREA 51
T—118 HOURS, 30 MINUTES

"Sir, we've got a shadow on Bouncer Three."

"A what?" Gullick spun around in his command chair. "What do you mean a shadow?"

Major Quinn pointed at the screen. "There's a bogey right behind Three. We didn't pick it up before because it's so small, but something's following Bouncer Three. I've checked the tapes and it's been there ever since Three left the hangar. Must have been somewhere in the vicinity when Three took off."

"What is it?" Gullick demanded.

"I don't know, sir. We were only able to catch it by tracking satellite and infrared signature."

The Cube was hooked in to the U.S. Space Command's Missile Warning Center, located inside Cheyenne Mountain outside Colorado Springs. The Space Command was responsible for the Defense Support Program (DSP) satellite system. DSP satellites blanketed the entire surface of the earth from an altitude of over twenty thousand miles up in geosynchronous orbits. The system had originally been developed to detect ICBM launches during the Cold

War. During the Gulf War it had picked up every SCUD launch and proved so effective that the military had further refined the entire system to be effective enough to give real-time warnings to local commanders at the tactical level—a valuable system that those in the Cube could tap into. Through the other members of Majic-12 Gullick had access to systems like DSP and many others.

Every three seconds the DSP system downloaded an infrared map of the earth's surface and surrounding airspace. Most of the data was simply stored on tape in the Warning Center, unless, of course, the computer detected a missile launch, or, as in this case, an authorized agency requested a direct line and keyed in a specific target area to be forwarded on a real-time basis.

"Is it a Fast Walker?" Gullick asked, referring to the code name for unidentified valid IR sources that the system occasionally picked up and could not be explained.

"It's definitely a bogey, sir. It doesn't match anything on record. It's too small to be even a jet aircraft."

The unspoken question was, what was that small yet fast enough to stay on the tail of Bouncer Three, which was moving at over thirty-five hundred miles an hour toward Nebraska?

"Put it on up front," Gullick ordered, turning his seat back to the main screen. He briefly touched the right side of his skull, then looked at the hand as he pulled it away. It was shaking slightly. Gullick gripped the edge of his chair to stop that.

Quinn transferred the information to the large screen in the front of the room. There was a small glowing dot just behind the larger dot indicating Bouncer Three.

"How far behind Three is it?"

"Hard to tell, sir. Probably about ten miles or so."

"Have you told Three?"

"Yes, sir."

Gullick spoke into the boom mike just in front of his lips, keying the send button strapped to his belt. "Bouncer Three, this is Cube Six. Do you have a visual on the bogey? Over."

"This is Three. Negative. We see nothing. Whatever it is, it's too far back. Over."

"This is Six. Give me some evasive maneuvers. Over."

The pilot of Three answered. "Wilco. Wait one. Over."

On the screen the dot representing Bouncer Three suddenly darted to the right just north of Salt Lake City. The smaller dot just as quickly followed. A quick series of zigzags didn't faze the bogey.

"Should I order an abort, sir?" Quinn asked.

"No," Gullick said. "Let's ride this out. Get Aurora on alert. I want to be on top of this bogey." He keyed the radio. "Three, this is Six. Forget about it. Just continue the mission. I'll take care of the situation from this end. Out."

Quinn's worry showed through and it irritated Gullick. "Should I inform Nightscape Six?"

"Negative, Major. Let these people do their job and let me worry about the bogey. You let me do the thinking and informing around here. You got that?" Gullick glared at the junior officer.

"Yes, sir!"

VICINITY BLOOMFIELD, NEBRASKA
T—118 HOURS, 15 MINUTES

"We have multiple heat signatures to the left," the pilot of the AH-6 announced, immediately swooping in that direction.

"Go get 'em, cowboy," Prague yelled into the intercom as he flipped up his goggles. He reached into the backseat, across Turcotte's lap, and grabbed a rifle that had been strapped down there. Hooking his arm into the sling, Prague leaned out of the helicopter, his safety harness keeping him from falling out to the ground below. Turcotte leaned forward and watched the same scene that Prague was following—cattle scattering in all directions from the sound of the helicopters.

Prague put the rifle to his shoulder and looked through the night scope mounted on top. He fired twice and two of the cows collapsed immediately. "Nerve agent," he said, glancing over his shoulder at Turcotte. "Knocks 'em down, but leaves no trace. We recover the dart."

The AH-6 pulled up and assumed a stationary position a hundred meters away from the two animals. The UH-60 Blackhawk came to a hover directly over the two bodies and Turcotte watched as ropes were thrown out of the Blackhawk and four men with rucksacks fast-roped down.

The four men gathered around the bodies and there was an occasional flash of light as they worked on the cows.

"Time hack?" Prague asked.

"Six minutes, thirty seconds until Bouncer Three is on station."

"Okay," Prague said. "We're all right."

"What are they doing?" Turcotte finally asked.

Prague turned to the rear, looking like a mechanical demon with a wide grin beneath the protruding bulk of his night vision goggles. "They're getting some prime filet down there. You like heart? Or maybe eyeballs? How about cow ovaries? We come back with all sorts of good stuff.

"They have top-of-the-line surgical lasers to make clean cuts. They also have suction to clean the blood up. What the locals are left with is a couple of dead cows with specific body parts surgically removed, yet no sign of vehicle traffic in the area. Also no blood, which is kind of disturbing. No one can explain it so no one really looks into it too hard, but it serves its purpose."

Which is what? Turcotte wondered. He had heard about cattle mutilations. It was in the paper every so often. Why was such a sophisticated operation being run just to do this? Was this why Duncan had sent him out here? To find out that the government people at Area 51 were behind cattle mutilations?

The Blackhawk had moved away while the men worked. Now it came back in, letting down two harnesses on winches—one on either side. The first two men were up with their gory load in thirty seconds. Then the next two.

"Initiate phase two," Prague ordered and they were heading farther to the southwest.

"You hear that?" Billy Peters asked.

"Huh?" Susie replied, her mind on other matters—in this case Billy's arm around her shoulders and her head on his broad chest. She could hear his heart beating, that was for sure.

"Sounds like helicopters or something," Billy muttered. He reached out with his free hand and wiped some of the fog off the front windshield of his '77 Ford pickup and tried to look out. They'd been parked here for a long time—since just before it had gotten dark, but there'd been a lot to say. Susie was leaving her folks and Billy was on the spot, not quite sure whether to go for it and invite her to live in his trailer down in Columbus or punt and go along with her plan to move to her sister's in Omaha.

He'd picked this spot because he was sure there'd be no one to interrupt them, but now he was almost glad there might be an interruption because he sure couldn't make his mind up tonight, not with her pushing up against him like she was: how was a man supposed to think clearly under those circumstances?

"Something's coming this way," Billy said, looking out the window into the night sky.

The Cube, Area 51
T—118 Hours, 4 Minutes

Gullick was watching the large map. The bogey was still behind Three. Both dots were currently near the conjunction of the Wyoming, Colorado, and Nebraska borders.

"Aurora's status?" Gullick asked.

"On the runway, ready to take off."

"Give her the go."

"Yes, sir."

"TOT for phase two?"

"Eighty-six seconds," Quinn answered.

Gullick flicked a switch on the console in front of him and watched the video feed from the control tower on the surface. A curiously shaped plane began rolling forward. Shaped like a rounded manta ray, the most significant features of the two-man reconnaissance plane were its huge intakes under the front cockpit and large exhausts behind the engines. Capable of Mach 7, over five thousand miles an hour, or almost a mile and a half a second at maximum speed, it could get to a target in a hurry.

The successor to the famous SR-71 Blackbird, Aurora had made its maiden flight in 1986. At a billion dollars a plane there were only five in the inventory, and they were used only when all other systems were exhausted. To the public that had financed it, the plane didn't exist. It was one of the most closely guarded secrets in the Air Force and Gullick had one at his disposal around the clock, an indication of the importance of this project to the Air Force.

With sufficient thrust built up, Aurora suddenly bounded

up into the air and accelerated while climbing at a seventy-degree angle, swiftly turning toward the northeast and disappearing from the screen.

VICINITY BLOOMFIELD, NEBRASKA

Turcotte's AH-6 was holding at two hundred feet while the Blackhawk passed them by and came to its own hover over a cornfield in front of Turcotte and to his left. The other AH-6 slid over and took up security four hundred meters in the opposite direction. The Blackhawk slowly lowered until it was about eighty feet above the ground, just above the point where the rotor wash would permanently disturb the stalks of corn.

A bright light flashed out of the cargo bay of the Blackhawk, the beam angling to a terminus in the field below, cutting through the corn and burning into the ground.

"The laser's computer aimed," Prague explained through the intercom, proud of his men and their toys. "Makes a perfect circle. Confuses the shit out of those eggheads who come and scratch their heads over it in daylight. Dumb fucks. They figure it's related to the dead cows in the next field, which it is," he said with a laugh, "but they don't know how and they'll never figure it out."

And? Turcotte thought. Why did Prague want to confuse people?

"Nightscape Six, this is Bouncer Three. ETA forty-five seconds. Over."

"Roger. Out." Prague turned to Turcotte. "You're going to love the last act of this play. Watch to the south."

Turcotte checked the Calico one more time. This was all so strange, but the thing that disturbed him the most was the way Prague was showing him everything now, but hadn't explained it before. What did Prague know about him? Turcotte wondered.

"Jesus, Susie, you see that!" Billy furiously wiped the windshield as the beam of light played down a quarter mile to their left into the field.

"What is it?" Susie asked, her living problems forgotten for the moment.

"I don't know, but I'm getting the hell out of here." He turned the key and the Ford's engine started up.

"I've got a heat source in the trees to the southwest!" the pilot of the other AH-6 announced. "It's a car engine!"

"Shit!" Prague exclaimed.

A bright glow came flying in from the south, low on the horizon, moving faster than anything Turcotte had ever seen. It swept by silently, followed closely by another, smaller glowing dot.

"What was behind Bouncer Three?" Prague asked out loud, his composure cracking for the first time since Turcotte had met him. Turcotte was surprised by *both* craft that sped by. This whole scenario was getting weirder by the second.

Turcotte watched as the large disk that Prague had called Bouncer Three made an abrupt jump move to the right, changed directions just short of 180 degrees in a split second, and did a pass over the small town of Bloomfield on the horizon before heading back toward the southwest.

"Get me to that heat source!" Prague ordered. The pilot of the AH-6 complied, pointing the nose toward the stand of trees. "You other guys, head for the MSS," he added.

The Blackhawk banked right and headed back to the northj, to the secure area of Devil's Nest, the other AH-6 flying escort. Turcotte flipped off the safety on the Calico as they headed toward the treeline. Whatever was going on, it was clear to Turcotte that it wasn't going according to Prague's plan.

THE CUBE, AREA 51

"Pass complete. Three's coming home," Quinn announced.

All eyes were on the screen. The bogey was still behind Three. It continued that way for about a minute, then suddenly the second dot broke away, heading back to the northeast, where it had just come from.

"Get Aurora on that bogey!" Gullick ordered.

VICINITY BLOOMFIELD, NEBRASKA

"We've got to get these people," Prague ordered as the helicopter banked toward the rapidly fleeing pickup truck.

"They're civilians," Turcotte protested, leaning through the door and checking out the truck.

"They saw too much. We can't have them talking about seeing helicopters here. Fire across the front of the truck," Prague ordered the pilot, who expertly sideslipped his helicopter so that they were now flying sideways, with the nose of the aircraft—and the chain gun hung off the skid—pointed toward the pickup. A stream of tracers arced out, right across the headlights of the pickup, and the brakelights flared.

"Goddamn!" Turcotte yelled. "Are you crazy?"

"Put us down on the road in front of them," Prague ordered, ignoring Turcotte.

"Who are these people, Billy?" Susie screamed. "Why are they shooting at us?"

Billy didn't waste time trying to explain. He slammed the

truck into reverse as the helicopter settled down in front of him in the glow of the headlights, blowing dirt and debris up into the air, blinding him.

The pickup's rear tires slipped into the drainage ditch on the side of the road. Dirt flew as Billy threw the gear into first, but they didn't move.

The skids touched ground and Prague was out the door, leaving the dart rifle behind in favor of his Calico. Turcotte followed, right on his heels. Turcotte's mind was trying to sort out all that had happened and was happening.

"Hands up and out of the truck!" Prague yelled.

The doors opened and a man stepped out, a woman following, hiding herself behind the man's bulk.

"Who are you people?" the man asked.

"Cuff them!" Prague ordered Turcotte.

"They're civilians." He stood still.

Prague shifted the muzzle of his Calico in Turcotte's direction. "Cuff them."

Turcotte looked at the weapon, looked at Prague, then pulled out two plastic cinches from his vest and secured the couple's hands behind their backs.

"Let me see your ID," the man demanded. "You can't be doing this. We didn't do nothing wrong. You ain't cops."

"Get in the helicopter," Prague ordered. He herded the procession toward the AH-6.

"Where are you taking us?" the man asked, standing stubbornly in the middle of the road just short of the helicopter, the girl still cowering at his side.

Turcotte looked at Prague and saw the way the man's body was set, saw his finger shifting from outside the trigger guard to inside, a sure sign he was about to fire. Turcotte had been trained just like Prague: the only safety was the finger off the trigger.

Turcotte quickly stepped in between. "Just do as he says.

We'll get this sorted once we get back to base. There's been an accident," he added lamely. "I'm Mike," he said, tapping the man on the shoulder and pointing at the helicopter, the sudden human gesture momentarily disorienting the couple.

The man looked at Turcotte. "Billy. This here's Susie."

Turcotte nudged them toward the helicopter. "Well, Billy and Susie, looks like the man wants you to go for a ride."

"Shut up, meat," Prague snarled, gesturing with the weapon.

They got into the helicopter and the pilot lifted.

THE CUBE, AREA 51

A third dot was now on the screen, popping on the screen over eastern Nevada and heading almost directly toward Bouncer Three, which was returning to base. Gullick knew that was Aurora on its way to intercept the bogey.

"The bogey is dropping off the chase, sir," Quinn reported. The bogey was circling, heading back in toward the Nightscape objective.

"Redirect Aurora toward Nebraska," Gullick ordered.

Quinn complied.

"Aurora ETA at the objective?" Gullick immediately demanded.

"Ten minutes," Quinn announced.

Not bad time to cover almost twelve hundred miles. But in this case it might be about nine minutes too late, Gullick reflected as he watched the symbol that represented the bogey close on the target site. He briefly considered ordering Bouncer Three to turn around, but that was beyond the present scope of his authority. Gullick smashed his fist down onto the desk in front of him, startling those in the Cube.

Vicinity Bloomfield, Nebraska

The AH-6 cleared the trees at the edge of a field and turned to the north. Turcotte had strapped the man and woman into the backseat and squeezed in next to them. Prague was twisted around in the right front seat, the barrel of his Calico pointed rearward, his finger caressing the outside of the trigger guard.

Turcotte looked at the muzzle, then at Prague. "I'd appreciate it if you didn't point that thing at me," he said into the boom mike. Turcotte was scared. Not so much because of the gun pointed at him, although that was a problem, but more because the man holding the gun was acting so irrationally. What did Prague think he was going to do with these two civilians?

"I don't give a fuck what you'd appreciate," Prague answered over the intercom. "You questioned me in the middle of a mission. That's a no-go, meat. I'm going to have your ass."

"These people are civilians," Turcotte said. The couple were ignorant of the conversation because they weren't wearing headsets.

"They're fucking dead meat now, as far as I'm concerned," Prague said. "They saw too much. They'll have to go to the facility at Dulce and get clipped."

"I don't know what the hell you're doing, or what you're talking about," Turcotte said, "but they're—" He halted as the helicopter suddenly jerked hard right, then dropped altitude.

"What are you doing?" Prague yelled at the pilot, keeping his attention on the backseat.

"We got company!" the pilot screamed in return. A brightly glowing orb—about three feet in diameter—appeared directly in front of the windshield. The pilot slammed the collective down and pushed the cyclic forward in evasive reaction, but the glow dipped right down with them and crashed into the front of the helicopter. There was a shattering of Plexiglas and Turcotte ducked his head.

"Prepare for crash!" the pilot yelled into the intercom. "We're going—" The rest of his sentence was cut off as the nose of the chopper impacted with the ground. The blades cartwheeled into the soft dirt and exploded off, miraculously pinwheeling away and not slashing through the body of the aircraft.

Turcotte felt a sharp rip in his right side, then everything became still. He lifted his head. The only sound was a high-pitched scream. He turned to his left. Susie's mouth was a wide-open O and the sound was emanating from it. Billy's eyes were open and he was blinking, trying to see in the dark.

Turcotte reached down and unbuckled Billy's seat belt, then whipped out his commando knife and cut the couple's hands free. "Get out," he said, nudging them toward the left door, before turning his attention to the front seat.

The pilot was hanging limp in his harness, his right arm twisted at an unnatural angle. Prague was beginning to stir. His Calico was gone, thrown from the aircraft on impact.

The smell of JP-4 aviation fuel was strong in the air. As soon as it hit a hot metal surface such as the engine exhaust, the helicopter would be an inferno.

Prague appeared to be fumbling with his seat belt. Turcotte leaned over between the two front seats, ignoring the explosion of pain that movement ignited on his right side. Prague's right hand was flipping open the cover to his holster. "Don't let them get away," he rasped at Turcotte. He had the gun out and pointed it back toward Billy, who was helping Susie out of the door.

Turcotte reacted, slamming the inside edge of his left hand across Prague's throat, feeling cartilage give way, while with his right hand he hammered down on Prague's gun hand, hearing the forearm bone crack against the edge of the seat. Prague's eyes bulged, and he gasped through his mangled throat.

Turcotte followed Billy and Susie out the left rear door. "Keep moving," he ordered, pushing them away. A flame flickered somewhere in the rear of the helicopter. Staying with the aircraft, Turcotte reached in the front seat and unbuckled the pilot. Prague's left hand suddenly moved, slashing across his body at Turcotte with his knife. The blade cut through the Gore-Tex jacket and inflicted a gash on Turcotte's right forearm.

Pinning Prague's left hand with his right, Turcotte leaned over the pilot and hit Prague again in the throat with his left, this time not holding back as he had the first time. The cartilage completely gave way and Prague's airway was blocked.

Turcotte threw the pilot over his shoulder. He jogged away from the helicopter as it burst into flames.

9

THE CUBE, AREA 51
T—117 HOURS, 45 MINUTES

"Nightscape Six is down, sir," Quinn announced. "I have a transponder location. No communication by radio."

"Launch a conventional crash recovery to the transponder location," General Gullick ordered. He continued to watch the dot representing the bogey. It was slowly moving about in the vicinity of Nightscape Six's transponder signal. Aurora was now approaching the Nebraska-Colorado border.

VICINITY BLOOMFIELD, NEBRASKA
T—117 HOURS, 42 MINUTES

"Get out of here," Turcotte said to Susie and Billy, who were staring at the burning helicopter. Turcotte had the pilot's flight suit ripped open and was going over the man's vital signs, doing a primary survey—for breathing first, then bleeding, then checking for broken bones. The pilot was good to go on the first two other than some scrapes and cuts. There was an obvious broken arm.

Turcotte couldn't tell for sure, but based on the large dent on the man's helmet and his unconscious condition, he felt the pilot had some sort of head injury, and he was not trained or equipped to deal with that. All he could do was leave the helmet on and hope that it contained the injury until he could get the man some professional medical help. The pilot was unconscious, and from his condition it did not appear that he would be gaining consciousness anytime soon, which was fine with Turcotte. He immobilized the broken arm as well as he could.

"But—" Billy said, confused. "What—"

"No buts; no questions; no memory," Turcotte snapped, looking up from the pilot's body. "Forget everything that happened tonight. Don't ever tell anyone, because if you do they won't believe you and then people who don't want you talking will come looking for you. Leave it here and go."

Billy didn't need any further urging. He took Susie by the arm and quickly walked away in the darkness toward the nearest road.

He looked down at himself. Blood was seeping out the right side of his Gore-Tex jacket and his right sleeve. He delt with the forearm first, wrapping a bandage from his combat vest over the sliced skin and stopping the bleeding. Carefully probing with his fingers, he reached in through the jacket and gasped when he touched torn skin. Turcotte carefully unzipped his Gore-Tex jacket and jumpsuit. An eight-inch-long gash was just over the outside of his ribs. As best he could, he bandaged the wound.

Turcotte looked up into the sky. He could see the small glowing object, about a thousand feet overhead. It was lazily moving about, as if to view the results of its actions. He watched for a few moments, but there did not appear to be any immediate threat. Although from the way that thing had been moving, Turcotte didn't think he would have much time to react if there were.

Turcotte scanned the horizon. The others would be here

soon. And then? That was the burning question. He'd
killed Prague on reflex. He didn't regret it, given what he'd
seen Prague do this evening, but the situation was very
confusing and Turcotte wasn't sure what his next move
should be.

Had Prague known he was a plant? That would explain
some of his actions, but not all of them. And if Prague
hadn't known he was a plant, then the man had been bor-
derline nuts; unless, Turcotte reminded himself, there was
another layer to everything that he had just witnessed. He
knew the actions, he just didn't know the motivation.

None of that was going to do him any good, Turcotte
knew, unless he could get back to Duncan with what he
had just seen, and to do that he was going to have to get
away from these Nightscape people. The pilot's unconscious condition would buy him some time once they were
picked up. It would simply be Turcotte's story, and he began working on what he would tell them.

THE CUBE

Gullick had complete telemetry feedback from Aurora and
he could listen in on the pilot and reconnaissance systems
officer (RSO) talking to each other.

"All systems on. We'll be in range of target in seventy-
five seconds," the RSO announced.

Gullick keyed his mike. "Aurora, this is Cube Six. I want
a good shot of this target. Get it on the first pass. You
probably won't have an opportunity for a second. Over."

"Roger that, Cube Six," the RSO said. "Fifty seconds."

"Descending through ten thousand," the pilot announced. "Slowing through two point five. The look will be
right," he told the RSO, giving a direction to orient all the
sophisticated reconnaissance systems on board the aircraft.

"Pod deploying," the RSO said as the speed gauge continued to go down. Gullick knew that now that the plane was under two thousand miles an hour the surveillance pod could be extended. Doing it at higher speeds would have destroyed the necessary aerodynamics of the plane and caused the plane to break and burn. Even now, according to the telemetry, the skin temperature of the aircraft was eight hundred degrees Fahrenheit. "Twenty seconds. All green."

"Leveling at five thousand. Steady at Mach two."

"All systems on."

Gullick looked up to the large screen at the front of the room. The red triangle representing Aurora closed on and passed the small dot indicating the bogey. Then the bogey darted away.

Gullick keyed the mike, "This is Cube Six. The bogey is running! Vector one nine zero degrees. Pursue!"

Aurora was fast, but maneuverable it wasn't. Gullick watched as the red triangle began a long turn that would encompass most of Nebraska and part of Iowa before it was through. The small dot was heading southwest, currently over Kansas.

"What's the bogey's speed?" General Gullick asked.

"Computer estimates it's moving at Mach three point six," Major Quinn replied.

As the bogey crossed the panhandle of Oklahoma, Aurora completed its turn over southern Nebraska. "She'll catch up," Gullick said.

The two dots continued, Aurora steadily closing the gap.

"Bogey's over Mexican airspace," Quinn reported. He hesitated, but duty required that he speak. "Are you authorizing Aurora to continue pursuit?"

"Shit," Gullick said. "The Mexicans won't even know it's there. Too high and too fast. And even if they get a blip on radar it will be gone in a blink and there's nothing they can do about it anyway. Damn right it's to pursue."

The length of Mexico was traversed in less than twelve minutes, Aurora now less than a thousand miles behind the bogey and closing rapidly.

"Intercept in eight minutes," Quinn announced.

VICINITY BLOOMFIELD, NEBRASKA

Turcotte heard the choppers long before they arrived. The Blackhawk landed on the opposite side of the crash and discharged a squad of men with fire extinguishers. Turcotte knew that by daylight there would be nothing in the field other than some charred cornstalks. The other AH-6 landed right next to his location.

"Where's Major Prague?" the man who ran off the helicopter asked.

Turcotte pointed at the crash site. "Killed on impact."

The man knelt down next to the pilot. "What's his status?"

"Broken arm. I think he has a concussion. I haven't taken his helmet off, to keep the pressure on in case his skull is fractured."

The man signaled for the pilot to be place on board the Blackhawk. He pointed to Turcotte. "You come with me. They want you back at the Cube."

THE CUBE

"Sir, Aurora already has a photo of the bogey," Quinn said. "What do you want it to do when it catches up?"

The Aurora was purely a reconnaissance plane. Mounting any sort of weapon system, even missiles, would have destroyed its aerodynamic form and reduced its speed drastically.

"I want to find out where this bogey comes from," Gullick said. "Then I can send other people to take care of the problem."

Both indicators were now over the eastern beginning of the Pacific Ocean.

The RSO's voice hissed in Gullick's ear. "Cube Six, this is Aurora. Request you lay on some fuel for us on the return flight. We will be past the point of no return in fifteen minutes. Over."

"This is Cube Six. Roger. We're scrambling some tankers for you. Keep on its tail. Out." Gullick pointed at Quinn, who was also monitoring the radio.

"I'll take care of it, sir," Quinn said.

The Mexican coastline was now long gone. Gullick knew that the Pacific Ocean off the coast of Central and South America—other than Canal traffic—was a very desolate place. They were still heading almost due south.

"We're close," the pilot announced. "It's about two hundred miles ahead of us. I'm throttling back to ease up on it."

Gullick watched the telemetry. It reminded him of being ground support when he was a test pilot. Reading the same gauges that the pilot overhead did, but not having hands on the controls. As the plane passed through Mach 2.5 the RSO extended the surveillance pod and activated his low-level light television (LLLTV) camera. Gullick immediately had the image relayed through a satellite onto the screen in front of him. The LLLTV was no ordinary television. The camera enhanced both the light and image, giving it the ability to display an image at night, while at the same time carrying a magnification of over one hundred. The RSO began scanning ahead, using the information fed to him from the satellites above to pinpoint the bogey.

"Eighty miles," the pilot announced.

"Sixty."

"I've got it!" the RSO yelled.

In the small television screen Gullick could see a small dot. As if on cue the dot suddenly jerked to the right, a splash of water shot up, and it was gone.

Gullick leaned back in his seat and closed his eyes, his forehead furrowed in pain.

"Cube Six, this is Aurora. Bogey is down. I say again. Bogey is down. Transmitting grid location."

10

General Gullick poured himself a cup of coffee, then took his chair at the head of the conference table. He took a pair of painkiller pills out of his pocket and swallowed them, washing them down with a swig of scalding coffee. Slowly the reports started coming back.

"Aurora is returning," Major Quinn reported. "ETA in twenty-two minutes. We have the exact location where the bogey went down into the ocean."

Gullick looked at the inner circle of Majic-12, who were in the room. Each man knew his area of responsibility, and as the orders were issued, each took the appropriate action. "Admiral Coakley, the bogey is in your area of operations now. I want whatever you have floating closest to the spot on top of it ASAP! I want you to be ready to go down and recover that thing.

"Mr. Davis, I want the information from Aurora downloaded to Major Quinn and I want to know what that thing is."

"Already working on the digital relay," Davis replied. "I'll have the hard copy from the pod as soon as it touches down."

Gullick was mentally ticking off all that had happened,

but it was very hard for him to think clearly. "What's the status at the crash site?"

Quinn was ready, the earplug in his right ear giving him a live feed from the man in charge on the ground in Nebraska. "Fire is out. Recovery team is en route and will be on site in twenty minutes. Those present on the scene from Nightscape are cleaning up the pieces and providing security. Still no response from locals. I think we'll make it clear."

Gullick nodded. If they got the remains of the helicopter out of there before daylight without being spotted, the Nightscape mission would be a success. The bogey was a whole different question. One he hoped he could answer shortly.

"What about the survivors of the helicopter crash? They here yet?" General Gullick asked.

Quinn checked his computer. "The pilot is in the clinic in Vegas being worked on. Major Prague was killed in the crash. The third man, a Captain Mike Turcotte, was slightly injured but is here, sir."

"Send him in."

A quarter mile up a bedraggled and hurting Turcotte had been waiting for a half hour now. His Gore-Tex jacket was partly melted and he was black from soot and dirt. The bandage he had hurriedly put on his arm in Nebraska was soaked with blood, but he thought the bleeding was stopped. He wasn't ready to peel the bandage off to check until he was someplace where he could get proper medical care.

The helicopter had swung by the airstrip outside, dropping him off before continuing on with the pilot to Las Vegas, where the program maintained its medical clinic close by the hospital facilities at Nellis Air Force Base.

Turcotte had been met by two security men who had hustled him inside the hangar.

The interior doors were shut, but there was a bouncer in the portion next to the elevator doors. Turcotte studied the craft, recognizing it as the sister of the one that had flown by earlier in Nebraska. For all he knew it could be the same one. It didn't take a genius to put together the cattle mutilations, the false landing signature lasered into the cornfield, and these craft to recognize that there was a cover-up operation of major proportion being operated here. Turcotte just didn't understand how the pieces fit together. The mission he had just been on in Nebraska seemed very high risk and he could see no clear-cut purpose to it. Unless it was to draw attention away from this site, but that didn't quite click.

One thing was for certain, Turcotte knew. He certainly had something to report on now. It would be someone else's job to put the pieces together. He was glad to have gotten out with his ass in one piece. He looked down at his right hand. The fingers were shaking. Killing Prague, although not the first time he had killed, weighed heavily on him. He turned his hand over and stared at the scar tissue there for a little while.

With great effort Turcotte brought his mind back to his present situation. He wasn't in the clear yet. He was confident that Prague's burned body would raise no questions. He knew that the other helicopter aircrews would return later this morning or maybe even the following morning once they had finished sterilizing the crash site in Nebraska. And as soon as they were debriefed, the detection of the two civilians by the other AH-6 crew would surface. Then there would be questions asked that he couldn't adequately answer. The clock on his career was already ticking, but looking at the alien craft told Turcotte that there were larger issues than his pension involved here. He also knew that the reaction of those in charge when they found out he had let the two civilians go might be more than a letter of reprimand in his official files. These people were playing hardball, and by killing Prague he had entered their playing field. He just hoped he could get out of here and that then Duncan would cover his butt.

The elevator doors slid open, and the guard inside gestured for him to come in. Turcotte walked in and the floor seemed to fall out from under him as they hurtled down. The doors opened again, and Turcotte stepped out into the control room of the Cube. He looked about but the guards hustled him through the room to a corridor in the back. He entered a conference room where the lights were turned down low. There were several people sitting in shadows near the end of the table. Turcotte walked up to the ranking general.

Turcotte made no attempt to salute; his arm wouldn't allow it. "Captain Turcotte reporting, sir." He noted the nameplate on the man's chest—Gullick.

Gullick saluted smartly. "What happened?"

That voice—the same one that had been giving the orders to Prague over the radio—Turcotte remembered now where he had heard it before: the board of inquiry that had investigated what had happened in Germany. That voice had been one of six that had questioned him via speakerphone in the secure holding area in Berlin. Turcotte took a deep breath and cleared his mind of everything but the story he now had to tell. There would be time later to deal with the other issues.

Turcotte proceeded to describe the events of the previous night, leaving out the important facts about intercepting the truck with the two civilians and killing Prague, of course. Gullick was most interested in the attack by the small sphere, but there was nothing Turcotte could really say about that as he had not been looking out the front when it had hit the helicopter.

Gullick listened to his account, then pointed back at the elevator doors. "They'll take you in to the clinic in the morning. You're dismissed."

So much for thank you, Turcotte thought as he left the room. Gullick had been the most outspoken in his praise of Turcotte's actions in Germany, praise that had confused and sickened Turcotte. But obviously, the events of the previous evening were not in the same league. Turcotte had no doubt that if he had killed the two civilians and presented their bodies like trophies, he would have received a hearty slap on the back.

The elevator doors closed off the control room to Turcotte, and he began his return trip to the surface. He should be able to get clear now.

General Gullick waited until the elevator doors had closed behind the Army captain. Then he returned his attention to Major Quinn. "That was no help. I want all the other personnel completely debriefed when they return from the MSS. Have you analyzed the data from Aurora?"

"Yes, sir. We've got several good shots of the bogey."

"Put one on the screen," General Gullick ordered.

A small glowing ball appeared on Gullick's computer screen.

"Scale?" Gullick asked.

Around the edges of the screen rulers appeared. "It's three feet in diameter, sir," Quinn said.

"Propulsion system?"

"Unknown."

"Flight dynamics?"

"Unknown."

"Spectral analysis?"

"The composition of its skin was resistant to all attempts to—"

"Unknown, then." Gullick slapped his hand on the tabletop, glaring at the picture as if he could penetrate it with his eyes. "What the hell *do* we know about it?"

"Uh . . ." Quinn paused and took a deep breath. "Well, sir, we've got it in our records."

"What?"

In response Quinn split the screen, the photo taken by Aurora of the bogey sliding to the left and an identical object appearing on the right in grainy black and white.

"Talk to me, Quinn," Gullick growled. "Talk to me."

"The photo on the right was"—Quinn paused again and cleared his throat with a nervous cough—"the photo on the right was taken by a gun camera in a P-47 Thunderbolt on February twenty-third, 1945, over the Rhine River in Germany."

There was a nervous rustle from the other men in the inner circle of Majic-12 who were at the table.

"A foo fighter," Gullick said.

"Yes, sir."

"What's a foo fighter?" Kennedy asked.

Gullick remained silent, digesting the revelation. Quinn looked at the information he had dredged up on his computer screen and continued for the others in the room who didn't know their aviation history. "The object on the right was called a 'foo fighter.' There were numerous sightings of these objects made by aircrews during World War II. Because they were initially suspected to be Japanese and German secret weapons, all information concerning them was classified.

"The foo fighter reports started in late 1944. They were described as metallic spheres or balls of light, about three feet in diameter. Since the bomber aircrews that reported them were usually veterans and gun cameras on board escort fighters occasionally recorded them also, giving factual support to those accounts, the reports were taken seriously."

Quinn was in his element. Before being assigned to the project he had worked in Project Blue Book, the Air Force's classified study group on UFOs—reports of unidentified craft *other* than the ones kept at Area 51. Blue Book has also been a smokescreen for the Area 51 project and a purveyor of disinformation to mislead serious researchers. The foo fighters were in the Blue Book files and most aviators had heard of them.

"The lid could not be kept on such a widespread occurrence, and reports of foo fighters did leak out to the general press, and they are even mentioned in some modern books about UFOs. What *didn't* leak out, though, is that we lost twelve aircraft to the foo fighters. Every time one of our fighters or bombers would try to get close to one or fire on them—they were bogies, after all—the foo fighters would turn and ram the attacker, leaving our aircraft the worse for the encounter. Just like what happened to Nightscape Six. Because of these encounters, classified standing orders were issued by Army Air Corps high command to leave the foo fighters alone. Apparently that worked, because there were no further reports of attacks.

"After the war, when intelligence went through Japanese and German records, it was discovered that they, too, had run into foo fighters and experienced the same results. We know they weren't behind them from what we found. In fact, the records showed they thought the spheres were *our* secret weapons.

"Of particular interest is an incident that is still classified Q, level five." Quinn hesitated, but Gullick gestured for him to go on and tell the others. "On August sixth, 1945, when the *Enola Gay* flew the first atomic mission toward Hiroshima, it was accompanied the entire way by three foo fighters. The mission was almost scrapped when the spheres appeared, but the commander on the ground at the departure airfield at Tinian decided to continue it. There was no hostile action by the foo fighters and the situation was repeated several days later during the mission to Nagasaki."

Kennedy leaned forward. "Von Seeckt was on the airfield there at Tinian back when they launched the *Enola Gay* carrying that bomb, wasn't he?"

"Yes, sir. Von Seeckt was there," Quinn replied.

"And we still don't know anything about these foo fighters, do we?" Gullick asked.

"No, sir."

"Russian?" Kennedy asked.

Quinn stared at him. "Excuse me, sir?"

"They couldn't have been Russian, could they? The sons of bitches did beat us with Sputnik. Maybe they made these things."

"Uh, no, sir, I don't believe there was any indication they were Russian," Quinn replied. "Once the war was over, reports about the foo fighters ended for a while."

"For a while?" Kennedy repeated.

"In 1986 a bogey was picked up in the atmosphere by space surveillance and tracked," Quinn said. "The object did not fit any known aircraft parameters."

Quinn pressed a key and a new picture appeared on the screen. It looked as if a child had gone crazy with a bright green pen. A line zigzagged across the screen and looped back on itself several times. "This is the flight path of a bogey they picked up back in eighty-six flying at altitudes ranging from four to one hundred and eighty thousand feet." Quinn hit another button. "This is the flight pattern of our bogey tonight superimposed on the one from eighty-six." The two were very similar. "There's something else, sir."

"And that is?" Gullick asked.

"There was another series of unexplained sightings right after this one. The Navy along with the DIA were running an operation called Project Aquarius. It was, um, well, what they were doing—"

"Spit it out, man!" Gullick ordered.

"They were experimenting using psychics to try to locate submarines."

"Oh, Christ," Gullick muttered. "And?" he wearily asked.

"The psychics were doing reasonably well. About a sixty-percent success rate on getting the approximate longitude and latitude of submerged submarines simply by sitting in a room in the Pentagon and using mental imaging of a photograph of each specific submarine.

"There was an unexpected thing that occurred every once in a while, though. One of the psychics would pick up the image of something else at the same coordinates as the submarines. Something hovering *above* the location of the sub."

"And, let me guess," Gullick said. "We don't know what that something was, correct?"

"Space surveillance picked up . . ." Quinn hit his keyboard and let the flight-path schematic speak for itself: another radical flight pattern.

"Did anyone ever explain any of these sightings?" Gullick asked.

"No, sir."

"So we have a *real* UFO on our hands now, don't we?" Gullick said.

"Uh, yes, sir."

"Well, that's just fucking fine!" Gullick snapped. "That's all I need right now." He glared at Admiral Coakley. "I want that thing recovered and I want to know what the hell it is!"

As the men filed out, Kennedy stopped by General Gullick and sat down next to him. "Maybe we should check with Hemstadt at Dulce about these foo fighters," he said. "There might be some information about them in the Machine."

Gullick looked up from the tabletop and stared into Kennedy's eyes. "Do you want to go to Dulce to hook up to the Machine?"

Kennedy swallowed. "I thought we could just call him and ask. It's possible that the Machine might be controlling—"

"You think too much," Gullick cut him off, ending the conversation.

11

Vicinity Dulce, New Mexico
T—113 Hours, 30 Minutes

Johnny Simmons awoke to darkness. At least he thought he was awake. He could see nothing, hear nothing. When he tried to move, panic set in. His limbs didn't respond. He had a horrible feeling of being awake but asleep, unable to connect the conscious mind with the nervous system to produce action. He felt detached from his body and reality. A mind floating in a black void.

Then came the pain. Without sight or sound it exploded into his brain, becoming all his mind, all of his world. It was coming from every nerve ending in jagged, climbing spikes, far beyond anything he had thought possible.

Johnny screamed, and the worst of it all was that he couldn't hear his own voice.

12

Las Vegas slowed down slightly at five-thirty in the morning. The neon still glowed, and there were people on the streets, most heading to their rooms for a few hours of sleep before starting over again on the games of chance. Kelly Reynolds was doing the opposite, starting her day after catching three hours of sleep in her motel room. The first thing she had done when the alarm went off was call Johnny's apartment on the slim chance that he might be there or have changed the message.

She looked up as a red-eye flight roared in toward the horizon. *Walk to the sounds of the planes,* she thought to herself, paraphrasing Napoleon. She'd rent a car at the airport. Right now she needed the fresh air and the time to think.

This is what dad would have done, go for the strongest link. The thought brought a sad smile to her face. Her father and his stories. The best time of his life had been over before he was twenty. What a horrible way to spend the rest of one's life, Kelly thought.

World War II. The last good war. Her dad had served in the OSS, the Office of Strategic Services, the precursor to the CIA. He'd jumped into Italy during the last year of the war and worked with the partisans. Running the hills with a band of renegades licensed to kill Germans and take what they needed by force. Then he'd worked in Europe as the war closed out, helping with the war crimes trials. Much of what he saw there had soured him on mankind.

Peace had never been the same. He'd turned to the slow death of the bottle and lived with his memories and his nightmares. Kelly's mom had retreated into her own brain and shut out the outside world. And because of them Kelly had grown up fast. She wondered if her dad had still been alive, if his liver had lasted a little longer, how the affair at Nellis would have turned out. She might have been able to go to him for help. At the very least, she would have considered what he would have done instead of blazing her own path to destruction. He certainly would not have bought into Prague's line so naively. He would have told her to approach the bait very slowly and to watch out for the hook.

The only legacy she had from her dad was his stories. But she was his legacy and that was more than she could say for herself at forty-two. No children and not much of a career to counterweight that. As she walked to the airport, Kelly felt an overwhelming depression. The only thing that kept her going was Johnny. He needed her.

She stopped in an all-night market and bought two packs of cigarettes and a lighter.

Area 51

Turcotte strapped himself into the plane seat and tried to get comfortable. He'd spent the last two hours, since leaving the underground control room, alone, waiting in a small room off of the hangar, until they rolled out the stairs to load the 737 to fly into Las Vegas and pick up the morning shift of workers. He was glad that he was going to be able to get out of here. First thing he would do in Las Vegas after getting his arm sewn up was call Duncan on the number he had memorized. He wanted to get everything off his chest. Then hopefully he could leave all this behind.

He noticed an old man come on board, accompanied by two younger men whose demeanor suggested they were bodyguards for the first man. Despite the fact that they were the only other passengers on board, the old man took the front row of seats on the other side of the plane from Turcotte. The bodyguards, apparently satisfied there were no immediate threats, sat down a few rows back as the plane's door was shut by the same hard-faced man who had greeted Turcotte with the breathalyzer a little less than forty hours ago. That man disappeared into the cockpit.

"They are fools," the old man muttered in German, his gnarled hands wrapped around a cane with a silver handle.

Turcotte ignored him, looking out the window at the base of Groom Mountain. Even this close—less than two hundred meters away—it was almost impossible to tell that there was a hangar built into the side of the mountain. Turcotte wondered how much money had been poured into this facility. Several billion dollars at least. Of course, with the U.S. government having a covert black budget somewhere between thirty-four and fifty billion dollars a year, he knew that was just a drop in the bucket.

"They will all die, just like they did last time," the old man said in perfect German, shaking his head.

Turcotte looked over his shoulder. One of the bodyguards was asleep. The other was engrossed in a paperback.

"Who will die?" Turcotte asked in the same language.

The old man started and then looked at Turcotte. *"Are you one of Gullick's men?"*

Turcotte lifted his right hand, exposing the blood-soaked fabric. *"I was."*

"And now who are you?"

At first Turcotte thought he had translated poorly, but then he realized he had it right, and he understood. It was a question he had struggled with all through the dark hours of the morning. *"I don't know, but I am done here."*

The old man switched to English. "That is good. This is not a place to be. Not with what they plan, but I am not sure any distance will be enough."

"Who are you?"

The old man inclined his head. "Werner Von Seeckt. And you?"

"Mike Turcotte."

"I have worked here since 1943."

"This is my second day," Turcotte said.

Von Seeckt found that amusing. "It did not take you long to get in trouble," he said. "You are going to the hospital with me?"

Turcotte nodded. "What were you talking about earlier? About everyone dying?"

The engine noise increased as the plane taxied toward the end of the runway. "Those fools," Von Seeckt said, gesturing out the window. "They are playing with forces they don't understand."

"The flying saucers?" Turcotte asked.

"Yes, the saucers. We call them bouncers," Von Seeckt said. "But even more, there is another ship. You have not seen the large one, have you?"

"No. I've only seen the ones here in this hangar."

"There is a bigger one. Much bigger. They are trying to figure out how to fly it. They believe if they can get it to work they can take it into orbit and then back. Then there will no longer be any need for the space shuttles, but more importantly they believe that it is an interstellar transport, that we can bridge centuries of normal development by simply flying the mothership. They think we can have the stars right away without having to make the technological breakthroughs to do it." Von Seeckt sighed. "Or, perhaps more importantly, without the societal development."

Turcotte had seen enough the past couple of days to accept what Von Seeckt was saying at face value. "What's so bad about just flying the thing? Why are you saying it's a threat to the planet?"

"We don't know how it works!" Von Seeckt said, stamping the head of his cane down on the carpet. "The engine is incomprehensible. They are not even sure which of the many machines inside *is* the engine.

"Or there may be two engines! Two modes of propulsions. One for use inside of a solar system or inside a planet's atmosphere and the other once the ship is outside significant effect of gravity from planets and stars. We simply don't know, and what if we turn the wrong one on?

"Does the interstellar drive create its own wormhole and the ship is pulled through? Maybe. So, maybe we make a wormhole on earth—not good! Or does it ride the gravitational waves? But in riding, does it disturb them? Imagine what that could do. And what will it do if we lose control?

"And who is to say the engine will still work properly? It is a flaw of inductive logic to say that just because the bouncers still work that the mothership will work. In fact, what if it is broken and turning it on makes it self-destruct?"

Von Seeckt leaned over and spoke in a lower voice. "In 1989 we were working on one of the engines from the bouncers. We had removed it from the craft and placed it in a cradle. The men working on it were testing tolerances and operating parameters.

"They found out about tolerances! They turned it on and it ripped out of the cradle holding it. They had not replicated the control system adequately and lost the ability to turn it off. It tore through the retaining wall, killing five men. When it finally came to a stop it was buried sixty-five feet into solid rock. It took over two weeks to drill into the rock and remove it. It wasn't damaged at all.

"I have seen it before. They never learn. I understood the first time. There was a war. Extreme measures were called for then. But there is no war now. And all the secrecy! Why? What are we hiding all this for? General Gullick says it is because the public will not understand, and his cronies produce all sorts of psychological studies to back that up, but I do not believe it. They hide it because they have hidden it for so long that they can no longer reveal what they have been doing without saying that the government has lied for so many years. And they hide it because knowledge is power and the bouncers and the mothership represent the ultimate power."

The plane was gathering speed and moving down the runway. "It all used to make sense," Von Seeckt said. "But this year something changed. They are all acting very strangely."

Turcotte had cued into something Von Seeckt had said. "What do you mean the 'first time'?"

"I have worked for the government of the United States a very long time," Von Seeckt said. "I had a certain"—Von Seeckt paused—"knowledge and expertise that they needed so they, ah, recruited me in mid-1942. I came out here to the West. To Los Alamos, in New Mexico."

"The bomb," Turcotte said.

Von Seeckt nodded. "Yes. The bomb. But in 1943 I moved to Dulce, New Mexico. That is where the real work went on. Los Alamos, they worked off of the information we gave them.

"It was all very, very secret. They pieced it all out. Fermi had already done the first piece even before they had the knowledge I brought with me. His chain-reaction experiment gave them the raw material. I gave them the technology."

"You did?" Turcotte asked. The plane was gaining altitude. "How did you know—"

Von Seeckt raised his cane. "Another time for that story, maybe. We worked nonstop until 1945. We thought we had it right, just like they think they understand the mothership. The difference was that there was a war then. And even so, there were many who argued we should not test the bomb, but everyone in power was tired. Then Roosevelt died. They hadn't even briefed Vice President Truman. Their great secrecy almost cost them there. The secretary of state had to go and tell him about the bomb the day after the President died.

"After understanding the significance of what he was told, Truman gave the go-ahead to test. But I don't think they fully informed him of the potential for disaster, just as they keep the President in the dark now. We took a chance then."

Von Seeckt muttered something in German that Turcotte didn't catch, then he continued in English. "They have a presidential adviser on the Majic committee, but there is much they do not tell her. I know they have not told her about the Nightscape missions. They believe this operation here, and much else that is secret in the government, is beyond the scope of the politicians who can be gone in four years."

Turcotte didn't respond to that. He had long ago decided that the country was run by bureaucrats who stayed in their slots for decades—not by politicians who came and went. At least he was beginning to understand why Duncan had sent him in to infiltrate Nightscape.

"On the sixteenth of July, in the year of our Lord 1945, at five-thirty in the morning, the first atomic weapon made by man was detonated. We placed it on a steel tower in the desert outside of ..lamogordo Air Base. No one quite knew what was going to happen. There were some—some of the finest minds mankind has ever produced—who believed the world would end. That the bomb would start a chain reaction that would not stop until it consumed the planet. Others thought nothing would happen. Because it was even riskier than history thinks. We were playing with technology we had *not* developed!"

That confused Turcotte. He had always understood that the U.S. had developed the A-bomb from scratch. He didn't have time to focus on that because Von Seeckt was still talking.

"It was children playing with something we hoped we understood. What if a simple mistake had been made? What if we had connected the red wire where the blue wire was supposed to go? And even if it did work we weren't quite sure of the limitations!

"Do you know what Oppenheimer said he was thinking about that morning?" Von Seeckt didn't wait for an answer. "He was thinking of the Hindu saying: 'I am become death, the shatterer of worlds.' And we had. It went just as planned. We had death under our control—because it did not start a chain reaction and it didn't just sit there on the tower and do nothing. It worked."

"Why are you telling me this?" Turcotte asked.

"Because I think you are done here, as you say. And I am dying. And there is nothing left for me."

Von Seeckt was silent for a few minutes, the plane rising up into the early-morning darkness. "Because I have lived in ignorance and fear for all my years but now I have nothing to fear. I am dead even as you see me, but it is only now in looking back with a different perspective that I know I was dead all those years." He turned. "Because you are young and have a life ahead of you. And they are playing

God down there below us and someone has to stop them. There are four days before they try to run up the mothership to full power. Four days. Four days until Armageddon."

Turcotte asked several questions but Von Seeckt wouldn't answer. The rest of the trip was made in silence.

McCARREN AIRPORT, LAS VEGAS

It was still dark. Kelly waited in the terminal, staring out at the runway. A plane roared overhead, and in the runway lights she could see the red stripe painted down the side. The plane touched down but didn't turn toward the terminal. It pulled off to an area about a quarter mile away, behind a fence with green slats. Show time.

Kelly ran through the main terminal dodging tourists and burst outside. She slid into the rental car she'd left at the curb, stuffing the ticket that had been placed on the windshield into her pocket. Following the airport service road, she paralleled the green fence, stopping as she neared a gate in it. She shut down the engine and turned off the lights. There was the faintest glow of dawn on the horizon.

"What now?" she asked herself. She opened one of the packs she had bought and lit up. The first breath in was awful, tearing down her throat. She felt lightheaded and nauseated. The second was better. "Three years down the tube," she muttered.

A bus pulled up to the gate and it swung open, admitting the vehicle. Kelly opened the door, stubbing out the cigarette. Just before the gate shut, a van with darkened windows pulled out.

"Shit," Kelly said, jumping back in the car. As it turned the corner she got the car started and followed. The van

turned onto Las Vegas Boulevard and headed north. They
passed the Mirage, Caesars Palace, and other famous casinos that lined the street. At the edge of town the van made
a right into the main gate for Nellis Air Force Base.

Kelly made a quick decision and followed, merging into
the flow of early-morning work traffic entering the post.
The air policeman waved her to a halt as she had expected,
because she had no access sticker on her rent-a-car, but she
was prepared.

"Could you tell me how to get to the public affairs officer?" she asked, holding up her press card as the line of
cars piled up behind her. She could see the van still ahead.

The air policeman hurriedly gave her directions and
waved her through, keeping the flow of traffic going. Kelly
had watched the van and followed in the direction it had
gone.

She was surprised to see it parked outside a building
next to the post hospital. Kelly drove past, looped around,
then parked in the lot outside a dental clinic across the
street.

The side door of the van slid open and two men in black
windbreakers stepped out, then an old man leaning on a
cane, followed by a fourth man wearing a dirty and torn
black parka.

The four disappeared into a door. Kelly leaned back and
exercised what her dad had told her was the most important trait a person could have—patience.

Inside the hospital annex the man in the white coat was
curt and to the point. "I'm Dr. Cruise. Please take a seat in
examining room two, Professor Von Seeckt. You," he said,
pointing at Turcotte, "follow me." They left the watchdogs
in the waiting room.

Turcotte followed the doctor into examining room one.
Turcotte estimated Cruise to be in his fifties, with carefully

styled silver hair and expensive glasses. He appeared to be in good shape and was coldly efficient in bedside manner.

"Strip down to the waist," Cruise ordered.

Turcotte remembered Prague's nickname for him— meat. He was beginning to feel more and more like that was apropos. Hell, Turcotte thought as he watched Dr. Cruise prepare a needle with painkiller, he'd have sewn the wound up himself if he'd had access to the proper medical equipment. He'd been hurt worse on training exercises.

"Have you seen the pilot who was injured?" Turcotte asked as Cruise slid the needle into his side.

"Yes."

Turcotte waited a few seconds but there was nothing further. "How is he?"

"Fractured skull. Some bleeding on the brain. He was lucky whoever was with him didn't take his helmet off, or he wouldn't have made it here alive."

Luck had nothing to do with it, Turcotte thought to himself. "Has he regained consciousness?"

"No." Cruise put the needle down and picked up a charged surgical needle. He seemed quite preoccupied with some other thoughts.

Turcotte watched with detachment as Cruise began to sew the edges of the tear on his side together. He considered his situation. If Prague had suspected him, then the word hadn't been passed along, because the two guards were obviously for Von Seeckt. That meant he was home free as soon as he was done here.

"Wait here," Doctor Cruise ordered after he'd finished putting a bandage on the arm. He went into the office next door. The door swung shut but the latch didn't catch and it was left slightly ajar. Looking at the mirror above the examining table, Turcotte could see into the office. Cruise was at the sink, washing his hands. Then the doctor placed both hands on the edge of the sink and stared in the mirror, saying something to himself.

Turcotte thought that quite odd. Then Cruise reached into a pocket inside his coat and pulled out a needle with a plastic protective cover over the tip. He stared at the needle, removed the cover, then took a deep breath and headed out of the office, through the far door, handling the needle very gingerly.

Turcotte hopped off the examining table and slowly opened the door to Cruise's office. He looked about. There was some paperwork on the desk. Turcotte noticed a folder with Von Seeckt's name neatly printed on the label. He flipped it open.

The top document was a certificate of death signed by Cruise with today's date in the top right block. Cause of death: pulmonary failure.

Turcotte twisted the knob and threw open the door to examining room two. Cruise froze, the needle a few inches away from the old man's arm. "Don't move!" Turcotte ordered, drawing his 9mm Browning High Power from his hip holster.

"What do you think you're doing?" Cruise blustered.

"Put the needle down," Turcotte said.

"I'll report you to General Gullick," Cruise said, carefully putting the syringe down on the countertop.

"What is going on?" Von Seeckt asked in German.

"We'll find out in a second," Turcotte said, keeping the muzzle of his pistol on Cruise as he walked over and picked up the needle.

"What's in it?" he asked.

"His treatment," Cruise said, his eyes on the syringe.

"It won't harm you, then, will it?" Turcotte asked with a nasty smile, turning the point toward Cruise's neck.

"I'm—I—no, but—" Cruise froze as the tip touched his skin.

"This wouldn't happen to be something that causes pulmonary failure, would it?"

"No," Cruise said, his eyes wide and staring down at the gleaming metal and glass tube.

"Then there's no problem if you get a dose," Turcotte said, pushing the point into Cruise's neck.

Sweat was pouring down Cruise's face as Turcotte's thumb poised over the plunger.

"No problem, right, Doctor?"

"Don't. Please. Don't," Cruise whispered.

Von Seeckt didn't seem too surprised by any of these events. He was putting his shirt back on. "What is in it, Dr. Cruise? My friend with the needle, he has had a hard night. I would not provoke him into doing anything rash."

"It's insulin."

"And please tell me what that would have done to me?" Von Seeckt asked.

"An overdose would cause your heart to stop," Cruise said.

"Your death certificate is filled out on the good doctor's desk," Turcotte said, looking at Von Seeckt. "He already signed it. The only thing blank was your time of death, but it was dated today."

"Ah, after all these years." Von Seeckt shook his head. "And you are a *doctor*," he added, shaking his head at Cruise. "I knew General Gullick was evil, but you should know better. You swore an oath to preserve life."

"Gullick ordered this?" Turcotte asked.

Cruise almost shook his head, but thought better of it given the steel needle in his throat. "Yes."

Turcotte slid the needle out, but before Cruise could even draw a deep breath, he slammed his elbow up against the doctor's temple. Cruise crumpled to the ground unconscious.

"Thank you, my friend," Von Seeckt said. He pulled his jacket on and picked up his cane. "And now?"

"And now we get the hell out of here," Turcotte said. "Follow me."

He opened the door and stepped out into the waiting room, pistol first. There was only one guard there, reading a magazine. He looked up and kept very still.

"Keys to the van," Turcotte ordered. "With your left hand."

The guard slowly took the keys out of his pocket.

"Put them on the table, then get on your knees, face to the wall." The man complied.

"Get them, Professor," Turcotte said. He edged toward the door, keeping his weapon on the guard. "Where's your partner?"

The man kept silent, which is what Turcotte would have done in his position. Turcotte slammed the barrel of his pistol down on the back of the man's head and he dropped to the floor.

"Let's go." Turcotte carefully opened the outside door and looked out. Because of the tinted windows he couldn't tell if the other guard was inside the van, which was parked. Turcotte stuck the hand with the gun inside his parka pocket. He walked out with Von Seeckt, straight up to the van, and slid the side door open. Empty. "Get in."

On the other side of the street Kelly watched the two men get into the van, the younger of the two holding a gun in his hand. She shifted her eyes and watched the other man, the guard who had come outside to smoke a few minutes ago, turn around and start walking toward the front of the building.

Turcotte turned the key and nothing happened. He tried again. "Fuck," he muttered.

Von Seeckt leaned over and pointed at a small device under the steering column. "Electronic theft protection," he explained. "There's a small conductor that is placed there. Without it, no electrical power. They have begun installing—"

"All right, all right," Turcotte cut in. He hadn't seen the driver take it out and it wasn't on the key ring. He looked back at the front door of the clinic. A shadow crossed his peripheral vision—the other guard coming around the corner of the building.

Then it all fell apart. The front door opened and the other guard staggered out, pistol waving about, firing, blinking blood out of his eyes.

Turcotte kicked open the driver side door. "Get out!" he yelled to Von Seeckt. He fired three rounds quickly, deliberately high, causing both guards to drop to the ground.

"Jesus!" Kelly flicked her cigarette out the window and started the car's engine. The man who had just fired swung around and looked at her, his eyes piercing right through the windshield from twenty feet away, then he spun about and fired again at the black-jacketed men. Too high, Kelly thought, and that decided her.

With a squeal of rubber she peeled out of the parking lot. She drove to the near side of the van, slamming on the brakes and skidding to a halt. "Get in!" she yelled, leaning over and throwing open the passenger door.

The man with the gun shoved the old man in, following right behind. "Go! Go! Go!" he exhorted her.

Kelly didn't need the advice. She fishtailed out of the parking lot. The two men ran out into the road behind, firing. A group of airmen waiting outside the dental clinic ran for cover.

There were a few plinks as bullets hit the trunk. Kelly took the next corner with her foot still pushing down on the accelerator. They were out of sight of the two gunmen. The main gate to the base was four blocks directly ahead.

"Steady through the gate," the man with the pistol said. "We don't want to attract attention."

"No shit, Sherlock," Kelly replied.

13

"So, Mr. Mike Turcotte and Professor Werner Von Seeckt, are you the bad guys or the good guys?" Kelly asked. Her hand shook as she lit a cigarette. "You don't mind, do you?" she asked, indicating the cigarette.

"If I was younger, I'd have one myself," Von Seeckt said. They were seated in her hotel room, belated introductions having just been made.

"Why were you following us?" Turcotte demanded. "You didn't just happen to be in that parking lot."

"I'm not telling you a thing, until you tell me who you are and why those guys were shooting at you," Kelly said.

Von Seeckt was looking at a piece of paper he'd pulled out of his coat. "To answer your first question, as you Americans say, we are the men in the white hats."

"And the guys back at Nellis," Kelly asked, "—the men in the black hats? Who are they?"

"The government," Turcotte said. "Or part of the government."

"Let's try this one more time," Kelly said. "Why were they shooting at you?"

Turcotte gave a concise explanation of the events of the previous twenty-four hours, from Area 51 to Devil's Nest, back to the Cube, to the hospital annex and Doctor Cruise's attempt to kill Von Seeckt.

"Whoa!" Kelly said when he came to a halt. "You expect me to believe that?"

"I don't give a shit what you believe," Turcotte said.

"Hey, don't get smart with me," Kelly said. "I saved your ass back there."

"You only saved our ass if what I just told you was the truth," Turcotte replied. To his surprise Kelly laughed.

"Good point."

"So, I've told you our story," Turcotte said. "Why were you there?"

"I'm looking for a friend of mine who has disappeared trying to infiltrate Area 51, and you got off the shuttle plane from that place. I didn't plan on getting caught in a gun battle. Have you heard about a reporter named Johnny Simmons getting picked up trying to get into Area 51 two nights ago?"

"There was a lot going on that night," Turcotte said. He glanced at Von Seeckt.

"If he disappeared trying to get into Area 51," Von Seeckt said, "he is either dead or he has been taken to a government facility at Dulce, New Mexico."

Turcotte remembered Prague mentioning that place.

"I don't think he's dead," Kelly said. "The man who was with him—a guy named Franklin—he was reported killed in a car crash that night. If they were going to kill Johnny, it would have been just as easy for them to put him in the car with Franklin. I think he's still alive and that means we have to go to New Mexico."

"Wait a second . . ." Turcotte began, but Von Seeckt was nodding his head.

"Yes, we must go to New Mexico. There is something there at Dulce we will need. Can you take us there in your car?"

"Yes. And I've got a place in Phoenix that we can stop at on the way," Kelly said.

Turcotte sat down on the couch and rubbed his forehead. He had a massive headache and it was getting worse. His side ached and he was tired. "No. We don't go anywhere," he said.

"You can stay here," Kelly said. "I'm going after Johnny."

"We need to stay together," Von Seeckt said in German.

"Why?" Turcotte asked.

"Hey!" Kelly yelled. "None of this talking around me."

"I was just telling my friend that we need to stick together," Von Seeckt said.

"No," Turcotte said. "I'm done with this. I've done my duty and now it's time for someone else to deal with this." He grabbed the phone.

"Who are you calling?"

"None of your business," Turcotte said. He began to dial the number that Duncan had given him. On the eighth digit the phone went dead. He looked up to see Kelly holding the cord, which she had unplugged from the wall.

"It's my phone," she said.

"This isn't a game!" Turcotte slammed the phone down.

"I know it isn't a game," Kelly replied just as loudly. "I just got shot at. My best friend has disappeared. He"—she pointed at Von Seeckt—"almost was murdered. I don't think anyone in this room thinks it's a game!"

"Plug the phone back in." Turcotte spaced the words out.

"No."

As Turcotte began to stand, Kelly held up a hand. "Listen to me. Before any of us does anything, let's get on the same sheet of music."

"I agree," Von Seeckt said.

"Who said we were voting?" Turcotte asked. He walked

over to the room door and opened it. *Screw these people,* he thought. He was tired and hurting and wanted nothing more than to forget all about Area 51 and this entire mess. He'd done his job and it had almost cost him his life. They couldn't ask any more of him.

He went down to the lobby and over to the first phone booth. Using his own phone credit card he dialed Duncan's number. It rang three times, then it was picked up, but the answer wasn't at all what he'd expected.

A mechanical voice came on. "You have dialed a number that has been disconnected. Please check the number and dial again."

Turcotte punched in the ten numbers again. He was certain he had them right. And received the same response. "Fuck!" he hissed as he slammed the phone down, earning himself a dirty look from a woman two phones over.

He went to the elevator. Had the number been bogus to start with? Or had he been cut off after going in? What the hell was going on?

He opened the door. Kelly barely looked up. She was grilling Von Seeckt. "But how did the government get the bouncers? And why are they hiding them and pulling all this deception shit? And what was the small sphere that made Turcotte's helicopter crash? And why were they trying to kill you if you were one of them—one of Majic-12?"

"Because they have gone too far," Von Seeckt said. "Are going to go too far," he amended. "In four days they will cross the line."

"What line?" Kelly asked.

"Welcome back, my young friend," Von Seeckt said. "Have you decided to stay with us?"

"I haven't decided anything," Turcotte muttered. He slumped down in one of the chairs by the window.

"This is the biggest story in years," Kelly said.

"And if you run it, your friend is dead," Turcotte couldn't help throwing in.

"Your phone call doesn't appear to have cheered you up," Kelly said.

Turcotte didn't reply.

"We must do this ourselves," Von Seeckt said.

"Do what?" Turcotte snapped.

Von Seeckt looked at the piece of paper in his hand and read. " 'Power, sun. Forbidden. Home place, chariot, never again. Death to all living things.' "

"What?" Turcotte was totally confused.

"May I please use your phone?" Von Seeckt asked Kelly.

"Certainly," Kelly said.

"How come you're letting him call?" Turcotte asked.

"He said please," Kelly replied.

"Wait one," Turcotte said to Von Seeckt, holding up his hand. "I'm pretty much in the dark here, like she is. But we're all in the same shit pile. I know what happened in Nebraska. And I saw what they tried to do to you at the medical annex. And I saw what they have in those hangars back there at Area 51, but I don't know what the hell is going on. Before you make any phone calls, tell us what is going on."

"They are going to try to engage the propulsion unit of the mothership on the fifteenth of this month. I fear that when the engine is engaged there will be disaster."

"I know that—" Turcotte began.

"Mothership?" Kelly cut in, which necessitated a brief description by Von Seeckt.

"How will engaging the engine be a disaster?" Kelly asked.

"I do not know exactly," Von Seeckt said. "But there is someone who might. Which is why I need to use the phone." He looked at Kelly. "Let me have the address of this place we will be stopping at in Phoenix." Kelly gave it to him and Von Seeckt dragged the phone into the bedroom suite and closed the door behind him.

Turcotte frowned but bowed to the situation. "Thanks for the ride."

"Better late than never," she said.

"What?"

"Forget it." She pointed at the closed bedroom door. "Is he on the level?"

"Your guess is as good as mine," Turcotte said.

"Great."

The Cube, Area 51

General Gullick steepled his fingers and looked around the conference table. Dr. Cruise was holding an ice pack to his temple. The other members of the inner circle were also there. Dr. Duncan, naturally, had not been informed of the meeting.

"Priorities," Gullick said. "One. Mothership run-up and propulsion engagement. Ferrel?"

"On schedule," Doctor Ferrel said. "We're analyzing the data from the run-up."

"What about the physical effect that Dr. Duncan complained about?"

Ferrel shook his head. "I don't know. She was the only one affected. The only change in variables was that she is female."

"What?" Gullick said.

"Maybe the wave effect of the engine affects females differently."

"Is it significant?" Gullick asked.

"No, sir."

"Any foreseeable problems?"

"No, sir."

Gullick moved on. "Two. This 'foo fighter.' Admiral Coakley?"

"I have three ships en route to the location where it went down. One is the USS *Pigeon,* a submarine rescue ship. It has the capability to send a minisub down to the bottom at that location."

"ETA and time to recover?" Gullick asked.

"ETA in six hours. Recovery—if they find it and it is intact—inside of twenty-four," Coakley responded.

"What do you mean if they find it?"

"It's a small object, General," Coakley explained. "It disappeared in deep water and we're not even sure it's still there."

"You *will* find it," Gullick said.

"Yes, sir."

"Sir . . ." Quinn paused.

"What?" Gullick snapped.

"What if this foo fighter wasn't the only one? The reports we have from World War II indicate multiple sightings. There were *three* flying with the *Enola Gay.*"

"What if it isn't the only one?" Gullick repeated.

"The pattern we observed with this one that went down in the Pacific indicated that it was waiting somewhere in the vicinity here and picked up Bouncer Three departing the Area."

"So?" Gullick said.

"Well, sir, then there might be another one of these foo fighters in the vicinity here and it might interfere when we run the mothership test flight. Obviously, the foo fighters are clued in to our operation here in some manner."

General Gullick considered this. He had spent a lot of time worrying about the test flight. This was a new wrinkle, and he struggled to deal with it. "Do you have any suggestions, Major?"

"I think we ought to check and see if there is another

one around. The last one reacted to a bouncer flight. If
there is another one about, maybe it would react to another bouncer flight, except this time we would be more
prepared."

Gullick nodded. "All right. We can't afford to have anything go wrong on the fifteenth. Let's prepare a mission for
tonight. Except have two bouncers ready. One as bait, the
other to follow and intercept. We'll also prepare some kill
zones if there's one of those things about and it takes the
bait."

"Yes, sir."

"Three," Gullick said. He looked at Dr. Cruise, then
General Brown, who was responsible for overall security.
The right side of Gullick's face twitched. "The *fuck-up* this
morning."

"Von Seeckt is gone," Brown said. "We have his apartment in Las Vegas covered in case he shows up there.
We—"

"Von Seeckt is old and a pain in the ass, but one thing
the man is not, is stupid," Gullick said. "If I'd have known
you were going to fuck up a simple termination I'd have let
nature take its course and listened to his shit for five more
months, then let him die. Now we have him on the loose
with his big mouth and his knowledge."

"He can't have gotten too far," General Brown said.

"The term that comes to mind," Gullick said, glaring at
Cruise, "is *anal retentive*. You had to have the death certificate typed up *before* you actually killed him?"

"Sir, I—"

Gullick silenced the doctor with a wave of his hand.
"What about this"—Gullick looked down at his computer
screen—"this Captain Turcotte?"

"He was new, sir." Brown had a file open. "He just arrived in time for the Nightscape mission last night." Brown
paused. "Since the events this morning, I had the other

surviving members of the Nightscape mission debriefed at the MSS via SATCOM. It appears that there was a civilian contact just as Bouncer Three arrived at the objective in Nebraska and the foo fighter interfered. Captain Turcotte was on board Major Prague's helicopter. Prague's bird stayed behind to deal with the civilians."

"There was no report of civilians. No report at all," Gullick said. "I debriefed Turcotte personally about the mission and he didn't say anything about that." He was shocked. "Turcotte lied to me."

"We don't know who the civilians were, but there has been no report filed with local authorities about the night's activities," Brown said.

"Of course not," Gullick said. "Turcotte would have told them to keep their mouths shut." He looked down again at the computer screen. "What's his background?"

"Infantry. Then Special Forces. We recruited him out of DET-A in Berlin."

Gullick slapped the conference tabletop. "I remember him now. He was involved in that incident in Düsseldorf with the IRA. I never saw him. We did the after-action inquiry by secure conference call, but I recognize the name now. He was there. So why is he lying to us and helping Von Seeckt flee? Is he a plant?"

General Brown shook his head. "I don't know, sir."

"He might be," Kennedy said. The others at the table all turned to look at the CIA man.

"Clarify," Gullick ordered.

"When we did our background on Dr. Duncan, my people picked up some information that she was working with someone inside our organization or was sending someone in to infiltrate us. The NSA had supplied her with a phone cutout to talk to this agent. That cutout was activated forty minutes ago. My people disconnected it."

"Could you find out who was calling?"

"Not without attracting the NSA's attention," Kennedy said. "But whoever was calling on that line, and I do believe it was Turcotte, given all that has happened, didn't get through."

"Why wasn't I informed of all this?" Gullick demanded.

"I thought I could take care of it," Kennedy said. "I warned Major Prague to be on the lookout and to check any new personnel extra carefully."

"Obviously that worked damn well!" Gullick exploded. He threw a file folder across the room. "Does anyone in here believe in letting me know what's going on before we fuck things up any further?"

The men of the inner circle of Majic-12 exchanged worried glances, not quite sure what to make of the question. Just as swiftly as he had exploded, Gullick calmed down. "I want everything you have on Turcotte." He checked the computer screen. "And who's this woman in the rent-a-car?"

"We've run the plates the guards copied. The woman renting the car is Kelly Reynolds. She's a freelance magazine writer."

"Just great." Gullick threw up his hands. "That's all we need."

"I'm working on getting a photo ID of her and her background."

"Track them down. Put out a classified alert through CIA channels into the police networks. No one should approach them. We have to get them ourselves. Quickly!"

"We also have a report from Jarvis," Kennedy continued. "This Reynolds woman interviewed him yesterday evening. Jarvis gave her the usual story, but she was better prepared than most and penetrated his backstop cover. She specifically asked about that reporter that we picked up the other night on White Sides Mountain."

"I wonder why she helped Turcotte and Von Seeckt," Quinn said.

Gullick stood. "Find her. Then you'll know. While you're at it, find Turcotte and find Von Seeckt and terminate them. Then we won't have to worry about the whys."

14

"Who did you call?" Turcotte asked, as he toweled his hair.

While Von Seeckt had been on the phone, Turcotte had taken a shower and cleaned himself up. Kelly had run out and gone to a Wal-Mart to buy him a loose-fitting pair of pants and a shirt to replace his torn and sooty jumpsuit. He felt more human now. The stitches that Cruise had put in his arm were holding up well.

"I left a message for a Professor Nabinger." Von Seeckt held up the crumpled piece of paper he had in his hand. "I believe he may hold the key to understanding the mothership."

"Who is Nabinger?" Kelly asked.

"An archaeologist with the Brooklyn Museum."

"Okay, time out," Turcotte said. "I thought I was halfway up to speed with all this, but now you've lost me."

"When they discovered the mothership," Von Seeckt said, "they also found tablets with what are called high runes on them. We have never been able to decipher the tablets, but it appears that Professor Nabinger might be able to." Von Seeckt's fingers ran over the head of his cane. "The only problem is that we have to get access to the tablets to show them to the professor."

"We are not going back into Area 51," Turcotte said flatly. "Gullick will have our heads if we go back in there. And they'll find us here soon enough too."

"The tablets aren't there," Von Seeckt said. "They're being held at the Majic-12 facility in Dulce, New Mexico. That is why *I* said we must go there."

Turcotte sat down in an easy chair and rubbed his forehead. "So you're agreeing with Kelly and say that we should go to Dulce. I assume whatever facility is there is highly classified also. So we're just going to break in, rescue this reporter Johnny Simmons, get these tablets, decipher them, and then what?"

"We make public the threat," Von Seeckt said. He looked at Kelly. "That's your job."

"Oh, I've been hired?" Kelly asked.

"No, sounds to me like you volunteered like I did," Turcotte said with a sarcastic laugh. "Sort of like people used to volunteer to charge across no-man's-land in World War I. Didn't your mother ever tell you not to pick up hitchhikers?"

Von Seeckt's voice was grim. "None of us in this room has any choice. We either expose what they are planning to do at Area 51 in four days and stop it or we—and many others—die."

"I'm not sure I buy into the danger this mothership holds," Turcotte said.

Von Seeckt shook the piece of paper with the message from Nabinger on it. "This confirms my suspicions!"

Turcotte glanced at Kelly and she returned the look. For all they knew Von Seeckt could be a total crackpot. The only reason Turcotte even began to believe the old man was the fact that Cruise had tried to kill him. That meant someone took him seriously enough to want to get rid of him. Of course, they might want to kill him because he *was* a crackpot, but Turcotte thought it best to keep that thought to himself. He didn't feel on very firm ground; after all, his phone call had been to a number that was disconnected, so his story didn't hold up much better than those of the other two people in the room.

Von Seeckt had told him about Duncan being in the Cube. She might be legitimate, she might not. Turcotte's training told him that when he didn't have enough information he had to make the best possible choice. Going to Dulce seemed like a good way to at least accumulate more information from both Von Seeckt and Kelly on the way there.

"All right," Turcotte said. "Let's stop yacking and get going."

BIMINI, THE BAHAMAS
T—108 HOURS, 50 MINUTES

Less than a hundred miles east of Miami, the islands that made up Bimini were scattered across the ocean like small green dots. It was in the sparkling blue water around those dots that massive stone blocks had been found that had fueled speculation that Atlantis had once been there.

Peter Nabinger didn't have the time to dive to see the blocks. Besides, he'd already seen pictures of them. He was here to see the woman who had taken the pictures and then stayed to study them further.

As he walked the short distance from the tiny dirt-strip airport to the village where Slater lived, Nabinger reflected on the only other time he'd seen the woman. It had been at an archaeological convention in Charleston, South Carolina. Slater had presented a paper on the stones in the shallow waters off her island home. It had not been received well. Not because her groundwork and research had been faulty, but because some of the conclusions she had proposed had gone against the prevailing winds of the world of academic archaeology.

What had fascinated Nabinger was that a few of Slater's slides showed forms of high runes etched into the under-water stonework. He'd gotten copies of the slides and they'd helped him decipher a few more high rune symbols. However, the chilly, in fact hostile, reception her presenta-tion had received had convinced Nabinger to keep his own studies quiet.

Nabinger wiped the sweat from his brow and adjusted his backpack. At the conference Slater had not seemed particularly perturbed at the attacks on her theories. She had smiled, packed her bags, and gone back to her island. Her attitude had seemed to suggest that they could take it or leave it. Until someone came up with some better ideas and supported them, she was sticking to hers. Nabinger had been impressed with that self-confident attitude. Of course, she didn't have a museum board of directors or an academic review board for tenure looking over her shoul-der, either, so she could afford to be aloof. –

He looked down at the card she had given him at the conference—a small map photocopied on the back pointed the way to her house. She'd given it to him when he'd asked for copies of the slides. "We don't have street names on my island," she had told him. "If you don't know where you're going, you won't get there. But don't worry, you can walk everywhere from the airfield or the dock."

Nabinger spotted a shock of white hair above a garden of green surrounding a small cottage. As the woman turned around, he recognized Slater. She put a hand over her eyes and watched him approach. Slater was in her late sixties and had come to archaeology late in life, after retir-ing from a career as a mineral- and geologic-rights lawyer representing various environmental groups—the reason she could afford to go her own way and another reason she irritated the archaeological old guard.

"Good day, young man," she called out as he turned into her drive.

"Ms. Slater, I'm—"

"Peter Nabinger, Brooklyn Museum," she said. "I may be old and getting a little long in the tooth, but I still have my mind. Did you take a wrong turn on the Nile? If I remember rightly, that was your area of expertise."

"I just flew in here from Cairo, via the puddle jumper from Miami," Nabinger said.

"Iced tea?" Slater asked, extending her hand toward the door and leading him in.

"Thank you."

They walked into the cool shadows of the house. It was a small bungalow, nicely furnished, with books and papers piled everywhere. She cleared a stack of papers from a folding chair. "Sit down, please."

Nabinger settled down and accepted the glass she gave him. Slater sat down on the floor, leaning her back against a couch covered with photographs. "So what brings you here, Mr. Egypt? Do you want more photos of the markings on the stones?"

"I was thinking about the paper you presented in Charleston last year," Nabinger began, not quite sure how to get to what he wanted to know.

"That was eleven months and six days ago," Slater said. "I would like to think your brain works a little quicker than that, or we might have a long day here. Please, Mr. Nabinger, you are here for a reason. I am not your professor at school. You can ask questions even if they seem silly. I've asked many silly questions in my life and I never regretted a one, but I have some regrets about the times I kept my mouth shut when I should have spoken up."

Nabinger nodded. "Are you familiar with the Nazi cult of Thule?"

Slater slowly put down her glass. "Yes." She was thoughtful for a moment. "Do you know that about ten years ago there was a great controversy in the medical community about using certain historical data to study hypothermia?" She didn't wait for an answer. "The best data ever documented on hypothermia was developed by Nazi doctors immersing concentration camp inmates in freezing vats of water and recording their decreasing bodily functions until they died. They also took some out of the water before they died and tried to resuscitate them by warming them up in various ways—which invariably failed to work. Not exactly something your typical medical researcher can do, but entirely realistic if you're looking for accuracy.

"The decision the American medical community made was that data gathered in such a brutal and inhuman manner should not be used, even if it advanced current medical science and eventually saved lives. I do not know how you would feel about that issue. I don't even know how I feel about it."

Slater paused, then smiled. "Now I am the one circling the subject. But you must understand the situation. Of course, I have read the papers and documents available on the cult of Thule and on the Nazis' fascination with Atlantis. It is part of my area of study. But there are those who would violently oppose any use of that information, so, as eccentric as some of my theories do seem, I have had to keep that particular piece of information out of my own papers and presentations."

Nabinger leaned forward. "What have you found?"

"Why do you want to know?" Slater asked.

Nabinger reached into his backpack and pulled out his sketchbook. He handed her the drawing and rough translation. "That's from the wall in the lower chamber of the

Great Pyramid." He checked his watch. He had to catch
his return flight to Miami in an hour and a half. He proceeded to quickly relate Kaji's story of Germans opening
up the chamber in 1942, ending it by showing her Von
Seeckt's dagger. He then described his efforts at deciphering the high runes and the message he had taken off
the wall of the chamber.

Slater heard him out. "This reference to a home place.
Do you think that is reference to a place on the far side of
the Atlantic?"

"Yes. And that's why I'm here. Because the Germans—if
they did go into that chamber in 1942, which I'm not absolutely convinced of yet despite the dagger—had to have
gotten their information about the chamber from somewhere. Perhaps the Germans found writing somewhere
that got them to that chamber, if you follow my logic."

"I follow your logic." Slater handed the drawing back.
"In the early days of World War II, German U-boats operated extensively along the East Coast of the United States
and here in the islands. They sank quite a bit of shipping.
But they also conducted some other missions.

"As you have talked with this Kaji fellow in Egypt, I have
talked to some of the old fishermen here in the islands,
who know the waters and the history. They say that in 1941
there were numerous sightings of German submarines
moving here among the islands. And that the submarines
did not seem interested in hunting ships—since we are off
the main shipping lanes here—but rather to be looking for
something in the waters around the islands."

Slater reached behind her and gathered some photos. "I
think this is what they found."

She handed them over. They appeared to be the same
photos that she had presented at the conference. Large
stone blocks, closely fitted together in about fifty feet of
water.

Slater talked as Nabinger looked at the photos. "They might have been part of the outer wall of a city or part of a quay. There is no way of knowing, with large portions covered with coral and other underwater life and the sea bottom close by sloping off into unexplored depths. This section with the stones might be just a tiny part of a larger ancient site, or may be the only site, built there thousands of years ago when that area was above water. Built by a people we don't know about, for a reason we can't yet figure out.

"The major pattern of the stones is a long J or more accurately a horseshoe with the open end to the northeast. All told it's about a third of a mile long in about fifty feet of water. Some of the stones are estimated to weigh almost fifteen tons, so they didn't get there by accident and whoever did put them in place had a very advanced engineering capability. You can barely get a knife point in the joints between some of those stones."

Slater stood up and leaned over Nabinger's shoulder and pointed. "There."

There was a large, ragged gouge in one of the blocks. "And this is?" Nabinger asked.

Slater shuffled through the photos. "Here," she said, handing him a close-up of the scar on the block.

Nabinger peered at it. There were other, very faint, older marks—writing around the edges of the gouge! Very similar to what was in his notebook, but the gouge had destroyed any chance of deciphering it!

"What happened to this stone?" Nabinger asked.

"As near as I can tell," Slater said, "it was hit by a torpedo." She touched the picture, running her fingers over the high runes. "I've seen others like these. Ancient markings destroyed sometime in the last century by modern weapons."

Nabinger nodded. "They're just like the ones I deci-

phered from the lower chamber. Not traditional hieroglyphics, but the older, high rune language."

Slater walked over to a desk buried under stacks of fold-
ers and books. She rummaged through, then found what
she was looking for. "Here," she said, handing Nabinger a
folder. "You are not the only one interested in the high
rune language."

He opened it. It was full of photos of high runes. Written
on walls, on mud slabs, carved into rock—in just about
every possible way by which ancient cultures had recorded
their affairs. "Where did you take these photos?" Nabinger
asked, his heart pounding with the thought of the potential
information he held in his hands. He recognized several of
the shots—the Central American site that had helped him
begin his breaking of the rune code.

"There's an index in the folder detailing where each
photo was shot—they're numbered. But, basically, several
locations. Here, under the waves. In Mexico, near Vera-
cruz. In Peru, at Tucume. On Easter Island. On some of
the islands in Polynesia. Some from your neck of the woods
in the Middle East—Egypt and Mesopotamia."

"The same symbols?" Nabinger asked, thumbing
through the photos. He had seen many of the same ones
before, but there were a few new ones in there to add to his
high rune database.

"Some differences. In fact, many differences," Slater answered. "But, yes, I believe they all stem from the same
root language and are connected. A written language that
predates the oldest recorded language that is generally accepted by historians."

Nabinger closed the binder. "I have been studying these
runes for many years. I've seen a lot of what you have in
here before—in fact I was able to decipher what I did of
the wall of the chamber in the Great Pyramid using symbols from a South American site. But the question that

bothers me—and why I have never made public my findings—is how can the same ancient writing have been found
in such vastly separated places?"

Slater sat back down. "Are you familiar with the diffusionist theory of civilization?"

"Yes, I am," Nabinger said. He knew what Slater was
referring to despite the fact that the prevailing winds of
thought this decade blew in favor of the isolationist theory
of civilization. Isolationists believed that the ancient civilizations all developed independent of one another. Mesopotamia, the Indus Valley, China, Egypt—all crossed a
threshold into civilization about the same time: around the
third or fourth century before the birth of Christ.

Nabinger had heard the argument many times. Isolationists cite natural evolution to explain this curious bit of syn-
chronicity. They also explain many common points in the
archaeological finds of these civilizations as due to man's
genetic commonality. Thus the fact that there are pyramids
in Peru, in Egypt, in Indochina, in North America—some
made of stone, some of earth, some of mud, but remark-
ably similar to one another given the distances between
those sites—all that is just because each society as it developed had a natural tendency to do the same thing.

Nabinger himself found this a bit of a leap. It would have
been quite a genetic coup if all these civilizations should
also have developed this same ancient high rune writing
and then abandoned it, well before the first hieroglyphics
were being etched on papyrus.

The diffusionists argued the other side of the civilization
coin, and Nabinger felt more affinity for their stance. They
believed that those civilizations rose at approximately the
same time on the cosmic scale—and exhibited all those
similarities, including the high runes—because those civilizations had all been started by people from a single earlier
civilization.

There were problems with the diffusionist theory, though—serious problems—and that is why Nabinger kept his views on the subject to himself. The strongest argument against the diffusionist theory was that there was no way for people from these different locations to have communicated with one another or have had any social or cultural intercourse. Those early people would have had to cross the Atlantic and the Pacific, according to diffusionist theory. They had a hard enough time even sailing around on the Mediterranean at that epoch, never mind crossing the oceans.

Slater's face wrinkled as she smiled. "And you know who the number-one spokesperson for the diffusionists is, don't you?" She didn't wait for an answer. "Leif Jorgenson. The man who sailed the Atlantic in a Viking ship to prove that Europeans were in North America long before Christopher Columbus. And who floated from Indonesia to the Hawaiian islands on a wood raft to support his theory that the islands were colonized from the west.

"But he's taken all that—and more—a step further in the last ten years. He's currently working the recently discovered ruins in Mesoamerica, looking at pyramids and the Mayan calendar and—guess what?—new high runes discovered there.

"Four years ago Jorgenson uncovered a massive site in Mexico near Jamiltepec. Over twenty large earthen and stone pyramids covering almost seven hundred acres on the west coast of Mexico, less than two miles from the Pacific Ocean. It had been covered by the jungle and because of the mountains around it was accessible only by sea.

"At the site he found further evidence of cross-cultural communication at a time earlier than traditional historians say is possible. There was jewelry made with gems that could only have been mined over two thousand miles away in South America. Stonework very similar to that at other sites, some on the other side of the Pacific in Oceania. He has in his possession hard evidence of a certain degree of interaction among widely spread peoples many centuries ago, but he is basically being ignored by the mainstream scientific community because they simply do not believe it is possible."

Nabinger was aware of the find, but he didn't want to offend Slater. After all, he'd come to her. "How does Jorgenson think civilization originated?"

"He believes that there was an original culture of white-skinned, long-eared, pyramid-building, rune-writing people living and flourishing at what he calls the 'zero point,'" Slater replied. "And that civilization spread out from that zero point at what he calls a 'zero time'—just prior to civilization developing simultaneously at all those other places that we are now studying. Civilization came from the zero point."

"And where is the zero point?" Nabinger asked, even though he had a very good idea of what the answer would be.

"It is the place so many legends call Atlantis."

"And that is why you are so familiar with his theories," Nabinger said.

"Yes. Because there *are* connections that have not been adequately explained." She paused. "Let me put it this way. Most people dismiss Jorgenson's zero-point theory based on physical impracticality. They say that there is no way man at that time—somewhere around four thousand B.C.—could have made it from the zero point to the other locations around the globe, regardless of where you place the zero point. They would have had to cross the oceans.

"Jorgenson's reply is that while there is not enough scientific evidence to convincingly support his theory, there is also not enough to *refute* it. *If* you assume there was a way ancient man could have crossed the oceans and spread, then the evidence falls into place. Thus all the sea journeys Jorgenson has undertaken in replicas of old sailing vessels."

She tapped the translation Nabinger had given her. "I must give you credit, young man, for pursuing your study of the commonalities among the high runes, in defiance of the common theories. Obviously it has brought you success that many other scientists and investigators have failed to find because they accepted the standard theories and could not see the greater possibilities in thinking differently. I have tried my own hand at translating the high runes, but it is not my area of expertise."

"Let's get back to the Atlantis idea," Nabinger said, checking his watch again.

"Jorgenson believes—and as you know there is scientific data to support this—that there was a major geological event in the Atlantic Ocean somewhere around 3400 B.C. Pretty much every culture around the globe refers to a great flood at about that time. Even the Tibetan Book of the Dead talks of a large land mass sinking into the sea at that time, and they are on the other side of the world from the Atlantic.

"And there are so many legends referring to the same thing: a great civilization in the middle of an ocean, destroyed by fire or flood! The Mayans called Atlantis Mu. The northern Europeans called it Thule. There was also the land called Lemuria—which a Madame Blavatsky picked up for her own cult of Thule—which is the question you started this meeting with.

"Lemuria was a land that scientists in the nineteenth century postulated must have existed because of the presence on Madagascar of a certain type of monkey, the lemur, that was also found in India. They believed Lemuria had been in the Indian Ocean. Blavatsky's followers, with the stroke of their pens, moved Lemuria to the Pacific, tying the legend in with the statues on Easter Island, which loops us back to Jorgenson's large-eared race. The statues on Easter Island are of, as you also know, a large-eared people."

Slater laughed. "I can tell you even better myths and stories. In 1922 another German published a book about Atlantis and claimed it had originally been occupied by a genetically perfect people. But the perfection was marred when an outside woman arrived and taught them how to ferment alcohol. So much for the perfect society. Because of this imperfection Atlantis was then destroyed by the tail of a comet! The continent burned and only a handful of people escaped."

"Where do these people get their ideas from?" Nabinger asked.

"Ah, ever the scientist," Slater said. "You want source material?" She went to her crowded desk and searched for a minute, before pulling out a dog-eared hardcover book. "This is the original mention of Atlantis from the *Timaeus*, a treatise on Pythagorean philosophy written by Plato. I have it here in the original Greek. Allow a little bit of leeway for my translation, as I don't often converse in the language."

She turned several pages and ran her finger down the writing. "As is traditional with the Greeks, this manuscript takes the form of a dialogue among several persons, Socrates being one of them. In this passage Solon is telling the story of some of the Greek legends—for example the flood of Deukalion and Pyrrha. He is rebuked by an older priest:

O Solon, you Greeks are children. There have been and will be many destructors of mankind, of which the greatest are by fire and water."

She turned a few pages.

Many are the truths and great are the achievements of
the Greeks. But there is one that stands out above all
the rest. It is in our history that a long time ago our
state stopped a mighty host which started from a distant point in a distant ocean and came to attack the
whole of Europe and Asia. For the ocean in that long
ago day was navigable outside of what we call the Pillars of Hercules—there, there was an island which was
larger than North Africa and Asia Minor put together
and it was possible for travelers to cross from it to our
land.

Slater looked up from the book. "There are many who
believe Plato is referring to North and South America, but
then those people run into the same problem that Jorgenson has. The technology of the day rules out an ocean
voyage across the Atlantic, so whatever Plato is referring
to, if it is real, had to be closer to Europe. Of course, Plato
is also saying something that goes against conventional
thought: that the ocean outside the Pillars of Hercules, the
Strait of Gibraltar, was navigable to people at that time."
She turned another page.

On this island of Atlantis there was a confederation of
very powerful kings who ruled the island and many
other islands and lands. Here, through the Pillars of
Hercules, they ruled North Africa as far as Egypt and
over Europe as far as Tuscany.

The kings of Atlantis at one time tried to enslave
both the people of Greece and Egypt, but the Greeks,
in a noble fight, stopped the invaders.

At a later time there occurred earthquakes and

floods, and on one grievous day the entire island of Atlantis was swallowed up by the sea and disappeared.

"And now for an especially interesting detail," Slater said.

Atlantis disappeared and the ocean at that spot has now been made impassable, being blocked up by mud which the island made as it settled into the ocean.

Slater smiled. "You know, of course, about the Sargasso Sea to the east of here. And the water around the islands here is relatively shallow in many places. If the ocean level were a bit lower, it would be almost impassable to most ships."

"So you believe you are sitting on the site of Atlantis?" Nabinger asked.

"I don't know," Slater said candidly. She pulled a volume off her bookshelf. "Take this with you, along with photographs of the runes. It has more about the legend of Atlantis that you might want to look at. I hope I have given you the information you wanted."

"That and more," Nabinger assured her, although there was little she had told him that he didn't know and he already had most of the high rune images on file. He had just enough time to get to the airport and catch the hop back to Miami and continue with his trip. He hoped Von Seeckt had more.

"One thing," Slater said as they walked to the door. "What do you think was in the black box that was taken out of the pyramid?"

Nabinger paused. "I don't have a clue."

Slater nodded. "My reference earlier to the use of data from the concentration camps: I did not make that idly. This man you are after, this German, Von Seeckt. If he is part of what I think he is part of, then you might be getting into something that you need to be very careful of."

"And that is?" Nabinger felt the minutes to his flight tick down.

"Ask him when you see him," Slater said. "If he evades answering, ask him specifically about Operation Paperclip."

"What was that?"

"Something I heard whispers about when I worked in Washington." Slater stepped back toward her house.

"Is there anything else I should know?" Nabinger asked, poised at her gate.

"I know you were humoring me," Slater said. "You knew nearly everything I told you, but you stopped by anyway. Why?"

"It was on the way," Nabinger answered honestly. "But also, I hoped you might have some new information, since you keep up with this area of research. Your information on Von Seeckt might prove helpful."

Slater was standing in the shadow cast by the peaked roof of the house. "They found something unusual at the Jamiltepec site in Mexico about eight months ago."

That *was* news to Nabinger. "What did Jorgenson find?"

"Jorgenson didn't find it," Slater said. "I have only heard rumors. Jorgenson was away lecturing. His people were deep under the main pyramid when they found a passageway leading down. They were getting ready to open it when they were shut down. The Mexican army came in claiming that it was an historical site, but anyone with enough cash could have had them do that."

"What happened?" Nabinger asked.

"From the whispers I've heard, it appears that Jorgenson's team had been infiltrated. Some say by the Mexican government, since it was their army that shut the dig down; others say it was the CIA. That's because there are rumors that Americans were seen working the site after Jorgenson's people had to clear out. He made a stink, but once the Mexican government pulled his authorization there was little he could do."

"Any idea what was down there?"

"Not a clue, my son. Not a clue. But you might want to ask Von Seeckt."

15

Turcotte drove, Kelly navigated, and Von Seeckt sat in the backseat, watching the countryside. They were in Kelly's rent-a-car heading southwest out of Las Vegas in the approximate direction of Dulce, New Mexico, via Phoenix.

Since there was only one road that went in that direction out of Las Vegas—Highway 93 to Kingman Arizona—Kelly's mind was not much preoccupied with the map on her lap. It was over eighty miles to Kingman with no turns in between. "You told me they found the mothership in its hangar, but you never said if they found the bouncers there too," she said, turning in the seat and glancing back at Von Seeckt.

"Ah, the bouncers," Von Seeckt said. "Yes, the mothership was the first find the Americans made. There were also two bouncers found near the mothership in the same chamber."

"And the other bouncers?" Kelly asked.

"They were not found there," Von Seeckt said. "They were recovered and transported to Area 51."

"Recovered from where?" Kelly asked.

"From another location." Von Seeckt's attention was on the desert flowing by.

Kelly met Turcotte's glance across the front seat, then returned to the backseat. "Another location? Where is that? Remember, you hired me, and my currency for payment is information."

Von Seeckt finally turned his attention inside the car. "I thought your payment was finding your friend."

"Johnny Simmons is not here in this car," Kelly said. "I hope and pray that we find Johnny at Dulce and can get him out safely. But *you* are here in this car and the more information we have, the better our chances are of getting Johnny out of there."

"The bouncers are back in Area 51," Von Seeckt countered. "Why are you concerned with their history?"

"You said we're going to Dulce to find tablets that related to them," Kelly argued.

Kelly was startled when Turcotte slammed a fist on the steering wheel. "Listen, Von Seeckt, I don't want to be here. I didn't want this damn assignment from the start. But I'm here and I'm helping you people. So you help back. Clear?"

"Your assignment?" Kelly asked, her reporter instincts still working. The two men ignored her question.

"I took an oath of secrecy," Von Seeckt said to Turcotte. "I am only violating that oath to prevent disaster."

"It's a little damn late for that now," Turcotte said. "And we're helping you. I took a few oaths of my own, and I violated one of those when I saved your life and the lives of that couple up in Nebraska. You've crossed a line and you can't go back. Understand that. We're in this now. All three of us. Whether you like it or not, and personally I can tell you I ain't too fucking thrilled, but I'm here and I accept what that means."

Von Seeckt pondered that for a few moments. "I know I crossed a line. I suppose much of what I feel is just habit. I have been so used to being quiet and not speaking. I have never talked to anyone outside of the program in all my life since being recruited in 1942. It is quite strange to speak openly about this.

"There are nine atmospheric bouncers. We know they are linked to the mothership because of their technology and the material they are constructed of and because there were two buried with the mothership—Bouncer One and Bouncer Two, as they are so elegantly called.

"We also know the others are related to the mothership because it is through material discovered in the mothership hangar that we were able to track down the other seven bouncers. When they found the mothership in 1942 they also not only found the first two bouncers, but several of the tablets we have already talked about. Although the people in the program could not decipher the symbols on the tablets, there were drawings and maps that could be understood."

"Wait a second," Kelly said. "You're telling me that the best minds the government could gather together couldn't decipher these high runes? We've got computers that can break codes in seconds."

"First," Von Seeckt said, "you must remember that it is extremely difficult to decipher a language or system of writing with so little material to look upon. That rules out effective use of computers—not enough data. Second, we did not necessarily have the 'best' minds, as you put it, working on this. We had those who could be recruited and pass a security check and also sign an oath of secrecy. In reality that left many of the best minds *out* of the field. And because of the secrecy of the program, those minds never got access to the data. Third, those who did work on the problem of deciphering the runes were limited by the conventions of their discipline. They did not understand that these runes found near the mothership could be related to runes elsewhere. Fourth, because of security requirements, the information they were working with was highly compartmentalized. They didn't have access to all the data that was available."

"Where else were these runes found?" Turcotte asked.

"I will go into that at another time," Von Seeckt said. "When Professor Nabinger is with us tomorrow."

Turcotte gripped the wheel tighter until the whites of his knuckles showed. Kelly noticed that and quickly tried to keep the flow of information going. "But even though they couldn't decipher the runes," Kelly said, "they were able to find other bouncers?"

"Yes," Von Seeckt replied. "As I said, there were drawings and maps. There seemed to be no doubt that much attention was being paid to Antarctica, although the specific location was not given. Just a general vicinity on the continent. We eventually broke it down to an eight-hundred-square-kilometer area.

"Unfortunately, the few expeditions that were mounted during the war years to Antarctica could not be fully equipped, due to other, more pressing requirements for the men and ships required for such an operation—such as defeating Germany and Japan.

"In 1946, as soon as the material and men were available, the United States government mounted what was called Operation High Jump. You can look the mission up. It was well documented. However, what no one seemed to wonder was why the government was so interested in Antarctica in 1946. And why did they dispatch dozens of ships and airplanes to the southernmost continent so quickly after the end of the war?

"It was a very extensive operation. The largest launched in the history of mankind up to that point. High Jump took so many pictures of Antarctica that they haven't all even been looked at yet, fifty years later! The expedition surveyed over sixty percent of the coastline and looked at over half a million square miles of land that had never before been seen by man.

"But the real success of High Jump occurred when they picked up signs of metal buried under the ice in that eight-hundred-square-mile box that special attention was paid to, which is what they were secretly after in the first place."

Von Seeckt leaned forward. "Do you know how thick the ice is down there? At some places it is three miles deep! The current altitude of the land underneath the ice is actually below sea level, but that is only because the weight of the ice on top depresses the continent. If the ice were removed, the land would rise up miles and miles! Even with all the expeditions—High Jump included—only about one percent of the surface area of Antarctica has been traversed by man.

"Antarctica contains ninety percent of the world's ice and snow and it is a most formidable foe, as those men who were operating secretly under the cover of Operation High Jump found out. A plane with skis landed at the site where their instruments had picked up the metal signal—which, despite the aid of the drawings on the tablets, was found only after five months of searching by thousands and thousands of men.

"But the weather down there is unpredictable and brutal at best. A storm moved in and the plane was destroyed, the crew frozen to death before they could be rescued. A second mission was mounted to the site. It was determined that the reflected signal was coming from over a mile and a half down in the ice. We did not have the technology at the time to do either of the two things required to explore further: to survive on the ice at that point long enough, and to drill down far enough.

"So, for nine years we bided our time and prepared. Besides, we had the two bouncers in Nevada to work on. We weren't sure what was down there in Antarctica, but from the symbols on the tablets it looked like there would be more bouncers, so the priority of the recovery effort was not as high as it might have been otherwise."

"You mean there were other sites and other symbols and other priority levels?" Kelly asked.

Von Seeckt looked at her. "Very astute, young lady, but let us stay with the subject at hand. In 1955 the Navy launched Operation Deep Freeze, under the leadership of Admiral Byrd, the foremost expert on Antarctica. The operation established five stations along the coast and three in the interior. At least that is what was announced to the press and recorded in the history books.

"A ninth, secret station was also established. One that has never been listed on any map. In 1956 I flew there in the beginning of what passes for summer in the Antarctic. Scorpion Station, as it was called, was over eight hundred miles in from the coast in the middle of"—Von Seeckt searched for the words, then shrugged—"in the middle of nowhere, actually. Just ice for miles and miles, which is why the spot was so hard to find in the first place. I was shown the location on the map, but what does it matter? The ice sheet was two and a half miles thick at that point.

"They had taken the entire summer of 1955 to simply move in the equipment they needed. They began drilling in 1956. It took four months to get down the mile and a half to the target. They finally punched through to a cavity in the ice, which was very fortunate. We had been afraid that perhaps the bouncers—if that was what was down there—had been covered over with ice and were frozen into the ice cap. If that had been the case we would have had no hope of recovery. But no, the drill bit broke through to open air. They sent down cameras and looked around. Yes, there were more bouncers in the cavity.

"Then they had to widen the shaft, make it big enough for a person to go down and look. It was amazing! There was a chamber hollowed out of the ice. Not quite as big as Hangar Two, but very big. There were the other seven bouncers. Lined up in a row. Perfectly preserved—everything left in Antarctica is perfectly preserved," Von Seeckt added. "Did you know that they found food at camps along the coast that had been left over a hundred years, and it was still edible?"

"Is that why those bouncers were left in that location?" Kelly asked. "So they would be so well preserved?"

"I do not believe so," Von Seeckt said. "The two left here in Nevada were functional. The desert air is very good at preserving things also, and they were out of the elements inside the cavern with the mothership."

"Then why Antarctica?" she asked.

"I do not know for sure."

"A guess, perhaps?" Turcotte threw in. "Surely you must have an idea or two?"

"I think they were left there because it is perhaps the most inaccessible place on Earth to leave something."

"So whoever left them didn't want them found?" Turcotte asked.

"It appears that way. Or at least they only wanted them found when the finders had adequate technology to brave the Antarctic conditions," Von Seeckt said.

"But they left the mothership and two bouncers back in Nevada," Kelly noted. "And that was more accessible than Antarctica."

"The terrain and climate in Nevada is more accessible to man," Von Seeckt agreed. "But the cavern the mothership was hidden in wasn't. We were very fortunate to stumble across it, and it required an effort to blast into the site. No, I believe the ships were hidden with the intention they not be found."

"Why seven in Antarctica and two in Nevada?" Kelly wondered out loud.

"I don't know," Von Seeckt said. "We would have to ask whoever left them."

"Go on with what happened in Antarctica," Turcotte prodded.

"It took us three years to bring the bouncers up. First the engineers had to widen the shaft to forty feet circumference—and remember, they could only work six months out of the year. Then they had to dig out eight intermediate stopping points on the way up, in order to bring them up in stages. Then, it was necessary to tractor the bouncers to the coast and load them onto a Navy ship for transport back to the States. All in all it was a fantastic engineering job.

"Then we began the real work back at Area 51 trying to figure out how they flew. We had been working on the first two, but with nine, we could afford to disassemble a few. After all these years we can fly them, but we still don't know how the engines work. And even though they can be flown, I do not believe we are able to use them to anywhere near the limits of their capabilities. There is still equipment on board the craft that we don't know how to operate and in fact whose purpose we're ignorant of." Von Seeckt then told Kelly the story about the engineering mishap on the bouncer engine. She found all this fascinating. If it wasn't for Johnny she'd be on the wire right now, breaking the story. But she knew this is what Johnny would do for her if she had disppeared.

"What else did the tablets show?" Turcotte asked.

"Some other locations. Other symbols. It was all very incomplete," Von Seeckt said.

"For instance?" Kelly said.

"I do not remember it all. The work was compartmentalized very early on. I was not allowed complete access to the tablets, which were moved down to the facility at Dulce early on in the project. Nor was I allowed to see the results of the research at Dulce. The last time I was in Dulce was 1946. I do not remember it very well. I do not believe they have had much success with the tablets, otherwise we would have seen the results at Area 51."

Kelly thought that was odd. Her reporter's instincts were tingling. Had they cut Von Seeckt out of the inner circle years ago? Or was Von Seeckt holding something back?

"That is why we need to link up with this Nabinger fellow," Von Seeckt continued. "If he can decipher the high runes, then the mystery may be solved not only of how the equipment works, but also of who left the equipment and why."

Kelly caught herself before the words came out of her mouth. This was not what Von Seeckt had said back in the hotel room. Just a few hours ago he was focused on stopping the mothership. Damn Johnny. She was stuck in this car with these two because of him. Kelly slumped down in the passenger seat and the miles passed in silence.

16

With only fifteen minutes before his flight was scheduled to depart, Peter Nabinger debated whether he should check his answering machine, but impatience won out. He punched in his long-distance code and then his number. Two rings and the machine kicked in. After the greeting he hit his access code, then the message retrieval.

"Professor Nabinger, this is Werner Von Seeckt returning your call. Your message was most interesting. I do know of the power of the sun, but I need to know about the rest of the message. Both what you have and what I have. I am going to a place where there are more runes. Join me. Phoenix. Twenty-seven sixty-five Twenty-fourth street. Apartment B-twelve. The twelfth. In the morning."

The message ended. Nabinger stared at the handset for a few moments, then headed toward the gate with a bounce in his step.

LAS VEGAS, NEVADA

Lisa Duncan was in her hotel room in Las Vegas. Gullick's reasoning about the accommodation was that there were no suitable quarters available at Area 51 for her. She thought that was a bunch of bullshit, just like a lot of what she had seen and heard so far about Majestic-12, more commonly known as Majic-12.

Lisa Duncan had everything that was available in the official files about Majestic-12, and it was a pretty slim reading file. Majestic-12 had been started in 1942 when President Roosevelt signed a classified presidential order initiating the project. At first, no one had quite understood the strange facts that were being uncovered with the transfer by the British in the fall of 1942 of a German physicist, Werner Von Seeckt, and a piece of sophisticated machinery in a black box.

The British had not known what exactly was in the box, since they couldn't open it, except that it was radioactive. Since, in those days of the Manhattan Project, nuclear matters were the province of the United States, Von Seeckt and the box were sent over the ocean.

At first, it had been thought that the box was of German development. But Von Seeckt was clearly ignorant, and the contents of the box, once it was opened, raised a whole new set of questions. If it had been German, then most certainly they would already have won the war. There were symbols on the inside of the box—which they now knew belonged to a language called high rune—that the early Majestic-12 scientists puzzled over. One thing was clear, though: there was a map outline of North America on which a location had been marked—somewhere in southern Nevada, they determined.

An expedition armed with detecting equipment was sent out, and after several months of searching they discovered the mothership cavern. The men of Majestic-12 had quickly identified the black metal of the box container with the metal used in the struts of the mothership. They now had more information, but were no closer to figuring out who had left the equipment, or why the box had been placed in the pyramid and the ships left out here in the desert. The other bouncers had been discovered in Antarctica from maps found in Hangar Two. And they had been able to piece together that the Germans had most likely been led to the hidden chamber under the Great Pyramid by maps they had discovered elsewhere.

The MJ-12 program had remained the most highly classified project in the United States for the past fifty-five years, at first because of the atomic information. Then, after the Soviets had finally detonated their own bomb—using information stolen from the United States—the existence of the mothership and the bouncers was kept secret for several reasons.

Duncan turned the page in the briefing book and looked at the official reasons. One was the uncertainty of the public's reaction should the information be released—a topic Dr. Slayden was supposed to cover in his briefing.

A second reason was that once flying the bouncers had been mastered, in the mid-fifties, the craft were incorporated into the Strategic Air Command on an emergency-use-only basis. All of the bouncers were fitted with external racks for nuclear payloads to be used in case of national emergency. It was felt that because of their speed, maneuverability, and nonexistent radar signature, the bouncers would be a last-ditch method to get to the heartland of the Soviet Union to deliver a fatal blow in case of all-out war.

Another reason, spawned by the Cold War, was simply security. The Russians had been able to develop their own atomic weapons off of plans stolen from the U.S. It was feared that, even though the American scientists couldn't figure out the propulsion system of the bouncers or even, for so many years, how to get into the mothership, the Russians might do a better job. That fear was especially heightened after the Russians lobbed Sputnik up into space, beating the United States to the punch.

One thing the report didn't mention, though, Duncan knew, was the existence of Operation Paperclip and its effect on the MJ-12 project. Paperclip was officially launched in 1944 as the war in Europe was winding down, but Duncan felt that Paperclip really began the day Von Seeckt was shipped over from England to the United States.

Paperclip—a rather innocuous name for a very deceitful operation. As the war in Europe was ending, the United States government was already looking ahead. There was a treasure trove of German scientists waiting to be plundered in the ashes of the Third Reich. That most of those scientists were Nazis mattered little to those who had invented Paperclip.

When Duncan had first read of Paperclip, she'd been shocked by the blatant incongruity of the situation. The end justifies the means was the motto of those who recruited and illegally allowed the scientists into the United States. Yet at the same time, colleagues of those same scientists were being tried for war crimes where the defense of the end justifying the means had been ruled immoral. In many cases intelligence officers from the JIOA, Joint Intelligence Objectives Agency, were snatching Nazi scientists away from army war-crimes units. Both groups were hunting the same men but with very different goals in mind.

Despite the fact that President Truman had signed an executive order banning the immigration of Nazis into the United States, the practice continued unabated, all in the name of national security.

Majestic-12 had started with Werner Von Seeckt—an undisputed Nazi—and it had continued over the years, using whatever means were required. Several of the scientists used in the early work on the bouncers and mothership were Nazis, recruited by Paperclip. While the names of some of the former Germans working on the NASA space project were highly publicized, the vast majority of the work covered by Paperclip went on unobserved. When news of the project became public, the government claimed that Paperclip had been discontinued in 1947. Yet Duncan had affidavits from an interested senator's office that the project had continued for decades beyond that date.

One of the things that disturbed Duncan the most about the present state of affairs was not so much the work being done at Area 51 with the mothership and the bouncers. What bothered her was what General Gullick was hiding. She was convinced he was holding something back. And she had a strong feeling it had something to do with other aspects of the MJ-12 program that they weren't showing her.

The senator who had provided Duncan with information on Paperclip was under pressure from several Jewish groups to disclose the history of the project, with the possibility in mind of prosecuting some of those involved. Duncan was concerned about the past, but she was more worried about the future.

While the German physicists had gone to MJ-12 and the German rocket scientists had gone to NASA, the largest group of Nazi scientists involved in Paperclip had yet to be uncovered: the biological and chemical warfare specialists. As advanced as German rocketry had been at the end of the war with the V-2 and jet aircraft, their advancements in the field of biological and chemical warfare had been chilling.

With plenty of human beings to experiment on, the Germans had gone far beyond what the Allies had even begun to fear. While the Americans were still stockpiling mustard gas as their primary chemical weapon, the Germans had three much more efficient and deadly gases by war's end:

tabun, soman, and sarin—the latter of which the American military immediately appropriated for its own use after the war.

Where were all these biological and chemical scientists whom Paperclip had saved from prosecution? Duncan wondered. What had *they* been working on all these years?

She put the briefing book down in aggravation. There were too many questions and everything was going too rapidly. Not only was this whole Paperclip issue a problem, but she also wondered about the Mothership test itself. Was Gullick moving ahead quickly with the flight for reasons that weren't apparent, and in doing so was he overlooking problems with the mothership and its propulsion system? She most definitely remembered the feeling of nausea she'd had in the hangar during the test.

She'd been sent here by the President's advisers to check on the situation and look into the potential problems that revealing the existence of the MJ-12 project might create. After all, the President had been in office three years already and his administration by default would be implicated in any cover-up.

She flipped open the lid on her laptop and went to work, typing out her findings so far.

CLASSIFICATION: TOP SECRET, Q
CLEARANCE, ADDRESSEE ONLY
TO: Chief of Staff, White House
FROM: Dr. Lisa Duncan, Presidential Observer
Majestic-12
SUBJECT: AREA 51 Inquiry.

I have studied the official inbriefing, toured the facilities at Area 51, and attended one meeting of Majic-12. Based on these initial inputs my impressions are:
1. The technology that is present at Area 51—particu-

larly the mothership—is beyond what you can imagine from reading the papers and viewing the video briefing.

2. Security at the facility is excessive in light of the present world situation.

3. The President's concerns about the psychological and sociological effects of revealing the project are to be addressed at a meeting tomorrow morning.

4. As for the upcoming test flight of the mothership, I request that the President withhold authorization pending further investigation. There is some dissension on the Majic-12 staff about the testing, and while it may turn out to be nothing, I believe more time is needed.

5. As expected, General Gullick and the other staff members are very evasive about the early days of the program and any links to Operation Paperclip. The one who would know the most is Werner Von Seeckt, but I have not been able to meet him since my initial inbriefing. He has not returned my calls. I will try to corner him tomorrow after the psychological briefing.

6. I have not received any communication from Captain Turcotte. I assume he has not found anything to report of significance.

END
CLASSIFICATION: TOP SECRET, Q
CLEARANCE, ADDRESSEE ONLY

She attached a cable from her laptop into a breadloaf-sized black box that she'd been given by a Secret Service man when she'd been inbriefed for her new job in Washington. All she knew was that the box was supposed to encrypt her message so that only the addressee could read it. She plugged the cord coming out of the box into her phone socket and waited until a green light glowed on the side—apparently it did its own dialing.

Duncan waited until the green light went out, then she unplugged all the machinery. She walked to the window of her hotel room and looked out, watching the people scurrying about, going into and out of casinos. How would they react if what was hidden in the desert beyond the buildings were revealed to them? If they learned that, at least once upon a time, mankind had not been alone in the universe? If it was shown that while their ancestors were still living in caves and struggling to make arrowheads, aliens were visiting the Earth in craft we still couldn't understand?

Those were the large, theoretical questions. Of more immediate concern to Duncan was to follow through on the instruction she'd received from the White House chief of staff. The President was concerned about what he had not been getting briefed on in the twice-yearly status reports from Majic-12. Because the organization had been around so long and had members from almost every major government agency of significance, he didn't trust using normal channels to check it out; thus Duncan's assignment. She'd had Turcotte assigned to her based on the recommendation of the President's national security adviser. Apparently Turcotte was some kind of hero for actions on a classified mission overseas. She'd briefed him personally, but he had not yet called with anything.

Duncan rubbed her forehead, walked over to the bed, and lay down. She sincerely hoped the people out at Area 51 would give her some good answers tomorrow and that they'd be of a higher quality than the ones she'd been given so far.

THE CUBE, AREA 51

Major Quinn noted the alert signal blinking in the upper right-hand corner of his computer screen. He finished the order he was working on and transmitted it, then accessed the signal that had caused the alert.

Since the Cube had access to every piece of top-of-the-line equipment the government possessed—and access to all codes and encryption techniques—Dr. Duncan's message to the White House chief of staff had taken less than six seconds for the Cube computer to decrypt. Quinn read the text. He connected the name "Turcotte" to the man injured on the Nightscape mission into Nebraska. Another complication he didn't understand. This was Gullick's territory.

He printed out a hard copy and walked to the rear corridor, taking the message with him. Gullick wasn't in his office. The code above the handle to Gullick's private quarters read DO NOT DISTURB. Quinn stood for a few seconds in thought, hand poised to knock. Then he turned and went back to Gullick's office. He clipped a top-secret cover on the message and placed it in General Gullick's reading file.

17

"I've told you my reasons for being here and helping you. How about telling me your reasons?" Kelly asked.

They were holed up in Johnny Simmons's apartment. Turcotte was less than thrilled about being there, given that it looked as if Simmons had been picked up by Gullick's people. But Kelly had argued that no one knew about their connection with Johnny, so there was no reason for someone to come looking for them here in Phoenix. Besides, they needed to stay somewhere en route to Dulce, and a motel was out of the question. The apartment was on the second floor of a modern complex, and it did not appear that anyone had been inside for several days.

Turcotte had expressed misgivings about stopping at all. He wanted to push on to Dulce and try to infiltrate it this evening. But Von Seeckt had told them of the planned rendezvous with Professor Nabinger the next morning at this location, and Kelly had agreed that they ought to wait. Turcotte had reluctantly accepted their decision.

Turcotte was slowly accepting that they all needed each other: Von Seeckt held the knowledge to get them out of their predicament; Kelly was to be the voice to the public that would ensure their safety once they acquired the information they were after; and he held the expertise to keep them safe and acquire more information.

"My story will have to wait until tomorrow," Von Seeckt said. He was seated near the window, looking down two stories at the parking lot. "Professor Nabinger will have the same questions, and I do not wish to tell it twice. It is difficult to tell and covers many years."

Kelly looked over at Turcotte. "Well?"

"I've already told you what happened. I just arrived in time for the Nightscape mission."

"Yeah, but you didn't come out of a hole in the ground prior to that," Kelly said. "How did you get sucked into working at that place? You said something earlier today about an assignment."

"I was in the army, and they cut orders assigning me there." Turcotte stood up. "I'm going out to the store. Anyone want anything?"

Without waiting for an answer he walked out and headed for the stairs. Kelly was two steps behind him. "You're not getting away that easy. There's something you aren't telling. Why'd you help Von Seeckt? You were one of the bad guys. Why'd you change sides?"

Turcotte went down the stairs, Kelly at his side. "I told you. My commander wanted me to apprehend some civilians in Nebraska. I didn't like that. Also, they tried to kill Von Seeckt. I don't approve of kidnapping or murder, even if the government is the one sanctioning it."

"Yeah and pigs have wings," Kelly said. "I don't buy it. You—"

Turcotte whirled and faced her, the action so swift that Kelly stepped back, startled. "I don't give a damn what you buy or don't buy, lady," he said. "You ask too many questions. You let Von Seeckt have his secrets. How about letting me have mine?"

"Von Seeckt is going to tell us his when Nabinger gets

here," Kelly countered, stepping in closer to Turcotte. "Come on. You didn't just abitrarily decide to go against your orders and your training. You must have had a reason. And I do have a reason for asking. I've been set up before by the government and I'm not going to naturally assume that you're telling me the truth. We only have your word about what took place in Nebraska. For all I know it never happened."

Turcotte looked off past her toward the western horizon, where the sun was balanced on the edge of the planet. "All right. You want to know about me? I got nothing to lose anymore and maybe if we survive this mess, you can print it somewhere and people can know the truth.

"I was involved in an incident at my last assignment before coming back to the States," Turcotte said. "That's what they called it: an incident. But people died in this incident."

He shifted his eyes back to her and the look was not kind. "You're a reporter. You'll like it. It's a good story. I was assigned to a CT—counterterrorist—unit in Berlin when it happened. Everyone thinks it's all great over there since the wall went down, but they still have a terrorist problem. Same as it was in the seventies and early eighties. In some ways worse because there's bigger and better weapons available to the bad guys from all the old Warsaw Pact stockpiles, and there're a lot of people in those countries who'd sell anything to get their hands on Western currency.

"The only difference between now and back in the eighties is that we learned our lessons from those old days and now we preempt terrorism. And that's why you don't hear about it so much anymore—not because the assholes have gone away. People are so naive."

"Preempt?" Kelly asked.

Turcotte gave a short, nasty laugh. "Yeah. When we were

getting held hostage by every two-bit terrorist or wacko with a bomb, someone high up in the workings of NATO got the bright idea that instead of sitting around and letting the terrorists hit us, we'd seek them out and hit them first. The only problem was that it wasn't quite legal." He looked down the street and spotted a café. "Let's get some coffee."

They walked over and took a corner booth. Turcotte sat with his back to the wall, watching the street outside. There was a constant clatter of dishes and utensils overlaid with the murmur of conversation from the other patrons. After the waitress had brought them a cup each, he continued, speaking in a low voice.

"So, anyway, we fought fire with fire. To stop the lawbreakers we broke the law. I was on a joint U.S.-German team. Handpicked men from the U.S. Special Forces DET-A out of Berlin and the Germans' GSG-9 counterterrorist force." Turcotte poured a load of sugar into his coffee and stirred. "Ever hear that slogan: We kill for peace?" Kelly nodded. "Well, that's what we did.

"I didn't mind doing it either. We were wasting people who'd put a bomb in a train station and didn't care who got caught in the blast. We pretty much broke the back of the remnants of the Baader-Meinhof gang in less than six months. I was in on six operations." Turcotte's voice was flat. "I killed four people on those ops.

"Then we got word that some IRA fellows were in town, trying to buy surplus East German armament that some former members of the army had stashed away for a rainy day when the wall came down. The word was these Irish guys were trying to get some SAM-7 shoulder-fired antiaircraft missiles.

"We don't know what they were going to do with them, although the best guess was they'd sit outside Heathrow and take out a Concorde just after takeoff. That would make the news, which is all those scumbags want. I know they signed a peace accord and ceasefire and all that happy shit, but that don't stop the guys who pull the trigger. They have to be on the edge. A lot of those people do what they do because they like it. They couldn't give a shit about the so-called goals they shout at the cameras. It's just an excuse to be a sociopath."

He paused when the waitress came by to take their order. Kelly ordered a bagel, Turcotte a glass of orange juice.

"Anyway, everything about the mission was rushed because the intel was late. The IRA had already purchased the missiles and had them loaded in a car and were heading for France when we were alerted. We were airlifted ahead of them and picked up some cars. The terrorists were taking back roads—staying away from the autobahn—which played right into our hands."

The angry undercurrent in Turcotte's voice grew. "We should have just stopped them and taken them into custody. But we couldn't do that, you see. Because that would have caused too much controversy—the trial and all. And it just compounds the problem to put them in jail, 'cause that gives every blood relative they have a reason to grab some hostages and demand their release. And the whole cycle starts again. So instead we were supposed to kill them. Make it look like we were terrorists ourselves, and that way no one looks bad except the local cops.

"So." Turcotte took a deep breath to steady his voice. "We were all set to hit them outside a small town in central Germany. They were heading up to Kiel to load the weapons on a freighter for transshipment to England. But the IRA guys—they were Irish after all—they had to stop in a *Gasthaus* for a few brews and lunch before making it to their rendezvous at the port.

"I was the team XO—executive officer. The commander was a German. We set up on the north side of the town—

the way they would have to leave. We had a good spot on a curve in the road.

"When the car didn't show after an hour, my CO—let's call him Rolf—got spooked. Surveillance told us they'd stopped in town. But maybe they'd left by another way. Rolf asked me what I thought. How the fuck was I to know?

"So Rolf and I went into the village and spotted the car outside a bar. We'd been told there were three of them. So old Rolf he decides, hey, fuck it, let's take them out right now and right here. You and me. He was still worried that they might have spotted the surveillance team that had been following them and that they might take a different route out of town to lose the tail and bypass the ambush our team had set up. Or that they might even be doing a dead drop with the missiles in the town and we might lose track of the ordnance.

"So I said, hey, yeah, sounds good to me. We had MP-5 silenced subs slung inside our long coats and pistols in our shoulder holsters. Rolf ordered surveillance to close up tight around the bar to make sure no one escaped and to pick us up when we were done."

The waitress brought the bagel and orange juice. Turcotte took a deep breath, then slowly exhaled as she walked away.

"We walked right in the front fucking door. The place is packed, people eating dinner and drinking. Must have been twenty, twenty-five people in there. But we spot our suspects right away and guess what? There's only *two* of these bozos seated in a booth, drinking. So Rolf looked at me like, hey where's number three? So again, like how the fuck do I know? Probably taking a piss. I started to the bar to order a brew, scanning the room as I went, but Rolf hesitated.

"I can't blame him too much. Shit, we had silenced sub-

machine guns under our coats and we were there to kill."
Turcotte gave Kelly a twisted grin. "Contrary to popular
fiction and what they show on the movies, we weren't stone
cold killers. We were good at our job, but we were also
scared. Most people are in that situation. If you aren't,
you're crazy—and I have met some of those crazies. Anyway, one of the IRA guys in the booth he looks at Rolf
standing there with his thumb up his ass and you could just
tell that the Irish guy *knew* who we were. Rolf wasn't exactly the greatest actor in the world, and I'm sure I wasn't
giving off the best vibes either.

"So the guy reached under his coat, and Rolf and I
hosed the two of them down lickety-split. We each fired
half a magazine—fifteen rounds each—and there was
nothing left in that booth but chewed-up meat. And the
most amazing thing was that after the first shot there
wasn't a single sound other than the sound of our brass
falling to the floor. Everyone in the place just fucking froze
and looked at us, wondering who was next. Then someone
had to scream, and everything went to hell."

Turcotte's eyes had taken on a distant look as he went
back into that room. "The smart ones just hit the deck.
That's what Rolf and I yelled at them in German to do
after the scream. But about half the people rushed for the
doors, and that's when we spotted the third guy. He was in
the middle of a group of four people, running for it. He
might have been taking a leak. He might have been around
the corner at the bar. I don't know. But there he was."

Turcotte shook his head. "And Rolf—fucking Rolf—he
just fired them all up. I don't know what short-circuited in
his head. Hell, the third guy couldn't have gone anywhere.
Surveillance had to have been sitting on top of his car outside by now and could have taken him out once they got an
open shot outside the *Gasthaus*. But Rolf just lost it."
Turcotte's voice briefly broke.

"The only good thing was he just had fifteen rounds in the mag. He got the IRA guy, but he also hit some civilians. I didn't know how many at the time. There was just this pile of bodies; at the very least the three that had been around the IRA man, plus some others who'd been in the line of fire. Rolf was even flipping his taped-together magazines, putting a fresh one in when I grabbed the gun out of his hand." Turcotte pulled out his right hand and put it in front of Kelly's face. The skin on his palm was knotted with scar tissue. "You can still see where the suppressor on the barrel of Rolf's sub burned my hand. At the time I didn't feel a thing, I was so freaked.

"So I took his weapon and grabbed him by the collar and made for the door. One thing for sure—people really got the hell out of our way now. Surveillance had a car waiting for us and I threw Rolf in and we split."

Turcotte took a drink of coffee. "I found out later that night that Rolf had killed four civilians, including a pregnant eighteen-year-old girl, and wounded three. The news was playing it up like an internal IRA hit and the whole country was in an uproar to catch the killers. But they couldn't catch the killers, could they? Because the country was the killers.

"For a while I even thought they might give Rolf and me up as sacrificial lambs, but then common sense kicked in. I was stupid for even thinking that. If they gave us up, the whole counterterrorist operation would be out in the open and those in power certainly didn't want that. Might lose a few votes at the polling booth. So you know what they did?" Turcotte looked at Kelly with red-rimmed eyes.

Kelly slowly shook her head.

"They held an inquest, of course. That's proper form in the military. As a matter of fact the head man I met down in the Cube, General Gullick, he was one of those appointed to look into the whole thing. For security reasons we never saw those who questioned us, nor did we know their names. They talked to us and then talked to each other, and guess what they decided? They gave us fucking medals. Yeah, Rolf and me. Ain't that great? A medal for killing a pregnant woman."

"You didn't kill her," Kelly quietly remarked.

"Does it matter? I was part of it. I could have told Rolf to wait. I could have done a lot of things."

"He was the commander. It was his responsibility," Kelly argued, remembering what her father had told her about the army and covert operations.

"Yeah. I know. I was just following orders, right?"

Kelly had no answer for that.

"So that's how my career in the regular army and Special Forces ended. I went to my American commander and told him where he could shove his medal, and they had me on the next thing smoking back to the States. But I had to stop in D.C. first. To meet someone." He proceeded to tell her about meeting Dr. Duncan, her orders to him, and the phone line out of commission.

"Why were you chosen?"

"Right person, right time," Turcotte said with a shrug. "There aren't that many high-speed dudes like me who have top-level clearances and can fire a gun."

Kelly shook her head. "You were chosen because you told them to shove the medal. It showed somebody, someplace, that you had integrity. That's even rarer than a top-level security clearance." Kelly reached across the table and squeezed his hand, feeling the rough flesh in the palm. "You got screwed, Turcotte."

"No." Turcotte shook his head. "I screwed myself the minute I started playing God with a gun. I thought I was in control, but I was just a pawn, and they used me up like one. And now you know why I turned on my commander out there in Nebraska and killed him and why I rescued

Von Seeckt and I don't give a shit whether you believe me or not. Because it's between me and all these high-speed assholes who pull strings and cause people to die. Fuck me once, shame on me—fuck me twice, I fuck back."

18

"Give me a status," Gullick ordered.

"Bouncer Three is ready for flight," Quinn reported. "Bouncer Eight is also prepped and ready. Aurora is on standby status. Our link to Cheyenne Mountain is live and secure. Anything moves, we'll be able to track it, sir."

"General Brown?" Gullick asked.

The Air Force deputy chief of staff frowned. His conversation with his boss in Washington had been anything but fun. "I talked to the chief of staff and he okayed the alerts, but he was not happy about it."

"I don't care if he was happy or not," Gullick said. "I just care that the mission is a go."

Brown looked down at his own computer screen. "We've got every base alerted and planes on standby for pursuit. The primary and alternate kill zones are a go."

"Admiral Coakley?"

"The carrier *Abraham Lincoln* is steaming toward the sight where the foo fighter went down. It's got planes on alert."

"We're all set, then," Gullick said. "Let's roll."

*　　*　　*

The hangar doors slowly slid open. Inside Bouncer Three, Major Paul Terrent checked the control panel, which was a mixture of the original fixtures and added-on human technology, including a satellite communications link with General Gullick in the Cube.

"All set," he announced.

"I don't like being the bait," his copilot, Captain Kevin Scheuler, remarked. They were both reclined in depressions in the floor of the disk. The cockpit was an oval, twelve feet in diameter. They could see out in all directions, the inner walls displaying what was outside of them as if the walls themselves were not there—another piece of technology they could use but still didn't understand.

The effect, while useful, was extremely disorienting, and perhaps the second greatest hurdle Bouncer test pilots had to overcome. Most particularly, the view straight down when the craft was at altitude, as if the pilot were floating in the air, was quite a shock to the system until one got used to it. For this night's mission both men were wearing night vision goggles on their flight helmets and the interior of the hangar was lit in red lights, meaning there was little difference in illumination for them between there and the outside night sky.

However, the greatest hurdle to flying the machine was the physical limitations of the pilots. The Bouncer was capable of maneuvers that the pilot's physiology could not handle. In the early days of the program there had been blackouts, broken bones, and various other injuries, including one fatal crash—the disk staying intact, the unconscious pilots inside being turned into crushed protoplasm on impact with the earth. The disk had been recovered, cleaned out, and was still capable of flight. The two pilots had been buried with honors; their widows told they had died flying an experimental aircraft and given their posthumous medals at the funeral.

There was machinery surrounding the depressions that the scientists had yet to figure out. The project's scientists believed that there was a built-in way for the pilot depressions/seats to be shielded from the effect of G-forces, but they had yet to discover it. It was as if a child who was capable of riding a tricycle were allowed into a car. He might understand what the steering wheel did, but he wouldn't understand what the small opening on the steering wheel column was for, especially if the child had not been given the keys.

The best that they had been able to come up with was allowing the test pilots enough flight time so that they understood their own limitations and did not push the machine past what they could handle. Beyond that, the shoulder and waist harnesses bolted around the depressions would have to do.

"There's nothing that can catch us," Major Terrent said.

"Nothing human," Scheuler noted. "But if this foo fighter thing was made by the same people who made this, or people like the people who made this, then—"

"Then nothing," Terrent cut in. "This ship is at least ten thousand years old. The eggheads know *that*, at least. Whoever left it behind has been long gone. And they probably weren't people."

"Then why are we flying this mission, trying to bait this foo fighter? Who made *it*?" Scheuler asked.

"Because General Gullick ordered it," Terrent said. He looked at Scheuler. "You have any further questions, I suggest you talk to him."

Scheuler shook his head. "No, thanks."

Terrent pressed a small red button added on top of the Y-shaped yoke in front of him, keying the SATCOM radio. "Cube Six, this is Bouncer Three. All systems ready. Over."

Gullick's deep voice answered. "This is Cube Six. Go. Out."

The airstrip outside was dark. Terrent pulled up on a lever to his side with his left hand and the disk lifted. The control system was simplicity itself. Pull up on the lever and the disk went up. Let go of it and the lever returned to center and the disk stayed at that altitude. Push down on it and the disk descended.

Terrent pushed the yoke forward with his right hand and they moved forward. The yoke worked in the same manner as the altitude lever. Letting go brought the disk to a halt. Constant pressure equaled constant speed in whichever direction the yoke was pushed.

Scheuler was looking at the navigation display—a human device tied in to a satellite positioning system. A computer display with a black rectangular outline to separate it from the surrounding view showed their present position as a small red glowing dot with state borders shown in light green lines. It was the easiest way to orient the pilots as to their location.

"Let's roll," Terrent said. He pressed forward and they were out of the hangar.

Behind them, still in the hangar, Bouncer Eight rose to a hover and waited. On the airstrip Aurora stood at the end, engines on, prepared for flight. On airstrips across the United States and down into Panama, and on board the *Abraham Lincoln* at sea, pilots sat in their cockpits and waited—for what, they had not been told. But they knew whatever it was, this was no game. The planes' wings had live missiles slung underneath and the Gatling guns were loaded with bullets.

"All clear," Quinn said, a rather unnecessary statement since everyone in the room could see the small red dot indicating Bouncer Three moving northwest out of the state. The computer had already screened out all commercial aircraft flights.

"Contact!" Quinn announced. A small green dot had suddenly appeared on the screen, well behind Bouncer Three. "Same reading as the first one!"

"Three, this is Six," Gullick spoke into his headset. "Head for Checkpoint Alpha. Over."

On board Bouncer Three, Major Terrent slowly pressed the yoke to the right and the disk began a long curve over southern Idaho, turning toward the Great Salt Lake. What was different about the turn from one made by an ordinary aircraft was the fact that there was no banking. The disk simply changed directions, staying flat and level. The bodies of the two men inside strained against their restraining harnesses during the turn, then settled back in the depressions.

"Give me a reading," Terrent said.

"The bogey's about three hundred miles behind us," Captain Scheuler responded. He was watching the same information on his small screen that the people in the Cube had displayed on their large one.

"Is it turning with us?" Terrent asked.

"Not yet."

"Get Aurora in the air," Gullick ordered. "Alert Kill Zone Alpha reaction forces and get them up too. Have you fed coordinates of the bogey to Teal Amber?"

Quinn was working quickly. "Yes, sir."

At Hill Air Force Base, just outside Salt Lake City, two F-16 Fighting Falcons roared down the runway and up into the night sky. As soon as they had reached sufficient altitude, they turned west, over the flat surface of the lake, heading for the desolate land on the far side.

* * *

"That's the lake," Terrent said. He pressed the yoke to the right a bit more.

"On course," Scheuler said, checking their projected direction.

"Is the bogey turning yet?"

"Yes," Scheuler said. "It's taken the bait. Right on our trail, about one hundred and fifty miles behind."

Terrent keyed his mike. "Six, this is Three. Kill Zone Alpha in one minute, forty-seven seconds. Over."

"Roger," Gullick answered. There were several more dots on the screen now. The red one indicated Bouncer Three heading directly toward a small orange rectangle—Kill Zone Alpha—a point directly over the center of the Hill Air Force Base Range. On the ground out there a helicopter and recovery crew from Nightscape waited. The green dot was the bogey, following Bouncer Three. Two red plane silhouettes showed the F-16's on an intercept course. A red triangle represented Aurora, en route directly from Area 51.

"Intercept in forty-five seconds," Quinn announced.

Bouncer Three went through the orange rectangle.

"What the fuck was that?" the pilot of the lead F-16 called out as Bouncer Three flashed by.

"Wolfhound One, this is Six. Stay on target!" General Gullick's voice in the pilot's helmet was a cold slap in the face. "Have you got a lock on the target?"

The pilot checked his instruments. "Roger, Six."

"Arm your missiles."

The pilot armed the air-to-air missiles under his wings. Still shaken by the image of Bouncer Three, he also armed his 20mm multibarrel cannon. His wingman did the same.

"This son of a bitch is moving fast," the wingman said over the secure link between the two planes.

"Not fast enough," the pilot said.

General Gullick was concerned about the same thing in the Cube. "What's the speed of the bogey?"

"Computer estimates twelve hundred miles an hour," Quinn replied. "It's pacing Bouncer Three." Which was the reason the disk was flying so slowly, trying to draw the bogey in to the kill zone at a slow enough speed to be hit by the conventional jets. Gullick was intimately familiar with the weapon systems on board the F-16's—he was checked out on the aircraft. They could handle that speed.

"Six, this is Wolfhound One. Target will be in range in ten seconds. Request final authorization. Over."

"This is Six. Fire as soon as target is in range. Over."

The pilot took a deep breath.

"Is this guy for real?" his wingman asked.

"No time for questions," the pilot snapped. The heads-up display indicated the target was in range. "Fire!" he yelled.

A Sidewinder missile leapt out from underneath the wings of both planes.

Even though they conceptually knew what the bouncers were capable of—and therefore could conceptualize what the foo fighters might be able to do—there was complete shock as the bogey simply left the orange square behind and was over fifty miles away by the time the Sidewinders had crossed the two miles from where the F-16's were to where the bogey had been.

"What the fuck was that?" the F-16 pilot said for the second time in less than two minutes. His heads-up display was clear. The Sidewinder he'd fired was an arc disappearing over the base range, running out of fuel and descending. Whatever he'd fired at was gone.

*   *   *

Gullick reacted first. "Get Aurora after it. Launch Bouncer Eight." He keyed his radio. "Bouncer Three, this is Six. Head for Kill Zone Bravo. Over."

"This is Three. Roger."

Gullick switched frequencies. "Wolfhound One, this is Six. Return to base for debriefing. Out."

As the two F-16's turned back toward Salt Lake City and Hill Air Force Base, the pilot of the lead aircraft looked across the night sky to his wingman.

"We're in for a long night," he said on their secure channel. "I don't know what it was we just saw—or didn't see—but one thing for sure, the security dinks are going to be all over us on the ground."

Major Terrent lined up Bouncer Three on an azimuth that would take them directly over the four corners—where Colorado, Utah, Arizona, and New Mexico met—the only place in the United States contiguous to four states.

Kill Zone Bravo was several hundred miles beyond that in the same direction. White Sands Missile Range.

"Where's the bogey?" Terrent asked.

"Holding, about fifty miles behind us," Scheuler reported.

"Let's hope they're better prepared at Bravo," Terrent said.

General Gullick was directing the situation to insure just that. He had Aurora and Bouncer Eight heading directly toward the kill zone. They would beat Three there by four minutes.

Four F-15's from the 49th Tactical Fighter Wing at Holloman Air Force Base were already in the air. He didn't expect them to have any more luck than the two F-16's had—except now he had the ace card of having Bouncer Eight in the air. Gullick planned on using both it and Bouncer Three to corral the bogey into a position where the F-15's could get a good shot at it. Aurora was to be on standby to chase, just in case it did get away again and moved outside the continental United States. It was a rule that even General Gullick could not break on his own initiative—the bouncers could not fly over the ocean or foreign territory on the remote chance they might go down.

The wall display was crowded now. Bouncer Three straight shot from Salt Lake to White Sands, the bogey just behind. Bouncer Eight and Aurora on line from Nevada. Four small airplane silhouettes lying in wait over White Sands.

"Amber Teal has the bogey," Quinn announced. "We're getting some imagery."

Gullick wasn't impressed or interested. They already had photos of the foo fighters. He wanted the real thing. He keyed his SATCOM link to the F-15 commander. "Eagle Leader, this is Cube Six. Target ETA in five minutes, twenty seconds. You're only going to get one shot at this. Make it good. Over."

"This is Eagle Leader. Roger. Over." Eagle Flight Leader glanced out of his cockpit at the other three planes. "Eagle Flight, take up positions. Get a fix on the first craft as it goes through. It will come to a halt on the far side of the kill zone. A second craft similar to the first is also en route from the west and will also hold on the western side of the kill zone. Launch on the bogey as soon as it crosses Phase Line Happy. Over."

The four planes broke into a cloverleaf pattern, the kill zone a large pocket of empty sky, crisscrossed with electronic energy as the planes turned on their targeting radar.

*   *   *

From Bouncer Three, Captain Scheuler could see the waiting F-15's on his display. "ETA thirty seconds," he said.

"Slowing." Major Terrent let up on the yoke.

"That's the first one," Eagle Flight Leader called out as Bouncer Three buzzed through, slowing as it went. His men were disciplined. No one questioned what it was. That would have to wait until the ready room after the mission. Even then, they all knew they could never speak openly of tonight's mission.

"Lock on," Eagle Leader confirmed.

"Locked," Eagle Two echoed, as did the other two pilots.

"Fire!"

On the display at the front of the Cube the foo fighter appeared to suddenly become motionless as a thin red line extended from each fighter toward the green dot.

"Jesus Christ!" Eagle Flight Leader swore. The bogey had disappeared—straight up! Then reality set in hard. "Evasive maneuvers!" he screamed as the Sidewinder missile from the F-15 opposite him locked onto his plane.

For four seconds there was absolute confusion as pilots and planes scrambled to escape friendly fire.

General Gullick didn't even watch the self-induced melee. "Bouncer Three, go! Direct angle of intercept. Break. Eight, loop to the south and catch it if it goes the way the other did! Aurora, get some altitude. Move, people! Move! Over."

"Seventy thousand feet and climbing," Quinn reported. "Seventy-five thousand."

*   *   *

"Please, Lord," Eagle Flight Leader whispered as he pulled out of the steep dive he'd gone into. A Sidewinder roared past to his left. He keyed his radio. "Eagle Flight report. Over."

"One. Roger. Over."

"Two. Roger. Over."

"Three. Took a licking, but I'm still kicking. Over."

Eagle Flight Leader looked up. Not to where the bogey had gone but farther. "Thank you, Lord."

"Ninety thousand and still climbing," Scheuler informed Major Terrent. His fingers hit the keyboard in front of him, his arms struggling against the G-forces pushing him down into his cutout seat.

"One hundred ten thousand and still climbing," Major Quinn said. "The F-15's are all secure and returning to Holloman," he added. "One hundred and twenty thousand." Well over twenty miles up and still going vertical.

"One hundred and twenty-five thousand. It's peaking over," Scheuler said.

Major Terrent let out his breath. The controls had started to get slightly sluggish. The record for altitude in a bouncer was one hundred and sixty-five thousand feet, and that had been a wild ride four years ago. For some reason, due to the magnetic propulsion system, which had not yet been figured out, at over a hundred thousand feet the disk started losing power.

The crew of the disk that had made the record flight had had the unnerving experience of peaking out while still trying to climb and gone into an uncontrolled descent before the disk had regained power.

"Heading?" Terrent asked, concentrating on keeping control.

"Southwest," Scheuler said. "Heading, two-one-zero degrees."

"What's it doing?" Gullick asked.

"Bogey heading two-one-zero degrees," Quinn said. "Descending on a glide path, going down through one hundred and ten thousand. Three is in close pursuit. Eight is—" Quinn paused. "The bogey's turning!"

"Uh-oh," Captain Scheuler said as things changed on his display.

"What?" The controls were getting firmer in Major Terrent's hands. They were just about down to one hundred thousand feet.

Scheuler snapped into action. "Collision alert!"

"Give me a direction!" Terrent yelled.

"Break right," Scheuler guessed.

On the large screen the red and green dots both curved in the same direction and merged. Gullick stood, his teeth biting through the forgotten cigar.

Scheuler watched the foo fighter tear by directly overhead, less than ten feet away. A beam of white light was flashing out of the small glowing ball and raking over and through their disk.

"Engine failure. Loss of all control," Terrent reported. They both felt their weight lighten, then they were peaking over and heading down.

Scheuler looked at his display. "Ninety thousand and in free fall."

The lever and yoke moved freely in Terrent's hands. "Nothing. No power." He looked over at Scheuler. Both men were maintaining their external discipline but their voices displayed their fear.

"Eighty-five thousand," Scheuler said.

"Bouncer Three is in uncontrolled descent," Quinn reported. "No power. Bouncer Eight and Aurora are still in pursuit."

The green dot representing the foo fighter was moving swiftly to the southwest.

"Sixty thousand," Scheuler reported.

Terrent let go of the useless controls.

"Fifty-five thousand."

"The bogey will hit the Mexican border in two minutes," Quinn reported.

"Bouncer Eight, this is Cube Six," Gullick said into his boom mike. "Get that son of a bitch!"

With no power other than the Earth's gravity, Bouncer Three was going down at terminal velocity. They had tipped over and the edge to both men's right was leading the way down.

They were actually descending more slowly than they had gone up, Scheuler reflected, watching the digital display count down in front of him. He felt strangely detached, his years of pilot training keeping the fear at bay. At least they weren't tumbling.

Scheuler glanced over questioningly at Terrent. "Forty-five thousand."

Terrent tried the controls again. "Still nothing," he reported.

"Thirty seconds to the border," Quinn said. He confirmed the bad news the screen was displaying. The gap between the bogey and Bouncer Eight was increasing rather than decreasing, despite the crew of the disk pushing it to the limits of human endurance.

Gullick spit out the mangled remains of his cigar. "Bouncer Eight, this is Cube Six. Break off. I say again, break off and return home. Aurora, continue pursuit. Over."

"This is Bouncer Eight. Roger. Over."

"This is Aurora. Roger. Over."

On the screen Bouncer Eight rapidly decelerated and curved back into airspace above the United States. Aurora continued following the bogey.

"Alert the *Abraham Lincoln* to launch pursuit," Gullick ordered Admiral Coakley. The general finally shifted his gaze to the upper part of the screen. The green dot representing Bouncer Three was still motionless. "Altitude?" he asked.

Quinn knew what he was referring to. "Thirty thousand. Still no power. Uncontrolled descent."

"Nightscape recovery status?" Gullick asked.

"In the air toward projected impact area," Quinn said.

"I'm going to initiate at twenty thousand," Terrent said. His right hand rested on a red lever. "Clear."

Scheuler pushed aside the keyboard and display from his lap as Terrent did the same. "Clear."

"Cable up," Terrent ordered.

Scheuler hit a button on the side of his seat. Anchored to the ceiling above and behind the two of them, a cable tightened, its near anchor point sliding along a track bolted onto the floor until it stopped right between the two depressions the men were seated in.

"Hook up," Terrent instructed.

Scheuler reached into the waist pocket of his flight suit and pulled out a locking carabiner and slipped it onto the steel cable, just above where Terrent put his. He made sure it was on and screwed tight the lock. He then traced the nylon webbing back from it to the harness strapped around his torso, making sure it was clear and not wrapped around anything.

"Hooked up," he confirmed. He glanced over at his display. "Twenty-two thousand five hundred."

Terrent grabbed the controls one last time and tried them. They moved freely. No response. He looked at Scheuler. "Ready, Kevin?"

"Ready."

"Blowing hatch on three. One. Two. Three." Terrent slammed down the red lever and the exploding bolts on the hatch at the other end of the cable blew. The hatch spun away and cold night air whistled in.

"Go!" Terrent screamed.

Captain Scheuler unbuckled his shoulder straps and pushed, sliding up the cable, slamming against the roof of the disk. He got oriented and looked down at Terrent, still in his seat. Then he let go and was sucked out of the hatch, the nylon strap reaching its end and deploying the parachute that he had been sitting on. The disk was already gone into the darkness below by the time the chute finished opening.

He watched but there was no other blossoming of white canopy below.

Major Terrent's hands were on the releases for his shoulder straps when his pilot's instincts took over one last time. He reached down and grabbed the controls. There was something—the slightest response. His focus came back inside the craft as he wrestled with the controls.

*   *   *

"Ten thousand feet," Quinn said. He looked at his computer screen and hit a few keys. "We're getting a slight change in downward velocity on Bouncer Three."

"I thought you said the readout said the hatch was blown and they had initiated escape." Gullick said.

"Yes, sir, the hatch is gone, but"—Quinn checked the data being sent in from the satellites and Bouncer Three itself—"but it's slowing, sir!"

Gullick nodded, but turned his attention back toward the screen and the green dot of the bogey, now over the Pacific far west of Panama.

Without Scheuler, Terrent had no idea what his altitude was. He'd pushed aside his own heads-up display when he'd hooked up. The power was coming back, but very slowly.

"Five thousand feet, continuing to decelerate," Quinn said.

"How come I don't see the F-14's from the *Abraham Lincoln* on the display?" General Gullick asked.

"I—uh—" Quinn's fingers flew over the keyboard and a cluster of small plane silhouettes appeared on the screen. They were heading toward an orange circle representing the spot where the previous foo fighter had gone into the ocean. The symbols for the bogey and Aurora were also heading there.

"I think I've got it!" Terrent yelled to himself. He had the altitude lever pulled up as high as it would go and could continue to feel power returning. "We'll make it, we'll—"

"She's down," Quinn said in a quiet voice. "Bouncer Three is down. All telemetry is cut."

"Make sure Nightscape recovery has the exact position

from the last readout," Gullick ordered. "Time to bogey intercept for the Tomcats?"

Quinn looked at General Gullick for a few seconds, then turned back to his terminal. "Six minutes."

"I don't see what good intercept will do," Admiral Coakley protested. "We've already tried twice. It's over the ocean. Even if we down the bogey it won't—"

"*I* am in charge here," General Gullick hissed. "Don't ever—"

"Bogey's gone, sir," Quinn said. "She's gone under."

The data was complex and much of it was not in the historical record. It counted at least six different types of atmospheric craft, only two of which were listed. And it was not action of this type that had awoken it twice before. Nevertheless, this new event was a threat because it was tied in to the place where the mothership was.

Valuable energy was diverted, and the main processor was brought up to forty-percent capacity to ponder the bursts of input that had occurred in this past cycle of the planet around its star. There had been conflict, but that did not concern it. There were larger issues at stake here.

VICINITY, DULCE, NEW MEXICO
T—93 HOURS, 30 MINUTES

There was something stuck in both his arms and on the inside of each thigh. Johnny Simmons also sensed tubes between his legs—a catheter, both fore and aft. There was also some sort of device hooked in the right side of his mouth, giving off a very light mist of moisture. Another tube ran into the left side of his mouth and that was how he was breathing. There was something over his face, covering it, pressing his eyes shut and blocking off his nose. Beyond that Simmons didn't have a clue as to his condition. And those discoveries had been made only in those few breaks between periods of excruciating pain.

He assumed that at least one of whatever was stuck in him was a nutritional IV. He had no clue as to the passage of time, but it felt as if his entire existence had been spent in this darkness.

If it had not been for the needles and catheters, Johnny believed he would have thought himself dead and his soul exiled to hell. But this was a living hell, a physical one.

He felt a coppery taste in his mouth. He didn't even wait for the pain now. His mouth contorted open and he silently screamed.

The first thing Colonel Dickerson did as his command-and-control helicopter zeroed in on the personnel beacon from Bouncer Three was have his aide, Captain Travers, remove the silver eagles on his collar and replace them with two stars. That was for any military personnel they might run into. The typical military mentality viewed generals as gods, and that was the way Dickerson wanted people responding to his orders this night.

"ETA to beacon two minutes," the pilot of the UH-60 Blackhawk announced over the intercom.

Dickerson glanced out the window. Three other Blackhawks followed, spread out against the night sky, their running lights darkened. He hit the transmit button for his radio. "Roller, this is Hawk. Give me some good news. Over."

The response from his second-in-command at the main White Sands complex was immediate. "This is Roller. I've got people awake here. The duty officer is rounding us up some transport. They've got two lowboys we can use and a crane rated for what we need for recovery. Over."

"How long before you can get them out to the range? Over."

"An hour and a half max. Over."

"Roger. Out."

The pilot came on the intercom as soon as Dickerson was finished. "There he is, sir."

Dickerson leaned forward and looked out. "Pick him up," he ordered.

The Blackhawk descended and landed. The man on the ground sat on his parachute to prevent it from being inflated by the groundwash of the rotor blades. Two men jumped off the rear of Dickerson's aircraft, ran over to Captain Scheuler, and escorted him back to the bird, securing the parachute.

Scheuler put on a headset as soon as he was on board. "Have you picked up Major Terrent's signal?" he asked.

Dickerson indicated for the pilot to take off. "No. We're going to the disk transponder."

"Maybe his equipment got damaged when he was getting out of the disk," Scheuler said.

Dickerson glanced across at the pilot, who met the look briefly, then went back to flying. There wasn't time to tell Scheuler about the slight slowing in descent of Bouncer Three just before impact.

"ETA to disk transponder?" Dickerson asked.

"Thirty seconds."

The pilot pointed. "There it is, sir."

"Shit," Dickerson heard the copilot mutter. And that was a rather appropriate comment on the current condition of Bouncer Three. He keyed his radio. "Roller, we're going to need a dozer and probably a backhoe too. Over."

His aide back at main base was ready. "Roger."

The pilot brought the aircraft to a hover, the searchlight on the belly of the helicopter trained down and forward on the crash site. Bouncer Three had hit at an angle. Only the trail edge was visible, sticking up out of the dirt ridge it had impacted into. Knowing the dimension of the disk, Dickerson calculated that it was buried at least twenty feet into the countryside.

"What about the beacon on the hatch?" he asked Captain Travers.

"Nightscape Two has it on screen and is closing on it. About four miles to the southwest of our location," Travers responded.

They had to clean up every single piece of gear and equipment. There was always the chance that someone they had to recruit to help with the recovery—such as the drivers of the lowboys or the bulldozer or crane operator— might talk, but as long as there was no physical evidence, they were good to go.

"Let's land," Dickerson ordered.

The Cube, Area 51

General Gullick scanned the haggard faces around the conference table. There were two empty seats. Dr. Duncan had not been informed of, or invited to, the night's activities, and Von Seeckt was, of course, absent. As recorder and data retriever, Major Quinn was seated away from the table, at a computer console to Gullick's left.

"Gentlemen," Gullick began, "we have a problem occurring at a most critical time. We have Bouncer Three down with one casualty at White Sands. We also have six aircrews currently being debriefed on the night's events. And all we have gained against those potential security breaches is a replay of the events of the other night. We have more pictures of this foo fighter to add to our records and we have almost the exact same location in the Pacific Ocean that it disappeared into."

Gullick paused and leaned back in his chair, steepling his fingers. "This thing, this craft, has beaten the best we could throw against it, including our appropriated technology here." He looked at Dr. Underhill. "Any idea what it did to Bouncer Three?"

The representative from the Jet Propulsion Laboratory held a roll of telemetry paper in his hands. "Not until I get a chance to look at the flight recorder and talk to the crewman who survived. All I can determine from this," he said, shaking the paper, "is that there was a complete loss of power on board Bouncer Three in conjunction with a near collision with the foo fighter. The power loss lasted for one minute and forty-six seconds, then some power began returning, but too late for the pilot to compensate for the craft's terminal velocity."

Dr. Ferrel, the physicist, cleared his throat. "Since we don't understand the exact workings of the propulsion system of the disks, it makes it doubly hard for us to try to figure out what the foo fighter did to Bouncer Three to cause the crash."

"What about something we do understand?" Gullick asked. "We certainly understand how helicopters fly."

Underhill nodded. "I've gone over the wreckage of the AH-6 that crashed in Nebraska, and the only thing I have been able to determine is that it suffered complete engine failure. There was no problem with either the transmission or hydraulics or else no one would have survived the crash. The engine simply ceased functioning. Perhaps some sort of electrical or magnetic interference.

"The pilot is still in a coma and I have not been able to interview him. I have some theories, but until I can work on them, I have no idea how the foo fighter caused the engine on that aircraft to cease functioning."

"Does anyone," Gullick said, with emphasis, "have any idea what these foo fighters are or who is behind them?"

A long silence descended on the conference table.

"Aliens?"

Ten heads swiveled and looked at the one man who didn't rate a leather seat. Major Quinn seemed to sink lower behind his portable computer.

"Say again?" Gullick said in his deep voice.

"Perhaps they are aliens, sir," Quinn said.

"You mean the foo fighters are UFOs?" General Brown sniffed.

"Of course they're UFOs," General Gullick cut in, surprising everyone in the room with the harshness of his tone. "We don't know what the fuck they are, do we? That makes them unidentified, right? And they fly, right? And they're real objects, aren't they?" He slapped a palm down on the table top. "Gentlemen, as far as the rest of the world is concerned *we're* flying UFOs here every week. The question I want an answer to is who is flying the UFOs that we aren't?" He swiveled his head to Quinn. "And you think it's aliens?"

"We have no hint that anyone on Earth possesses the technology needed for these foo fighters, sir," Quinn said.

"Yes, Major, but the Russians sure as shit don't think we possess the technology to make the bouncers either. And we don't," Gullick hissed. "My point is, has someone else dug up some technology like we have here?"

Kennedy, from CIA, leaned forward. "If I remember rightly from my inbriefing, there were other sites listed on the tablets that we never had a chance to look at."

"Most of those sites were ancient ruins," Quinn said quickly, "but the thing is, there are more high runes at those sites. Who knows what might be written there? We haven't been able to decipher the writing. We *do* know that the Germans deciphered some of the high runes, but that was lost in World War II."

"Lost to us," Gullick amended. "And it's not certain that the Germans were able to read the high runes. They might have been working off of a map like we did when we went down to Antarctica and picked up the other seven bouncers. Remember," Gullick added, "that we just uncovered what was at Jamiltepec eight months ago."

That caught Major Quinn's attention. He had never heard of Jamiltepec or of a discovery having been made there related to the Majic-12 project. Now, though, was not the time to bring it up.

Kennedy leaned forward. "We do have to remember that the Russians picked up quite a bit of information at the end of World War II. After all, they had a chance to go through all the records in Berlin. They also knew what they were doing when they conquered Germany. If people only knew the fight that went on over the scientific corpse of the Third Reich between us and the Russians."

The last comment earned the CIA representative a hard look from General Gullick, and Kennedy quickly moved on.

"My point is," Kennedy said quickly, "that maybe the Russians found their own technology in the form of these foo fighters. After all, we have no reports of Russian aircraft running into them during the war. And it is pretty suspicious that the Enola Gay was escorted on its way to Hiroshima. Truman did inform Stalin that the bomb was going to be dropped. Maybe they wanted to see what was going on and try to learn as much as they could about the bomb."

"And remember, they put Sputnik up in 1957." General Brown was caught up in Kennedy's theory. "While we were dicking around with the bouncers and not pursuing our own space program as aggressively as we should have, maybe they were working on these foo fighters and reverse-engineering them with a bit more success than we had. Hell, those damn Sputniks looked like these foo fighters."

Gullick turned to Kennedy. "Do you have any information that might be connected to this?"

Kennedy stroked his chin. "There's several things that might be of significance. We know they have been carrying out secret test flights at their facility at Tyuratam in southern Siberia for decades, and we've never been able to penetrate the security there. They do everything at night and even with infrared overhead satellite imagery, we haven't been able to figure out what they've got. So they could be flying foo fighters."

"But these things went down into the Pacific," General Brown noted.

"They could be launching and recovering off a submarine," Admiral Coakley said. "Hell, their Delta-class subs are the largest submarines in the world. I'm sure they could have modified one to handle this sort of thing."

"Any sign of Russian submarine activity from your people at the site?" General Gullick asked.

"Nothing so far. Last report I had was that our ships were in position and they were preparing to send a submersible down," Coakley replied.

Major Quinn had to grip the edge of his computer to remind himself that he was awake. He couldn't believe the way the men around the conference table were talking. It was as if they had all halved their IQ and added in a dose of paranoia.

Gullick turned his attention back to Kennedy and indicated for him to continue. "This might not have anything to do with this situation, but it's the latest thing we've picked up," Kennedy said. "We know the Russians are doing work with linking human brains directly into computer hardware. We don't know where they got the technology for that. It's way beyond anything worked on in the West. These foo fighters are obviously too small to carry a person, but perhaps the Russians might have put one of these biocomputers on board while using magnetic flight technology such as we have in the disks. Or they simply might be remotely controlled from a room such as we have here."

"We've picked up no discernible broadcast link to the foo fighter," Major Quinn said, trying to edge the discussion back to a commonsense footing. "Unless it was a very narrow-beam satellite laser link we would have caught it, and such a narrow beam would have been difficult to keep on the foo fighter, given its speed and how quickly it maneuvered."

"Could Von Seeckt have been turned?" Gullick suddenly asked. "I know he's been here from the very beginning, but remember where he came from. Maybe the Russians finally got to him, or maybe he's been working for them all along."

Kennedy frowned. "I doubt that. We've had the tightest security on all Majic-12 personnel."

"Well, what about this Turcotte fellow or this female reporter? Could either of them be working for the other side?"

Quinn started, remembering the intercept of Duncan's message to the White House chief of staff. Gullick mustn't have gotten to it yet. Again, he decided to keep his peace, this time to avoid an ass-chewing.

"I have my people checking on it," Kennedy said. "Nothing has turned up so far."

"Let's see what Admiral Coakley finds us in the Pacific. Maybe that will solve this mystery," Gullick said. "For now, our priorities are sterilizing the crash site at White Sands and continuing our countdown for the mothership."

Major Quinn had been working at his computer, reading data from the various components of the project spread out across the United States and the globe. He was relieved when information began scrolling up. "Sir, we've got some news on Von Seeckt."

Gullick gestured for him to continue.

"Surveillance in Phoenix has picked up Von Seeckt, Turcotte, and this female reporter, Reynolds."

"Phoenix?" Gullick asked.

"Yes, sir. I ordered surveillance on the apartment of the reporter who tried to infiltrate the other night once I found out that Reynolds was asking about him. The surveillance just settled in place this evening and they've spotted all three targets at the apartment and are requesting further instructions."

"Have them pick up all three and take them to Dulce," Gullick ordered.

Quinn paused in sending the order. "There's something else, sir. The men we sent to check out Von Seeckt's quarters have found a message on his answering service that might be important. It was from a Professor Nabinger."

"What was the message?" General Gullick asked.

Quinn read from the screen. " 'Professor Von Seeckt, my name is Peter Nabinger. I work with the Egyptology Department at the Brooklyn Museum. I would like to talk to you about the Great Pyramid, which I believe we have a mutual interest in. I just deciphered some of the writing in the lower chamber, which I believe you visited once upon a time, and it says: 'Power, sun. Forbidden. Home place, chariot, never again. Death to all living things.' Perhaps you could help shed some light on my translation. Leave me a message how I can get hold of you at my voice-mail box. My number is 212-555-1474.' "

"If this Nabinger knows about Von Seeckt and the pyramid—" began Kennedy, but a wave of Gullick's hand stopped him.

"I agree that is dangerous"—Gullick was excited—"but of more importance is the fact that it seems Nabinger can decipher the high runes. If he can do that, then maybe we can . . ." Gullick paused. "Did our people check to see if Von Seeckt has contacted Nabinger?"

Quinn nodded. "Yes, sir. Von Seeckt called Nabinger's service at eight twenty-six and left a message giving a location for them to meet tomorrow, or actually this morning," he amended, looking at the digital clock on the wall.

"The location?"

"The apartment in Phoenix," Quinn answered.

Gullick smiled for the first time in twenty-four hours. "So we can bag all our little birds in one nest in a few hours. Excellent. Get me a direct line to the Nightscape leader on the ground in Phoenix."

WHITE SANDS MISSILE RANGE, NEW MEXICO

The engine on the crane whined in protest, but the earth gave before the cable, and inch by inch Bouncer Three was pulled up out of its hole. As soon as it was clear, the crane operator rotated right, bringing the disk toward the flatbed that was waiting. In the glow of the hastily erected arc lights, Colonel Dickerson could see that the outer skin of the disk appeared to be unscathed.

As soon as Bouncer Three was down on the truck, Dickerson grabbed hold of the side of the flatbed and clambered up onto the wood deck and then onto the sloping side of the craft itself. His aide and Captain Scheuler were right behind him. Balancing carefully, Dickerson edged up until he was at the hatch that Scheuler had thrown himself out of two miles above their heads.

The interior was dark with the power off. Taking a halogen flashlight off his belt, Dickerson shone it down on the inside. Despite having fought in two wars and seen more than his share of carnage, Dickerson flinched at the scene within. He sensed Scheuler coming up next to him.

"Oh, my God," Scheuler muttered.

Blood and pieces of Major Terrent were scattered about everywhere inside. Dickerson sat down with his back to the hatch, trying to control his breathing while Scheuler vomited. Dickerson had been a forward air controller during Desert Storm and had seen the destruction wrought on the highway north out of Kuwait near the end of the war. But that was war and the bodies had been those of the enemy. *Goddamn Gullick,* he thought. Dickerson grabbed the edges of the hatch, and lowered himself in. "Let's go," he ordered Scheuler, who gingerly followed.

"See if it still works," Dickerson ordered. He'd sure as hell rather fly it back to Nevada than have to cover it up and take back roads by night.

Scheuler looked at the blood- and viscera-covered depression that Terrent had occupied.

"You can take a shower later," Dickerson forced himself to say. "Right now I need to know whether we have power, and we don't have time to clean this thing up."

"Sir, I—"

"Captain!" Dickerson snapped.

"Yes, sir." Scheuler slid into the seat, a grimace on his face. His hands went over the control panel. Lights came on briefly, then faded as the skin of the craft went clear and they could see by the arc lights set up outside.

"We have power." Scheuler stated the obvious. He looked down at the altitude-control level and froze. Terrent's hand was still gripped tightly around it, the stub of his forearm ending in shattered bone and flesh. He cried out and turned away.

Colonel Dickerson knelt down and gently pried the dead object loose. *Goddamn Gullick, Goddamn Gullick;* it was a chant his brain was using to hold on to sanity. "See if you have flight control," he ordered in a softer voice.

Scheuler grabbed the lever. Space appeared below their feet. "We have flight control," he said in a rote voice.

"All right," Dickerson said. "Captain Travers will fly with you back to Groom Lake. We'll have pursuit aircraft flying escort. Got that, Captain?"

There was no answer.

"Do you understand?"

"Yes, sir," Scheuler weakly said.

Dickerson climbed back out of the disk and gave the appropriate orders. Finally done, he walked away from the lights and behind the sandy ridge that the disk had crashed into. He knelt down in the sand and vomited.

THE CUBE, AREA 51

The lights were dim in the conference room and Gullick was completely in the shadows. The other members of Majic-12 were gone, trying to get some long-overdue sleep or checking in with their own agencies—except for Kennedy, the deputy director of operations for the CIA. He had waited as the others filed out.

"We're sitting on a fucking powder keg here," Kennedy began.

"I know that," Gullick said. He had the briefing book with Duncan's intercepted message in it. It confirmed that Turcotte had been a plant, but of more import was the threat that Duncan would get the President to delay the test flight. That simply couldn't be allowed.

"The others—they don't know what Von Seeckt knows, what you and I know, about the history of this project," Kennedy said.

"They're in it too far now. Even if they knew, it's too late for all of them," Gullick said. "Just the Majestic-12 stuff is enough to sink every damn one of them."

"But if they found out about Paperclip—" began Kennedy.

"We inherited Paperclip," Gullick cut in. "Just as we inherited Majic. And people know about Paperclip. It's not that big of a secret anymore."

"Yeah, but we kept it going," Kennedy pointed out. "And what most people know is only the tip of the iceberg."

"Von Seeckt doesn't know Paperclip is still running, and he was only on the periphery of it all back in the forties."

"He knows about Dulce," Kennedy countered.

"He knows Dulce exists and that it's connected somehow with us here. But he was never given access to what has been going on there," Gullick said. "He doesn't have a clue what's going on there." The right side of Gullick's face twitched and he put a hand up, pressing on the pain he felt in his skull. Even thinking about Dulce hurt. He didn't want to speak about it anymore. There were more important things to deal with. Gullick ticked off the problems on his fingers.

"Tomorrow, or more accurately this morning, we take care of Von Seeckt and the others there in Phoenix. That will close that leak down.

"By dawn we'll have the mess at White Sands all cleaned up and the aircrews involved debriefed and cleared.

"We have the eight o'clock briefing by Slayden, which should help get Duncan off our back for a little while. Long enough.

"Admiral Coakley should be giving us something on these foo fighters soon.

"And last but not least, in ninety-three hours we fly the mothership. That is the most important thing." General Gullick turned, facing away from Kennedy to end the discussion. He heard Kennedy leave, then reached into his pocket and pulled out two more of the special pills Dr.

Cruise had given him. He needed something to reduce the throbbing in his brain.

AIRSPACE, SOUTHERN UNITED STATES

Checking the few photos that he had not seen before helped Professor Nabinger's fledgling high rune vocabulary grow by a phrase or two. The seats on either side of him were empty and there were photos spread out all over the row. He drank the third cup of coffee the stewardess had brought him and smiled contentedly. The smile disappeared just as quickly, though, when his mind came back to the same problem.

How had the high rune language been distributed worldwide at such an early date in man's history, when even negotiating the Mediterranean Sea was an adventure fraught with great hazard? Nabinger didn't know, but he hoped that somewhere in the pictures an answer might be forthcoming. There were two problems, though. One was that many of the pictures showed sites that had been damaged in some way. Often the damage appeared to have been done deliberately, as in the water off Bimini. The second, and greater, problem was that many of the pictures were of high runes that were, for lack of a better word, dialects. It was a problem that had frustrated Nabinger for years.

There were enough subtle, and sometimes not-so-subtle, differences in the high rune writing from site to site to show that although they had very definitely grown from the same base, they had evolved differently in separate locales. It was as if the root language emerged in one place, been taken at a certain point to other locales, then evolved separately at each place. Which made sense, Nabinger allowed.

It was the way language worked. It also fit the diffusionist theory of the evolution of civilization.

The real problem for Nabinger—beyond the fact that the dialect made translation difficult—was that the content of the messages, once translated, was hard to comprehend. Most of the words and partial sentences he was translating referred to mythology or religion, gods and death and great calamities. But there was very little specific information. Most of the high runes in the pictures seemed related to whatever form of worship existed in the locale they were found in.

There was no further information about the pyramids or the existence or location of Atlantis. There were several references to a great natural disaster sometime several centuries before the birth of Christ, but that was nothing new. There was much emphasis on looking to the sky, but Nabinger also knew that most religions looked to the sky, whether to the sun, the stars, or the moon. People tended to look up when they thought of God.

What was the connection? How had the high rune language been spread? What had Von Seeckt found in the lower chamber of the Great Pyramid? Nabinger gathered up the photos and returned them to his battered backpack. Too many pieces with no connection. With no *why*. And Nabinger wanted the why.

22

"You gave Nabinger this address?" Turcotte asked for the third time.

"Yes," Von Seeckt replied from the comfort of the couch. The living room of the apartment was dark.

"You left it on his voice mail?"

"Yes."

"And he left the first message on your voice mail?" Turcotte persisted.

"Yes."

"For God's sake," Kelly muttered from underneath a blanket on a large easy chair, "you sound like a cross-examining attorney. We went through all that earlier today in the car. Is there a problem?"

Turcotte peered out the two-inch gap between the curtain and the edge of the window. He'd been standing there for the past hour, unmoving while the other two slept, the only sign that he was conscious his eyeballs flickering as he took in the view.

He had awakened them both a few minutes ago. It was still dark out and in the glow of the streetlights there was nothing moving on the street. "Yeah, there's a problem."

Kelly threw the blanket aside and reached for the lamp.

"Don't do that." Turcotte's voice froze her hand on the knob.

"Why?"

Turcotte turned his gaze into the room. "If I have to explain everything I say, we're going to get our shit wasted when there's no time to explain. I'd appreciate it if you just do what I say when I say it."

Kelly's clothes were wrinkled and she had not had the most comfortable night's sleep in the chair. "Are we in the middle of a crisis that you don't have time to explain?"

"Not this minute," Turcotte said. "But I'm preparing you both for the minute when that's going to happen. Which," he said, jerking his thumb at the window, "is going to be sometime this morning."

"Who's out there?" Von Seeckt asked, sitting up on the couch and trying to pull his beard into some semblance of order.

"Less than an hour ago a van pulled in across the street and down that way"—Turcotte pointed to the left—"about two hundred feet. For fifteen minutes no one got out. Then a man exited, went over to our rent-a-car, and placed something under the right rear quarter panel. He went back and got in the van, and there's been no movement since then. I assume they have surveillance on the back of this building also."

"What are they waiting for?" Kelly tossed aside the blanket, stood, and began gathering her few belongings.

"If they got the messages off Von Seeckt's answering service, probably the same thing we are. Waiting for Nabinger to show."

Kelly paused, seeing that Turcotte was standing still. "Couldn't they just have had this place under surveillance after kidnapping Johnny?"

"Maybe," Turcotte said. "But that van wasn't there when we pulled in last night, and when you and I were out for our little walk I did a sweep of the area and didn't spot any surveillance. I think they only came on the scene this morning. Which makes me think they got around to checking the good professor's answering service."

Von Seeckt nodded. "Yes. They would do that. I made a mistake, did I not?"

"Yes. And by the way, next time, you tell me what you're doing *before* you do it." Turcotte reached inside his coat. He pulled out a pistol, pulled out the magazine, checked it, put it back, and pushed the slide back, chambering a round.

"What's the plan?" Kelly asked.

"You ever read the book *Killer Angels*?" Turcotte asked, shifting over and looking back out the thin crack.

"About the Battle of Gettysburg?" Kelly asked.

Turcotte spared a glance back at her. "Very good. Do you remember what Chamberlain of the Twentieth Maine did when he was on the far left of the Union line and about out of ammunition after continuous attacks by the Confederates?"

"He ordered a charge," Kelly said.

"Right."

"So we're going to charge?"

Turcotte smiled. "Just when they do. They'll be overconfident and think they have the initiative. Timing is everything."

"Ah, fuck," the major muttered to the other men crowded into the van. He glared at the sophisticated communications rig bolted to the left rear wall of the van, then keyed the mike hanging from the ceiling. "Roger that, sir. Anything else? Over."

"Don't screw it up." General Gullick's voice was unmistakable, even after being digitized and scrambled, then unscrambled and deciphered by the machines. "Out here." The radio went dead.

The major pushed the ceiling mike out of the way and looked at the other men. "We wait until the other target links up at the apartment. They have to be taken alive. All of them."

"It'll be daylight by the time the other guy gets here," one of the men said in protest.

"I know that," the major said in a tone that was not conducive to discussion. "I'll clear it with the locals and keep them out of the way." He lifted a sophisticated-looking gunlike object. "Remember—they are all to be taken alive, so use your stunners only."

"What about Turcotte?" one of the men asked. "He's going to be trouble."

"He's the priority target when we go in the door. The others will be easy," the major said.

"I don't think Turcotte's going to worry about keeping *us* alive," one of the men muttered.

Despite a long night with an extended layover at Dallas– Fort Worth International, Professor Nabinger felt thoroughly alive and alert as the taxi turned the corner and the apartment building appeared. There was just the slightest hint of dawn in the air in the east.

After removing his bags Nabinger paid the driver. He left the suitcase on the curb and tucked his leather case with the photos Slader had given him under his arm as he searched for the appropriate apartment. He knocked on the door and waited. It swung open, but no one was there.

"Hello?" Nabinger called out.

"Step in," a woman's voice came from inside the dark room.

Nabinger took a step forward and a man's arm reached

around the door and grabbed his collar, pulling him into the room. The door slammed shut behind him.

"What is going—" Nabinger started.

"Quiet," Turcotte said. "We're going to be attacked in a few seconds. Go with her." He had one of the flash-bang grenades he'd kept from the Nightscape mission in his hand. He pulled the pin and leaned against the door, listening.

Kelly took Nabinger's arm and led him to the far corner of the room, where Von Seeckt also waited. She handed him a strip of dark cloth cut from the curtain. "Hold this over your eyes."

"What for?" Nabinger asked.

"Just do it!" Kelly said.

The door exploded in under the impact of a hand-held battering ram and men tumbled in, their eyes searching for targets. They were greeted with a bright bang and flash of white light, immediately blinding all of them.

Turcotte dropped the dark cloth he'd held to protect his vision and stepped among the four men, his arms moving in a flurry of strikes, sending two of them down unconscious in less than a second. He scooped up one of the stun guns from an inert hand and finished off the other two with it as they tried to regain their senses.

"Let's move!" Turcotte yelled.

Kelly grabbed hold of Nabinger and they headed out the door.

In the van the major tore the headset off and bounced it off the wall, his ears still ringing from the transmission of the flash-bang grenade going off in the apartment across the street.

"They're coming out!" the lookout man in the front seat of the van yelled.

The major pulled open the side door and stepped out into the street, a silenced submachine gun at the ready.

Turcotte froze, the other three members of his group stacking up behind him. The officer with the submachine gun was joined by a man from the front seat, both pointing their weapons directly at Turcotte.

"Don't move an inch!" the officer ordered.

"What're you going to do? Shoot me?" Turcotte said, hefting the stun gun. "Then why'd you use these? You're supposed to take us alive, aren't you?" He took another step toward the two men. "Those are your orders, aren't they?"

"Freeze right where you are." The officer settled the stock of the gun into his shoulder.

"General Gullick will be mighty pissed if you put holes in us," Turcotte said.

"He might be pissed, but you'll be dead," the major returned, centering his sights on Turcotte's chest. "I'll make damn—" The major's mouth froze in midsentence and a surprised look ran across his features.

Turcotte fired at the driver and the stun round caught the man in the chest, and he collapsed next to his leader. Turcotte glanced over his shoulder. Kelly slowly lowered the stun gun she'd picked up on the way out. "Took you long enough," he said, gesturing for them to get into the van.

"The conversation was interesting," Kelly said. "So very macho." They helped Von Seeckt and a thoroughly confused Nabinger into the back of the van. The street was still deserted.

"You drive," Turcotte said, standing in the opening between the two front seats. "I want to play with the toys in the back."

"Next stop, Dulce," Kelly said, throwing the van in gear and pulling away with a squeal of tires.

THE CUBE

"Sir, the team leader in Arizona reports that they've lost the targets." Quinn carefully kept his eyes down, looking at his computer screen.

Three hours of sleep were all that General Gullick seemed to need to operate on. He wore a freshly pressed uniform and the starched edge of the light blue shirt under his dark blue coat pressed into his neck as he turned his attention from reading reports on the mothership. "Lost?"

"Professor Nabinger showed up and the Nightscape team moved in to secure all the targets." Quinn recited the facts in a monotone. "Apparently, Turcotte was prepared. He used a flash-bang grenade to disorient the entry team. Then, using the stun guns from the entry team, he and the others subdued the van team and took off, driving the van."

"They have the van?" General Gullick leaned back in his chair. "Can we trace it?"

Quinn closed his eyes briefly. This day was starting out very badly and it wasn't going to get better as the new information scrolling up on his screen told him. "No, sir."

"You mean we don't have a tracer on our own vehicles?" Gullick asked.

"No, sir."

"Why not?" Gullick raised his hand. "Forget it. We'll deal with that later. Put out a 'sight and report only' to the local authorities. Give them a description of the van and the people."

He looked up at the large display at the front of the room. An outline of the United States was currently displayed. "I want to know where they're heading. We've got to prevent them from going to the media. Alert Mr. Kennedy to have his domestic people monitor the wires. We get a peep that Von Seeckt has gone to anyone, I want Nightscape there." Gullick's eyes flickered across the map. "Tell those in Phoenix to stay there. I also want Tucson and Albuquerque covered. They'll stay away from the airports, so we have them on the ground. The longer they're out there the bigger the circle grows."

Quinn plunged on. "There's something else, sir."

"Yes?"

"The *Abraham Lincoln* task force is reporting negative on any sign of the foo fighters. They've scanned the ocean bottom for a twenty-kilometer circle around where the first one went down and they've found nothing. The minisub off the USS *Pigeon* has combed the bottom and—"

"They stay there and they keep looking," Gullick ordered.

"Yes, sir." Quinn shut the lid on his laptop computer, then nervously flipped it open again. "Sir, uh . . ." He licked his lips.

"What?" Gullick growled.

"Sir, it's my duty to, uh, well . . ." Quinn rubbed his hands together, feeling the knob of his West Point ring on his right hand. The questions had been building for too long. His voice became firmer. "Sir, this mission is going in a direction that I don't understand. Our job is to work on the alien equipment. I don't see how Nightscape and—"

General Gullick slammed his fist into the tabletop. "Major Quinn!"

Quinn swallowed. "Yes, sir?"

Gullick stood. "I'm going to get some breakfast and then I have to attend a meeting. I want you to relay a message to all our people in the field and everyone working for us." Gullick leaned over the table and put his face a foot away from Quinn's. "We have three goddamn days before we fly the mothership. I'm tired of being told of failures and mistakes and fuckups. I want answers and I want results. I've dedicated my life and my career to this project. I will not see it be tarnished or destroyed by the incompetence of others. You don't ask questions of me. No one asks questions of me. Is that clear?"

"Yes, sir."

23

"I think I'll just stay here," Nabinger said. They were stopped at a small rest area off Highway 60 on the Natanes Plateau. There was a brisk wind blowing out of the northwest and Turcotte was making instant cups of coffee for all of them, using the microwave inside the van and supplies he'd found in a cabinet there. They were seated in the captain's chairs inside with the side door open.

"We can't let you do that," Turcotte said.

"This is a free country!" Nabinger said. "I can do whatever I want. I didn't plan on being in the middle of a fight."

"We didn't plan it either," Kelly said. "But we're stuck. There's more going on here than any of us know."

"I just wanted some answers," Nabinger said.

"You'll get them," Kelly said. "But if you want them, you have to stick with us." Nabinger had not reacted too badly to being basically kidnapped and taken away in the van. But Kelly knew his type, as she'd interviewed scientists just like him. Many times the quest for knowledge became more important than everything else around them, including their own personal safety.

"This is all so incredible," Nabinger said. He looked at

Von Seeckt. "So you believe this message refers to the mothership?"

Von Seeckt nodded. "I believe it is a warning that we must not fly the mothership. I believe the *chariot* obviously refers to the mothership and I would take very seriously the *never again* and *death to all living things* writings."

"If this is true," Nabinger said, "it means that the ancient humans were influenced by the aliens that left these craft behind. It would help explain so many of the commonalities in mythology and archeology."

"Let's hold on here a second," Kelly said. "If these writings in the Great Pyramid in Egypt refer to the mothership—which was abandoned on this continent—then it had to have been flying once upon a time."

"Of course it flew at one time," Von Seeckt said. "The real question is: Why did they *stop* flying it? What is the threat?"

"I've got a better question for right now." Turcotte handed a mug of steaming coffee to Von Seeckt. "You told me on the plane out of Area 51 that you were recruited by the U.S. military during the Second World War. Yet Professor Nabinger tells us that you were with the Nazis in the pyramid. I'd like an explanation. Now."

"I second that," Kelly said.

"I do not think—" Von Seeckt paused as Nabinger reached into his backpack and pulled out a dagger.

"I was given this by the Arab who guided you into the pyramid back then."

Von Seeckt took the dagger and grimaced, then placed it down on the table. He cradled his wrinkled hands around the mug and looked out over the bleak terrain of the Indian reservation. "I was born in Freiburg in 1918. It is a town in southwest Germany, not far from the border with France. The times I grew up in were not good years in Germany. In the twenties everyone was poor and angry over the way the war to end all wars had ended. Do you know that at the end of the First World War no foreign troops had yet set foot on German soil? That we were still occupying French soil when the government surrendered?"

"Spare us the history lesson," Turcotte said. He had picked up the dagger and was looking at the symbols carved into the handle. He knew about the SS. "We've heard it all before."

"But you asked," Von Seeckt said. "As I said, in the twenties we were poor and angry. In the thirties everyone was crazy from having been poor and angry for so long. As Captain Turcotte says, you all know what happened. I was in the university in Munich studying physics when Czechoslovakia fell. I was young then and I had that—ah, what are the words—myopic, self-centered vision that the young have. It was more important to me that I pass my comprehensive exams and be awarded my degree than that the world was unraveling around me.

"While I was at the university, I did not know that I was being watched. The SS had established early on a special section to oversee scientific matters. Their commander reported directly to Himmler. They put together a list of scientists and technicians that could be of use to the party, and my name was on the list.

"They approached me in the summer of 1941. There was special work being done, they told me, and I must help." For the first time Von Seeckt brought his gaze out of the desert. He looked at each person in turn. "One of the advantages of being an old man who is dying is that I can tell the truth. I will not pretend and whine as so many of my colleagues did at the end of the war that I worked against my will. Germany was my country and we were at war. I did what I considered my duty to my country and I worked willingly.

"The question that is always asked is 'What about the

camps?' " Von Seeckt shrugged. "The first truth is that I
did not really know about them. The higher truth is that I
did not care to know. There were rumors, but I did not
care to pursue rumors. Again my focus was with myself and
my work. That does not excuse what happened or my role
in the war effort. It is simply what happened.

"I was working near Peenemünde. The top men—they
were working on the rockets. I was with another group,
doing theoretical work that we hoped would have future
application. Some of it touched on the potential of an
atomic weapon. You can find out what you need to know
about that from other sources.

"The problem was that our work was mainly theoretical,
laying the groundwork, and those in command did not
have much patience. Germany was fighting a war on two
fronts and the feeling was that the war had better be over
sooner rather than later, and we needed weapons now, not
theory."

"You say you worked at Peenemünde?" Kelly cut in. Her
voice was harsh.

"Yes."

"But you also say you didn't try to find out about the
camps?"

Von Seeckt remained quiet.

"Don't bullshit us," Kelly said. "What about the Dora
concentration camp?"

The wind blew in the door from the desert floor, chilling
the group.

"What was Dora?" Turcotte asked.

"A camp that supplied workers to Peenemünde," Kelly
said. "The inmates were treated as terribly as the people at
the other, better-known camps. When the American Army
liberated it—the day before Roosevelt died, as a matter of
fact—they found over six thousand dead. The survivors
weren't far from dead. And they worked for people like

him," she added, thrusting her chin toward Von Seeckt's back. "My father was with the OSS, and he was there at Dora. He was sent in to find information on what had happened to some OSS and SOE people who had tried to infiltrate Peenemünde during the war to stop the production of the V-2's.

"He told me what it was like at the camp and the way the Allies acted when they arrived—the intelligence people and the war-crimes people showing up and fighting over the German prisoners and how some of the worst were scooped up by the intelligence people and never came to trial. The intelligence people treated the German scientists better than they did the survivors of the camps, because of the knowledge those men possessed. They just stepped over the bodies, I guess."

As Kelly paused to catch her breath, Von Seeckt spoke. "I know *now* what happened at Dora. But I did not know then. I left Peenemünde in spring of 1942. That was before"—his voice broke—"before it got bad."

He held up a hand, forestalling Kelly, who had begun to speak. "But over the years I have asked myself the question: What if I had not been ordered away? What would I have done?"

He turned back to the other three. "I would like to believe I would have acted differently than the majority of my colleagues. But I spoke earlier of the honesty an old man should have. The honesty to come to peace with oneself and one's God—if one believes in a God. And the honest answer I came up with after many years was no, I would not have acted differently. I would not have stood up and spoken out against the evil.

"I know that for certain because I did not do so here, in this country, when I saw things happen out at Area 51. When I heard rumors of what was going on at Dulce."

Von Seeckt slapped his palm on the tabletop. "But now I

am trying to make my peace and be honest. That is why I am here."

"We're all trying to make our own peace," Turcotte said. "Go on with your story. You say you left Peenemünde in the spring of 1942?"

Von Seeckt nodded. "Spring 1942. I remember it well. It was the last spring I spent in Germany. My section chief came to me with orders, reassigning me. I was a very junior member of the research staff and would not be missed. That is why I was selected. When I asked my chief what I would be doing and where I would be going, he laughed and said I was going wherever the Black Jesuit's vision said."

Seeing the uncomprehending looks, Von Seeckt explained. "That is what those on the inside called Himmler: the Black Jesuit." He paused and closed his eyes. "The SS was very much a religious order. They had their own ceremonies and secret rites and sayings. If I was asked by an SS officer why I obeyed, my verbatim answer must be: 'From inner conviction, from my belief in Germany, the Führer, the Movement, and in the SS.' That was our catechism.

"There was much whispered talk of Himmler and the others at the top. Of how they believed in things most did not believe in. Did you know that in the winter of 1941 our troops were sent into Russia without an adequate supply of cold weather equipment? But not because we didn't have cold weather gear sitting in supply depots in Germany, but rather because a seer told Hitler that the winter would be very mild and he believed that. It turned out to be one of the most brutal on record, so tens of thousands of soldiers froze and died because of a vision.

"So my colleagues in the scientific community saw a ridiculous task and they sent the junior man. Ah, but the men I linked up with to carry out this mission, they did not think it a ridiculous task. They had information that they did not share with me. There was no mistaking the seriousness with which they set out to pursue the mission."

Von Seeckt smiled. "I myself got very serious when I found out where our mission was taking us: Cairo, behind enemy lines. All I was told was to be prepared to find and secure something that might be radioactive.

"We traveled by train south to Italy. Then we were taken by submarine across the Mediterranean to Tobruk, where we were put on trucks and given local guides. The British Eighth Army was in disarray and in retreat so it was not as difficult as I had feared for us to infiltrate their lines and make it to Cairo, although there were a few adventures along the way."

Turcotte took a sip of his now cold coffee. The story was interesting but he didn't see how it helped them much with their present situation. And he could tell Kelly was very disturbed by Von Seeckt's revelations about his past. Turcotte himself wasn't happy about the SS connection. Von Seeckt could admit whatever he wanted, but that didn't make it clean as far as Turcotte was concerned. Confession didn't make the crime go away.

"A Major Klein was in charge," Von Seeckt continued. "He did not share his information with us. We went to the west bank of the Nile and then I saw our destination: the Great Pyramid. I was very much confused as I carried my radioactivity detector into the tunnel in the side of the pyramid in the dead of night. Why were we here?

"We went down, and Klein kept turning to a man who had a piece of paper he consulted. The man pointed and Klein ordered his men, a squad of SS storm troopers, to break through a wall. We went through the opening into another tunnel that sloped down. We went through two more walls before we entered a room."

"The bottom chamber," Nabinger said. "Where I found the words."

"Where you found the words," Von Seeckt repeated as a tractor trailer loaded with cattle roared past.

"What did *you* find in the chamber?" Nabinger asked.

"We went down and broke through the final walls into the chamber. There was a sarcophagus there—intact. Klein indicated for me to use my machine. I did and was surprised to see a high level of radiation in the chamber. Not dangerous to humans, but still, it should not have been there. It was much higher than what would be normal background radiation. Klein didn't hesitate. He took a pick and levered off the lid.

"I was stunned when I looked over his shoulder. There was a black metal box in there. I could tell the metal had been carefully tooled and was not the work of ancient Egyptians. How, then, could this have gotten in here? I asked myself.

"I had no time to think on it. Klein ordered me to take up the box and I did, putting it in a backpack. It was bulky but not overly heavy. Perhaps forty pounds. I was much stronger in those days.

"We left the pyramid the same way we had come in. We linked up with our two trucks and headed west while we still had darkness to cover our movement. At daylight we hid in the dunes. We had the two Arab guides that had stayed with the trucks to show us the way and they took us west.

"On the third night they led us right into an ambush." Von Seeckt shrugged. "I do not know if it was deliberate. The Arabs—they always worked for whoever would pay them the most. It was not uncommon for the same guides to be working for both sides. It does not really matter.

"The lead truck took a direct hit from a British tank. There were bullets tearing through the canvas sides of the truckbed I was in. I dived down next to the box. That was my job—protect the box. Klein was next to me. He pulled out a grenade, but he must have been shot before he could throw it because he dropped it and it fell next to me. I pushed it away—out of the back onto the sand, where it exploded. Then there were British Tommies everywhere. Klein was still alive. He tried to fight, but they shot him many times. They took me and they took the box."

Turcotte interrupted. "Klein didn't drop that grenade."

"Excuse me?" Von Seeckt was out of his story momentarily.

Turcotte was looking out the door down the road, where the cattle truck was a disappearing spot on the horizon. "Klein was under orders to kill you and destroy the box."

"How do you know that?" Von Seeckt asked.

"It might have been fifty years ago, but many things don't change. If they couldn't get the box home safely, then they most certainly didn't want the other side to get it or the knowledge you possessed. That's the way any mission like yours would have worked. The British did the same thing when they sent specialists over to look at German radar sites along the French Coast during the war. Their security men had orders to kill the specialists rather than allow them to be captured because of their knowledge of British radar systems."

Von Seeckt nodded. "After all these years, do you know, that never occurred to me? It should have, after all I have seen since."

"All that is fine and well," Nabinger said impatiently, "but not important right now. What is important is—what was in the box?"

"The box was sealed when we found it and Klein refused to allow me to open it. As my friend Captain Turcotte so aptly has noted, Klein was a stickler for following orders.

"The British took me, and the box, and I was hustled away. First back to Cairo. Then on a plane. . . ." Von

Seeckt paused. "Suffice it to say I eventually ended up in England in the hands of the SOE."

"SOE?" Nabinger asked.

"Special Operations Executive," Kelly said.

Von Seeckt nodded. "Quite correct, as the English would say. They interrogated me, and I told them what I knew. Which wasn't much. They also checked the box for radioactivity. And got a positive reading." He looked at Kelly, sensing her change in mood. "You know something of the SOE?"

"As I said earlier, my father was in the OSS. The American counterpart to the SOE."

Von Seeckt stroked his beard. "That is most intriguing. The SOE turned me over to the OSS. Apparently radioactivity was the Americans' province."

"The British didn't open the box either?" Nabinger was trying very hard to control his patience.

"They *couldn't* open the box," Von Seeckt corrected. "So they shipped me off to the United States. The box was on the same plane. After all, the British did have a war to fight and apparently more important things to attend to. Also, as I was to find out, radioactivity *was* the province of the Americans."

"Did the box ever get opened?" Nabinger almost groaned the question.

"Yes, yes, it did," Von Seeckt said. "The Americans did that. They kept me in a place outside of Washington, somewhere out in the country. To this day I could not tell you where it was. The box went somewhere else and I was interrogated. Then they seemed to forget about me for several weeks. One day two men showed up at my jail cell. One was a lieutenant colonel and the other a civilian. They took me to a new place." Von Seeckt pointed to the northeast, along the road. "To Dulce."

"The box?" Nabinger's patience was exhausted.

"There was a small nuclear weapon in the box," Von Seeckt said.

"Oh, fuck," Turcotte said. "What have we gotten into here?"

Nabinger slowly sat back in his seat. "Buried under the Great Pyramid for ten thousand years?"

"Buried under the pyramid for approximately ten thousand years," Von Seeckt confirmed. "Of course, we only guessed in the beginning that that was what it was. The Americans were just at the start of the Manhattan Project at the time, so our knowledge was rather primitive by today's standards. Ten years earlier and we probably would not have had a clue what was in the box.

"We took the bomb apart. Very carefully." Von Seeckt chuckled. "The Americans always thought I knew more than I knew. After all, I had been found with the damn thing. But the longer I was there, the more I *did* know as we worked. Even with today's technology, though, I do not believe they are able to make a bomb as small and lightweight and efficient as that one we worked on. It was amazing. There were parts that I still don't understand. But we were able to learn enough from it—along with the work being done in other places—to put together the bombs we did use to end that war."

"So this bomb from the pyramid—it was from the same people who built these disks and the mothership?" Nabinger's question was rhetorical. "That raises so many questions and issues about the pyramid and why it was built. Perhaps—"

"Professor." Turcotte's voice cut through like the cold wind that was blowing in the door. "Those questions can wait. Right now we need to get a little farther up the road. It's not that far to Dulce, and we have to wait until dark to try anything, but I'd like to take a look around during daylight. You can discuss this on the way."

As Von Seeckt and Nabinger climbed into the back of the van, Kelly tapped Turcotte on the arm and leaned close. "Did you ever see this mothership that Von Seeckt is so worried about?"

"No. I only saw the smaller bouncers." Turcotte looked at her. "Why?"

"Because we only have Von Seeckt's word that it exists. And his story about what he admits to doing during World War II doesn't thrill me. What if there's more that he's not telling us? He was SS, for Christ's sake."

"Is there anything specific that makes you doubt his story about what is going on now?" Turcotte asked.

"I've learned to question things, and my question is, if the mothership doesn't exist, then maybe this whole thing is a setup. And even if it does exist, maybe this whole thing is a setup."

"A setup for what?" Turcotte asked.

"If I knew that, I'd know if it was a setup," Kelly said.

A small smile crept along Turcotte's lips. "I like that. Paranoid thinking. Makes me feel almost sane."

"Next chance we get, I'll tell you my story, and you'll understand why I'm paranoid."

THE CUBE, AREA 51

"General." Dr. Slayden inclined his head toward Gullick, then took in the other people in the room. "Gentlemen and lady."

Slayden was an old man, formerly the second oldest on the committee after Von Seeckt, now the oldest with the one empty chair on the right side of the table. Slayden was bald and his forehead was wrinkled. His major distinguishing feature was his bushy white eyebrows, quite startling given his naked skull.

General Gullick had always thought Slayden a worthless member of Majic-12, but Duncan's visit had forced him to search for ways to gain time. The psychologist had been the answer.

Slayden began. "There have been numerous movies and books published in the field of science fiction about the reaction of people on Earth to alien contact—either here on Earth if the aliens come to us or in the future when we expand to the stars. There have, in fact, been several government work groups over the last several decades dedicated to projecting possible reactions to contact with extraterrestrial life forms.

"While Project Blue Book was the Air Force's official watchdog for unidentified flying objects, there were classified study groups composed of social psychologists and military representatives, whose purpose was to prepare contingency plans for alien contact. These projects fell under the province of DARPA—the Defense Advanced Research Projects Agency. I was one of the original members of DARPA's contact committee.

"The problem we were given was initially a theoretical one." Slayden smiled. "Of course, at the time, we on the committee did not know of the existence of this facility. We were also severely restricted by ethical and security considerations. We were working with the subject of large-group dynamics: how the people of Earth would respond to an outside entity. The ability to conduct realistic experimentation was almost nil. In fact our most valid research data base was the public reaction to the broadcast of *The War of the Worlds* by Orson Welles in 1938.

"The major result of that broadcast was mass hysteria and fear. As this chart shows . . ."

As Slayden went through his reportoire, General Gullick shifted his attention to the computer screen built into the desktop in front of him. Everyone around the table already knew that what Slayden was saying was unimportant. Everyone, that is, except Dr. Duncan—that was the whole purpose of this briefing.

There was nothing new from the *Lincoln* task force on the foo fighters and nothing on Von Seeckt and the other three targets. Gullick reluctantly returned his attention to the briefing.

"However, no one had ever really considered the possibility of our exposure to alien life coming in the form of the discovery of the bouncers and mothership—a sort of archaeological discovery of extraterrestrial life. There have been people, most labeled crackpots, who have pointed to various artifacts and symbols on the planet as signs that we have been visited in the past by alien life forms. The bouncers and mothership are incontrovertible proof that this has happened. This presents us with several challenges but also a great opportunity."

Slayden had forgotten that this was mainly a propaganda briefing for Duncan, and he was totally immersed in his material. "You see, one of the greatest uncontrolled variables in contact theory was that the contact would occur at the discretion of the extraterrestrials. That they would come to us. Or that the discovery of evidence that the planet had been visited in the past by aliens would hit the news in an uncontrolled manner. Here at Area 51, though, we control that variable. We have the evidence and it is at our discretion that the information be revealed. Because we control that variable, we can also prepare both ourselves and the public for the moment of disclosure."

Slayden looked at Duncan. "You may have noticed over the course of the last several years an increasing number of reports in the news media about Area 51. These reports did not start in a vacuum. We have done many things to deliberately lay the groundwork for the public to accept the revelation of what we have here.

"Contrary to what the press has reported, our security here has been designed not to keep observers out, but to actually *allow* observers to see what we want them to see. We could have easily blocked access to all vantage points into the Groom Lake area. Instead we put holes in our security net at certain times and places and allowed designated visual and auditory stimuli to be observed and recorded.

"We also used agents of misinformation. One noted example is a man called Steve Jarvis, who has claimed for years to have worked out here at Area 51. In reality, Jarvis is an agent of ours who reveals information to media people. Some of the information he gives is actually true, some is false. All of it is specifically designed to prepare people to accept without fear what we have here.

"We actually even ran a small test of disclosure several years ago when the Air Force rolled out the F-117 Stealth fighter and displayed it publicly. There was no valid military or security reason to reveal the existence of the Stealth fighter. In fact, the Air Force vigorously fought the disclosure. However, the operation was done to test media and popular reaction to a government revelation of something the government had previously kept secret from the populace.

"As you can see from my data on that . . ."

Gullick remembered that event well. The Air Force had screamed bloody murder about publicizing the F-117. But the interesting thing to Gullick was that Slayden and his spin doctors had turned the tables on the Air Force General Staff, pointing out to them the beneficial possibilities disclosure would bring in the arena of budgeting with Congress. In the end the Air Force had been enthusiastic about the event. Gullick wasn't foolish enough to believe, though, that the F-117 disclosure was anything like announcing the existence of the mothership. It sure sounded good, though.

Of course, Slayden was only giving Duncan the tip of the iceberg. Slayden and his people had early on presented one of the truths of psychological preparation: overstimulation. And making people believe the truth to be much worse than it really was, was one of the major purposes of the Nightscape missions.

Nightscape had conducted numerous animal mutilations, rural overflights by the disks, and even human abductions. There was no way they would let Duncan know about that. And even Slayden didn't know the extent of Nightscape; he didn't know of the need at Dulce for the people who were abducted or the animal parts that were brought back. Gullick rubbed the right side of his skull, irritated at the timbre of Slayden's voice. Goddamn academic assholes. Gullick checked his screen one more time, looking for an update on the search for both the foo fighters and Von Seeckt's group.

Gullick looked across the conference table at Duncan. He was disgusted with outsiders whining and complaining about government secrecy and security. He thought it the most amazing paradox and could not understand why others didn't see it the way he did: If the public could handle knowing everything, then there wouldn't be any need for the secrecy because the world would be living in harmony. It was the same people who decried the government that made the government necessary. If they all had the self-discipline that he and other military people had, the world would be a hell of a better place, Gullick thought as he waited impatiently for the briefing to be over so he could get back to real work.

24

They still had the same van. Kelly had argued to ditch it, but Turcotte insisted they might need the equipment. They'd compromised by switching the government license plate for a private one.

Kelly had assumed driving chores and watched in the rearview mirror as Turcotte sat in one of the four captain's chairs in the back, beside the communication and computer console that took up most of the left side. They both were listening as Von Seeckt and Nabinger put together what they had shared and tried to postulate some reasonable theories to explain what they had.

"We have to assume that the bomb you found in the pyramid was of the same technology as the disk and mothership," Nabinger said.

Von Seeckt nodded. "Yes, that is reasonable."

"Going beyond that, I think that many of the commonalities among ancient civilizations can now be explained." Nabinger took out of his backpack the papers Slater had given him. "The high rune language that has been found at various spots across the world must have originated with these aliens. In fact, I would say that these aliens must have affected the natural progression of mankind's development." He then proceeded to explain the diffusionest theory of the rise of civilization.

When he'd finished Von Seeckt was deep in thought. "I have thought about this often over the years, wondering who left this marvelous technology behind and why. About ten thousand years ago there was an alien outpost on this planet. It was—"

"Why aliens?" Turcotte asked suddenly, echoing the question that had popped up in Kelly's head.

"Excuse me?" Von Seeckt said.

"Why does it have to be aliens? All along everyone is assuming that these craft were left by another species, but why couldn't they have been developed by some ancient civilization of man that perished, and we're the recycles?"

Nabinger smiled. "I have considered that, but the facts argue against it's being even a remote possibility. The level of civilization needed to develop craft such as they have out at Area 51 would have left much more of a trace than simply those craft and the bomb found under the Great Pyramid. We have been scouring the surface of the planet for a long time. Certainly an advanced human civilization would have left more of a trace. No, these things had to have come from an alien culture."

In the rearview mirror Kelly could see Turcotte raise his hands, ceding the point.

"However, it is good that we not close our minds to other possibilities," Von Seeckt said. "As I was saying, it appears that we are back at the original problem. We are not any closer to understanding why the ships were abandoned by the aliens."

"Maybe they had no place to go," Kelly offered. "Maybe their home world was destroyed and they came here on a one-way colonizing mission, and that is why the mothership was hidden in that cave—so they couldn't go back."

"But what about the bouncers?" Turcotte asked. "They

were still capable of flight. Hell, we're flying them now. Surely they wouldn't have hidden them like that."

"And why the bomb hidden in the pyramid?" Kelly asked.

That question was one Nabinger must have been pondering. "No one has ever really determined why the pyramids were built. Originally they were assumed to be burial monuments, but that theory was debunked when no bodies were found in the chambers inside. Then it was assumed they were cenotaphs—monuments to dead pharaohs whose actual burial place was hidden to guard against future grave robbers.

"But with this new information there's another theory we ought to consider. It is a bit strange, but as Doctor Von Seeckt has said, we must consider all possibilities. Let me give you a little information about the construction of the Great Pyramid.

"There are two small tunnels coming out of the uppermost chamber, also known as the king's chamber. The exact purpose of these tunnels is not clear, as they are too small for people to go through. An interesting fact, though, is that if you follow their exact azimuth out to the stars, one is aligned with Alpha Centauri and the other with Alpha Draconis, two nearby star systems."

"Maybe our aliens came from one of those systems," Von Seeckt said.

"Another interesting theory, but one previously considered outrageous," Nabinger said, "is that the pyramids are space beacons. Originally, the entire exterior of all three in the Giza group was covered with very finely crafted flat limestone." He looked at the other two men in the back of the van. "Can you visualize what they must have looked like then?"

Turcotte nodded. "I imagine you would probably have been able to see them from space."

"Visually, yes, when they reflected sunlight," Nabinger said. "But even more importantly, given the angle of the sides of the pyramid, if they are viewed above thirty-eight degrees from the horizon—i.e., from space—they would have painted a radar picture with a directivity factor of over six hundred million for a two-centimeter wavelength."

"Not exactly the Stealth bomber," Turcotte noted.

"No. Such a radar picture could be seen from a long way away from the planet, to say the least." Nabinger leaned forward. "The first question I asked myself when I originally saw the pyramids many years ago was the most basic. Why did the ancient Egyptians choose that form? No one has ever been able to give an adequate reason. If, given the building capability of the time, you wanted to build a massive structure that could be detected from space, the pyramid is the best choice."

The archeologist was warming to his subject matter. "Hell, think about all the other symbols that have been etched into the surface of the Earth by the ancients! The giant bird symbols on plateaus in South America. Symbols in chalk in England. We've always wondered why early man was so intent on drawing symbols that could only be seen from above when they themselves would never have been able to see it from that perspective."

"That still doesn't answer any of the questions that we need answers to," Turcotte said. "If we don't come up with something to support Von Seeckt's contention that the mothership mustn't be flown, all we've done is put ourselves in a deep shit-pile with no way out."

"That is what we will find at Dulce," Von Seeckt said.

"Well, we're just about there," Kelly said. "I hope someone's got a plan."

"I'll have one by the time we get there," Turcotte said, looking in the drawers below the console and checking out some of the equipment stored there. He glanced up at Von Seeckt. "Mind telling us what's at Dulce?"

Kelly nodded slightly to herself. She was beginning to like Turcotte more and more. There was a lot of fog swirling about this situation: different agendas by the four people in this van, unclear government objectives, secrets piled on top of secrets. She just wanted Johnny and then she was going to break this wide open. To get Johnny, though, she was going to have to trust Turcotte's skills. She knew that Turcotte was going to have to trust Von Seeckt to the same degree—and he didn't. She didn't either. Her reporter's sixth sense told her the old man was holding back.

"I told you," Von Seeckt said. "It is another government installation, an offshoot of the installation at Area 51."

"Have you ever been there?" Turcotte asked.

"I told you. Once. Just after the end of World War II. It was very long ago and my memories are not that good."

"I know you said that," Turcotte said. "And I asked you again because I don't understand why you never went there again if this place was such an important part of Majic-12 and you were one of the founding members of the board, so to speak."

The sound of the van engine and the tires rolling sounded abnormally loud in the silence. Kelly decided to see if she could keep the ball rolling. "Want to hear what is suspected to go on there?" she called out.

"I'd appreciate any information, even rumors, at this point," Turcotte said.

Kelly brought her research to the forefront of her brain. "Among the UFO community it's said that Dulce is the site of a bioengineering lab. That it's a place where our government turns over people to the aliens whose craft we are flying at Area 51. We know the first part is true."

"And we know the part about turning people over to aliens isn't true," Turcotte noted.

"Are you sure?" Kelly asked.

"No, it cannot be!" Von Seeckt cried out. "I would have known if we'd had contact with whoever left the bouncers and mothership. We would not have had to struggle so hard for so many years. We just got into the mothership this past year. It sat for so long, a puzzle we couldn't break."

"Maybe something changed this year," Kelly suggested. She had Von Seeckt off balance and she knew from experience that she had to keep up the pressure. "I have heard that the government is doing testing on mind control at Dulce. They are supposedly working with memory-affecting drugs and EDOM."

"What's EDOM?" Turcotte asked.

"Electronic dissolution of memory," Kelly said. "I did an article on it a few years back. Of course, the people I interviewed were only talking about it theoretically, but it always seems that our government likes to take theory and see if it can work. EDOM is used to cause selective amnesia. It creates acidic croline, which blocks the transmission of nerve impulses, which in the brain stops the transmission of thought in the affected area."

"Ever hear of that?" Turcotte asked Von Seeckt.

"I have heard . . ." Von Seeckt began, then he paused. When he spoke again, his voice was hesitant. "I will tell you the truth. I will tell you why I never went back to Dulce after my visit in 1946."

They all waited.

"Because I knew who was working there." Von Seeckt's voice dripped disgust. "I met them. My fellow Germans. The biological and chemical warfare experts. And they were continuing their experimental work that they had started in the concentration camps. I could not go there. I could not stand to see what they were doing." Von Seeckt told them about Paperclip.

"Surely most of these people are dead now," Kelly said when he was done. "But I imagine that the work is still continuing there and that explains a lot of the Nightscape stuff and why everything is classified. But what's the connection with the mothership?"

"I have not been there, true," Von Seeckt said, "but Gullick and the others he trusted—they traveled to Dulce often. Something changed this year. They changed."

Kelly sensed blood in the water. "Changed? Changed how?"

"They began acting irrationally," Von Seeckt said. "We always had secrecy in Majic-12. And Dulce has existed for many years, as Captain Turcotte says. But something is different now. The urgency to fly the mothership. What is the rush? Even getting into it. For so many years we could not penetrate the skin, then suddenly they pick a certain spot and try a new technique, and they succeed after decades of trying.

"Even how quickly they have mastered the controls and the instruments. It is as if they know much more than they should."

"Could they have broken the code on the high runes?" Nabinger asked. "That would explain some of it."

"Some of it, yes," Von Seeckt agreed. "But I do not think they have broken the code, or if they have, it does not explain why they are acting so strangely and in such a rush." Von Seeckt threw his hands up in the air. "I do not understand."

"Do you know where the facility is?" Turcotte asked.

"Not exactly. Just somewhere on the outside of the town of Dulce. I do remember a large mountain behind the town and that we went around the mountain on a dirt road. Then we went into a tunnel and it was all underground."

Turcotte rubbed his forehead. "So you don't exactly know where it is and you don't exactly know what goes on there?"

"No."

Kelly looked up in the rearview mirror. Turcotte met her eyes, then spoke. "Well, we'll be there shortly. And we'll find out what's going on and get Johnny Simmons out of there."

Kelly opened her mouth to say something, then shut it. She turned her eyes back to the road and drove.

VICINITY, DULCE, NEW MEXICO

Johnny Simmons could see. He didn't know how long ago it had started, but it had begun with the slightest tinge of gray infiltrating the blackness surrounding him. Then the difference between light and dark grew, and he was able to make out some forms moving around on the periphery of his vision. He couldn't move his head, nor could he move his eyes.

But as time went by, he wished the slight improvement that had occurred had not. Because there was something wrong about the forms he caught glimpses of. They were human shaped, but they weren't human and that is what scared him. The silhouetted forms were all wrong—heads too large; arms too long; torsos too short. Once he thought he saw the outline of a hand, but there were six fingers instead of five and the fingers were much too long.

Johnny was concentrating so hard on his eyes that it was a while before he noticed other changes in his environment. There was a scent in the air. A very unpleasant scent. And he could hear sound, albeit as if from a long distance away. It was a clicking sound, but not mechanical. More like insect clicking.

The copper taste flooded Johnny's mouth and his world went black again. But this time he could hear his own screams, sounding as if it were some other person a long way away. But the pain was close.

25

ROUTE 64, NORTHWEST NEW MEXICO
T–79 HOURS

The road curved around a small lake to the left and passed between tree-covered hills. Turcotte checked the map. They were close to Dulce. According to Rand McNally the town was just south of the border with Colorado, nestled between the Carson National Forest and the Rio Grande National Forest. The terrain was rocky and mountainous, with occasional clusters of pine trees adorning the hillsides. It was the sort of relatively unpopulated area the government liked to build secret facilities in.

They hit a straight section of road and a long-distance view opened up directly ahead. Von Seeckt leaned forward between the seats. "There. That mountain to the left. I remember that. The facility is behind it."

A long ridge extended from left to right about ten miles ahead, culminating in a peak slightly separated from the main body of the ridge.

"Where should I go?" Kelly asked.

"Stay on this road," Turcotte said. "I'll tell you where to stop."

As they got closer, the town of Dulce appeared at the base of the ridgeline, a scattering of buildings along the valley floor running up to the base of the large mountain.

Route 64 passed along the south side of the community, and Kelly carefully kept to the speed limit as they drove through. As the town slipped behind them, Turcotte told her to pull off on a dirt road and stop.

"You say the facility is behind that mountain?" he asked Von Seeckt.

"Yes. It was night when I came here and over fifty years ago, though. There wasn't much here in those days. I don't remember all these buildings."

Turcotte looked to the north. "All right. We have about two hours of daylight left. Let's check out what we can see from the van." He pointed back toward town and Kelly turned them around.

They cruised in past the sign marking the city limits and took a right, going past the local elementary school. The road slowly sloped up. Within a quarter mile they were at the base of the ridge. Turcotte kept Kelly taking turns that directed them to the right. It was the only way he could see around the mountain. Left would only run along the south side of the ridgeline.

An arrowhead with a 2 inside it marked a road leading to the northeast. The other roads all appeared to be local residential streets. Kelly turned onto the arrowhead road and they began climbing the shoulder of the mountain. A sign indicated they were now on the Jicarilla Apache Indian Reservation. A white Ford Bronco rolled past with two men seated inside and Turcotte twisted his head and watched it go by.

"Government plates," he noted.

"Yeah," Kelly said.

"Probably from the facility."

"I don't want to burst your bubble," Kelly said, "but you see a lot of U.S. government plates out here. We're on federal land, actually Indian land, but the Bureau of Indian Affairs, which helps run the reservations, is federal."

"But it could be from the base," Turcotte said.

"Ah, optimism," Kelly said, mimicking his Canuck accent. "I like that."

"There." Turcotte pointed to the right shoulder. "Stop there."

The road split. To the right it went down into a valley. To the left a wide, well-maintained gravel road curved along the back of the ridgeline and disappeared.

"It's around there," Turcotte announced firmly.

"Why not to the right?" she asked.

"Von Seeckt said it was behind the mountain. To the right is not behind the mountain." He looked to the back. "Correct?"

Von Seeckt concurred. "I believe to the left."

Turcotte continued. "Also, since we left Phoenix that's the best maintained and widest gravel road I've seen." He smiled. "But mostly, the thing that convinces me that the facility is down that road—besides Von Seeckt's opinion, of course—are those little lines of what appears to be smoke hanging above the road." He pointed to the gravel road. "See them? There and there?"

"Yes. What are they?"

"That's dust caught in a laser beam. A car goes down that road, the beam gets broken and a signal is sent. There's two of them, so they can tell if a vehicle is coming or going depending on the order the beams get broken. I don't think the Bureau of Indian Affairs guards the reservations that tightly, do you?"

"What now?" Kelly asked, glancing over her shoulder at the other two men in the rear.

"I don't think this place will be as well guarded as Area 51," Turcotte said. "All the work here must be done inside, so it obviously doesn't attract as much attention as the other facility. So that's to our advantage.

"The other thing to remember is a basic fact about most

guarded facilities. The goal of a lot of the security is not, as you would think, to prevent someone from actually breaking in. The goal is deterrence: to keep someone from considering breaking in."

"I don't understand," Nabinger said from the rear.

"Think of the security cameras in banks," Turcotte explained. "They work through deterrence. They keep most people from robbing the bank because those people know their picture will get taken and the police will eventually catch them. The same with most security. For example, if I wanted to kill the President, I could most definitely kill him. The problem lies with killing him and getting away afterward."

"So, you're saying we can get in to this facility but we can't get out?" Kelly asked.

"Oh, I think we should be able to get out. It's just that they'll know we did it."

Kelly shrugged. "Hell, that ain't a problem. They're already after us. We get Johnny, we go public. That's the only way we'll make it."

"Right," Turcotte said.

"So, back to my original question," Kelly said. "What now?"

"Back to town," Turcotte said. "We need a ticket to get us in. Once inside I'll get us to Johnny."

"And the high rune tablets," Nabinger added. "Von Seeckt told me that Dulce is where they keep all the ones the government has."

"And the high rune tablets," Turcotte amended. "Whatever you can find."

"Anyplace in particular in town?" Kelly asked as she turned them around and headed to the south.

"Know how cops always hang out at the local doughnut shop?" Turcotte said.

"Yes."

"We need to find where the workers from the base get their doughnuts."

T—73 Hours, 15 Minutes

"That one," Turcotte said. They'd watched a dozen or so cars with small green stickers on the front center of the windshield pull in and out of the convenience-store parking lot over the course of the past several hours. Turcotte had pointed out the stickers and explained that they were decals used to identify cars that had access to government installations. As night had fallen, the lights had come on, illuminating the parking and leaving their van in the darkness across the street.

"I've got him." Kelly started the engine to the van and followed the Suburban out of the parking lot of the Minit Mart.

They followed the truck as it went north through town and then turned onto Reservation Route 2. They were a quarter mile from the split in the road.

"Now," Turcotte ordered.

Kelly flashed her high beams and accelerated until they were right on the bumper of the Suburban. She swung out and passed, Turcotte leaning out the window and giving the finger to the driver of the truck as he screamed obscenities.

Kelly slammed on the brakes and they skidded to a halt at the intersection with the gravel road. The driver of the Suburban came to a stop on the gravel road, headlights pointing at the van.

"What the fuck is your problem, asshole?" the burly driver of the truck demanded as he stepped out and started walking toward the van.

Turcotte jumped out of the passenger side of the van and

met him halfway between the two vehicles, caught in the glow of the headlights.

"You an idiot or what?" the driver demanded. "You pass me and—"

Without a word Turcotte fired the stun gun, dropping the man immediately. He cuffed him with plastic cinches from his vest and dragged the body into the back of the van. "Get into the truck," he ordered Von Seeckt and Nabinger. The two men scuttled over into the backseat of the Suburban.

Kelly drove the van a hundred meters down the tar road, where the turn concealed them from the intersection. There was no place to conceal the van, so she just pulled off to the shoulder. Turcotte made sure the man was secure and quickly frisked him.

"This isn't much of a plan," Kelly muttered as she locked the van and pocketed the keys. "And I'm not sure I buy your easy-to-get-in-and-out theory."

"One of my commanders in the infantry used to say any plan was better than having Rommel stick it up your ass on the drop zone," Turcotte said as they jogged up the road toward the truck.

"I don't get it," Kelly said.

"I never did, either, but it sounded good. What's really interesting," he said, pausing for a second and looking at her in the starlight, "is that you're the first person who ever said that about that quote. I never told my commander I didn't get it."

"And?" Kelly said.

He began jogging again. "It means you listen and you think."

Turcotte took the wheel this time. He scanned the interior and reached above the visor; an electronic card key was there, such as those used in hotels to open doors. He checked the name: Spencer. "The plan is getting better by the minute." He tucked the card between his legs next to the stun gun. "Everyone down. We're going to be on camera in a second."

Throwing the engine into gear, he rolled down the gravel road, past the laser sensors. There was no way he could see it, but he had no doubt that the vehicle was being surveyed by infrared cameras to check for the decal and insure it was authorized. He knew the decal was covered with a fluorescent coating that could easily be seen through such a device. He watched the road carefully, hoping that there would be no more forks where a decision had to be made.

A sign appeared in the headlights warning that they were now entering a federal restricted area and the fine print listed all the dire consequences unauthorized personnel would face and all the constitutional rights that they no longer had. Four hundred meters past the sign a steel bar stretched across the road. A machine such as those used at airports to give out parking tickets was on the left side. Turcotte pulled up and inserted the card key into the slot. The steel bar lifted.

He continued on, then the road split. Turcotte had less than three seconds to make a decision. To the left loomed the mountain. To the right the valley floor. He turned left and immediately was in a narrow valley. The sides closed in and camouflage netting covered the road, staked down on the rock walls on either side, confirming his decision. A thirty-foot-wide opening in the base of the mountain appeared directly ahead, carved into the side of the mountain. A dull red glow came out of the opening.

A bored security guard in a booth just inside the cave opening hardly looked up, waving the Suburban in. A large parking garage was off to the right and Turcotte turned that way. The man-made cave was dimly lit by red lights. That was both to defeat detection from the outside by not having bright white light coming out of the entrance, and also to allow people to begin getting their night sight when departing.

The slots were numbered, but Turcotte took his chances and went to the far end, out of sight of the guard, and parked. There were about ten other cars in the garage. Over fifty spaces were empty, which meant that the night shift was a skeleton crew, for which Turcotte was grateful.

There was a pair of sliding doors set in the rock twenty feet from where he had parked. "Let's go."

Turcotte glanced over his shoulder at the three people following him—Kelly short and compact, Von Seeckt leaning on his cane, and Nabinger bringing up the rear. Kelly smiled at him. "Lead on, fearless one."

He slid the card key into the slot on the side of the elevator. The doors slid open. They crowded inside and Turcotte examined the buttons. They ranged from HP, Garage, down through sublevels 4 to 1. "I'd say *HP* stands for 'helipad.' They probably have one cut into the side of the mountain or maybe even on the top of the mountain above us. Any idea what floor we should go to?" he asked Von Seeckt.

The old man shrugged. "They had stairs when I was here last, but we did go down."

"I'd say bottom level," Kelly suggested. "The greater the secret, the deeper you go."

"Real scientific," Turcotte muttered. He hit sublevel 1. The elevator dropped, the lights on the wall flashed, then halted at sublevel 2. A message appeared on the digital display above the number lights:

ACCESS TO SUBLEVEL 1 LIMITED TO
AUTHORIZED PERSONNEL ONLY.
TOP SECRET Q LEVEL CLEARANCE REQUIRED.
DUAL ACCESS MANDATORY.
INSERT ACCESS KEYS NOW.

Turcotte looked at the two small openings—made for small round objects—one just below the digital display and the other on the far wall. They were far enough apart that one person could not operate both keys—just like the launch systems of ICBM. "I don't have the keys for that, and our Mr. Spencer didn't have them on him either."

"Let's try this level," Kelly suggested.

Turcotte pressed the open button and the doors slid apart, revealing a small foyer and another door and another warning sign:

SUBLEVEL 2
AUTHORIZED PERSONNEL ONLY.
RED CLEARANCE REQUIRED.

An opening for a card key to be passed through was just below the sign. Turcotte held up the card key he'd appropriated from the Suburban. It was orange. "We're still out of the depth of Mr. Spencer's security range." He stepped forward and shrugged off the small backpack he had on. "But I think I can handle this little roadblock." He removed a small black box.

"What's that?" Kelly asked.

"Something I found in the van. They had all sorts of goodies back there." A card key was attached to the box by several wires. Turcotte slid it into the slot in the direction opposite that indicated by the arrow. "It reads the door code backward, memorizes it, and then reverses the code. I've used similar devices in some of my other assignments." He slid it down in the proper direction and the two doors slip open to reveal a guard seated at a desk ten feet away.

"Hey!" the guard yelled, bounding to his feet.

Turcotte dropped the box and reached for the stun gun. It got caught in his pocket and he abandoned the effort, sprinting forward. The guard's gun had just cleared his hol-

ster when Turcotte jumped into the air, feet leading, and
flew over the desk. The bottom of his boots caught the
guard in the chest, knocking him back against the wall.

Turcotte was back on his feet first and he slammed a turn
kick into the side of the guard's skull, knocking him out.
He turned to the desktop and looked at the computer
screen that was built into it. It showed a schematic, with
rooms labeled and green lights in each little box. The others quickly gathered around.

"Archives," Turcotte said, resting a finger on a room. He
looked up at Nabinger and Von Seeckt. "That's yours." He
reached into his pocket and pulled out the stun gun. "You
meet anyone, use this. Just aim and pull the trigger, the
gun does the rest. You've got five minutes. Then be back
here whether you found what you're looking for or not."

Nabinger oriented himself with the diagram and looked
down the corridor. "Right. Let's go." He headed off with
Von Seeckt.

Turcotte pointed. "I'd say your friend is in one of these
two places." One was labeled HOLDING AREA and the other
BIOLAB.

"Biolab," Kelly said.

They sprinted in the opposite direction from the one
Von Seeckt and Nabinger had taken. The hall was quiet
and they passed several doors with nameplates on the outside—obviously offices for the people who worked here in
the daytime.

"Left," Kelly said. A set of swinging double doors waited
at the end of a short corridor. They halted and Kelly
arched her eyebrows at Turcotte in question as they heard
someone cough on the other side.

"We charge," Turcotte whispered.

"You don't have much of a tactical reportoire," Kelly
replied quietly.

Turcotte pushed the doors open and stepped in. A middle-aged woman in a white coat was bent over a large chest-high rectangular black object. Her hair was pulled back tight in a bun and she peered up over a pair of glasses.

"Who are you?" she demanded.

"Johnny Simmons?" Turcotte asked.

"What?" the woman replied, but Turcotte caught the shift of her eyes to the black object.

He walked past her and looked down. It reminded him of an oversized coffin. There was a panel on the top—what the woman had been looking at. "What is this?" he asked.

"Who are you people?" The woman looked past them at the door. "What are you doing here?"

There were a number of cables coming out of the ceiling, going into the black top. Some of the cables were clear and there was fluid in them. He turned on the woman. "Get him out of there."

"Johnny's in there?" Kelly stared at the casing. She walked over and picked up a clipboard hanging on a hook. She checked the papers on it.

"Someone's in there," Turcotte said. "Those are IV tubes. I don't know what they're carrying, but someone's in there on the receiving end."

"It's Johnny," Kelly said, holding up the clipboard.

"Get him out of there," Turcotte repeated.

"I don't know who you are," the woman began, "but—"

Turcotte slid his Browning High Power out of its holster. He pulled the hammer back with his thumb. "You got five seconds or I put a round through your left thigh."

The woman glared at him. "You wouldn't dare!"

"He would," Kelly said. "And if he didn't, I would. Open it!"

"One. Two. Three." Turcotte dropped the barrel and aimed at the woman's leg.

"All right. All right!" The woman held up her hands.

"But I can't just open it. The shock will kill the obj—" She caught herself. "The patient. I have to do this in proper procedure."

"How long?" Turcotte asked.

"Fifteen minutes to—"

"Make it five."

At the other end of this level of the facility Von Seeckt and Professor Nabinger were staring at an intellectual treasure trove. The archives had been dark when they opened the doors. When Nabinger hit the lights, a room full of large filing cabinets had come into view. Opening drawers, they found photos. The drawers were labeled with numbers that meant nothing to the two men. At the far end of the room there was a vault door with a small glass window. Von Seeckt peered through. "The original stone tablets from the mothership cavern are in there," he said. "But they must have photographs of them in these cabinets."

Nabinger was already opening drawers. "Here's the same high runes from the site in Mexico that Slader showed me," Nabinger said, holding up large ten-by-fifteen-inch glossies.

"Yes, yes," Von Seeckt said absently, throwing open drawer after drawer. "We need to find ones she didn't show you—the ones from the mothership cavern. I do not believe our Captain Turcotte will have much patience once his five-minute limit is up."

Nabinger started going through drawers more quickly.

The woman's hands shook as she worked on the panel. Most of the cables had been disconnected and she was checking some readings.

"What did you people do to him?" Kelly asked.

"It's complicated," the woman said.

"E-D-O-M?" Kelly spelled out the letters.

The woman stiffened. "How do you know of that?"

"Finish the job," Turcotte said.

The woman hit a key and the box began beeping. "It will be safe to open in thirty seconds."

Von Seeckt had paused at one drawer, looking at the photos more carefully. At the end of the aisle Nabinger was moving on to the next cabinet when he noticed something in a glass cabinet on the wall. He moved over and stared at the object inside.

Von Seeckt held up a handful of pictures. "These are the photos from the mothership cavern! Let us rejoin the good captain."

The beeping stopped and the woman pointed at a lever on the side of the box. "Lift that."

Turcotte grabbed the red handle and pulled it up. With a hiss the lid came up, revealing a naked Johnny Simmons submerged inside a pool of dark-colored liquid. Needles were stuck in both arms and tubes led to his lower body. A tube was inserted in his mouth, a clear plastic-type material wrapped around the tube and molded to his face, ensuring a seal to keep the fluid out.

"I have to remove the oxygen tube and the catheters and IVs," the woman said.

"Do it." Turcotte said. He turned as Von Seeckt and Nabinger appeared in the doorway. Nabinger's hands were bleeding and he held something wrapped in his jacket.

"You were not at—" Von Seeckt halted in midsentence when he saw the body inside the black box. "Ah, these people! They never stopped. They never stopped."

"Enough," Turcotte ordered. The woman was done. He leaned over and scooped Johnny up. "Let's go."

"What do I do with her?" Kelly asked.

"Kill her," Turcotte snapped as he headed out the door.

Kelly looked at the woman.

"Please don't," the woman begged.

"The change starts here," Kelly said. She shot the woman with the stun gun, then hurried after the others. They piled into the elevator. Turcotte leaned Johnny up against the wall and Kelly kneeled to support him.

Turcotte punched in the button labeled G and the elevator rose. He poked Nabinger in the chest. "You and Kelly carry him out to the van."

"What are you doing?" Kelly asked.

"My job," Turcotte said. "I'll link up with you in Utah. Capitol Reef National Park. It's small. I'll find you."

"Why aren't you going with us?" Kelly demanded.

"I'm going to see what's on sublevel one," Turcotte said. "Plus, I'll create a diversion so you can get away." He hustled them out into the garage, then stepped back into the elevator.

"But—" The shutting doors cut off the rest of her words.

Turcotte punched in sublevel 2 and the elevator went back down to where he had just left. The doors opened on the unconscious guard. Turcotte ran out and grabbed the guard's body. He dragged the body back, wedging it in the doorway to keep the doors from shutting. Then he shrugged off the backpack of gear he had appropriated from the van. He knew it was only a matter of time before some alarm was raised. They had to have some sort of internal checks with the guards, and when the sublevel 2 guard didn't respond . . . well, then things would get exciting.

He laid out two one-pound charges of C-6 explosive he'd found in the van on the carpeted floor of the elevator. He molded the puttylike material into two foot-long half circles, placing them about two and a half feet apart in the center of the floor. He pushed a nonelectric blasting cap into each charge. He'd crimped detonating cord into each fuse in the van, so all he had to do was tie the loose ends of the det cord together with a square knot, leaving enough to put on the M60 fuse igniter. The igniter was about six inches long by an inch in diameter with a metal ring at the opposite end from the det cord.

The det cord was just long enough for him to step outside the elevator doors. He pulled the unconscious guard out of the way and held one of the doors open with his left hand. Then he checked his watch. It had been almost five minutes since he'd let the others out in the garage. They ought to be getting near the metal gate. He'd give them another two minutes, then showtime. The seconds dragged by slowly.

Time. Turcotte put the M60 in his mouth, clamping down on it with his teeth. He pulled the metal ring with his right hand.

The detonating cord burned at twenty thousand feet per second. The result was that Turcotte was still pulling when the charges exploded. He threw down the igniter and stepped into the elevator. A three-foot hole was in the floor. Turcotte jumped in, falling ten feet, landing on the concrete bottom of the elevator shaft. He heard alarms screaming in the distance.

The sublevel elevator doors were at waist level. Turcotte reached up and jammed his fingers between them and pulled. He felt some of the stitches Cruise had put in his side pop. The doors grudgingly gave six inches, then the emergency program kicked in and they began opening of their own accord.

Turcotte had his Browning out in his right hand as he peeked up over the lip. There were two guards standing in the corridor and they were ready, the explosion having alerted them. Bullets ripped in above Turcotte's head. He ducked and heard the rounds thump into the wall above his head. He removed a flash-bang grenade from his pocket, pulled the pin, and tossed it toward the sound of the guns. He squeezed his eyes shut and put his hands over his ears.

As soon as he felt the concussion, he sprang up. In his last assignment Turcotte had fired thousands of rounds from the pistol every day. It was an extension of his body and he could put a round into a quarter-sized circle at twenty-five feet.

One guard was kneeling, submachine gun dangling on the end of its sling, his hands rubbing his eyes. The other still had his weapon ready but was disoriented, facing toward the wall, blinking and shaking his head. Turcotte fired twice, hitting the first man in the center of his forehead, throwing the body back. The next round hit the second man in the temple. As he keeled over, his dead finger jerked back on the trigger, sending a stream of bullets into the wall.

Turcotte slowly slid on his belly up into the corridor. He got to his feet, staying low in a crouch. The hall extended about sixty feet, to a dead end. There were several doors to the left and another corridor turning to the right. There were red lights flashing and a teeth-jarring low-frequency siren wailing. One of the doors to the left opened and Turcotte snapped a shot in that direction, causing whoever it was to slam the door shut. There were name plaques next to each door on the left and Turcotte surmised that those rooms were quarters for sublevel 1 staff.

He abandoned his cautious approach and ran forward, turning the corner to the right. The hall he faced was ten feet long, ending in a double set of doors with more dire warnings in red posted on them. Turcotte pushed the doors open and stepped in. The rough concrete floor angled down to a large cavern carved out of the mountain. The ceiling was twenty feet high and the far wall a hundred meters away. What caught Turcotte's attention first were several dozen large vertical vats that were full of some am-

ber-colored liquid and each one holding something in it.
Turcotte stepped up to the nearest one and peered in. He
recoiled as he recognized what was a human being. There
were tubes coming in and out of the body and the entire
head was encased in a black bulb with numerous wires
going into it. It reminded Turcotte of what had been done
to Johnny Simmons, except on a more sophisticated level.

A golden glow to the right caught Turcotte's attention.
He ran in that direction and stopped in surprise as he
cleared the last vat. The glow came from the surface of a
small pyramid, about eight feet high and four feet across
each base side.

Several cables hanging from the ceiling were hooked
into it, but it was the texture of the surface that caught and
held Turcotte's attention. It was perfectly smooth and solid
appearing. The surface seemed to be some sort of metal
and when Turcotte touched it, it was cool and as unyielding
as the hardest steel. Yet the glow seemed to come right out
of the material.

There were markings all over it. Turcotte recognized the
high rune writing from the photos Nabinger had shown
him.

There was a noise. Turcotte spun and fired. A guard
racing through the double doors returned fire with a submachine gun, his rounds hitting several of the vats, shattering glass, the liquid pouring out. The man was disoriented
by the layout of the room and had fired instinctively at the
sound of Turcotte's gun.

Turcotte fired again, more carefully, and hit the man
twice, killing him. He felt nothing. He was in action mode,
taking care of what needed to be done. He needed information and he had plenty from what he had seen in this
room. He didn't expect any more guards soon. One of the
Catch-22's of a place like this was that the more guards you
had, the more people you had who were security risks. This

time of night he didn't think there was a platoon of men hanging around "just in case."

A humming noise drew his attention back to the pyramid. A golden glow was flowing out of the apex, forming a three-foot-diameter circle in the air above. Turcotte staggered back. His head felt as if an ax had split his brain from ear to ear. He turned and ran, heading away from the corridor he'd come down. When he'd first come into the room he'd realized they hadn't gotten all this equipment in here through the elevator he'd destroyed. There had to be another way. He fought to keep his concentration against the tidal wave of pain that surged through his skull.

The floor began sloping up again. A large vertical door beckoned. Turcotte grabbed the strap on the bottom of it and pulled up. It lifted to reveal a large freight elevator. Stepping in, he pulled the door back down and checked the control panel. It had the same two-key system, but the keys were only needed to go down. He punched in HP and the floor jerked.

The pain in his head slowly subsided as he got farther away from sublevel 1. He went up past 2, 3, then 4. The parking garage passed by, then almost ten seconds of movement passed until the light came on for HP. The elevator came to a halt. Turcotte pulled up on the inside strap and the door opened onto a large bay carved into the side of the mountain. Camouflage netting overhung the open end and the place was dimly lit with red night-lights. Crates and boxes were stacked about. If there had been a guard up here he must have responded to the alarm on the lower level, because the place was deserted. Turcotte ran across to the netting and peered out. A steel platform large enough to take the biggest helicopter in the inventory had been erected out there. He walked out onto it. The side of the mountain was very steep here. Turcotte looked down. The valley below was in darkness, giving no idea how far down it went. Eight hundred feet above, the top of the mountain was silhouetted against the light of the moon. Turcotte slid over the edge of the platform onto the rock-and-dirt mountainside and began climbing.

After a few minutes he could see lights moving in the valley below. Reinforcements. It would take them a while to get air assets in—he hoped. Having been in Special Operations for years, Turcotte knew that there just weren't packs of men sitting around with high-speed helicopters waiting around every corner.

He moved from rock to rock, clinging to bushes at times. He'd learned mountain climbing during a tour in Germany and this slope wasn't technically very difficult. The darkness was a bit of a problem, but his eyes were adjusting.

He reached the top of the mountain after forty-five minutes. He turned to the west, following the ridgeline that he had seen coming into town during the day. He moved quicker now that he was gradually descending. His head still hurt, feeling as if a massive headache was worming its way around his head, moving from section to section. What had that pyramid been? It definitely wasn't man-made. He knew it was connected to the bouncers and mothership. But how was it connected to the bodies in the vats? What the hell was going on down there?

He saw the lights of Dulce to his left and he curved downslope in that direction, heading for the western edge of town. As the ridgeline leveled out to valley floor he passed the first houses. An occasional dog barked, but Turcotte moved swiftly, not worried right now about the locals.

He spotted a pay phone outside a closed bowling area and jogged up to it. He picked up the receiver and dialed the number Dr. Duncan had given him. After the second ring a mechanical device informed that the number was no longer in service. Turcotte pushed down the metal lever, disconnecting. Then he dialed a new number with a 910 area code. Fort Bragg, North Carolina.

A sleepy voice answered. "Colonel Mickell."

"It's Mike Turcotte, sir."

The voice woke up. "Jesus, Turc, what the fuck have you done?"

Turcotte leaned against the phone booth, energy draining out of his body. "I don't know, sir. I don't know what's going on. What have you heard?"

"I haven't heard shit except somebody wants your ass bad. One of those agencies with a whole bunch of letters has put out a classified 'grab and hold' on you. I about shit when I saw it come through in my reading file."

Mickell was the deputy commander of the Special Forces Training Command at Fort Bragg and an old friend.

"Can you help me, sir?"

"What do you need?"

"I need to find out if someone is for real and, if she is, how to contact her."

"Give me her name."

"Duncan. Dr. Lisa Duncan. She told me she was the President's adviser to a thing called Majic-12."

Mickell whistled. "Oh, man, you're in some deep stuff. How do I reach you?"

"You don't, sir. I'll get back in contact with you."

"Watch your butt, Turc."

"Yes, sir."

Turcotte slowly hung up the phone. He wasn't one hundred percent certain that Mickell would back him up. He didn't know why Duncan's number didn't work. The only means of communication she'd given him as he went undercover and it had been out now for a couple of days. Not good. Not good at all. He'd just killed three men this evening. "Fuck," Turcotte muttered. *What the hell was that pyramid?*

Turcotte rubbed his forehead. He'd played his last cards. When it got down to it, he had to admit that the only people he could trust right now were heading for Utah and the rendezvous he had planned. He didn't want to go there, but it was the only place he could go.

He looked about. There was a pickup truck parked on the street. Goddamn, his head hurt. Turcotte drew deep inside, relying on years of harsh training. He drew up strength where most would find nothing. And headed for the pickup truck.

26

ROUTE 64, NORTHWEST NEW MEXICO
T—70 HOURS, 40 MINUTES

Johnny Simmons started screaming and Kelly's best efforts couldn't stop it. She wrapped her arms around him and held him tight, whispering words of comfort in his ear.

Getting out of the facility had been even easier than getting in. They'd piled into the Suburban, driven out past the unsuspecting guard, and linked back up with the van. Returning the still-unconscious driver to his own truck, they'd jumped into the van and driven back down through town and turned left on Route 64.

"Can't you keep him quiet?" Von Seeckt asked from the driver's seat, checking the rearview mirror.

"I'd be screaming too," Kelly answered, "if I'd been locked in that thing for four days. You just drive. No one can hear him except us."

Johnny quieted down and appeared to fall asleep or, Kelly thought, slip into unconsciousness. She turned to Nabinger, who had his hands wrapped in a bloodstained towel. Kelly pulled out the first-aid kit. "What happened to you, Professor?"

"There was something I had to get and it was in a glass case. I couldn't find a key so I broke the glass," Nabinger replied.

"Couldn't you have used something other than your hand to break the glass?" Kelly asked as she pulled out the gauze and tape.

"I was in a hurry," Nabinger replied. After a moment's silence he added, "I wasn't thinking about my hands."

"What was so important?" Kelly inquired.

Nabinger carefully unwrapped something from his jacket. He held a piece of wood, slightly curved, about two feet long by one foot high and an inch thick. Even in the dim light in the back of the van she could see that it was covered with small carved characters.

"It's a *rongorongo* tablet from Easter Island," Nabinger said. "Do you know how rare these are? Only twenty-one are known to be in existence. This must be one that was secreted away."

Kelly pointed at the eight-by-ten glossies that the two men had gathered. "What are those?"

Nabinger reluctantly looked from the tablet to the table, where the photos were piled. "Von Seeckt told me those are the photographs taken by the first team to enter the mothership cavern. They found flat stones with high runes."

"What do they say?" Kelly asked as she finished one hand and began working on the other.

Nabinger looked at the photos. "Well, it's not like reading the newspaper, you know. This will take time."

"Well, you've got some time, so get to work," Kelly said as she finished the second hand, then picked up a road map. She found where they had to meet Turcotte. "You've got all night," she announced. "I think we should get off this main road and take back roads through the mountains, heading west until we get to the linkup spot."

"How soon do you think they'll be after us?" Nabinger asked.

"They're *already* after us," Kelly said. "After us following this latest escapade, you mean. I think we'll be okay. I just hope Turcotte made it out all right."

"I am not concerned about them being after us," Von Seeckt said. "I am concerned that we only have seventy-two hours before the mothership flies."

The Cube, Area 51

General Gullick did not look like a man who had just been awakened five minutes ago. His uniform was well pressed and his face clean shaven. Major Quinn had to wonder if Gullick shaved his face and skull before he went to bed every night for just such an occurrence as this—always ready for action. It suddenly occurred to Quinn that maybe the general never slept. Maybe he just lay there in the dark, wide-awake, waiting for the next crisis.

"Let me hear it from the beginning," Gullick ordered as the other members of Majic-12, minus Dr. Duncan, straggled in.

There wasn't much to tell. Quinn summarized the information an excited security chief had called in from Dulce. In reality, Quinn realized, as he recited the brief list of facts concerning the break-in and the abduction of the reporter Simmons and the theft of photos from the archives, they knew more here at the Cube, because it was obvious from the description from the guards and the female scientist who'd been on shift that it had been Von Seeckt, Turcotte, Reynolds, and Nabinger acting in concert.

"I underestimated all of them," Gullick said when Quinn was done. "Especially Von Seeckt and Turcotte."

Kennedy leaned forward. "We're in trouble. They're going to go to the media with this Simmons fellow."

"How far into conditioning was Simmons?" Gullick asked.

Quinn was puzzled. What were they talking about?

Kennedy consulted his notepad. "They were sixty percent into phase four."

Gullick looked at Doctor Slayden. "What do you think?"

Slayden considered it. "I can't say for sure."

"Goddammit!" Gullick's fist smashed into the desktop. "I'm tired of people bullshitting me when I ask them a question."

The room was silent for several moments, then Slayden spoke. "They disconnected Simmons before treatment was complete. That had to be a shock to his system, and the way his mind will react to that, nobody knows. If nothing else happens, the sixty percent he did have will be enough to assure that Simmons will be discredited if he speaks publicly. He'll fit in with all the other wackos, to use a rather unscientific term."

"What about the photos they stole?" General Brown asked.

"They were of the high rune tablets," Gullick said. "Even if Nabinger can decipher the language, it will be quite a while before other scientists can verify his translation. The tablets are not a problem. Even if they go to the media, it will take a little time before anyone starts believing their story. They really don't have any proof."

Gullick's voice was void of emotion, but a vein throbbed in his forehead. "All right. Then we're still back at the original problem—Von Seeckt and Turcotte. They're the threat, but I think at this point we can handle them for a little while. Long enough, at least, for us to finish the countdown. That's all that matters."

Quinn found that a little hard to believe. What about afterward? he wanted to ask, but he kept his mouth shut. He knew that question would only earn him grief, so he chose another one. "What about the foo fighters?"

"We'll deal with that and this new problem too," Gullick

snapped. "Prepare everything to move up twenty-four hours."

"But—" Quinn began. The general cut him off again with a glare.

"I want the hangar opened tomorrow," Gullick said, "and I want the flight to be tomorrow night." Gullick looked around the table. "I think everyone has a lot of work to do, so I suggest you get moving." As they all got up, his voice halted them. "By the way. I want the orders on capturing Von Seeckt and his crew changed. It's no longer capture at any cost. It is terminate with highest sanction."

27

CAPITOL REEF NATIONAL PARK, UTAH
ADJUSTED T—44 HOURS

Just north of Monument Valley, Capitol Reef National Park was right in the middle of the Rocky Mountains. This time of year it was virtually deserted. In fact, in a few weeks the gates would be locked for the winter snows. The lack of people, and out-of-the-way location, were two reasons Turcotte had selected it as their meeting point. The location put a lot of distance between themselves and Dulce.

He drove in past the empty Ranger station and followed the road around. At the first campsite he spotted the van. Kelly was standing outside, stun gun in hand, watching his truck. She relaxed when she saw him step out. There was a concrete walkway at the end of the campsite, going along the top of the cliff on which the site was located. It afforded a beautiful view of the surrounding mountains—or would have if the sun was up.

"Good to see you," Kelly said.

"How is everyone?" Turcotte asked, stretching his arms out.

"Johnny's semiconscious. Whenever he gains consciousness, he's delirious. I don't know what those people did to him, but it's bad. Von Seeckt's sleeping inside. Nabinger is looking at photos from the mothership hangar."

"Has he gotten anything?" Turcotte asked.

"What about you?" Kelly asked in response. "What happened? What was done on sublevel one?"

"I don't really know," Turcotte answered honestly and vaguely. He walked to the side door and slipped in, Kelly following.

"What have you got?" he asked the archaeologist.

"Better wake up Von Seeckt," Nabinger said. "He'll want to hear this."

It took Von Seeckt a few minutes to get fully awake and then they all gathered around Professor Nabinger. He held a legal pad covered with pencil marks.

"First you have to understand that my knowledge of the high rune language is very rudimentary. I have a very small working vocabulary, and to compound that fact, there are symbols here that—although I believe they mean the same as similar symbols from other sources—have slight differences in the way they are marked.

"The other problem is that the symbols that represent what we could call verbs are most difficult to make out because of the variations in tense, which change the basic symbol.

"Beyond the simple deciphering of the symbols and the words they might mean," Nabinger continued, "there is an additional problem to working with a picture language. The ancient Egyptians called hieroglyphics 'medu metcher.' That means 'the gods' words.' The word hieroglyphs, which is Greek, refers specifically to the drawings in temples. It is difficult for us in the modern day to understand a language that was developed to explain the religious and mythical—"

"Wait a second." Turcotte was tired and had had a long

night. "You're talking about hieroglyphics now. Let's stick with the high runes and what they say."

Nabinger was tired also. "I'm trying to explain all this to you so that you can take my few translations in the proper context. It would be wrong of us to superimpose our own culture and ideas upon what was written by a culture with a totally different set of values and ideas." He tapped the photos. "And here we are dealing with what appears to be an alien culture. We don't have a clue if their perception of reality is the same as ours."

"We're flying their ships," Turcotte noted. "It couldn't be that far off." He thought of the pyramid and the golden glow above it and mentally reconsidered his last statement.

"And not only that," Kelly added, "but didn't you tell us earlier that it appears this high rune language was the precursor to all of mankind's written languages and probably served as the starting point for those languages? So if the roots are common, we must be able to understand it better than if they were totally alien."

"Yes, yes," Nabinger said. "But there is just enough of a common root for me to decipher some of this text. This is—"

Turcotte placed a large hand on Nabinger's shoulder. "Professor. It's late. We all need to get some sleep. But before we sleep we need to decide what we're going to do next. To do that we need to know what you have, as good as you have been able to get it."

Nabinger nodded. "All right. There were two main stones set up in the cavern. Those are the two I have spent all my time on. There are others I will have to get to tomorrow. But here is what I do have.

"Please note where I have question marks after certain parts. That means that I am not quite certain of what—"

"Just show it to us!" Turcotte said.

Nabinger slid the first page under the small dome light.

THE CHIEF(?) SHIP/CRAFT NEGATIVE(?) FLY
ENGINE/POWER(?) DANGEROUS
ALL SIGNS NEGATIVE/BAD(?) AND MUST BE
   NEGATIVE/STOPPED(?)
MUST BE SOON

"That must refer to the mothership," Von Seeckt said. "The negative with the question mark in the first sentence—you don't know for sure what that word is?"

"A verb," Nabinger said. "It might be *cannot* or *should not* or *will not.*"

"Makes a bit of difference," Turcotte noted. "I mean, what if the damn thing just broke? That would cover the old *won't,* wouldn't it? What if these aliens got stuck and their triple A plan didn't cover Earth? And maybe that's why that thing shouldn't get cranked."

Kelly put an arm on Turcotte's shoulder. "See? You said 'shouldn't.' "

"Hard, isn't it?" Nabinger said.

Turcotte rubbed the stubble of his beard. "Yeah, I get it. All right, go on."

THE OTHER (A)???? NOT WANT TO STAY
BE GONE BEFORE ARRIVAL OF (B)????
(C)???? STANDS FIRM
NO CONTAMINATION/INTERFERENCE(?)
   WITH (WORD EQUALING *HUMANS)*
NATURAL COURSE MUST BE ALLOWED

"No idea what was arriving?" Kelly asked. Her hand was still on Turcotte's shoulder.

"It was a special symbol. One that I had never seen before," Nabinger said. "From the basic set of the symbol I would say it represented a proper noun: a specific name. I've designated each unidentified symbol by a different letter before the question marks to show that they aren't the same. As you will see on the next page, one of the noun symbols does repeat."

"So they decided to leave us alone?" Kelly said.

"But obviously that didn't happen," Von Seeckt said. "That bomb had to get into the pyramid somehow."

"Yes," Nabinger agreed. "And the high runes all over the planet. Somehow humans picked up some of that."

"Probably because it didn't work out the way they had planned. Apparently everyone didn't go along so easily with getting stuck on Earth." Nabinger turned over the last page.

DECISION MADE BY MEETING
(C)???? PREPARES TO IMPLEMENT
DISAGREEMENT
BATTLE
OTHERS (D)???? FLEE FIGHT
CHANGE HAS ARRIVED
IT IS OVER
DUTY IS (E)????

"So they fought among themselves?" Kelly said.

"Looks like it," Nabinger said.

"And in the end they did their duty," Turcotte said.

"But not perfectly," Von Seeckt said. "We are still dealing with the repercussions."

"I've got a stupid question," Turcotte said. "Why would the people who built the mothership leave their messages on stone tablets?"

"Because that's what whoever was left there had to work with," Nabinger said.

"This is big," Kelly said. "Bigger than what they have at Area 51. This means history is not at all what we think it is.

Hell, evolution is not what we think. Do you know how that will affect people? Think about religion? About—"

"No," Von Seeckt disagreed. "It is not bigger than what is happening at Area 51. That is the first problem. Because in just under three days they are going to try to fly the mothership, and the marker left by the people who abandoned the mothership says don't do it. We've got to stop it."

"I've got another stupid question," Turcotte said.

The other three waited.

"Why is Gullick in such a goddamn rush to fly the mothership? That's bugged me from the very beginning."

"I do not know," Von Seeckt said. "It troubled me ever since he came up with the countdown to fly it. It was ridiculous. He wanted to to fly it before we even ran a basic series of tests on it."

Turcotte felt a pounding on the right side of his head. "Something isn't right about all this."

"Ever since they went to Dulce early this year," Von Seeckt said, "it all changed."

Turcotte thought of the pyramid, the vats, the golden glow. The small orb that had destroyed the helicopter he was on in Nebraska. Too many pieces that didn't fit. The only thing he knew for sure was that this was bigger than him right now.

"Let's get a little sleep first," Turcotte suggested. "We're all tired and we'll be able to think better with a couple of hours of rest. We'll decide what to do in the morning. We still have forty-eight hours."

28

HANGAR TWO, AREA 51
ADJUSTED T−42 HOURS

Major Quinn blinked hard, trying to keep his eyes open against the lack of sleep. He pulled the collar of his Gore-Tex parka tighter around his neck and shivered. It was cold in the desert at night, and the wind whipping in the open windows of the humvee did not help. They had left Hangar One ten minutes ago and were racing around the base of Groom Mountain, General Gullick at the wheel and Quinn in the passenger seat. He wondered why the general had had to choose the single vehicle from the motor pool that had no top to it, instead of one of the others, but he knew better than to ask.

There was no road. There never had been one. Roads showed up in satellite photos. They had stayed on the runway most of the distance, until they turned off and headed directly for the mountainside. Now they rolled across the desert floor, the suspension of the vehicle easily handling the rough terrain. Gullick leaned over and checked their GPS, ground positioning system, linked in to satellites overhead. It gave their location to within five feet, even on the move. The headlights on the jeeplike vehicle were off, and Gullick was using night vision goggles, allowing them to travel unseen to the naked eye. The outer security net was tight: no unwanted watchers on White Sides Mountain this evening. And the skies were being carefully watched with the invisible fingers of radar to keep out unwanted overflights. Helicopter gunships were ready on the flight line outside Hangar One.

Still, Gullick wanted to take no chances. He braked as a figure stepped out of the darkness. The man walked up to the humvee, weapon at the ready. The man snapped to attention when he recognized General Gullick. Despite the night vision goggles there was no mistaking the general's presence.

"Sir! The engineers are just ahead, under that camouflage net."

Gullick accelerated. Quinn was grateful when they finally stopped near several trucks parked under a desert camouflage net. An officer walked up to the humvee and smartly saluted.

"Sir, Captain Henson, Forty-Fifth Engineers."

Gullick returned the salute and stepped out, Quinn following. "What's your status?" Gullick asked.

"All charges are in place. We're completing the final wiring now. We'll be all set by dawn." He held up a remote detonator the size of a cellular phone. "Then all it will take is a simple command on this. It's linked into the computer that controls the sequence of firing." Henson led the way to a humvee parked under the camouflage net and showed the general a laptop. "The sequence is critical to get the rock in the outside wall to come down in a controlled manner. Very similar to what happens when they demolish tall buildings in a built-up area—making the rubble come down on itself but not hit the ship."

The general took the remote and turned it around in his hands, almost caressing it.

"Be careful, sir," Captain Henson said.

Gullick reached down and pulled out his pistol. He

pushed the barrel into the underside of Henson's jaw. "Don't you ever dare speak to me like that, mister. Do you understand?" His thumb cocked the hammer back, the sound very loud in the clear night air.

"Yes, sir," Henson managed to get out.

Gullick's voice rose. "I have had to take shit from civilian pukes for thirty years! I'll be goddamned if I will accept even the slightest disrespect from a man in uniform. Is that clear?"

"Yes, sir!"

Quinn froze, stunned at the outburst.

"You fucking people." Gullick's voice had dropped to a mutter, and although the gun was still pressing into Henson's skin, his eyes had become unfocused. "I've given my life for you people," Gullick whispered. "I've done all . . ." The general's eyes refocused.

He quickly holstered the gun and turned to the mountainside, behind which the mothership rested. "Show me the charges," he said in a normal voice.

CAPITOL REEF NATIONAL PARK, UTAH

A voice yelled out shrilly. "They're here! They're here!"

Turcotte had his gun out, hammer cocked, as he kicked open the driver's door of the van and went down into a squat, peering around in the dark for a target. The screaming continued and Turcotte slowly relaxed and stood up as he recognized the voice. He walked around to the right side and opened the door.

Kelly held Johnny, gripping him tightly around the shoulders. "It's not real Johnny. It's not real."

Simmons was pressed up in the left rear corner, staring wide-eyed straight ahead. "I can see them! I can see them! I'm not going to let them take me again! I won't go back!"

"It's Kelly, Johnny! It's Kelly! I'm here."

For the first time since they'd picked him up, Johnny showed some awareness of his surroundings. "Kelly." He blinked, trying to focus on her. "Kelly."

"It's okay, Johnny. I came and got you like you wanted. I came and got you."

"Kelly—they're real. I saw them. They took me. They did things to me."

"It's okay, Johnny. You're safe now. You're safe."

Johnny turned away and curled into a ball and Kelly held on to him. Turcotte looked at Von Seeckt and Nabinger. "Get some sleep. We'll be leaving shortly." He turned and walked back outside, sliding the door shut behind him.

Turcotte walked out into the darkness. The stars glistened above the mountains that surrounded him on all sides. It would be dawn soon. He could sense it in the slightest change in the sky to the east. Most people would have not been able to tell, but Turcotte had spent many dark nights waiting for the dawn to come.

He thought of the people in the van. Von Seeckt with his demons from the past and fears for the future. Johnny Simmons and the demons that had been forced on him. Nabinger with his questions from the past and his quest for answers. Kelly—Turcotte paused—Kelly had her own ghosts, it seemed.

He turned as the van door opened. Kelly slipped out and walked over. "Johnny's asleep. Or passed out. I can't tell which it is."

"What do you think they did to him?"

"Screwed with his brain," Kelly said bitterly. "Made him think he got picked up by aliens and taken aboard a spaceship and had all sorts of experiments run on him."

"Think he'll get over it?" Turcotte asked.

"Why should he? He did get picked up by aliens," Kelly said.

"What?"

"Whatever they did to his brain is real. So for him it's all real. So, no, I don't think he'll ever get over it. You never get over reality. You just get on with your life."

"What reality happened to you?"

Kelly just looked at him.

"You said that you'd tell me, first chance you got," Turcotte said. He waited.

After a minute Kelly spoke. "I was working for an independent film company. Actually, I was part of an independent film company. I owned a piece. We were doing well. We did documentaries and freelance work. *National Geographic* in its early TV days had us work a couple of their pieces. It was before all these cable channels—Discovery and the like. Hell, we were before our time. We were on the right path.

"Then I got a letter. I still have the damn thing. Eight years ago. From a captain in the Air Force at Nellis Air Force Base. The letter stated that the Air Force was interested in making a series of documentaries. Some on the space program, some on their work in high-altitude medicine and other things.

"It sounded interesting, so I went to Nellis and met this captain. We talked about the various subjects he had mentioned in the letter, then, almost as an aside, he mentioned that they had some interesting footage in the public affairs office there.

"So I say, 'Of what?' And he says, 'Of a UFO landing at the air base here.'

"I about choked on my coffee. He said it like you would mention the sun came up this morning. Very calm and almost uninterested. I should have known from that, that it was a setup. But like I said, I was hungry. We were still struggling and this was the biggest thing ever thrown our way.

"Then, of course, he showed me the film. That removed all doubt. It was shot in black and white. He told me it had been taken in 1970. They had picked up a bogey on radar at Nellis. At first they thought it might be a stray civilian aircraft. They scrambled a pair of F-16's to check it out. The first half of the film they showed me was from the aircraft's gun cameras. It starts out with blank sky, then you catch a glimpse of something moving fast across the sky. The camera centers in and there's a saucer-shaped object. It's hard to tell the size because there's no reference scale. But I could see the desert and mountains in the background, moving. The disk cut across a lot of terrain. If it had just been against sky I might have questioned it more. The disk looked to be about thirty feet in diameter and silvery. It moved in abrupt jerks back and forth.

"If it was a fake, it was a very good fake—not someone hanging a hubcap out the window of their car and taping it with a videocamera as they drove. Believe me, I've actually seen a couple of those." She walked a little farther along the edge of the overlook and Turcotte followed.

"So the camera tracks this saucer and it descends. I can see an airstrip at the base of some mountains come into view. At the time I thought it was Nellis Air Force Base, but now I know it must have been the airstrip at Groom Lake. The saucer goes down, almost to the ground, and the F-16 goes by and that's it for the gun camera. There's a splice in the film and then I get it in color from the ground. Shot from the control tower, Prague tells me."

"Wait a second," Turcotte interrupted. "Give me that name again."

"Prague. That was the Air Force captain who I met and who sent me the letter. Why?"

"I'll tell you when you're done," Turcotte said. "Go on."

"So the saucer comes to a hover over the runway and stays there for a few minutes. I could see emergency vehicles being deployed—fire trucks with their lights on. I could see the reflection of the lights off the skin of the saucer—a very difficult effect to fake. Pretty much impossible to do, given the technology of the time. Then Air Force police vehicles being deployed. Then the saucer starts to go straight up and it just outraces the ability of the camera operator to track it and it's gone.

"I asked Prague why he wanted to give me this film, and he said the Air Force was trying to get people off its back concerning Project Blue Book. That they wanted to show that the Air Force wasn't covering things up and that there wasn't this great conspiracy that many UFO enthusiasts claim.

"So I left Nellis and went straight to two major distribution companies and told them what I had just seen. Of course they didn't believe me and of course, Prague hadn't given me a copy of the film. He had to clear release with his superiors, he told me, and for that he needed to know who I was going to distribute it through.

"So when these companies call Nellis and try to get hold of Prague, they're told that such a person doesn't exist. When they mention the film, they get laughed at, which doesn't do their disposition much good. I got trashed. I was labeled a nut and nobody wanted to deal with me. I was bankrupt within three months."

"Describe the saucer you saw again," Turcotte said.

Kelly did.

"The film was real," Turcotte said. "That sounds like one of the bouncers in the hangar. They really set you up good."

"I know," Kelly replied. "I wouldn't have gone to the distributors for financing if I didn't believe the film was real. That's what really pissed me off about the whole thing." The sky was getting noticeably brighter in the east. "That's what's so cunning about what they've been doing there in Area 51. It *is* real, but they set up the people who could truly expose it as frauds or kooks."

Kelly pointed at the van, which was fifty feet away. "They destroyed Johnny the same way. In his mind, after what they did to him in that tank, he thinks he was really abducted by aliens. And the fact is that he *was* abducted. That he probably did see things they didn't want him to see. But if he goes public with it, he's laughed at. Yet in his mind it is real. That's about the worst thing you can do to a person next to physically killing him. It can drive you insane."

She turned back to face Turcotte. "So now you know why I'm not too trusting."

"I can understand that."

"What was on sublevel one?" Kelly asked.

Turcotte succintly told her, leaving out his two phone calls after escaping.

Kelly shuddered. "These people have to be stopped."

"I agree," Turcotte said. "We've made a start on that. You might be pleased to know that Prague was—" He paused as there was a thumping sound inside the van.

They both turned as the door to the van shot open and Johnny appeared, holding the arm of one of the captain's chairs in his hands and swinging it about wildly. "You won't get me!" he screamed.

Turcotte and Kelly ran forward, but Johnny turned from them and sprinted along the path.

"Johnny, stop!" Kelly yelled.

"You won't get me!" Johnny screeched. He halted, brandishing the chair arm. "You won't get me."

"Johnny, it's Kelly," she said, slowly taking a step forward. The others were piling out of the van, Nabinger rubbing the side of his head.

"I won't let you get me!" Johnny turned and climbed up on the railing.

"Get down, Johnny," Kelly said. "Please get down."

"I won't let them get me," Johnny said, and he stepped out into the darkness and disappeared.

"Oh, God!" Kelly cried out as she ran up to the edge and looked over. Turcotte was right behind her. In the early-morning light they could just make out Johnny's body lying on the rock, two hundred feet below.

"We have to get him!" Kelly cried out.

Turcotte knew there was no way down into the gulley without climbing equipment. He also knew Johnny was dead; not only could no one could have survived that fall, the twisted and still way the body was lying confirmed it.

He wrapped his arms around Kelly and held her.

Fifteen minutes later a very somber group was seated inside the van. Nabinger had a bump on his head where Johnny had hit him with the arm of the chair before bolting from the van. It had taken ten of the past fifteen minutes for Turcotte to convince Kelly that they couldn't get to Johnny and that he would have to stay where he had fallen.

"All right," Turcotte began. "We have to decide what to do. The first thing is to agree on our goal. I think—"

"We get these bastards," Kelly said. "We get them and we finish them. I want to see every one of them—every single one out at Area 51 and in Dulce—be brought to justice."

"We have to stop the mothership from flying first," Von Seeckt cut in. "That must be our primary goal. I understand your desire for vengeance, but the mothership is a danger to the planet. We know that now from the translation of the tablets. We must stop that first."

"It's the one with the shortest fuse," Turcotte said. "We have to stop what they're doing there and in Dulce, but that can come after we stop the mothership test flight." He looked at Kelly. "Do you agree?"

She reluctantly nodded, her eyes red rimmed from crying.

"All right," Turcotte said. "If that's our primary goal, the way I see it, we got two choices. One is to go public with this. Head to the nearest big town—maybe Salt Lake City—and try to get the attention of someone in the media. That way we use public opinion to stop the test. The other option is to take matters into our own hands, go back to Area 51, and try to stop the test ourselves."

Turcotte turned to Kelly. "I know it's hard, but we need your input on this. Will going to the media work?"

She closed her eyes for a few moments, then opened them. "To be blunt, going public is the way you would think we should go. It's the way I would like to go. The problem is that going to the media does not guarantee that your story will get to the public. We have no proof of—"

"We have the photos of the tablets," Nabinger cut in.

"Yes, Professor," Kelly said, "but you're the only one who can translate them. And since you're with us, I think people are going to look at that a bit skeptically. There was a stone found in America—I think in New England—that the finder claimed showed that ancient Greeks were in the New World a millennium before the Vikings. Unfortunately, the man's proof rested on *his* translation of the markings on the stone. Other scholars, once they had a chance to study the stone, disagreed. Even if we find scholars who would agree with your translations, it would take too long. Certainly more than two days."

Kelly looked around the circle. "The same is true of all of us. Von Seeckt could tell his story but no one would believe it for a while, if ever, without proof. People in the media don't report or print everything that comes to them, because a lot of what comes to them is bogus and our stories are, to say the least, somewhat outrageous." She looked out the window. "Johnny's dead now. We don't even have him."

"Another thing we must keep in mind," Turcotte said, remembering the conversation he'd had earlier that morning with Colonel Mickell, "is that we have committed crimes. I've killed people. We all entered the facility at Dulce illegally. We might not get much of a chance to tell our story before we're hauled off to jail, and once that happens we'll be under the control of the government."

"Then we must do it ourselves," Von Seeckt announced. "It is what I said must happen all along."

"This isn't going to be as easy as Dulce," Turcotte said. "Not only do they have better security at Area 51, but they are going to be prepared. You can be sure that General Gullick is going to tighten things down the closer the test gets."

"You know the area and the facility," Nabinger said, turning to Von Seeckt. "What do you think?"

"I think Captain Turcotte is correct. It will be next to impossible, but I also believe that we must try."

"Then let's start planning," Turcotte said.

29

"I've got to make a phone call," Turcotte said. Things had been quiet for the past hour as they got closer to Area 51. Nabinger and Von Seeckt were in the back, napping.

"To whom?" Kelly asked.

The dark pavement went by under their wheels with a soothing, rhythmic thump. Turcotte had been thinking things through for the past couple of hours and he'd made a decision. He quickly told Kelly about Dr. Duncan and the reason he'd been sent into Area 51. He told her about trying to call twice and the line being disconnected and calling Colonel Mickell at Fort Bragg.

"So are you going to try her number again or are you trying Mickell?" Kelly asked when he was done.

"Mickell. We're going to need Duncan if she's legitimate."

"If she's legitimate, why is your line to her dead?" Kelly asked.

"That might be something out of her control and awareness," Turcotte said. He spotted an all-night gas station. He pulled over and left the engine running while he went to the phone booth. When he was done, he hopped back in the driver's seat, handing Kelly a slip of paper. "Duncan's phone number in Vegas," he said. "Mickell says that as far as he can find out, Duncan's legitimate."

"Do you trust Mickell?" Kelly asked.

"I'm not sure I trust anyone anymore," Turcotte responded.

Several miles went by, then Kelly spoke softly. "This is the road on which Franklin was reported to have been killed."

Turcotte glanced over from the driver's seat. "It's not your fault."

Kelly returned his glance. "Maybe we should have left him there. He wouldn't be dead at least."

"He'd be worse than dead if he was still in that damn coffin they had him in," Turcotte said. "We didn't kidnap him, we didn't take him to Dulce, and we certainly didn't mess with his mind. Gullick's people did that. Remember it. Don't start what-iffing. We did the right thing."

"I'm going to miss him," Kelly said. "He was a good friend."

"You'll have to save that for later," Turcotte said. "Right now we have a job to do." The road was a long black ribbon in front of them, the headlights punching a cone of brightness down the center. "This might help. Remember that guy Prague? The one who set you up?"

"Yes."

"He was my commander in Nebraska."

Kelly sat up straighter. "The one you killed."

"The very same."

"Good."

The Cube, Area 51
Adjusted T—31 Hours

"Utah State Police found Simmons's body thirty minutes ago," Quinn announced. He had been working in the conference room, away from the hustle of the control center, when General Gullick had walked in.

"Where?" Gullick asked.

"Capitol Reef National Park. It's in the south-central part of the state."

"Any sign of the others?"

"No, sir."

"How did he die?"

"It appears he fell off a cliff."

Gullick thought about it for a few moments. "They're heading to Salt Lake City. Send some Nightscape people there. Have them watch all media outlets."

"If we send people out, we'll have to cut back on some of our security here, sir."

Gullick glared at his subordinate.

"I'll get right on it, sir."

"I want the body policed up, also," Gullick said.

"Yes, sir."

"One less loose end to deal with," Gullick muttered. He turned back to his computer and the after-action report from Dulce, which he had been reading. "What's this *rongorongo* thing they took?"

"From Easter Island, sir," Quinn replied. "It's one of the rune sources."

"So they can read the damn thing and we were never able to?" Gullick asked.

"If Nabinger is legitimate, yes, sir, they can." Quinn had brought up the same file the general was reading. "They also took the photos of the tablets from Hangar Two."

Gullick tapped his large forefinger on the desktop. "Nothing in the media?"

"No, sir."

"Nothing from any of our sources?"

"No, sir."

"They just disappeared and left Simmons's body there?"

The tone indicated it was a rhetorical question and Major Quinn remained silent.

"Where's Jarvis? Is he out of town?"

The question caught Quinn off guard. His fingers flew over the keyboard. "Uh, he's in Las Vegas, sir."

"I want him nearby. Tell him to monitor the kooks at the mailbox. We're too close to have some flake on the perimeter like we had during the last Nightscape mission—the one that helped start all this shit."

"Yes, sir. I'll relay that."

Gullick stood. "Stay on top of everything. Let me know the second there's a peep from those people or from any of our media sources."

"Yes, sir." Quinn waited until General Gullick had left the room. Then he left his side chair and sat down in the seat at the end of the table: Gullick's chair. He pulled out the keyboard that was stashed underneath the tabletop and turned the general's computer on.

He began searching, going through files, looking for some clue as to why things were happening here the way they were. What was the rush for the mothership flight? Why had the Nightscape missions changed from being relatively benign to now including abductions and mutilations? Was there a national security objective involved here that Quinn had not been included on?

Quinn gave himself ten minutes, knowing that Gullick was a creature of habit, then he shut the computer down. He hadn't found anything, but the next time the general came in and left, he'd go back to looking.

30

"Do you think this will work?" Kelly asked.

Turcotte was applying burnt cork to his face, turning the already dark skin black. "It's a good plan. The best one we've had so far."

Kelly stared at him. "Hell, we barely had any plans before."

"That's why it's the best," Turcotte said. "I think we've got a chance. That's all you can ask for. We've got two chances at this. One of them should work. I don't think they'll be expecting us, which, as I've explained before, is to our advantage." He looked out at the darkening sky. "It's strange—General Gullick should be expecting us, but he won't be."

"Why should he be and why isn't he?" Kelly asked, confused.

"He should be because it's what he would do," Turcotte said, checking the magazine in his pistol. "He won't be because he's had his ass down in that underground bunker too long. He's forgotten the feel of being out in the field and in action."

He slammed the magazine home, chambered a round,

and put it back in the shoulder holster on his combat vest. "Ready?"

"Ready," Kelly said. She looked at the others. Von Seeckt was in the passenger seat up front. Nabinger was in the rear. The van was parked off the shoulder of a dirt road on the edge of the perimeter of the base range. Large signs were spaced along the west side of the road, warning that the land that lay beyond was restricted. A large mountain about four miles away was silhouetted against the setting sun to their direct west.

"You all take care of each other," Turcotte said.

"Shouldn't we be synchronizing watches or something?" Kelly asked. "It's what they do in the movies, and timing is rather important to this plan—at least what I've caught of it."

"Good idea." Turcotte peeled back the Velcro cover on his watch. "I've got eight on the dot in two minutes."

Kelly checked her watch. "Okay or check, or whatever you're supposed to say." She reached out and put her hand on Turcotte's shoulder. "You can count on us. We'll be there."

Turcotte smiled. "I know. Good luck." He turned and was gone, loping off into the darkness, lost in the shadow of the mountain.

"Let's go," Kelly ordered.

Nabinger turned the van around and they headed north.

AREA 51

The rhythm of the run had settled in to Turcotte's muscles a half hour ago. The various weapons and other equipment attached to the combat vest had required a bit of cinching down shortly after he'd left the van, and now everything on him was silent—just as he had been taught in Ranger school so many years ago. The only sound he heard was his own breath.

The knee was holding up so far, and he was careful to keep his stride shortened to reduce strain. He was presently moving along the base of the mountain he had initially set out for. He was scanning the slope with the off-center portion of his retina. He finally spotted what he'd been looking for. A thin animal trail headed up and Turcotte turned onto it. After a quarter mile it switched back on itself. Turcotte halted and caught his breath. He looked up. There was a long way to go. He started running.

TEMPIUTE, NEVADA

There was a phone on the outside of the AleInn, the local bar in the town of Tempiute. The same town where Johnny Simmons had met Franklin the previous week. The town's main claim to fame was its proximity to Area 51, and the Inn was a watering hole for the itinerant UFO watchers who passed through continuously.

Kelly parked the van next to the phone, and she and Von Seeckt got out and ambled over, he leaning on his cane. He patted his pockets, then looked at Kelly. She shook her head. "Use my phone card." She rattled off instructions and the number Turcotte had given her earlier.

LAS VEGAS, NEVADA

It was just before ten in the evening local time and Lisa Duncan was seated by the small desk in her hotel suite, watching CNN, when the phone rang. She picked it up on the third ring, expecting to hear her son's voice on the other end. Instead a heavily accented voice that she immediately recognized began speaking.

"Dr. Duncan, this is Werner Von Seeckt. General Gullick has been lying to you about what is going on at Area 51 and at the facility in Dulce, New Mexico."

"Professor Von Seeckt, I—"

"Listen. We don't have much time! Have you ever heard of Nightscape in conjunction with Area 51?"

"Yes. They run psychological prep—"

"They do much more than that," Von Seeckt cut in. "They kidnap people and brainwash them, and I am sure even much worse than that. They conduct cattle mutilations. They do much more."

"Like what?"

Von Seeckt didn't reply to that. "How about Operation Paperclip?"

Duncan picked up her pen and pulled the small pad of hotel stationery close. "What do you know about Paperclip?"

"Do you know what's going on at the lab in Dulce? The experiments with implanted memories?"

Duncan wrote the word DULCE on her notepad. "Back up to Paperclip. I'm interested in that. Is there a connection between Paperclip and what is going on at Dulce?"

"I do not know exactly what is going on at Dulce," Von Seeckt said, "but I just rescued a reporter who was being held prisoner there, and he killed himself in response to what they did to him there."

"I don't—" Duncan began, but Von Seeckt cut her off again.

"To reply to your question, does the name General Karl Hemstadt mean anything to you?"

Duncan wrote the name down. "I seem to remember hearing that name somewhere."

"Hemstadt was the head of Wa Pruf 9, the Wehrmacht's

chemical warfare branch. Hemstadt was taken in by Paperclip. I saw him in 1946 in Dulce. During the war he was responsible for supplying the death camps with gas. He also participated in much experimentation with new gases—of course, such experimentation had to be done on living humans to be truly valid.

"Since 1946 I have not been allowed into Dulce nor have I heard a word about Hemstadt again. However, I do not believe he just vanished. Such a man was notorious, and such people don't disappear without much help from powerful people—government people."

"There is someone else you must speak to," Von Seeckt said, and there was a brief pause, then a woman's voice came on the line.

"Dr. Duncan, my name is Kelly Reynolds. I was given your name by Captain Mike Turcotte. He has tried twice to contact you using the number you gave him. Both times the number was reported to be out of order. He says that you must trust no one."

"Where is Captain Turcotte now?" Duncan asked.

"He's on his way into Area 51."

"Why are you telling me all this?" Duncan asked.

"Because we want to meet you at the Cube in Area 51 tonight. You must not inform General Gullick or any of the other members of Majic-12 that you are coming."

"What is going on?" Duncan demanded.

"Be at the Cube tonight. No later than midnight local time. We'll explain everything then." The phone went dead.

Duncan slowly put the receiver down. She picked up another binder. This one had a cover identifying it as coming from the Justice Department and indicating that it was copy two of two copies made. She flipped it open and thumbed through, rapidly scanning. On page seventy-eight she found what she was looking for: General Karl Hemstadt was indeed listed as having likely been taken in by the Paperclip operation.

She gathered together her binders and threw them in a briefcase, then headed for the door. She had a taxi to catch.

TEMPIUTE, NEVADA

Von Seeckt walked back to the van with Kelly. "What do you think?" she asked.

"She finally bit when I mentioned Paperclip," Von Seeckt said.

"Do you think she'll alert Gullick?" Kelly asked as she got in the driver's seat. Von Seeckt sat to her right. Nabinger was in the back, looking at the *rongorongo* tablet.

"No," Von Seeckt said. "She's not one of them. The presidential adviser was usually on the outside. After all, the slot was a political appointment that could change every four years. I know for certain she was not fully inbriefed."

"Well, we'll find out soon enough," Kelly said, throwing the van into gear and leaving the parking lot.

AREA 51

Turcotte cut a hole for his head in the center of the thin silver survival blanket and pulled it down over his shoulders. He wrapped the blanket around his torso and cinched it tight with cord. It hung down to his knees and fit him like a poncho. Designed to keep heat in during an emergency, Turcotte was counting on it to keep him from being identified by the thermal sights that were part of the outer security perimeter of Area 51. He would still show up—

especially the heat rising from his head—but he hoped that the signature would be so much smaller than man shaped, that the monitors might assume it was a rabbit or other small creature and ignore it.

What he could not ignore any longer was the pain from his knee. He reached down and felt the swelling. Not good. But he also knew he had no choice. He checked his watch. He was ahead of schedule, so he could move more slowly. It would not do him any good to go over the mountain early, thermal blanket or no blanket. He continued on his way up the mountain, at a pace that kept the pain to a minimum.

NELLIS AIR FORCE BASE, NEVADA

"I want to see the duty officer," Lisa Duncan said to the sergeant seated behind the counter at the flight operations center at the base of the Nellis Air Force Base tower.

"And you are?" the sergeant asked without much interest.

Duncan pulled out her wallet and flipped open the special ID she'd been given upon getting her appointment. "I am the President's chief scientific adviser."

"The president of . . . ?" the sergeant began, then he halted as he saw the seal on the laminated card. "Excuse me, ma'am! I'll get the major right away!"

The major wasn't quite as impressed with the ID card when he heard what she wanted. "I'm sorry, ma'am, but the Groom Lake area is completely off limits to all flights. Even if I could get you a helicopter at this time of the evening, they would not be authorized to fly into that airspace."

"Major," Duncan said, "it is imperative that I get flown out to Groom Lake this evening."

The duty officer reached for the phone. "I can call out there and see if they will authorize a flight and then—"

"No," Duncan cut in. "I don't want them to know I'm coming."

The major shook his head. "I'm sorry, then. There's nothing I can do."

"Who do you work for?" Duncan asked, her voice cold.

"Uh, well, I work in the ops section for Colonel Thomas."

Duncan shook her head. "Higher."

"The base commander is—"

"Higher."

The duty officer glanced nervously at the sergeant who had first talked to Duncan. "This base falls under the command of—"

"Who's your commander-in-chief?" Duncan asked.

"The President, ma'am."

Duncan leaned over the counter and picked up a phone. "Do you want to talk to him?"

"Do I want to talk . . ." the major repeated dumbly. "No, ma'am."

"Then I suggest you get me a helicopter right away to take me where I want to go."

The major looked at the ID card lying on the counter one more time, then turned to the sergeant. "Get me the PR on duty."

"PR?" Duncan asked.

"Pararescue," the major explained. "We always have one crew of pararescue men on call for emergencies."

"They have a helicopter?"

"Yes, ma'am, they have a helicopter." The major glanced at the sergeant on the phone. "And they know how to fly it."

THE MAILBOX, VICINITY AREA 51

"That's it," Von Seeckt said. "The mailbox."

There were a half-dozen vehicles parked off the side of the dirt road and a group of people scattered about. Some were well prepared, seated in recliners, while others stood, scanning the horizon with a variety of binoculars and night vision devices.

"Dim your lights," Von Seeckt said.

Kelly pushed the button in and with their parking lights on they pulled off to the side of the road. She put the parking brake on, then stepped out. Von Seeckt joined her, while Nabinger remained in the back of the van.

Kelly walked up to an old couple who were comfortably seated in front of a pair of telescopes, with a cooler between their chairs. "Excuse me," Kelly began.

"Yes, dear?" the old woman replied.

"Do you know a man named the Captain?"

She chuckled. "Everyone here does." She pointed to a van parked about twenty feet away. "He's there."

Kelly led Von Seeckt over. The van was parked so that the rear end pointed toward the mountains that marked the edge of Area 51. The back doors were wide open and a very large scope was sticking out. Behind it a man in a wheelchair had his face pressed up against the eyepiece. He pulled back as Kelly stepped up. He was a black man, his lower half covered by a blanket draped over his lap. His hair was white and he looked to be about sixty years old.

"I'm Kelly Reynolds."

The man simply looked at them.

"I'm a friend of Johnny Simmons," she continued.

"So he got the tape," the man growled.

"Yes," Kelly said.

"Took you long enough. Where's Simmons?"

"He's dead." She pointed to the west. "He tried to infiltrate Area 51 and got caught. They took him to Dulce, New Mexico. We broke him out but he killed himself."

The old man didn't seem too surprised. "I heard they do strange things to people down at Dulce."

Kelly stepped closer. "I'll tell you the full story real quick. Then we need your help."

Nellis Air Force Base, Nevada

The officer in the flight suit stuck out a hand. "Lieutenant Haverstaw at your service, ma'am."

"Call me Lisa," Duncan said.

The officer smiled. "I'm Debbie." She pointed at the other people in flight suits. "That's my copilot, Lieutenant Pete Jefferson; our PRs are Sergeant Hancock and Sergeant Murphy." The two men were stowing gear on the back of the UH-60 Blackhawk.

"What are they loading?" Duncan asked.

"Our standard rescue gear," Haverstraw said.

"I just need you to fly me out to Groom Lake," Duncan said.

"SOP—standing operating procedures," Haverstraw said. "We always carry our rescue gear when we fly. Our primary mission, other than flying presidential scientific advisers around, is to rescue downed aircrews. You never know if we might get diverted to a mission." She smiled. "Besides, from what the duty officer briefed me, we're flying an unfiled mission into Area 51 airspace. Who knows what we'll run into? I've heard some strange stories about that place."

"Do you have a problem with running this mission?" Duncan asked, slipping her professional mask back on.

"No problem. I've been ordered by the post duty officer, who represents the post commander, to fly you wherever you want." Haverstaw put her flight helmet on. "My ass is covered." She opened the door on the pilot's side. "Besides, I hate seeing those big no-fly areas on the flight maps. Kind of view them as a challenge. Hell, I'm looking forward to this." She extended her hand toward the rear. "Climb on board."

VICINITY AREA 51

Taking a deep breath, Kelly called out. "Excuse me, everyone! I have something to say that you all might be interested in."

The UFO watchers all turned and looked at her, but no one moved until the Captain's voice boomed out behind her. "Get over here!"

They gathered round, a loose circle of figures in the dark.

"These people need our help," the Captain said. "You all know I been here a long time watching. Twenty-two years, to be exact. Tonight we're going to be doing more than just watch."

As the Captain spoke, outlining what Kelly had asked, a figure at the back separated from the group and slipped away into the darkness. When the car drove away, lights out, no one noticed, so caught up were they in what the Captain was saying.

AREA 51

The glow from the aboveground Groom Lake complex was off to Turcotte's right as he finished descending the mountain he had just crossed. The runway cut across his front,

and beyond that, the mountainside under which the
mothership rested, according to Von Seeckt's directions.

So far, so good, Turcotte thought to himself. But for the
rest of the way he was going to need help. He checked his
watch. Fifteen minutes. Gritting his teeth, Turcotte set to
work on his knee, keeping the tendons from tightening up
by jabbing his fingers into the swollen flesh and massaging
it.

NELLIS AIR FORCE BASE

Sergeant Hancock showed Lisa Duncan how to put on the
helmet and talk on the built-in radio.

"We're clear to lift," Lieutenant Haverstraw announced
from the front. "You all set back there?"

"All set," Duncan said.

"We're going to fly at one thousand feet until we get
close to the boundary. Then I'm going down low. It'll get a
little rough then, but I want to stay off their screens as long
as possible. Give us a better chance of getting you to
Groom Lake."

With a shudder the Blackhawk lifted and then banked to
the north.

VICINITY AREA 51

"I've got something here," Nabinger said, holding up the
wooden tablet he'd taken out of the Dulce archives.
Through all the phone calls and driving he'd never stopped
working on the translation.

"We don't have time for that right now," Kelly replied.
She tapped her wristwatch. "Show time."

She pulled onto the dirt road and turned west, the Captain's van next, then the rest of the UFO watchers' vehicles. They rolled down the road, past the warning signs and past the first set of laser detectors.

31

The Cube, Area 51
Adjusted T—22 Hours, 9 Minutes

"What do you have?" Major Quinn had been alerted by the duty officer and he'd quickly shut down Gullick's computer and gone out to the main control center in the Cube.

"Multiple vehicles in sector three," the operator announced, pointing at his computer screen. "Moving west along the road."

"Give me IR and thermal from the mountain," Quinn ordered.

The operator hit the proper command. A line of vehicles showed up rolling down the road.

"What does the mailbox look like?" Quinn asked.

Another scene came on screen: a lone mailbox, nothing around it, which confirmed to Quinn where the vehicles had come from.

"What the hell are they doing?" Quinn muttered to himself as the camera shifted back to the line of vehicles. "Alert the air police and have them stop these people."

"I've got Jarvis on the phone," another man called out.

Quinn picked up the phone and listened for a minute. He grimaced as he put the phone down. He turned and quickly walked over to a wooden door and knocked. He opened it without waiting for an answer. A figure lay on a cot inside and Quinn reached out and touched the man on the shoulder. "Sir, we've got multiple penetrations on the mailbox road. Looks like our UFO watchers are coming in for a closer look. Jarvis just called and said that Von Seeckt and that female reporter are with them, so this may be more than it appears."

Gullick swung his legs onto the floor. He was already dressed for action in camouflage fatigues. "Alert Night-scape and get the choppers ready," he ordered. As soon as Quinn was gone, he reached into his pocket and popped another pill. His heart rate immediately accelerated and he was ready for action. Then he followed Quinn into the control room.

"They're turning off the road!" the operator announced. "Or at least a couple of them are," he amended as he tried to keep up with the vehicles. "They're spreading out over the desert and still coming this way." He pressed a finger over an earpiece in his right ear. "The air police don't have enough vehicles in that area to get them all in time. Some of them are going to breach the outer perimeter."

Gullick looked over the man's shoulder at the tactical display. "I want Nightscape airborne in one mike. Also get the standby bouncer crew ready."

"Yes, sir."

Twenty miles to the south Lieutenant Haverstraw keyed the intercom. "We're going down to the carpet now. Hold on."

The Blackhawk swooped down toward the desert floor and Lisa Duncan looked out the right side window and *up* at a rocky ridgeline less than forty feet away. Her fingers dug into the webbing strapped across her chest and she did exactly as Haverstraw had suggested—she hung on.

*   *   *

"We've got a hot IR source coming in sector six," Quinn announced. "Low and fast."

"What is it?" Gullick demanded.

"Helicopter. It's below radar but we're picking it up from above."

"Check FFI," Gullick ordered, referring to the friend or foe transponder every military aircraft carried.

"It's one of ours," Quinn said. He hit the keys rapidly. "A Blackhawk assigned to the 325th Pararescue unit at Nellis."

"Tell them to get the fuck out of my airspace," Gullick snapped. He turned back to the ground tactical display, watching as the air police stopped seven of the thirteen vehicles coming in. The remaining six were inside the outer perimeter now. Past the air police cordon and spread out across two security sectors.

"They're calling us," Haverstraw announced. "We're being ordered to turn back."

"Ignore them," Duncan ordered.

"Yes, ma'am."

"No response from the Blackhawk, sir," Quinn reported.

General Gullick rubbed his forehead.

"Should I authorize Landscape to engage when in range?" Quinn asked.

"Tell them to track but hold on firing until I give the order," Gullick said.

"Nightscape is airborne," Quinn said.

Kelly spun the wheel of the van violently and a plume of sand spun out from beneath the rear wheels. She could see the lights of the Groom Lake complex less than two miles ahead.

"We're going to make it," Nabinger said from the seat next to her.

Flashing lights were separating from the steady lights marking the buildings. The lights were going up.

"You spoke too soon. We're going to have company."

"I'll see what I can do to help," Von Seeckt called out from the back. He was working on the computer keyboard attached to the communications console, his fingers flashing over the keys.

Turcotte's boots touched hardtop and he began sprinting across the runway. He felt naked, and he instinctively tucked his chin into his chest and bent forward, half expecting a shot to come out of the dark. On the far side of the runway, about a half mile away, at the base of the mountainside, he could make out a dark mass against the rocks—camouflage netting covering something. He felt a bit of hope seeing that. At least it appeared Von Seeckt's guess wasn't wrong.

"We've got someone on the runway," Quinn announced.

"Put it on the main screen," General Gullick said.

The IR scope mounted on top of the nearby mountain had a resolution of 300 power and it clearly showed a man running.

"How come we didn't catch his thermal signature earlier?" Gullick asked.

Quinn hit a few keys and the picture changed. The man's figure disappeared and there was only a small blob of red moving on the screen. "That's thermal imaging of the target. He's wearing some sort of thermal protection." Quinn changed the view and a map overlay of Area 51 came up. "He's heading for the engineer site outside Hangar Two," Quinn added.

"Divert one of the Nightscape aircraft," Gullick ordered. "Stop that man, number one priority."

"Yes, sir." Quinn began speaking into his microphone, then suddenly turned back to the general. "We've got interference, sir! I can't talk to Nightscape. Someone's cutting in and out on the radio."

In the back of the van Von Seeckt smiled as he heard the excited voices of the Nightscape pilots trying to communicate back to the Cube and with each other to coordinate their actions. He pressed down on the transmit button for the van's HF radio again, then let it up after a few seconds. Then again.

Gullick looked at the overlay of Area 51 and tried to make sense of the various symbols. He had three threats: the man nearing the engineer site, the inbound helicopter, and the vehicles coming in over the desert. This had to be a highly coordinated infiltration, and he could take no further chances. Even without radio he could still control things. He called out his orders.

"Alert the Landscape antiair sites by land line that they are in weapons-free status."

"Yes, sir."

"Warn the engineer site of the man infiltrating their position. He is to be stopped with extreme sanction."

"We have no land line to the engineer site," Quinn reported. "Their guard net is the Nightscape frequency. We can't get through to them."

"Goddammit!" Gullick yelled in frustration.

A tone screeched in Duncan's headset. Up front in the cockpit a red light flashed on the control panel.

"Missile lock!" Lieutenant Haverstaw called out. "Evasive maneuvers. Hancock and Murphy, watch our rear and get ready if it's a heat seeker!"

The Blackhawk turned on its left side and then jerked back right. Duncan watched as the two crewmen in the rear slid open the cargo doors and cold air swirled in. They were wearing harnesses around their bodies and leaned out the aircraft, looking down.

"I see a launch!" Murphy yelled. "Four o'clock. Climbing fast!" He was holding a flare and he fired it out and up, hoping the heat of the flare would divert the missile. At the same time Haverstraw slammed the cyclic forward and they rapidly began losing what little altitude they had left.

The missile roared by the right side of the helicopter, missing the outer edge of their rotor blades by less than ten feet. "That was close," Haverstraw said over the intercom, understating the obvious, as she reeled in collective and cyclic and stopped their descent barely above the desert floor.

"*That* was close," Duncan said, looking out at the ground less than twenty feet below.

"I don't think they want us here," Haverstraw said dryly.

"Put me on the radio to their headquarters," Duncan said.

"No can do," Haverstraw replied. "The frequency listed for Groom Lake is filled with interference."

"Halt!" a voice called out in the dark to Turcotte's right. He could make out a figure wearing night vision goggles and carrying a submachine gun moving toward him.

In reply Turcotte fired twice, both rounds low, hitting the man in the legs and dropping him. There was no need for another death. He regretted what had happened in the lab. Circumstances and anger had forced his hand there. He dashed forward and kicked the Calico submachine gun out of the man's hands and ripped the goggles off his head.

"Fuck!" the man cursed, reaching for his sidearm. Turcotte rapped him upside the head with the barrel of the Calico and the man was out. Turcotte checked the wounds—no arteries hit. He quickly wrapped a bandage from the man's own combat vest around each thigh to stop the bleeding, then continued on his way.

An AH-6 Little Bird gunship flashed by just overhead. Kelly pressed down on the accelerator. The lights of the complex were less than a half mile away.

"The doors to the hangar are closed," Nabinger said. "What are you going to do?"

"I just want to get there in one piece. Then I'll figure something out," Kelly replied.

"The helicopter is still inbound," Quinn reported. "Whoever is flying it is damn good. They're below tracking by ground radar. We can't relay from satellite tracking to the AA sites because of the jamming."

"Launch the alert bouncer," Gullick ordered. "Have it bring down the helicopter."

Haverstraw looked out her windshield. There was a lot going on. She could see vehicles down below in a circus of headlights running about. There were several helicopters flitting about also. One of those turned toward her.

"We've got company," Lieutenant Jefferson said.

Haverstraw didn't reply. She watched the AH-6 come straight toward them from a half mile away.

"Uh, we're on a collision course," Jefferson said.

There was a quarter mile between the two aircraft. The pilot of the AH-6 was flashing his spotlight at them.

"I think he wants us to land," Jefferson said.

Haverstraw remained silent, her hands tight on the controls.

Lisa Duncan twisted in her seat and looked forward as Jefferson spoke again. "Uh, Deb, he's—oh, Christ!" the copilot screamed out as the AH-6 filled up the entire forward view. At the last moment the other chopper suddenly veered, averting the midair collision.

"Chicken," Haverstraw muttered. She raised her voice. "We'll be there in thirty seconds."

"The hangar doors are opening!" Nabinger called out as a sliver of red light appeared ahead.

"I'm heading for it," Kelly said.

"Hey!" the sergeant seated inside the humvee called out as the muzzle of a submachine gun appeared in the door. "Watch that thing!"

"No, you watch it," Turcotte said, edging into the vehicle. He looked at the computer system and the wires leading out of the black box hooked up to it. "This is to blow the charges to open up Hangar Two?"

The sergeant was most definitely watching the end of the muzzle, the black hole seeming to grow larger every second it was fixed between his eyes. "Yes."

"Turn it on and bring up the firing sequence program."

"Geez, look at that," Haverstraw said as she set the Blackhawk down two hundred meters away from the large door that was sliding open in the side of the mountain. Red light spilled out onto the concrete and a disk was hovering there. It moved forward when the door was wide enough. "What the hell is that thing?"

"Thanks for the ride," Duncan said. "You'd better shut down and wait here until things get cleared up."

"Roger that," Haverstraw said. "And you're welcome."

Duncan took off her headset and got out of the helicopter. She turned her head as a van came to a screeching halt between her and the disk.

Turcotte looked at the screen. The charges were listed along with order and timing of initiation. He quickly began typing.

Armed guards ran out of the hangar as the bouncer hovered overhead, shining a light down on the scene being played out.

"Get out of the vehicle with your hands up!" one of the men ordered, pointing his weapon at the windshield of the van.

"Let's go," Kelly said. "We did all we can do. Let's hope we gave Turcotte enough time to do his end."

She opened the driver's door and stepped out along with Nabinger, the latter still holding the *rongorongo* tablet and wearing his backpack. Von Seeckt got out of the rear.

"Face down on the ground!" the man ordered.

"Wait a second!" a woman's voice called out. All eyes turned to the figure walking over from the Blackhawk helicopter. "I'm Dr. Duncan." She held out an ID card. "Presidential adviser to Majic-12."

The senior Nightscape man paused, confused at this sudden apparition and wrinkle in the chain of command. The three groups were all gathered in a thirty-foot circle just in front of the doors to Hangar One.

"I want General Gullick and I want him here now!" Duncan demanded.

"We have to secure these prisoners first," the guard said.

"I'm Kelly Reynolds," Kelly said, stepping forward, making sure her hands were away from her sides. "You know Dr. Von Seeckt, and the other man is Professor Nabinger of the Brooklyn Museum. We called you earlier."

Duncan nodded. "I know you called me earlier. That's

why I'm here. We're going to get to the bottom of this." She turned back to the guard. "Your *prisoners* are not going anywhere. None of us are. Get General Gullick up here now!"

"Sir," Quinn said tentatively, putting down the phone.

General Gullick's eyes were transfixed on the main screen, which showed the overlay of Area 51. All the vehicles had finally been corralled and the UFO watchers placed under arrest.

"Yes?"

"Dr. Duncan was on board that Blackhawk. She's up at Hangar One right now demanding to see you. Von Seeckt, Nabinger, and the reporter are there too."

A nerve began twitching on the side of Gullick's face. "Do we have commo yet?" Gullick demanded.

Quinn checked. "Yes, sir. The interference has stopped."

"Do you have contact with the engineer site?"

"No response, sir."

"Order Bouncer Four to check it out, ASAP!"

Gullick spun away from the screen and walked to the elevator. Quinn relaxed slightly as the doors shut behind the general and he relayed the orders.

The bouncer suddenly darted away to the west, leaving the tableau outside the hangar frozen in a standoff between the weapons of the Nightscape men and the tentative shield of Duncan's position.

A large figure walked out of the hangar, casting a long shadow from the backdrop of red light. General Gullick walked up and looked about. "Very nice. Very nice." He stared at Duncan. "I'm sure you have an explanation for this circus you've orchestrated?"

"I'm sure you have an answer for attempting to shoot down my helicopter," she returned.

"I am authorized by law to use deadly force to safeguard this facility," Gullick said. "*You* are the one who violated law by coming into restricted airspace and failing to respond when challenged."

"What about Dulce, General?" Duncan retorted. "What about General Hemstadt—formerly of the Werhmacht? What about Paperclip? Where is Captain Turcotte?"

Kelly saw the change come over Gullick and she reached out to stop Duncan's harangue.

As he finished typing, Turcotte saw a bright light coming out of the east through the camouflage netting. The same bright light he had seen his first night out here. The bouncer came to a halt forty feet away and landed. A man came out of the hatch on top, weapon in hand.

Duncan and Gullick both stopped their arguing and turned as a new voice called out. "You both don't understand!" Nabinger yelled. He looked about wildly, holding up the *rongorongo* tablet. "None of you do." He pointed at the hangar. "You don't understand what you have in there and where it came from. You don't understand any of it."

Gullick snatched a submachine gun from one of the Nightscape guards. "No, I don't understand, but you never will either." He pointed the muzzle at Duncan.

"You've gone too far," Duncan said.

"You signed your own death warrant, lady. You said too much and you know too much." His finger had already closed over the trigger when he was blinded by the searing glow of a bright searchlight. Without a noise Bouncer Four settled down behind Duncan's group.

"Get over here!" Turcotte yelled from the hatch on top of the saucer.

"Let's go," Kelly said, grabbing Duncan by the shoulders and pushing her toward the bouncer. The others followed.

Turcotte saw Gullick raise the muzzle of the submachine gun in his direction. "Do it and I fire the charges!" Turcotte called out, holding up the remote detonator for Hangar Two.

Gullick froze. "What did you do?"

"I did a little resequencing. I don't think it will quite work the way you'd like," Turcotte said, keeping an eye on his people as they moved in his direction and climbed the slope of the disk.

"You can't do that!" Gullick cried out.

"I won't if you let us get out of here," Turcotte promised.

"Back off," General Gullick ordered, waving to his security men.

Turcotte stepped aside, allowing the others to climb in the hatch. When all were on board, he slipped down inside, shutting the hatch behind him. "Take off!" he yelled at the pilot.

On the ground Gullick whirled. "I want Aurora ready for flight now!" He didn't trust this alien technology anymore.

"Yes, sir!"

"Where do you want to go?" Captain Scheuler asked from the depression in the center of the disk. He'd put up no argument at the engineer site when Turcotte had dropped through the hatch, weapon in hand, and ordered him to fly back to Hangar One. The others were sitting gingerly on the floor of the bouncer, gathered around the center. Von Seeckt had his eyes closed, trying to keep from being disoriented by the view out.

Turcotte still held a submachine gun pointed in the general direction of the pilot. "Turn right," he ordered the pilot.

"What are you doing?" Kelly asked.

Turcotte was looking out the clear skin of the bouncer as

they went around the mountain that hid the hangar complexes. He flipped open the cover on the firing button on the remote, then pressed the trigger.

"You told Gullick you wouldn't do that!" Lisa Duncan said.

"I lied."

Hangar Two was deserted, which was fortunate. The outer wall caved in, not in the orderly manner that had been planned, but in a cascade of rock and rubble crashing down onto the mothership, burying it under tons of debris.

In the Cube, Major Quinn felt the rumble of the explosions and watched the first rocks begin falling in Hangar Two on the remote video screens before the cameras were consumed by the man-made earthquake. "Oh, fuck," he muttered.

Gullick knew what had happened even as the last of the aftershocks of the explosions settled away. He staggered, then sank to his knees. He pressed his hands to the side of his head as pain reverbrated back and forth from one side to the other, searing through his brain. A moan escaped his lips. "I'm sorry," he whispered. "I'm sorry."

"Sir, Aurora is ready for flight," a young officer said with much trepidation.

Maybe it could be salvaged, Gullick thought, seizing upon that single idea. He slowly got to his feet. The manta ray of the high-speed plane was silhouetted against the runway lights. Yes, there was still a way to salvage things.

32

AIRSPACE, NEVADA

"What now?" Kelly asked. The others were gathered around, now standing on the floor of the bouncer, trying to get used to the eerie view straight through the skin of the craft. It was a bit tight with everyone inside. They were currently heading south out of Area 51 at two hundred miles an hour and slowly gaining altitude.

"I don't know." Turcotte turned to the others. "I got you out of there and the Mothership won't be flying for several weeks at least. So I did my part. Where to?"

"Nellis," Duncan said. "I can—"

"Las Vegas has got a good media hook-in," Kelly said, excited. "We fly this damn thing right downtown! Land in the fountain at Caesars Palace. That'll wake them up."

"This isn't a media circus," Duncan said. "I'm in—"

"No!" Nabinger held out the wooden tablet that he'd been hauling with him throughout the entire adventure at Area 51. "You're all wrong. We have to go to the place where the answers are."

"And that is?" Turcotte asked.

Nabinger pointed with his free hand at the tablet in the other. "Easter Island."

"Easter Island?" Duncan asked.

"Easter Island," Nabinger repeated. "From what I've decoded on this, the answers are there."

"No way," Kelly said. "We have to go public."

"Agreed," Duncan said. "As soon as we land, I can contact the President and we can stop this insanity." She tapped Scheuler on the shoulder. "Land us at Las Vegas."

The pilot laughed with a manic edge as his hands worked at the controls. "Lady, you can shoot me if you want, but I don't think we're going to land in Las Vegas."

Turcotte still had his submachine gun ready for use. "Why not?"

The pilot held up his hands. "Because I'm no longer flying this thing."

"Who is?" Turcotte asked.

"It's flying itself," Scheuler said.

"Where are we going, then?" Turcotte demanded.

"Just east of south right now on a heading of eighty-four degrees," the pilot said. "More than that I can't tell you until we get there."

"Does the radio work?" Duncan asked. "I can call and get us help."

Scheuler tried it. "No, ma'am."

"Give me a direction, Quinn," Gullick growled into the radio as Aurora powered up.

Quinn's voice came back through the headset. "South, sir."

"You heard him," Gullick said to the pilot as he settled into the RSO's seat. "Due south."

The plane hurtled forward and lifted. Out of the small window Gullick could just make out the silhouette of the mountain that hid the mothership. He felt the pain intensify in his head. "Stay busy," he whispered to himself. He knew they couldn't catch the bouncer, but at least they could track it. Eventually it would land. He ordered tankers along their projected flight path for inflight refueling.

Kelly knelt down next to the pilot. "Do you have a map of the world?"

Scheuler nodded. He swung in the laptop control and brought up a world overlay on the screen.

"Show me where Easter Island is," Kelly said.

Scheuler tapped a few keys. "Easter Island is in the Pacific. Off the coast of Chile. I'd say about five thousand miles from where we are right now."

"And on what azimuth from us?" Kelly asked.

Scheuler checked, then looked up. "Eighty-four degrees."

"It appears we're going to Easter Island whether we want to or not," Kelly announced. "How long until we get there?"

Scheuler did some calculations. "We're not maxed out but we're going fast enough. I estimate we'll be there in about an hour and a half." *

"Well, now that we have time," Kelly said, "and we know where we're going, let's find out as much as we can. Talk to me, Professor. What does the tablet say is on Easter Island?"

Nabinger was sitting cross-legged on the floor, the *rongo-rongo* tablet in his lap. "I've only managed to decipher part of this, but what I have . . ." He looked at a small notepad in his lap.

"Wait one," Turcotte said. "Let's not go through this guessing game again. Just tell us what you think it says rather than the literal translation."

Nabinger obviously wasn't happy about that unscientific approach, but he nodded. "All right. First, the tablet makes reference to powerful beings from the sky. People with hair of fire—red hair, I assume. They—the red-haired people—

came and lived for a while at the place of eyes-looking-at-heaven. That's how they describe it. From there they ruled after the month of the dark sky.

"Long after the month of the dark sky, the people with hair of fire went up in the great ship of the sky and left, never to return. But their . . ." Nabinger paused. "I am not quite sure what the next word is. It could mean 'parent,' but it doesn't seem to fit in context. Perhaps 'guardian' or 'protector'—remained and ruled.

"Even after the people with fire hair were gone, though," Nabinger continued, "the little suns carried the word of the, hmm, let's use the word *guardian.*"

" 'Little suns'?" Von Seeckt asked.

Turcotte remembered the foo fighter up in Nebraska and reminded the others. "So these things most definitely are connected to the bouncers and the mothership?"

"I'm certain of it," Nabinger said. "There is more here, but it has to do with the worship of the guardian. I have only the one tablet. If I had the others I might know more."

"How many are there?" Kelly asked.

"There used to be thousands on the island," Nabinger answered, "but most were eventually used up as firewood or destroyed by missionaries who thought they were part of old pagan rites. There are just twenty-one in existence now—or at least there were only twenty-one suspected to be in existence. I don't believe that counted this one, since it was hidden in Dulce."

"How did it get to Dulce?" Kelly asked.

"Majic-12 has studied the high runes for years," Von Seeckt said. "They never had as much luck as our good professor here has in translating them, but they have continued to collect whatever they can."

"So maybe people for MJ-12 already have checked out Easter Island?" Kelly ventured.

"They may have," Von Seeckt said, "but I believe I would have heard if they had discovered anything."

"What do you know about Easter Island?" Kelly asked.

"It is the most isolated island on the face of the planet," Nabinger said, remembering what was in Slater's notes. "It is the place that is farthest from any other landfall. It wasn't discovered by Europeans until 1722, on Easter Sunday—that's how it got its name. The islanders themselves call their island Rapa Nui."

"That remote location also helps explain why these aliens might have wanted to use it as a base camp," Von Seeckt added. "Remember the part of the tablet from Hangar Two about not interfering with the local inhabitants?"

"What is the island like?" Turcotte asked, more focused on the immediate future as always.

For that Nabinger did have to consult the notes he'd carried in his backpack through all their adventures. "The island is shaped like a triangle with a volcano at each corner. Land mass is about sixty-two square miles. It doesn't really have any beaches, one reason early visitors had a hard time getting ashore. It is very rocky. Almost no trees were left on the island when it was discovered. There are some now that have been planted.

"And, of course," Nabinger said, "there are the statues, carved out of solid rock in a quarry on the slopes of one of the volcanoes. The largest is over thirty-two feet tall and weighs over ninety tons. There are over a thousand of them scattered all about the island."

"I've seen pictures of those things," Kelly said. "How did those ancient people move such large and heavy objects?"

"Good question," Nabinger said. "There are several theories, none of which quite work."

"Ah," Von Seeckt said, "but perhaps our red-haired ancients might have had something to do with that. Or maybe left something lying around that the natives used to move the statues. Perhaps an antigravity sled or magnetic—"

"Is there any evidence of this guardian?" Turcotte cut in. "Anything like the bouncers or the mothership or even what was found in the pyramid?"

Nabinger shook his head. "No, but not as much is known about the island as people would like to think. We don't know why the statues were built, never mind how they got to their locations around the coast. There is much that is hidden about the history of the island. Archaeologists are still making new finds as they explore. The island is volcanic and honeycombed with caves."

That caught Turcotte's interest. "So maybe there is something there?"

"Perhaps this guardian still exists," Kelly suggested.

"I hope something's down there," Turcotte noted, looking over Scheuler's shoulder at the tactical display. "Because we've got someone hot on our tail. I don't believe General Gullick has given up yet."

33

AIRSPACE, PACIFIC OCEAN

"It's going to get worse before it gets better," Turcotte said.

"What now?" Kelly asked.

"Our satellite link shows we've got company up ahead too. Looks like a bunch of interceptors waiting for us to hit their kill zone."

"So what's the get-better part?" Kelly asked.

"Well, it always gets better after it gets worse," Turcotte said. "Either that or you're dead."

"Great philosophy," she muttered.

A covey of F-16's from the *Abraham Lincoln* waited over the Pacific, circling on the flight path the target was projected to follow. That is, until small glowing orbs suddenly appeared and all craft lost engine power.

General Gullick closed his eyes, hearing the panicked reports from the pilots as their engines flamed out. He took the headset off and looked at the pilot. "Where are we headed?"

"I've projected out the flight path of Bouncer Four," the pilot reported. He nodded his head at the screen. A line went straight from their present location over a thousand miles west of Colombia, due south.

"Antarctica?" Gullick asked. "There's nothing out here."

"Uh, actually, sir, I checked. There is an island along this route. Easter Island."

"Easter Island?" General Gullick repeated. "What the fuck is on Easter Island?" He didn't wait for an answer. He immediately got on the radio with the admiral in charge of the *Abraham Lincoln* task force. That resulted in a five-minute argument, as the admiral's priorities were some-what different from Gullick's. He wanted to recover the downed aircrews. A compromise was reached and the majority of the task force turned to the south and steamed at flank speed for Easter Island, while several destroyers stayed behind to pick up the crews.

Turcotte watched the dots of the waiting aircraft disappear off the screen. He felt the anxiety level in his gut kick up a notch higher despite this apparently positive development. "Talk to me, Professor. Tell me more about Easter Island."

"There are two major volcanoes on the island," Nabinger said. "Rano Raraku in the southeast and Rano Kao. Both have lakes inside the crater. On the slopes of Raraku are the quarries where the stone statues were cut and fashioned out of solid rock. Quite a few statues have been found there in various stages of creation. The inhabitants shaped each statue lying on its back, then cut down on the spine until it was free. Then they hauled it to its site, where it was raised onto a platform.

"It is interesting to note," he continued, "that the main road leading away from Raraku is lined with statues and there are some who think this was a processional route."

"To worship the fire-heads?" Kelly asked.

"Maybe. There are some who think the statues were simply abandoned there when the people rose up against the priests who oversaw the making of the statues. Those peo-

ple put a tremendous, almost unbelievable, amount of re-
sources into the creation and moving of those statues. It
had to severely strain the economy of the island, and the
theory is that eventually the common people revolted."

"So Raraku is the place to look?" Turcotte cut in.

"Maybe." Nabinger shrugged. "But on the rim of the
other significant volcano, Rano Kao, over a thousand feet
high, is where the ancient people built the village of
Orongo—their sacred village. The lake inside the crater is
almost a mile in diameter. Offshore of Kao lies a small
island called Moto Nui, where birds—terns—nest. In ancient times the cult of the Birdman occurred every year in
September, when young men would go from the volcano
rim, climb down the cliffs to the sea, swim to Moto Nui,
recover a tern egg, and the first man back was birdman for
the year."

Turcotte rubbed his forehead. "Okay, okay. They have
birdmen. They have volcanoes. They got big statues. They
got strange writings on wood tablets. But what the hell are
we looking for? Has anything strange been found there
that might suggest this guardian?"

"No."

"Then what are we—" Turcotte paused as the pilot
called out.

"We've got company!"

They looked out as six foo fighters bracketed their craft.

"I don't like this," Scheuler muttered. The foo fighters
were making no threatening movements, hanging in position as they flew south.

"How far out are we?" Turcotte asked.

"ETA at Easter Island in two minutes."

The foo fighters were slowing and closing in around their
craft, forming a box on all sides.

"I don't think we're going to have any choice about

where to look on the island," Kelly said. "I think the guardian has decided all of that for us."

"We're going down," Captain Scheuler announced unnecessarily, since all inside Bouncer Four could see the island below growing closer. The bouncer was being slowed by whatever force had taken over the controls.

"We're heading for Rano Kao's crater," Nabinger said, pointing at the moonlit surface of the lake in the center of the large volcano.

"This thing waterproof?" Turcotte asked Scheuler.

"I hope so," was the optimistic reply.

"Everyone hold on to something," Turcotte called out as they descended below the edge of the crater's rim. They splashed into the lake without much of a jar and then were enclosed in total darkness. For half a minute there was silence, and it was impossible to tell which way they were moving. A point of light appeared ahead and slightly above them, growing closer.

The light grew brighter, filtered through water, then suddenly they broke out into air again, into a large cavern. The bouncer lifted up above the surface of the water, which filled one half of the floor, and settled down on dry rock on the other half.

"We're shut down," Scheuler announced as the skin of the disk grew opaque. He tried the controls. "It won't power up."

Four thousand feet above Easter Island, General Gullick watched helplessly as the bouncer disappeared into the waters of the crater.

"Can you set us down on the airfield on the island?" he asked the pilot.

"Sir, that's a public airstrip. If we land there, the secret about this aircraft will be out."

Gullick's laugh had a edge of mania to it. "Major, there's

a lot of things that aren't going to be secret come daybreak if I don't get on top of all of this, and I can't do it up here. Land."

"Yes, sir."

"Let's see what we have," Turcotte said, heading for the ladder leading to the top hatch. He climbed up and unfastened the seal, flipping the hatch open. He climbed out onto the upper deck of the bouncer and looked about as the others gathered around him.

"I'd say go that way." He pointed toward a tunnel on the land end.

"After you," Kelly said, with a sweep of her hand.

Turcotte led the way with Nabinger at his side, the others following, with Kelly bringing up the rear. The tunnel was lit by lines of light that seemed to be part of the ceiling. The floor sloped up at first, raising faint hopes that it might go up to the surface, but then it leveled out and turned to the right.

They entered a cave, somewhat larger than the Cube. Three walls were rock, but the far wall was metal. On it was a series of complex control panels with many levers and buttons. What caught everyone's attention, though, was the large golden pyramid, twenty feet high, that sat in the center of the cave. Turcotte paused. It was similar to the one at Dulce, but larger. There was no glow above it, and Turcotte didn't pick up any of the negative feelings he'd experienced in Dulce.

He reluctantly followed the others as they walked in silence up to the base of the pyramid, staring at its smooth surface in awe. Faintly etched in the metal were high runes.

"What do you think?" Turcotte asked of no one in particular. "I'm sure this thing controls whatever took over the bouncer and is keeping us from getting out of here."

"Why are you in such a rush to get out of here?" Kelly asked. "This is the whole reason we came."

"I was trained to always have a way out ready," Turcotte said, staring at the pyramid suspiciously.

"Well, cool your spurs," Kelly replied.

"My spurs are cool," Turcotte replied. "I have the feeling the only thing waiting for us outside of this cave is going to be a lot of big guns."

"This must be the guardian," Kelly said.

They all held their place as Nabinger ran his hands over the high runes. "Amazing. This is the greatest find in archeological history."

"This isn't history, Professor," Turcotte said as he walked forward into the room. "This is here and now, and we need to figure this thing out."

"Can you read it?" Kelly asked.

"I can read some of them, yes."

"Get to work, then," Turcotte said.

Five minutes after Nabinger began, they were all startled when a golden glow appeared above the apex of the pyramid. Turcotte was pleased to note that he didn't get the sick feeling that the other pyramid had produced. He was disturbed, though, when a gaseous golden tendril from the globe reached out and wrapped itself around Nabinger's head.

"Take it easy," Kelly said as Turcotte started forward. "This thing, whatever it is, is in charge. Let Nabinger find out what it wants."

The first helicopter from the *Abraham Lincoln* came in at one hour and twenty minutes after Gullick had landed at the Easter Island international airport. Given that there were only four flights into the airport every week—and today was one of the off days—they had no trouble taking over the airfield.

The fact that the island was Chilean and they were violating international law didn't overly bother General Gullick either. He ignored the agitated requests from the admiral in charge of the *Lincoln* task force and the relays from Washington as people in charge woke up to the fact that something unusual was going on.

"I want an airstrike prepared," Gullick ordered. "Target is the Rano Kao volcano. Everything you have. The target is under the water in the crater."

The admiral would have ignored Gullick except for one very important thing: the general had the proper code words to authorize such a mission. On the deck of the *Abraham Lincoln* smart bombs were rolled out and crewmen began attaching them to the wings of aircraft.

Two hours after beginning, Nabinger had a dazed look on his face as the tendril unwrapped itself and flowed back into the golden globe.

"What have you learned?" Kelly asked as they all gathered around.

Nabinger shook his head, his eyes slowly focusing back to his surroundings. "Unbelievable! It's unbelievable! It spoke to me in a way I couldn't explain to you. So much information. So much that we never understood. It all fits now. All the ruins and discoveries, all the runes, all the myths. I don't know where to start."

"At the beginning," Von Seeckt suggested. "How did all this get here? Where did the mothership come from?"

Nabinger closed his eyes briefly, then began. "There was an alien colony—more an outpost than a colony as far as I can gather—on Earth. The aliens called themselves the Airlia.

"As best I can determine, the Airlia arrived here about ten thousand years ago. They settled on an island." The professor held up a hand as Turcotte started to ask a question. "Not this island. An island in the other ocean. In the Atlantic. An island that in human legend has been called Atlantis.

"From there they explored the planet. There was a species native to this planet very much like them." Nabinger smiled. "Us.

"They tried to avoid contact with humans. I'm not totally sure why they were here. I would have to have more contact. I get the impression it might simply have been a scientific expedition, but there is also no doubt that there was a military aspect to it."

"They were taking over the Earth?" Turcotte asked.

"No. We weren't exactly an interstellar threat ten thousand years ago. The Airlia were at war with some other species, or perhaps their own species. I can't quite figure that out from what it told me, but I think it is the former. The word it used for the enemy was different. And if the enemy had been some of their own I think I would be able to tell because . . ." Nabinger paused. "I'm getting ahead of myself here.

"The Airlia were here for several millennia, rotating personnel in and out for tours of duty. Then something happened—not here on Earth, but in their interstellar battle." Nabinger ran his hand through his beard.

"The war was not going well and some disaster happened and the Airlia here were cut off. It seems that the enemy could find the Airlia by detecting their interstellar drives." He looked at Von Seeckt. "Now we know the secret of the mothership. The commander of the colony had to make a decision: pack up and try to make a run for it back to safety in their home system or stay. Naturally, the majority of the Airlia wanted to go back. Even if they stayed and weren't spotted, there was always the chance the enemy would find them anyway.

"Of course, if they left, they would be spotted and then it

would be a race through space. There was an additional factor too. One that the Airlia commander apparently considered very important. He was the one who programmed the guardian, so most of what I learned is from his perspective. His name was Aspasia.

"Aspasia knew that even if they got away, the trace of their engine would be examined by the enemy and backtracked, and Earth would then be discovered by the others. He pretty much considered that equivalent to sentencing the planet to destruction. He felt that factor by itself ruled out leaving. The regulations he worked under also said that he could not endanger this planet and the life on it.

"But there were others among the Airlia who weren't so noble or so entranced by the regulations. They wanted to go back and not be stuck on this primitive planet for the rest of their lives. The Airlia fought among themselves. Aspasia's side won, but he knew that as long as they had the capability to return, it would always be a threat. He also knew that even their enclave on the island, Atlantis, would eventually violate their noninterference regulation.

"So he moved the mothership and hid it. He scattered his people. Some—the rebels—had already dispersed to other parts of the planet. Aspasia hid the seven bouncers down in Antarctica and"—Nabinger pointed over his shoulder—"he moved their central computer, the guardian, here to Easter Island. It was uninhabited then. He took the last two bouncers back to rest with the mothership." Nabinger took a deep breath. "That is, he did that after he did one last thing. He destroyed their outpost on Atlantis so that if the enemy did come through this solar system, they would not discover that the fire-heads had ever been here. He completely wiped out that trace of their existence here on Earth and hid the rest."

Nabinger looked at the screen. "Aspasia left the guardian on with the foo fighters under its control in case the way of the war changed and his own people came back to this sector of space. Obviously, they never did."

The professor turned from the computer. "Others among the Airlia, those who did not agree with Aspasia, must have tried to leave their own message to their people, knowing the guardian had been left on.

"Now I know the why and how of the pyramids. They were space beacons, built by rebels using the limited technology they found and the human labor they could exploit to try to reach out to their own people if they ever came close enough.

"And the bomb the rebels took. Aspasia knew about that, but he couldn't go in and take it away, not without letting the humans know of his power and existence or without having the rebels set it off.

"You see, the rebels, there weren't many of them. There were never more than a few thousand of the Airlia on the planet at any one time. And they went other places and worked their way in among the humans. Jorgenson's diffusionist theory is correct. There *are* many connections between all those ancient civilizations, and there is a reason they all started at roughly the same time, but it wasn't because man crossed the ocean. It was because Atlantis was destroyed and the Airlia spread out across the planet."

"I saw a pyramid just like the guardian but smaller, down on the lowest level in Dulce," Turcotte said.

"Yes, that was the computer the rebels hid," Nabinger said. "Not as powerful as the guardian but still far more advanced than anything we could comprehend. Gullick and his people must have just recovered that this year when the find was made at Jamiltepec in Mexico."

"And Gullick turned it on," Turcotte said, all the pieces falling into place.

"Yes," Nabinger said. "And it didn't work the way Gullick thought. He was no longer in control—the rebel computer was in control of him. It wanted the mothership. That was the thing the rebels wanted more than anything else: the only way to get home."

Von Seeckt turned to Duncan. "I told you we must not try to fly the mothership. General Gullick and his people might have brought the wrath of this enemy down upon our planet!"

"I don't think Gullick really knew what he was doing," Turcotte said, rubbing the right side of his head.

"The threat the Airlia faced was thousands of years ago," Duncan noted. "Certainly—"

"Certainly, nothing!" Von Seeckt cut her off. He pointed at the screen behind him. "This thing still works. The foo fighters this computer controls still fly. The bouncers still fly. What makes you think the enemy's equipment isn't still functioning out there somewhere, waiting to pick up a signal and go in and destroy Earth? The Airlia turned the mothership off because they were obviously *losing* their war!"

Lisa Duncan nodded. "This is beyond us. We have to bring the President here."

The golden glow suddenly went white, then a three-dimensional picture appeared. It showed the early-morning sky and a phalanx of small dots moving across.

"What's that?" Duncan asked.

"You might not get the chance to talk to the President," Turcotte said. "Those are F-16's coming this way."

34

Rapa Nui (Easter Island)

Gullick sat in the back of the large Navy helicopter parked on the runway and listened in on the command frequency as the strike force moved in. There was enough ordnance on those planes to reduce the volcano to rubble. After that—Gullick shook his head, trying to get rid of a pounding headache and think clearly. They would have to dig down to the mothership again. And then, then—

"Are you all right, sir?" The navy lieutenant was worried. He didn't know what was going on, but one thing for sure, the shit was hitting the fan.

"I'm fine," Gullick snapped.

"We've got bogeys!" the radar man called out. "Coming up out of the volcano."

The flight leader saw the foo fighters rising up to greet his planes. He'd been in the wardroom when the flight that had been dispatched to set the trap had gone down, their engines shut down by these very same craft.

"Eagle Flight, this is Eagle Six. Abort! Abort!"

The F-16's banked hard and kicked in afterburners, the foo fighters in hot pursuit.

*   *   *

In the guardian cavern everyone relaxed as they watched the warplanes turn away, followed by the foo fighters.

"Seems like this guardian can take care of itself," Turcotte said.

"Is there any way we can get hold of Washington?" Duncan asked. "I need to get this madman Gullick relieved."

"Can you ask the guardian to let us use the SATCOM radio in the bouncer?" Turcotte asked Nabinger.

"I'll try," Nabinger replied.

Gullick had one last card up his sleeve. He knew there was an Aegis-class cruiser in the *Lincoln* battle group. He grabbed the microphone and called the admiral.

The three-dimensional glow suddenly shifted perspective and showed four trails of flame coming off a warship. "What the hell are those?" Kelly asked, freezing Turcotte and Duncan in their tracks.

Turcotte spun around. "Tomahawk cruise missiles."

"He's going nuclear?" Duncan was shocked.

"No, those probably aren't nuclear, but they carry a hell of a wallop," Turcotte said.

"Do you think the foo fighters can stop them?

"No time. The foo fighters are chasing away the jets," Turcotte said. "They're out of position."

They watched, mesmerized, as the four missiles hit supersonic speed and crossed the shoreline of Easter Island, less than three miles away.

"We've got maybe four seconds," Turcotte said.

The image blanked out, then returned, showing the island unchanged.

"What happened?" Kelly asked.

*   *   *

On the *Lincoln* the admiral was asking the same question of his staff on the battle bridge. He ignored General Gullick's screamed demands as he talked to the officers working there.

"Near as I can tell, sir, there's some sort of force field around the volcano. The Tomahawks were destroyed when they hit it."

The admiral rubbed his forehead. He didn't have a clue what was going on. He'd already lost six multimillion-dollar fighters, and now four Tomahawks.

"I demand you launch another strike!" Gullick was yelling on one frequency.

"Sir, I've got communication with someone claiming they are inside that volcano," one of the men said.

"Give me that frequency," the admiral said, ignoring Gullick. He picked up a mike. "This is Admiral Springfield."

"Admiral, this is Lisa Duncan, the President's science adviser. You'd better listen up and listen good. Who authorized you to attack this place?"

"General Gullick, ma'am."

"General Gullick is insane."

"He had the proper authorization codes and—"

"Admiral, I want you to get me a direct line to the President. I'll give you *my* authorization codes to get that call through, and we'll get this all sorted out. Clear?"

The admiral gave a relieved sigh. "Clear, ma'am."

The golden tendril unwrapped itself from around Nabinger's head and returned to the orb. The orb pulsed and seemed to grow larger.

"What's happening?" Kelly asked.

"I don't know," Nabinger replied. "As much as I'm getting information from the guardian, it's getting information from me."

*   *   *

On Easter Island, Gullick was still yelling into the radio in the back of the helicopter when the navy lieutenant took off his headset and looked at the general. "Sir, I'm under orders to take you into custody."

Gullick's face twitched and he ripped off his own headset. "What? Who the hell do you think you are?"

"I have orders to take you into custody," the lieutenant repeated. He laid a hand on Gullick's arm and Gullick ripped it away.

"Don't you dare! I had served my country for over thirty years. This can not happen. We must succeed. We must fly the ship."

The lieutenant had almost lost friends on the previous night's F-16 mission and he had his orders. He drew his pistol. "Sir, we can do this the easy way or we can do this the hard way."

Gullick drew his pistol. The lieutenant froze, stunned that his bluff had been called.

AIRSPACE, DULCE, NEW MEXICO

From its perch watching the mothership hangar the foo fighter came out of the north at over five thousand miles an hour. It stopped abruptly and hovered, three miles over the mountain housing the Dulce facility. A tightly focused beam of golden light came out of it, aimed straight down. It passed through the mountain as if it didn't exist.

On the bottommost level the small pyramid was touched by the beam and instantly imploded. The layers of the facility pancaked on top of each other and the entire facility was destroyed in less than two seconds.

RAPA NUI (EASTER ISLAND)

Gullick turned to the north and his mouth opened wide. A high-pitched scream came out. He fell to the floor of the helicopter, dropping the pistol and pressing both hands against the side of his head. Dark red blood flowed out his ears and nose.

The lieutenant stepped back, shocked by what he was watching. Gullick reached a hand up, the fingers twisted in pain, in a gesture of supplication. Then he collapsed in a fetal position and was still.

The lieutenant stepped forward and rolled the body over. Lifeless eyes stared up at the morning sun.

35

RAPA NUI (EASTER ISLAND)

The view from the rim of Rano Kao was spectacular. Waves roared into the rocks a thousand feet below and the sea stretched out to the horizon, the setting sun creating hundreds of sparkles in the wave crests. The only thing marring the view was the silhouette of an aircraft carrier six miles off the coast.

A jet roared past, carrying another load of politicians. The *Abraham Lincoln* task force was spread out around the island and the local airfield was packed with incoming aircraft. Turcotte squatted and picked up a rock, tossing it up and down in his hand. Kelly was standing nearby.

Von Seeckt and Nabinger were still down in the cavern, studying the guardian computer. Nabinger had found the control that opened a shaft to the rim of the crater shortly after briefing them about the history. Then the others had begun to arrive, Duncan taking them down to see what had been found.

Nabinger had communicated with the guardian again. There was so much information. Medical theory; physics; the universe; even the instructions on how to fly the mothership. It was all there.

"So what now?" Turcotte asked.

"We're sitting on the biggest story of the century," Kelly

said. "Hell, it's the biggest story of the last two thousand years."

She and Turcotte had seen Gullick's body. He told her his theory that Gullick had been controlled by the pyramid uncovered in Mexico. That Gullick had turned it on and powered it up, but then it had taken over. It all fit together now, and Kelly would very shortly have to leave to do her job and tell the rest of the world the story.

"I miss Johnny," she said. "This is his story more than mine."

"His death wasn't in vain," Turcotte said.

"He helped bring to light the greatest story in history," Kelly agreed.

Turcotte threw the rock out toward the ocean and watched it disappear. "I think about that alien commander so many years ago. Aspasia. The decision he had to make."

"And?" Kelly asked.

"And it took a lot of guts." Turcotte stood. "And he made the right decision. It was what was meant to be."

"I didn't know you had this philosophical side to you," Kelly said.

"This all had to happen. I grant you that. But"— Turcotte looked out to sea—"but I don't know if we're making the right decision to continue down there with the guardian. I don't know if this is meant for us, this knowledge, this technology ahead of our time. I talked to Von Seeckt. He said they're already giving the guardian more power, putting it totally on line."

"You sound . . ." Kelly hesitated.

Turcotte looked at her. "Scared?"

She nodded.

"I am."

EPILOGUE

Rapa Nui (Easter Island)

It felt the power come in like a shot of adrenaline. For the first time in over five thousand years it was able to bring all systems on line. Immediately it put into effect the last program it had been loaded with in case of full power-up.

It reached out and linked with sensors pointed outward from the planet. Then it began transmitting, back in the direction it had come from over ten millennia ago, calling out: "Come. Come and get us."

And there were other machines out there and they were listening.

Robert Doherty is the pen name for a bestselling writer of military suspense novels. He is also the author of *The Rock, Area 51: The Reply, Area 51: The Mission, Area 51: The Sphinx, Area 51: The Grail, Area 51: Excalibur, Area 51: The Truth, Psychic Warrior,* and *Psychic Warrior: Project Aura.* Doherty is a West Point graduate, a former infantry officer, and Special Forces A-Team Commander. He currently lives in Boulder, Colorado.

For more information, you can visit his website at: www.nettrends.com/mayer.